A HEART'S FORGIVENESS

A LOVE'S ROAD HOME NOVEL - BOOK 2

LENA NELSON DOOLEY

WILD HEART
BOOKS

This book is dedicated to to Fred Johnstone, a long-time Christian friend who's shared many of my ministry experiences. Fred thought it was fun for me to borrow his last name for my villain.

And to Beverly and Fernando Henry, who adopted all three of their children. I also borrowed their last name for a character.

And, as always, my book is dedicated to my husband, James Dooley, who has filled my adult life with the knowledge that I've always been loved and cherished. Thank you for the wonderful fifty-six years we've shared. I'm game for 56 more if you are.

And I thank my Lord Jesus Christ for creating me to be a writer, and Who always walks through each story with me. Your presence in my life is what keeps me going.

And the land shall yield her fruit,
and ye shall eat your fill,
and dwell therein in safety.

Leviticus 25:19 (KJV)

CHAPTER 1

EARLY SPRING, 1890
GOLDEN, NEW MEXICO

"*A*re you plumb crazy?" Jeremiah Dennison's loud retort bounced around the main room of the adobe house and returned to mock him. "Where did you get such a harebrained idea?"

Trying to control his anger, he shoved his clenched fists into his denim trousers' pockets, paced to the window, and stared out, paying scant attention to the piñon trees bending in the wind. He loved Philip Smith like a father, but the man could vex the weather. And this latest idea was the most farfetched yet.

Philip gave a snort. "Harebrained?" He put his rocking chair into motion that sent out a rhythmic squeaking. "Why'd ya say that? It's worked fer other men."

Jeremiah tried to calm down. He wanted to measure his words, season them with wisdom that would awaken his elderly friend to all the pitfalls he would face. "What would you do with a mail-order bride?"

The old miner stilled the chair and stared at Jeremiah,

1

obsidian eyes piercing under his bushy white brows. "Some-thin""—he smothered a hacking cough with his fist, then swiped a clean handkerchief across his face—"has a deadly grip on me."

"I know you're sick. I take care of you, don't I?" Jeremiah resented the fact that what he'd done wasn't enough. Otherwise, Philip wouldn't even consider such a preposterous proposition.

His old friend reached up to scratch the scraggly beard he'd worn all the years he was a miner, but it no longer covered his clean-shaven chin. Old habits died hard. "Jerry, I don't wanna be a burden on ya."

"You'd rather be a burden to a woman you don't even know?" Jeremiah regretted his cynical tone the moment the words flew from his lips. He softened his tone. "I've never considered you a burden any more than you thought I was a burden when I came to the gold fields as a greenhorn."

Philip clutched the arms of the rocking chair and slowly rose. He took a moment to steady himself before he ambled toward Jeremiah. "I ain't come to this decision easy." He squinted up into Jeremiah's face. "I done studied on it fer a while."

Jeremiah straightened the fingers he'd gripped into fists and relaxed his stiff spine. "What do you mean, 'studied'?"

"Well, I figure a woman who'd answer them ads in the news-paper must be purty needy, maybe even desperate to get out of a particular bad situation." He gave a vigorous nod that riffled his snowy hair. "Made me a fortune when I sold my mine. More money than any man can spend in his lifetime. What good is a fortune to an old-timer like me? Won't never have a family of my own. Maybe I'll git me a woman with children. She can take care a me, and my money can take care a her." Another nod punctuated his last statement. "And her young'uns, if she has any."

How could Jeremiah deny his mentor's request? Philip never asked for much. If he didn't do this, the stubborn old man would look for help from someone else. A lesser friend might have a wagging tongue and spread the story all around Golden. Philip didn't need people gossiping about him sending for a bride. And other miners might try to nab her for themselves when she arrived. If Jeremiah had his way, it would be fine with him if they did, but his friend would be too disappointed. He didn't want to break Philip's heart, just talk him out of making this mistake.

"Jerry, ya ain't mad 'cause I'm plannin' to give my money to someone else, are ya?"

The words stabbed Jeremiah's heart. How could Philip believe that about him? "I don't need your money. I have more than enough of my own, thanks to selling my own mine and starting the ranch like you told me to."

The hoary head nodded. "That's what I figured."

"Where you going to send the ad?" Jeremiah couldn't believe he was considering being a part of this crazy scheme. But what else could he do?

Philip limped toward the sturdy pine dining table where a stack of newspapers was piled haphazardly beside blank paper, an inkwell, and a pen. "I read all these, and I think I'll send it to the *Boston Globe*." He picked up the top newspaper and shoved the rumpled pages toward Jeremiah.

Taking the newsprint, Jeremiah glanced at the headlines on the front page. An unusually hard winter had left many people out in the cold. "Why Boston?"

"Don't want jist anybody. Wanna help a *lady* in distress." Philip folded his scrawny arms across his bony chest. "Figure most a the women in Boston are ladies. My aunt Charlotte come from Boston, and she was a lady." He stopped and cleared his throat, then wheezed out a slow breath. "You do the writin', 'cause mine looks like hen scratchin'."

Judging from the stubborn tilt to the older man's chin, Jeremiah knew Philip's mind was made up. He dropped the newspaper back on the stack and pulled out the chair beside the stationery. "What do you want to say?"

He picked up the pen with the golden nib—another of the things the old miner had bought after he'd sold the mine. It had never been dipped into the inkwell until now.

Philip leaned both hands on the table, puffed out his chest, and wrinkled his forehead in concentration. "How about, *Wanted, a*... No. Makes it sound like she's an outlaw, or some- thin'. Do it this way. *A Christian man in Golden, New Mexico, is seekin'* ..." He waited for Jeremiah to finish writing the phrase. "Sound all right so far?"

Wanting to laugh, Jeremiah kept his eyes trained on the words before him. Philip was so serious. "What are you seeking?"

The old miner scratched his head. "I want a lady. Done already told ya that."

"Maybe we could say, *a Christian lady*. That should cover it."

Jeremiah dipped the pen in the inkwell. When he held it poised over the paper, waiting for Philip to agree with his suggestion, a small drop fell and quickly spread into an unsightly blob. "I've messed up this sheet. Do you have a pencil? I could use it while we figure out the wording. Then I'll copy it in ink."

Philip made his way to the sideboard against the back wall of the large open room and pulled out a drawer. He shuffled through the contents before holding up the stub of a pencil. "Here's the onliest one I got."

"It'll do." Jeremiah reached for the pencil and continued, "*A Christian man in Golden, New Mexico, seeks a Christian lady...* where do we go now?"

Once again, Philip was deep in thought. "*...who needs a chance at a new life.*"

Jeremiah nodded and added the words. "I like it. Do you

want to say anything else, or should I just put your name and address?"

"That's enough, but put General Delivery as my address." A smile crept across the older man's face, bringing a twinkle to his rheumy eyes.

He returned to his rocking chair while Jeremiah copied the words with ink, folded the message, inserted the paper in an envelope, and wrote the address for the *Boston Globe* on the front.

"I suppose you want me to take this to the post office." He knew Philip didn't get out much in the chilly spring air of the Ortiz Mountains, because it aggravated his breathing problem.

"If ya don't mind." Philip reached into the watch pocket of his trousers and pulled out a coin. "Here's the money."

"I don't need your money." Jeremiah headed toward the front door. "I just hope you aren't making a mistake."

Philip cleared his throat. "Jerry?" Huskiness colored his tone. "I'm thankful fer all ya do to help me." He paused until Jeremiah gave him a nod. "I've talked to the good Lord about this. I'm sure He agrees with what I'm doin'."

What could Jeremiah say to that? *Nothing.* He couldn't explain why, but when Philip Smith talked to his Lord, things happened. Jeremiah pushed his hair back before donning his Stetson and exiting through the front door, being careful it latched behind him. He didn't want Philip to have to get up and close it again if it should blow open after he was gone. Let him rest in his rocking chair. After all his long years of mining, he'd earned it.

Marching down the cobblestone street toward the post office, Jeremiah hoped he wouldn't meet anyone who wanted to talk. The sooner he got this letter mailed, the sooner he could wash his hands of the whole situation. Maybe no one would answer the ad. Or maybe he could just tear the whole thing up and not tell Philip he didn't mail it.

If he wasn't honorable, he could get away with that. But he couldn't lie to the man who meant more to him than anyone in the world. Wouldn't be right. He'd make sure to look over any letters Philip received. He wouldn't let some floozy use his friend as her meal ticket and think coming here was her golden opportunity—in more ways than one. No sirree, he'd watch anyone who came with an eagle eye. She would have to pass his inspection before he'd introduce her to Philip. Even if his old friend did say he'd talked to God about it.

As Jeremiah walked into town, he fastened the top button on his long-sleeved shirt. The day would heat up later, but spring brought cool breezes in the early morning. When he passed the hotel, Caroline Oldman stepped through the door and started sweeping the boardwalk.

"Morning, Caroline." He tipped his hat to the proprietress, who was also the wife of the preacher. They'd been good friends to Jeremiah since they arrived in Golden. Their influence had calmed the rowdy town a lot.

He kept walking toward the post office. Would Philip hear from a woman before summer? Jeremiah hoped the old miner wouldn't receive a single answer to his ad.

Jeremiah thought back to when he came from Missouri to New Mexico searching for gold. Philip was the first miner he'd met. Thin and wiry, the old man's face was almost hidden behind his long beard and thin gray hair that reached to his shoulders, but he had a heart of gold. He'd befriended Jeremiah and helped him learn all about mining. He was even there when Jeremiah's partner was killed in a cave-in at the mine they owned together.

Philip had listened to all of Jeremiah's rantings and guided him toward becoming a cattleman. He knew Philip prayed for him all the time. But Jeremiah couldn't accept all that God nonsense himself. Where had God been when train robbers killed his mother and he was left in the clutches of his cruel uncle and father?

With a shudder, he shook his head to dislodge the images invading his thoughts. The less he thought about the past, the better. Too much pain and suffering there.

He was sure Philip had prayed about sending this letter, but Jeremiah wasn't convinced there was a God. And if there was, why would He care whether some greedy woman came to fleece the old miner?

No, Jeremiah would guarantee that didn't happen.

CHAPTER 2

EARLY SPRING, 1890
BOSTON, MASSACHUSETTS

*M*addy Mercer pressed trembling fingertips against the throbbing ache in her temples. "I need to see how Loraine is faring."

"But Miss Madeline, your dear father has been gone only a few weeks." A deep frown marred Sarah Sneed's face, even though the words held compassion. "You're still in mourning. You shouldn't go traipsing down to that shanty town."

The usually cheerful woman, who had been more than a servant to Maddy since her mother died when she was only a child, turned to stir a pot on the stove. "Frank has been taking food to her. She hasn't gone hungry." The swirls of the long-handled spoon kept cadence with her words. "He'll take the basket to her this morning. There's no need for you to venture out into the cold."

Maddy closed the fasteners on the black, woolen, full-length mackintosh, ending at her neck, then straightened the double cape attached at the top. "I know, Sarah, but I've been praying for her, and I feel a strong urgency to see her myself."

At the sound of Sarah's huff, the outside kitchen door flew open, letting in Sarah's husband and more cold air than the stove could stave off. After he shut the heavy door, he stomped his feet on the doormat.

"Tell her, Frank. Miss Madeline shouldn't be out in this weather."

The ruddy-faced handyman and driver studied Maddy's face but said nothing.

"I've been cold before, and I can't continue to stay in this house. All I do here is mope and dwell on what I've lost." Maddy pulled a knitted hood over her hair, tucking in the few stray curls that refused to stay in her bun, and tied the strings in a bow under her chin. "Going to see Loraine will help me forget my sorrow for a little while."

Frank nodded and picked up the basket on the table and the heated brick his wife had prepared for him. He offered his other arm to Maddy and escorted her to the waiting surrey. "You're doing a good thing, helping these women. Most of the young people in your circle never think about what the poor are going through."

She turned tear-filled eyes toward this man, who more often than not was silent. His words touched her heart. "Father taught me about benevolence. How can I not help them? I'd want someone to help me if I were in their situation."

"I'm always glad to visit them for you, but Loraine sorely needs a woman right now." Compassion haunted his somber eyes. "It's a good thing you're going today."

After helping her into the back seat, he placed the brick wrapped in wool beneath her feet and tucked a heavy lap robe around her. Then he took his place in front and picked up the reins.

"Let's go." As his tongue clicked, the two matching black horses pranced down the slushy street.

Even though Frank had lowered the heavy side and back curtains on the large, leather-topped buggy, the wind clawed at Maddy with chilled fingers, sneaking toward the lump of ice that had settled in her heart when she lost her father. She ached with loneliness, an emptiness that nothing had been able to fill, not even the loving ministrations of this loyal couple who attempted to bring her comfort.

The surrey's strong springs couldn't keep the buggy from rocking as the wheels bumped over the cobblestones. On any other day, the swaying motion would have soothed Maddy, but her thoughts were so jumbled about losing her father and Loraine's immense needs that heaviness clouded her mind. And each breath of icy air burned her lungs.

When the buggy finally stopped outside the tumbledown shack, Maddy took a deep breath, immediately regretting it. She pressed a white linen square against her nose to block out the unpleasant odors of garbage mixed with human waste and who knew what else. She closed her eyes for a moment. This cluster of ramshackle shanties was an eyesore that should be torn down, but where else would the poor occupants go? It was the only place available to them. Boston wasn't ready to welcome these people inside the borders of the town.

Why hadn't someone forced the property owners to take better care of their renters? She knew most people didn't give a thought to the plight of the poor, focusing instead on their own sumptuous lives. Only a few residents like Maddy even ventured here.

The Bible, however, said that the poor would always be among us, so Maddy wanted to do whatever she could to help. Still, her offerings seemed so insignificant against such a vast problem, even where Loraine was concerned.

"Miss Madeline?" Frank offered his hand to help her alight from her carriage.

She took hold of his steadying grip and tried to find a place where her shoes wouldn't become bogged down in the muck and mire. After she perched on two small, convenient rocks, Frank startled her by sweeping her up in his arms and carrying her to the larger flat stone that served as a tiny stoop. He was careful when he set her down, keeping his arm around her until she steadied on her feet. He hadn't carried her since she was thirteen, but his strong arms felt comforting in a way she needed right now. While she knocked on the sagging, splintered door, he returned to the buggy to retrieve the basket of provisions.

She waited a long moment. When no one came, she knocked a little louder.

After another long wait, the door opened only a crack, and Loraine peeked out before she pulled the door wider. "Miss—"

"Just Maddy." She gave a trembling smile. "Remember what I told you."

Loraine clutched her gaping, tattered robe over the bulge of her stomach and moved back to allow Maddy's entrance. Maddy tried not to stare. In the weeks since she'd been here, the first-time mother had expanded at an alarming rate. Perhaps her baby was due sooner than she believed. She wouldn't last another month. She looked about to explode right now.

Frank followed through the gaping doorway and set the basket on the rickety table leaning against the wall near the open fireplace. Maddy shut the door, but it didn't latch. Must be some trick to making it stay.

Her servant lifted the lid of the basket and started removing cans of fruits and vegetables that had been bought at Shale's Mercantile. When he brought out a loaf of bread wrapped in a tea towel, she watched the enticing aroma capture Loraine's attention. Her eyes strained toward the food, hunger painting a terribly needy expression across her face. Then Frank left to retrieve the basket of coal they had brought.

"Come over and let's eat." Maddy didn't have to urge Loraine again.

The pregnant woman waddled to the table and dropped into the chair closest to the fire. "That smells so good."

Loraine's raspy voice didn't sound right to Maddy. Worry climbed with spidery feet up her spine.

Frank hastened across the room. "I'll keep watch over the horses and buggy."

He scooped a tattered curtain back and peeked between the boards nailed across the broken window. With his back to them, Maddy knew Loraine would feel less conspicuous and have a sense of privacy. She was grateful to Frank for being so astute.

Maddy lifted the lid from the crockery jar filled with warm, home-made soup and filled a bowl for the young woman. To make her feel less embarrassed, Maddy also ladled a small amount into a bowl for herself. They were sitting far enough from each other that Loraine couldn't see how little she had taken. She ate tiny bites while Loraine gobbled the soup and bread. All the while, the woman's plight tore at Maddy's heart.

After a few moments, Loraine slowed her eating, and her manners reflected Maddy's. "Thank you. I don't know what I would've done if you hadn't come. I didn't have a bit of food in the house."

Maddy reached across the table and clasped one of Loraine's dry, cracked hands. "Tell me how long it's been since you've eaten."

Loraine's head drooped as if in shame. "Not since I ran out of what your driver brought me last time. That was day before yesterday."

Maddy couldn't imagine being in such straits. This woman's parents should be horsewhipped. Disowning their daughter because she married someone they didn't approve of was unconscionable. They didn't even know her husband had died or that they were going to have a grandchild.

Her brows knit with concern. "Have you seen a doctor?"

Loraine shook her head, tears streaming down her pale cheeks.

"What about a midwife?"

"I don't have money for either of them."

Maddy barely heard the whispered words. She stared across the bleak, cold room at the small fire. "How much money do you have?"

Sobs erupted from Loraine. Maddy waited for them to subside, praying for the poor young woman sitting before her. She couldn't have been much more than Maddy's twenty-one years, but she appeared decades older.

"Not even a penny." A hiccough punctuated the sentence, and she swiped at her eyes with the backs of her hands. "When the landlord comes, he'll probably turn me out. I haven't paid him anything this month."

Each word battered Maddy's heart, chipping away some of the sadness hardening there. Her life was so much better than Loraine's. Her losses paled in comparison. "How much do you owe him?"

Loraine stiffened her spine. "I couldn't let you pay him, Madeline. Somehow God will take care of me. He has so far."

"Miss Madeline." Frank had turned away from the window. "We can't stay long. The horses will get too cold."

She opened her reticule and extracted what little money she carried with her. She pressed the coins and one crumpled bill into Loraine's hand. "Don't think about refusing me. Perhaps God sent me to you. I did feel a strong impression that I had to come."

Loraine smiled through her tears. "Thank you again."

Maddy pulled Loraine into a warm hug. "Either I or Frank will come to check on you and bring you food every day."

When Loraine looked as if she would protest, Maddy stepped back and gently took her cold hand, rubbing it to bring warmth. "Loraine, just look at it as God doing His work through us."

Tears made tracks down Loraine's smudged cheeks as she slowly nodded. "All right. Thank you."

Once back in the buggy, Maddy felt the cold clear to her bones. The heated brick had long since lost all its warmth. Even in the comfort of the covered double surrey, with a blanket wrapped around her skirt, she shivered—and from more than just the temperature. She had to think of another way to help Loraine. During the trip through Boston toward her home, she tried to come up with a solution. Since she had never quite warmed up in the hovel where Loraine lived, the cold numbed her body and clouded her mind.

"Whoa!" Frank Sneed called to the horses. After they came to a full stop, he stepped down from the front seat and lifted the heavy woolen side curtain. "Let me help you, Miss Madeline."

He extended his callused hand, and she grasped it, feeling the warmth through her black kid leather gloves. If only more of it would reach her heart.

She let Frank help her to the house. Thankful for the heat that whooshed from the open door, she was even more grateful for Frank as he hurried to care for the horses, knowing he must be as chilled as she was. The dependable man always put duty first.

Sarah greeted her with a welcome cup of hot chocolate and a plate of her favorite oatmeal cookies. Spices scented the air, reminding Maddy how little she'd been eating lately, and suddenly she felt hungry.

"Join me." She pointed toward another chair at the kitchen table. "I want to talk to you."

Sarah poured a cup of tea from the teapot she always kept steeping and sat with Maddy. "How was Loraine today?"

"I'm very worried about her." Maddy took a sip, welcoming the warmth the sweet liquid brought. "I think she'll have the baby soon, but she hasn't been to a doctor. She can't even pay her rent."

Sarah *tsked* before biting into her own warm cookie.

"I'll have Frank take our doctor to check her. I can't just sit here and not do anything for her." Maddy glanced around the warm, welcoming kitchen so different from the one-room, bare, cold shanty she had just left. Life could be so unfair.

She'd change that for Loraine, if she could find a way.

CHAPTER 3

GOLDEN, NEW MEXICO

*J*eremiah stepped from the cooler interior of the post office into the heat of midday. The spring-like weather he'd loved while growing up in the Missouri Ozarks didn't last long in New Mexico—a few days at the most. But he'd gotten used to the rapid change.

It had been only a week since he'd mailed the letter for Philip, and his friend had already asked him to check to see if an answer had come. This mail-order bride idea had become like a burr under his saddle, and Philip wouldn't let it go.

Jeremiah returned empty-handed to the adobe house built higher up Main Street than any other building in Golden, nestled in the Ortiz Mountains. When Jeremiah opened the door, Philip was giving pacing a valiant try, but shortness of breath had slowed him almost to a shuffle.

Eagerly, the older man turned a questioning gaze on Jeremiah. "So, did I git a letter?"

"Nothing."

"Well, I'll be danged. I was sure I'd a-heard by now." He slumped into his favorite chair and began rocking.

"I didn't expect an answer yet," Jeremiah said kindly. "Mail's slow, and who knows how long it'll take the paper to publish the ad?"

"Oh, I know all that." Philip reached toward his chin but stopped halfway, letting his hand drop into his lap. "I jist feel this urgency." His bony index finger tapped twice against his chest.

"Urgency? You planning on kicking the bucket anytime soon?" Jeremiah chuckled at his own joke, but his friend didn't join him.

"Ain't no laughin' matter, Jerry." Hurt threaded through the words. "I havta prepare a place fer her." Intensity blazed from Philip's eyes. "Cain't take too long with it neither."

Jeremiah rubbed at the tension tying knots in the muscles on the back of his neck. He didn't want to call Philip a pain in the neck, but this crazy notion about a bride brought on all kinds of aches in him. Getting a woman to come for his friend was bad enough, but he'd never considered the idea of sending off for a wife for himself. The likelihood of him never having a wife stung a place deep in his heart. Baking soda wouldn't ease this kind of heartburn.

Sure the saloons employed women, but who wanted to hitch himself to one of them? The only decent ladies in town were already married when they arrived. Respectable women, especially single ones, didn't want to come to a rough mining town, even if Golden did have several businesses besides the saloons.

Success was a cold bed partner. He'd felt that chill far too long. He wanted someone to share his life with besides an old miner who seemed determined that he wasn't long for this world. Much as he loved the old man, he knew he would love the right woman even more.

Memories from his childhood intruded. His mother rocking

17

him to sleep was the earliest memory he could dredge up. Another of her soothing hand on his brow when he was sick. Her warm kiss on his cheek that he'd been embarrassed for his school friends to see. Then she was gone. If she had lived longer and taught him about love, he might not have given in to the lust of the gold fields. But if he'd stayed in the Ozarks, he'd probably have been a dirt farmer just like his old man. Trying to eke out a living from the thin, rocky soil and barely getting by.

He jerked his thoughts back to his friend's last statement. "What do you mean, 'prepare a place for her'?"

The retired miner pulled his Bible off the table beside his rocker. "Been readin' the Good Book. Says God's goin' to prepare a place fer us."

Jeremiah leaned against the closed door and crossed his ankles. "So?" How could there be a heaven, when he wasn't even sure there was a God? If there were, where was God when his mother was jerked from his life, leaving him a frightened, lonely little boy? He shook his mind from that thought before it pulled him back into a dark place deep inside that no one else knew about.

"Cain't ask no woman to come here and not prepare a place fer her." Philip closed the book and looked up, a challenge in his piercing eyes.

Might as well agree with the older man. If he didn't, Jeremiah would never have any peace. "You have a nice house." He glanced around the bright, sunny room filled with factory-made furniture. Not many people in Golden had furnishings this nice. They'd worked long and hard on repairing this place when Philip sold his mine. Looked like a mansion to Jeremiah already. "Much too large for just one man."

"Yeah, but not if'n she has kids." Thin fingers drummed on the carved wooden armrest as Philip ceased rocking. He raked the room with a critical eye. "Won't be enough then."

Jeremiah straightened. "Couldn't you turn the storeroom in the back into a place for her?"

Any woman who'd answer a newspaper ad surely wouldn't be too picky. She should welcome any shelter if she was in such dire straits. Then again, it'd be a lot of unnecessary work if no one answered the ad.

"I ain't stickin' her out there." Steel laced Philip's words and cooled the atmosphere in the room as his thumb jabbed the air toward the back of the house. "Wouldn't be fittin'."

"So what did you have in mind?" Jeremiah knew he wouldn't like what was coming, but there was no way around it. And keeping Philip happy mattered to him. Probably more than anything else in his life.

"Want to add two large rooms 'cross the side a the house." Excitement filled the old miner's visage, twinkling his eyes. "And we'll need new furniture fer both. As good or better'n what I got fer me."

Philip talked as if Jeremiah didn't have a ranch to run. He figured he'd get stuck with finding the laborers to build the addition, obtaining the building supplies, and seeing to the furniture. Probably have to oversee the whole job too.

"I've already drawed the plans." The older man shuffled to the sideboard and grabbed a large rolled-up paper. He hobbled over to the dinner table and spread the sketch out. "See this." His finger followed the lines. "This room. And here's my bedroom. This'n's the kitchen." He glanced up from under bushy white brows, as if making sure Jeremiah paid attention. "She oughta be comfy in these two rooms." His forefinger tapped each area.

She sure should. They would almost double the size of the house. Philip must have bats in his belfry. All this work could be a complete waste. Jeremiah didn't realize he'd mumbled those last words until one of Philip's eyebrows rose toward the ceiling.

Jeremiah held up his hands in surrender. "I understand. You won't consider it a waste, even if no one answers your ad."

"Right on the nose!" Philip's index finger tapped the side of his nose on each word.

"So." Jeremiah heaved a sigh. "What do you want me to do?"

While Philip explained, Jeremiah's thoughts jumped around. He tried to listen to his friend while figuring how much time he could spend in town helping him and how much he really had to be on his own ranch. Those cattle wouldn't take care of themselves. With all the gold fever, he had a hard time keeping good help. Sometimes when he returned to the ranch after going to town, all the hands had abandoned their jobs. But the miners certainly liked eating the beef he produced. Selling meat to them and other people in town kept his bank balance healthy.

"I'll order the lumber and plaster tomorrow." He forced a smile instead of the grimace he felt like making. "I can come into town by eleven."

"Won't have to." Philip started rolling up the paper. "Done already ordered it all. Should come in on the train any day."

That was a surprise. "How'd you know how much to order?"

"Wasn't always a miner." The older man shuffled toward the rocker and settled into it. "Useta be a carpenter."

"I never knew that."

The twinkle returned to Philip's eyes. "Lotta things ya don't know 'bout me, son." He chuckled. "Whole lotta things."

What could Jeremiah do but join in the laughter? Philip was right. No matter how many times they talked together, new things were always popping up.

"So." He studied Philip to see his reaction. "You ever been married? We never talked about that."

The shaggy head nodded. "Sure was. Some of the happiest years of my life."

"And you never told me about it?" How could they have missed something that important?

"Never came up."

"Until now."

Why hadn't he asked Philip more about his life before the mining?

Because Jeremiah was too interested in his own misery. He hadn't looked beyond himself. If they'd discussed this part of Philip's life sooner, maybe the mail-order bride thing wouldn't have come as such a surprise to him.

"Want to tell me about her?"

Philip's eyes glazed over while he stared out the window. "Not much to tell. I loved her until the day she died. Still carry her and our son in my heart." Once again his finger tapped his chest. "Wish I'd a-had a pitcher made a-them."

Stunned, Jeremiah looked at Philip with new understanding. "Is that why you want to help a woman? Why you'd welcome children?"

"Partly." Philip rested his chin on his chest. Jeremiah thought he'd dropped off to sleep until one finger wiped a tear from each rheumy eye. "Lots a times, I've wondered what my son woulda been like if he'd a-lived. And I miss my Maggie every day. But I'm not lookin' to replace them. This is jist what God done told me to do."

Always came back to God. Everything with Philip returned there eventually. Even if he didn't force his ideas on Jeremiah, they were part of who Philip was. No doubt about it.

Just seemed like he talked more about God the older he got. Might as well humor him and agree. Jeremiah didn't want to discuss his friend's beliefs or his own lack thereof. The sooner this mail-order bride fiasco was over and done with, the better. He sure hoped no one would answer the letter. If no replies came, Philip would have a much larger house to rattle around in. But it was his money, and if he wanted to waste it that way, Jeremiah wouldn't be the one to argue.

∾

BOSTON, MASSACHUSETTS

*T*he brass knocker on the front door resounded through the downstairs as Sarah ran a wooden spoon in a figure eight through a pot of beef stew. "For some reason, the potatoes and carrots are sticking to the bottom of the pan. Must not be enough fat in the meat."

The warmth of the large stove and the companionship had drawn Maddy to the kitchen. She stood and tried to shake the wrinkles from her skirt. "I can answer the door. You're busy."

"I don't know why we had to let the other servants go." Sarah shook her head. "Your dear father is probably turning over in his grave."

"We can hire them back after Father's solicitor works out the details of the will." Maddy headed toward the door to the hallway. "I really don't mind answering the door."

Wonder who could be calling at this time of day? Usually visitors came in the early afternoon. That way ladies could be dressed and prepared to receive them. She turned the ornate knob, and the heavy wooden door creaked as she opened it. She'd have to ask Frank to oil the hinges again. The cold seemed to dry them out almost as much as the heat of summer.

A young boy dressed in rags stamped his feet on the porch. She could hardly believe how little protection he had from the frigid air and wondered where his parents were. She glanced toward the street but saw no one else.

"I got a message for Miz Madeline Mercer," the boy announced. "Could you tell her to come to the door, ma'am? I ain't s'posed to give it to anyone else."

She held out her hand. "I'm Madeline Mercer."

After placing the slightly wrinkled envelope in her palm, he started to leave.

"Would you like to come in? I believe there's hot stew and bread in the kitchen."

Madeline's words stopped the boy in his tracks. For a moment hunger pleaded from his eyes, then they hardened. "I'm s'posed to go back immediately and tell the man I give it to you. He's paying me extra for that." With those few words, the boy jumped down the steps and ran up the stone walkway to the front gate.

After thrusting the missive into her pocket, Maddy closed the door and hurried to the kitchen. Just those few minutes had chilled her to the bone. How could that young boy stand being out in such weather? She pulled her chair close to the large stove and held out her hands until the stinging left her fingers.

"So, Miss Madeline, who was at the door?" Sarah still bustled around finishing the lunch they would share when Frank arrived home.

"A young boy brought a message to me."

"What does it say?"

Madeline sighed. "I don't know yet. I was more concerned about the poor child. The rags he wore did nothing to ward off the cold. I asked him to come back to the kitchen. I could tell he was hungry, but he refused. Said he had to get back to the man who sent the letter." She pulled the envelope from her pocket, broke the seal, and skimmed the letter. "It's from Horace Johnstone. He says he'll arrive this evening at seven to dine with me."

Both women's gasps filled the room.

"When did you invite him, child? I must've missed it when you told me to prepare the meal."

"I didn't invite him." Her harsh tone grated in her own ears.

Indignation brewed like a storm in her chest. Invite him, indeed! Never would she ever have invited that man for a meal. What was he thinking just announcing his impending arrival this way?

The presumption of the man galled her. How dare he? Didn't he know a real gentleman waited for an invitation? She'd always considered him uncouth, and this was one more example of his lack of proper training.

"Then send him a message that you aren't receiving guests tonight." Sarah's bosom heaved, and her fists rested on her hips.

"He was Father's business partner, though I never understood why Father made him one. I will not be as ill-mannered as he is. Perhaps he wants to talk about the business. Maybe I should ask Mr. Sanderson to come too."

Sarah went back to stirring the stew. This time the spoon flew around inside the pot. "He could just be offering his condolences."

"He did that at the funeral, and that was sufficient." Even the thought of the man in her house gave Maddy the willies, as Frank was wont to say. "I don't like the man. Something about him doesn't feel right. I'll have to be alert."

After putting the spoon on its rest, Sarah enveloped her in a hug. "Neither do Frank and me. But surely he wouldn't do anything wrong in your own house."

❦

That evening, Maddy chose her mourning gown that had the highest collar. She wanted as much of herself covered as possible. She also desired to appear drab. She didn't like the way Horace sometimes leered at her.

Before her father died, she had understood he was only an employee, but now she wasn't too sure. Mr. Sanderson, her father's solicitor, had sent word that he hadn't finished working on all the papers about her father's estate. It shouldn't have taken a month or more, should it? Everything must be in order by now. Perhaps Mr. Johnstone had somehow slowed the process. Was there any way he could do that? She wished she knew.

She pulled her hair back into a severe bun, using extra pins to make sure no curls broke free. The bombazine dress she'd chosen was really a day dress, not one for entertaining guests in the evening, but that crass man probably wouldn't know the difference. Actually, she hoped he did. She wanted him to know that she held his insistence on coming to dinner in disdain. She'd thought she'd never have to see the odious man after her father's funeral.

A soft knock at her bedroom door brought Maddy out of her troubled musings. "Come in."

Sarah wore a dark dress with a black band circling the upper part of one arm. "Do you need any help getting ready?" At the end of the question, her eyes widened. "Whatever are you wearing, child?"

Maddy gazed at her servant but stood her ground against the censure she felt emanating from her.

"I mean, even though you're in mourning, that's not a proper dress for dinner guests," Sarah stammered.

"The man's manners are atrocious—inviting himself to my house. I want to let him know what I think about it." Maddy wouldn't give in.

"Your dear mother would be appalled if she were still with us." The wrinkles deepened between Sarah's graying brows. "She'd never have treated a guest in her home this callously."

"I have another reason for choosing this gown." Maddy fingered the black lace edging the stand-up collar. "I don't like the way Mr. Johnstone looks at me. It makes my skin crawl."

Sarah opened her arms and pulled Maddy close. "And so it should, child." The comforting pats on her back soon calmed Maddy's heart.

After the hug, she stepped back. "Will you do something for me?"

"Anything." The smile had returned to Sarah's kind face.

"Don't leave me alone with that man—even for a moment."

Sarah shook her head. "I don't know how we'll handle that. It wouldn't be right for Frank and me to sit at the table with you and your company."

Maddy was so angry she raised her foot to stomp it. However, remembering that Sarah would disapprove of this type of behavior, she lowered the foot and began tapping her toes in a soundless, rapid staccato against the Persian carpet. "I'm tired of following all the rules of etiquette. I really want you at the table with me." She crossed her arms and ran her hands up and down her sleeves, trying to take away the chilled feeling and willing away the terror striking her heart.

"I know, but we mustn't bring dishonor to your name." Sarah thought for a moment. "Frank could act as footman and stand inside the room wherever you are."

"That would work." For the first time since hearing the man was coming to dinner, Maddy felt a glimmer of hope. "Do you think Frank'll mind?"

"Of course not. He loves you as much as I do."

A heavy hand abused the brass doorknocker, sending repeated metallic thuds reverberating through the whole house. She was sure that if Sarah and Frank had been in their quarters on the third floor, they would have heard it even there.

"He's here." Sarah once again patted Maddy's shoulder. "You'll be all right, child. Remember the good Lord will be with you. Wait in your room until Frank comes to get you." She slipped out the door and turned down the hallway toward the back stairs.

Panic gripped Maddy's heart. If only this night were over, and she'd never have to see Mr. Johnstone again.

"Miss Madeline." A quiet knock accompanied the words.

The gentle sound of her name on Frank's tongue brought Maddy out of her dark thoughts. She opened the door and accompanied him down the front stairs, her hand resting inside his crooked elbow.

Horace Johnstone stood near the closed front door, his black hair slicked back and his leering gaze following her progress. How was she ever going to get through the evening? If she could think of a way to cut it short, she would. *Lord, I could use Your help right now.*

She stepped onto the marble tile in the foyer, and her heels clicked as she crossed to stand in front of her unwelcome guest. "Mr. Johnstone."

Even though she didn't want to touch him, she held out her hand. She didn't have to give him an enthusiastic shake.

Instead he grasped her fingers and lifted them to place a moist kiss against the back of her hand. "Madeline, you are so enchanting."

His glib words slid through the air and danced in chills down her spine. She quickly extricated her fingers and thrust her hand behind her. She wished she could wipe every evidence of the contact against her skirt, but she refrained.

"Dinner is served." Frank's words drew her attention.

"Thank you." She nodded toward her servant and led the way into the formal dining room.

Maddy smiled for the first time since the doorbell rang. Sarah had set two places on the polished rosewood table that could comfortably seat twenty people. One at each end. She hurried to her place, but Mr. Johnstone reached it first, pulling out the chair for her. She settled onto the cushioned seat her dear mother had embroidered.

"Thank you."

After sliding her chair in, the imperious man surveyed the room. "This will never do. We won't be able to carry on a conversation sitting so far apart. Have your servant move my place closer." He sounded as if he were used to having his commands obeyed.

Frank started to comply, but Maddy gave her head an imperceptible shake. "Actually, Mrs. Sneed has worked so hard on this meal, I don't want to give her anything extra to do." She forced herself to smile up at Mr. Johnstone.

With a fleeting grin, Frank straightened and stood still as a statue against the wall beside the doorway.

Oblivious, Mr. Johnstone stalked to the other end of the table. "That's all right. I'll move the dishes myself." His gruff words didn't bode well for the rest of the evening.

He grabbed the silverware and napkin and stacked them on the charger plate in a haphazard manner. He topped the stack with the cup and saucer, then brought the water glass in his other hand. When he arrived at the chair to Maddy's right, he set everything down, scattering them in no apparent pattern. The man evidently didn't know the proper way to arrange the items in a place setting. She gritted her teeth to keep from giving a very unladylike growl.

Since they'd had short notice, Sarah and Maddy had planned a very simple menu. Sarah brought in a large soup tureen on its matching platter. Frank hurried to help her set it on the table, then went to stand at attention beside the door. When Sarah turned to retrieve the individual bowls, Mr. Johnstone dipped into the soup with his own spoon, dripping the liquid onto the table linen, then slurping the hot liquid when his spoon reached his mouth.

Maddy sighed. This was going to be a long, dreadful meal.

~

*M*addy led the way into the parlor when she really wanted to march to the front door and bid her guest a swift good-bye. She chose a side chair, instead of the couch, not wishing to leave him any opportunity to sit beside her. "Would you like me to have Sarah bring tea or coffee?"

He frowned before he sat across from her on the sofa. "Didn't your father keep anything stronger in the house?"

When Maddy didn't answer him, he finally mumbled, "Coffee."

She rang the bell on the table beside her.

Frank left his post beside the doorway. "Yes, Miss."

After glancing up at him, she almost cried from the sympathy she read in his eyes. "Have Sarah bring tea for me and coffee for Mr. Johnstone." She hoped Frank would quickly be back at his post.

She clasped her hands in her lap and finally looked to her guest.

"Madeline, as I told you at the funeral, I'm sorry for your loss."

She didn't discern any sincerity in the man, and it grated on her that he assumed he could call her by her given name. She hadn't given him that permission. "Thank you again, *Mr. Johnstone.*"

He cleared his throat. "I know it's hard for a woman alone in the world."

Sarah swept through the doorway, carrying a silver tray. She set it on the coffee table between them. "Would you like for me to pour, Miss Madeline?"

"No, I can take care of it."

Maddy filled a dainty china cup with the darker pungent liquid before handing the saucer to her guest. Then she poured her tea, adding sugar and a little milk.

Before she finished stirring her own beverage, Mr. Johnstone had already gulped down the steaming coffee, and his empty cup clattered against the fragile dish. Maddy winced. Her mother's treasured china was in danger with this man around.

"I usually drink a large mug of coffee." He leaned back with his arms along the back of the red velvet sofa. "That little teacup is like drinking from a thimble." He laughed at his own joke.

She was surprised he even knew what a thimble was. "Would you like more?" She lifted the silver coffee server.

He shook his head. "Actually, Madeline, I've come to talk to you."

The doorway was on the other side of the sofa. Thankfully, Frank continued to stand sentinel. She saw his eyes widen for an instant at that statement, as did hers.

"I'm sure we don't have anything else to discuss." She had tired of trying to think of topics of pleasant conversation during the meal.

"Oh, I think we do." He sat forward and leaned his hands on his knees.

She felt uncomfortable with him moving even that short distance closer to her. "And what might that be?"

"I've come to tell you that we are going to be married."

She couldn't contain the horrified gasp that escaped. "Married?" Frank started toward the man, but she stopped him with a shake of her head. "Whatever gave you such a ridiculous notion?"

Mr. Johnstone winced when she said *ridiculous*, but she didn't care.

"That was your father's plan all along." He bit out the words in rapid succession.

Maddy stood up, her hands balled at her side. "That's absurd. He wouldn't have decided anything so momentous about my future without discussing it with me first."

He rose to his feet, his bulk towering over her. "Now just get down off your high horse, missy. You don't understand what a precarious situation you are in." He took a step to go around the table, but she shifted her position to keep it between them.

"You are not making any sense, Mr. Johnstone."

"Horace." He glared at her. "You must call your bridegroom by his first name."

"You are not my bridegroom, and you never will be!" Her

shrill words cut through the suddenly stifling air. Her chest tightened, and tears seeped into her eyes, but she refused to let them fall.

Mr. Johnstone—she could never call him *Horace*—held up his hands. "Now calm down. I need to explain things to you. Have a seat." He dropped back onto the sofa.

"What is there to explain? Nothing will change my mind." Her clipped words didn't seem to affect the man.

"I've been in touch with Sanderson—"

"Father's solicitor?" She perched on the front of the chair where she'd been sitting.

He nodded. "Your father made several poor decisions, and the business was in trouble when he died. You, my dear, are almost penniless."

Icy cords wrapped instantly around her heart. With all the strength she could muster, she willed her body not to respond to his words.

"I've saved most of the money I made, so I promised your dear father that if anything happened to him—" he paused, apparently for effect, before continuing—"I would marry you and take care of you in his stead."

Black dots appeared before her eyes, but Maddy fought against them. She would not give him the satisfaction of fainting. It would give him more reason to *need* to take care of her. She took a deep breath. "I'll take up a trade or become a governess before I would ever marry you." She raised her chin to a haughty angle and stood. Her belief that what he had said was a lie kept tears from trailing down her cheeks. "Frank, please see Mr. Johnstone out."

She turned to go, but Johnstone's words stopped her from leaving the room.

"I will give you two weeks to get used to the idea. Then we *will* wed."

Not in a million years.

CHAPTER 4

*S*hocked, Maddy returned to the chair and dropped as gracefully as she could with Mr. Johnstone's words hanging in the air between them like an adder ready to strike. She took a deep breath and slowly let it out, shivers coiling up and down her spine. Frank looked as if he were ready to explode. She'd better give an answer before her servant crossed the line and assaulted her guest.

"Where did you get such an insane idea, *Mr. Johnstone*? I would not marry any man, *even one I loved*, while I mourn my father." She hoped he understood the implication behind her words. How could she state her feelings any more plainly?

Mr. Johnstone steepled his fingers and stared at her over their tips, as if he were studying an interesting insect. "I don't think you understand, Madeline. You have no say in the matter."

His words, encased in iron, pierced her heart, stealing her breath. How could he be so calm and matter-of-fact about her life? If what he said was true, he'd ripped apart her world and turned it completely upside down. She quaked inside, afraid she would lose her fragile hold on her emotions. She didn't want Johnstone to know how much his words affected her.

"I don't think *you* understand, Mr. Johnstone." She stiffened her spine and didn't try to keep the disdain out of her tone. "I will not dishonor the memory of my father by shortening my time of mourning to only one more week."

Frank gave an approving nod. Maddy was glad she sat where she did, because Mr. Johnstone couldn't see her servant.

Johnstone relaxed his grim expression. "All right, Madeline, I will give you one month. A month from today. We. Will. Wed. Understood?"

Maddy didn't answer. If she said one thing, she'd lose all control and collapse. Instead she stood and swept from the room before tears betrayed her. Frank left right behind her.

"One month. Not a day longer." Mr. Johnstone's final, threatening words followed her and wound around her heart, almost strangling the life out of it.

Although Frank stopped at the bottom of the staircase, she continued up and didn't turn to look until she heard the heavy footsteps recede and the outside door close behind her tormentor. Crumpling onto the top step, she dropped her head into her hands and sobbed.

"Sarah, come in here!"

Maddy had never heard Frank raise his voice, but this bellow reverberated throughout the entrance hall.

Sarah must have been close, because she immediately clambered up the stairs and dropped beside Maddy, pulling her into her arms. "It's going to be all right, dear. We'll think of something." Soothing words accompanied soft hands as they rubbed her back and snuggled her into a warm, safe haven.

She melted into the woman's embrace as if Sarah were her mother. A rushing torrent of tears soaked the shoulder of Sarah's dress, but the servant didn't seem to notice as her gentle whispers and crooning continued to console Maddy.

When Maddy finally stopped crying, she stood and took a deep breath. Frank's hand rested on the banister a few steps down from the women. As she perused the worry on his face, she remembered he'd taken the doctor to check on her friend Loraine that day.

"I'm sorry, Frank. I've been so immersed in my own troubles that I didn't even ask what the doctor said." She mustered a brave, though wobbly, smile.

Balancing against the wall with one hand, Sarah rose from the step. "Let's go into the kitchen. We can talk by the stove, and I'll fix a cup of chocolate for you."

Sarah led the way, and Maddy and Frank followed. They settled on two kitchen stools beside the worktable while Sarah bustled around preparing the hot drink.

"What did the doctor say?" Maddy studied his face.

"He's afraid for her and for the babe. That shanty isn't a place for a dog, much less a woman in her condition. He said she should have a midwife on hand at all times at this late stage of her confinement, especially in her weakened condition." Compassion colored his deep brown eyes.

Maddy sat for a moment contemplating his words. She had to do something, and taking food or paying Loraine's rent wasn't enough. "Let's bring her here. There's plenty of room, and no one will have to go out in the weather to check on her. We can even have a midwife move into the bedchamber next to hers."

Frank relaxed a bit. "Are you sure, Miss Madeline? It'll mean a lot of work."

"I'll take care of her." The more she thought about it, the more she realized that's what she needed. Serving another would help take her mind off her own problems. Isn't that what the Bible told everyone to do? Serve those who needed help?

Sarah gave an unladylike snort. "It won't be too much work for me. We can both care for her—and for the wee one when it arrives."

A tiny spark of hope entered Maddy's heart. "I'm exhausted.

I'll take my chocolate up to my room." She arose and, when she swayed, caught hold of the edge of the table.

"Can you make it upstairs by yourself, Miss Madeline?" Frank stood beside her, ready to help.

She took a deep breath. "Yes, I can now."

Frank nodded. "I'll bring up the tray when Sarah has it ready."

As Maddy made her way upstairs, the flicker of hope began to grow. The problem with Mr. Johnstone hadn't gone away, but she didn't feel so desperate about it now. Somehow she would get out of marrying that terrible man. Even if she had to go work somewhere as a governess...or a housemaid.

~

Sarah stood by the stove stirring the chocolate drink to keep it from sticking and burning. "What's wrong, Frank?"

While her husband told her about all that went on with Horace Johnstone, Sarah grimaced. "What are we going to do? We promised Madeline's dear father we'd always take care of her. And I don't believe a word of what Mr. Johnstone said about Mr. Mercer wanting her to marry him."

"I've never liked the man myself." Frank paced the floor. "Now I like him even less. If I weren't a Christian, I'd say I hate him. And you're right. Something's false about all of this. What he told Madeline has to be a lie. Her father was a shrewd businessman—"

"Well, we know he made one mistake." When Frank gave her a quizzical look, she continued. "He did make the man a partner. That doesn't sound like a good decision to me. But did you ever hear Mr. Mercer call him 'a partner'? I never did."

"You're right. And it shouldn't have taken this long for the will to be settled. I wonder if Johnstone is causing the delay.

Tomorrow morning, I'm going to see Mr. Sanderson. Maybe he'll tell me something, since we're all Madeline has left in the world."

Sarah set the pan on a trivet and slipped her arms around his neck. "You're a good man, Frank Sneed." She gave him a quick kiss before fixing the tray for Madeline.

A smile lit his face. "And you're a good woman." He gave her a playful pat on her posterior. "I'm thinking I shouldn't wait until tomorrow morning to go for Loraine. After I take the tray upstairs, I'll go fetch her."

No wonder she loved that man. His thoughtfulness and thoroughness had carried them a long way together. And she knew she could trust him to take care of their sweet girl.

"You go ahead. I'll take this on up to Madeline."

The cold night wind kept Frank huddled under a lap robe as he drove the enclosed surrey toward shanty town, but the cold didn't feel as bitter as last night. And the moon's silvery light painted the landscape like a fairyland.

He hoped the warmth of spring would soon arrive. The closer he got to the hovels hunkering in the mire, the fewer signs of life he saw around him. A hard crust of ice covered everything, masking the usual malodorous scent.

When he stopped the horses, he couldn't detect even a glimmer from inside the thrown-together, tar-papered shack. Usually in the evening, flickers from the fire peeked between the boards on the windows and door.

He hurried to the door and knocked. In the stillness of the night, he didn't hear a sound from within. Not a creak of timber, and certainly not a whisper of a voice.

"Miz Loraine, it's Frank Sneed. Miss Madeline sent me. Miz Loraine, I'm coming in."

As he opened the door, he saw that the open stove held only dying embers. It took a moment for his eyes to adjust to the dimness of the room. He searched the shadows for the woman, at first not finding her. Then he realized that what he thought was a cast-aside quilt wadded on the floor beside the stove was actually Loraine.

He rushed toward her and grabbed her bony frame up into his arms. She felt so light, as if she was wasting away. And what of the babe she carried? Could the poor thing possibly still be alive?

Without shutting the door behind him, he stomped out, moving quickly toward the waiting vehicle, glad he'd put in several blankets and heated bricks. He wedged the limp woman on the floor between the seats and placed the bricks around her. After covering her with everything in the surrey, even the lap robe he'd used on his way there, he pulled the heavy leather side curtains closed and fastened them down. He hoped they would keep most of the frigid air out of the enclosed space.

"Lord, please protect her until I can get her to the house." With that prayer, he climbed into the driver's seat and clicked his tongue at the horses.

Trying to avoid the many rough patches in the road, he drove as fast as he felt he should toward home, keeping in mind his passenger's safety. Sarah must have been watching for him, because she opened the front door before he stopped the carriage.

"She's in a bad way." He jumped down and began shoving the curtains aside. He unwound most of the covers and lifted the young woman into his arms.

"I prepared a room near Madeline's." Sarah stopped wringing her hands and pushed the door open wider as he approached the front porch, then hurriedly closed it behind them.

Madeline stood at the top of the stairs. "Is she all right?"

Frank shook his head. "I couldn't tell." He took the stairs two at a time. "She was lying on the floor beside the dying fire. I just grabbed her and got here as soon as I could."

He brushed past Madeline, careful not to jar his burden. He hurried into the room and laid her on the bed. Both Madeline and Sarah followed on his heels.

Sarah started pulling the filthy quilt away from the girl. "She's breathing, but it's shallow. You go ahead and get the doctor. Miss Madeline and I will try to warm her up."

He ran back downstairs, knowing Loraine was in good hands.

~

*M*addy helped Sarah remove Loraine's tattered rags. Maddy's heart broke when she saw her skin, fragile as the thinnest china teacup, with each bone underneath defined. Why hadn't she brought Loraine here sooner? She had been so concerned for her own welfare. It didn't matter that the girl hadn't wanted so much charity. She should have insisted.

Lord, please don't let us be too late.

She hurried into her own bedchamber and rummaged through the bottom drawer in her wardrobe. Her heaviest flannel nightgown was buried under everything else. She jerked it out, not bothering to straighten the mess she'd made.

When she returned to the other bedroom, she helped Sarah slip the gown over Loraine's body and ease the unconscious woman under the thick bedcovers. "Is she going to be all right?" Concern laced the words together.

"She's alive," Sarah said softly. "And the babe moved when I gently pushed against the wee one." She brushed Loraine's matted hair from her face and placed a gentle kiss on her cheek. "Rest now, dear, and let the warmth soothe you. I'll be back soon."

"I'll stay beside her until you return." Maddy pulled the chair close to the bed and took Loraine's hand, rubbing it to get more warmth into the chilled fingers.

"I'm going to heat some broth and bring it up. We need to get nourishment into her, and it'll help warm her from the inside." Sarah hurried out.

Maddy continued massaging her friend's hand while she stared into the yellow, orange, and blue flames dancing in the fireplace across the room. If Loraine didn't warm up soon, maybe they should move her closer to the fireplace. They could shift the chaise longue from her own bedchamber and set it near the heat source. When Frank returned with the doctor, he could help them lay Loraine on it. Maddy knew she wouldn't spend the night in her own room. She would stay right beside Loraine until she started to recover.

Maddy climbed up on the bed and cradled her friend in her arms, hoping the warmth from her own body would help. *Father God, please help Loraine and protect the baby she's carrying.*

What would Maddy have done if she were in Loraine's shoes? But the very idea that her father would disown her for marrying someone he didn't approve of was inconceivable. She wouldn't have ended up in a ramshackle hovel in shanty town. So she had no idea how she would have handled a situation like Loraine's.

Soon she was very warm herself and nodded off to sleep.

~

"*M*iss Madeline."

Frank's voice, coming from the hallway, awakened Maddy. She wondered how long she'd slept. Even in slumber, her arms hadn't released their hold on the fragile woman with child. She eased away from Loraine, leaving her sleeping on her side. Just as she sat up, Frank entered the bedroom.

Dr. Thomas followed close behind. He set his black medical bag on the bedside table and extracted his stethoscope. After studying Loraine briefly, he gently pulled back the covers, turned her onto her back, and pressed the black cone of the instrument to her chest.

Loraine's eyes fluttered open for a moment. She moaned and closed them again.

The doctor turned toward Maddy. "Things aren't looking good."

Her heart ached for her friend. "We're going to keep her here at the house. Do you think good food and tender care will help Loraine?"

He ran his fingers through his snow-white hair, leaving some strands sticking straight up. "Of course it will help. I just can't tell you if it will be enough."

Leaning forward, he gave a light tap on Loraine's swollen belly. An answering movement brought the hint of a smile to the doctor's face. "The baby is alert and reacting to stimulus." He pressed the stethoscope on the spot where the baby had moved. "The heartbeat is stronger than the mother's."

Sarah bustled in carrying a tray, which she set on the table near the fireplace. "I've brought some nice beef broth and weak tea for our patient."

Dr. Thomas returned the instrument to his bag and turned toward Sarah and Maddy. "Go ahead. Try and wake her. See how much of the broth and tea you can get her to take. Then allow her to sleep for at least four hours before you try again. She needs to warm up and have nourishment to gain strength."

"Would it help to bring the chaise longue from my room, so she can be closer to the fireplace?" Maddy started pulling the covers up around Loraine.

The doctor moved back toward his patient. He slid his hands

beneath the quilts. "Her extremities are warming up, and I think she'd be more comfortable in the bed. She wouldn't roll off if she turns over in her sleep."

Maddy watched the doctor leave, then turned to help Sarah try to awaken Loraine. She would do all she could for her friend, and while she sat with the ill woman, she'd come up with a way to foil Mr. Johnstone's plans for her. She just *had* to. The alternative would be inconceivable.

CHAPTER 5

$\mathcal{F}$rank didn't want to upset things for Madeline, but he had to find out what was really going on so he could protect her. Sanderson Law Firm occupied the entire second floor of the National Bank building. After climbing the stairs, he stood before the door and read the gold letters on the frosted glass window. Dressed in clothes he usually wore only to church, he felt he looked more like a businessman than a servant. He hoped Mr. Sanderson would see him that way too. Frank had to get to the bottom of what was going on so he could help Madeline. He gave a quick rap on the gleaming mahogany door.

"Enter," an impersonal-sounding voice called.

He took a deep breath before grasping the doorknob. A law clerk or secretary, Frank wasn't sure which, sat behind the desk that matched the wainscoting around the room. Even the bookcases lining one wall were mahogany. Must have cost a pretty penny. And some of that money probably came from the Mercer estate. Frank was here to see that more of it went to the only heir. Wasn't right for Madeline to have to dismiss the other servants. What was Sanderson thinking?

The man behind the desk looked up. "May I help you?" His tone was no more cordial than before.

"I'd like to see Mr. Sanderson."

"Would that be Mr. Isaiah or Mr. Henry?" Not one gleam of interest lit the man's eyes.

"Which one is handling the Mercer estate?"

"That would be Mr. Isaiah." He shuffled papers on his desk as if he were looking for something. "Is he expecting you? I don't see an appointment on his calendar."

Frank cleared his throat. "I don't have an appointment, but I won't take much of his time. Name's Frank Sneed."

The other man stood, gathering some of the papers in his arms. "Wait here. I'll see if he has time for you." He went through the doorway behind his desk, pulling the door shut with a snap.

Frank dropped onto one of the chairs. He hoped he wasn't making a mistake, but he needed to know details about some things. Nothing made any sense right now. Madeline needed answers, and he planned to give them to her.

After almost an hour, the man returned. Good thing no one else needed to see either of the Sandersons. They'd be sitting here beside him, too, probably as impatient as he was.

"Mr. Isaiah will see you now." He dropped a stack of papers on his desk. "Follow me."

Frank took in the surroundings as they walked down a long hallway. Closed doors lined each side at regular intervals. Luxurious, polished-hardwood floor covered with a fancy runner, flocked wallpaper above the mahogany wainscoting, even electric lights with cut-crystal shades. He shook his head. All this abundance when some people had so little.

The man in front of him opened one of the doors and waited until Frank entered before closing it, leaving the two men alone.

Isaiah Sanderson rose from behind an enormous desk. His well-cut suit set off his snow-white hair, and the crinkles around his eyes revealed that he often smiled. However, he wasn't smiling now. He gestured toward a straight chair across from him.

"Have a seat, Mr. Sneed. What can I do for you?" The lawyer perched in his chair and clasped his hands on his desk, his stiff back held away from the cushions.

What's eating at him? Frank leaned forward and intently studied Mr. Sanderson's face. "I've come about the Mercer estate. Shouldn't there have been a reading of the will by now?"

Mr. Sanderson turned his gaze toward the bookcase lining the wall to his right. Surely the man knew every volume it contained. "Sneed? Aren't you Mr. Mercer's *servant*?"

The man didn't look at Frank when he asked the question, and the way he emphasized the last word told Frank what he thought about him. The Sunday clothes hadn't mattered one bit.

"That's right, sir. My wife and I are all Miss Madeline has left."

Without even glancing at him, Sanderson cleared his throat. "I thought Horace Johnstone and Miss Mercer were to be wed."

Frank shook his head even though he doubted the man could see it the way he kept glancing away from him. Frank's uneasiness intensified. A lawyer shouldn't be so evasive.

"Mr. Mercer never said anything like that."

"I'm sure the man didn't talk to you about everything that went on." Clipped words, sharp like a well-honed knife.

"No, he didn't. But he did trust me. And more than once, he asked that Sarah and I take care of Miss Madeline if anything happened to him. Never did mention her possible marriage to his business partner. Johnstone almost never came to the house, so Miss Madeline hardly knows the man."

Frank expected a reaction from the lawyer, but the man simply gripped his hands tighter until his knuckles whitened. "I'm not at liberty to discuss those things with you, and I'm meeting with a client shortly."

His pointed words hit their mark, but his eyes never left

their journey over the spines of the books. What could Frank do but leave quietly?

When he reached the street, the disquiet in his spirit had increased. If Mr. Sanderson didn't have anything to hide, why did he brush Frank off so quickly? An honest man would look him straight in the eyes.

~

*H*orace Johnstone glared at the man exiting the elevator across the lobby of the bank building. He had to have been in Sanderson's office. Why was Madeline's servant talking to the lawyer? Horace had better get up there and remind Isaiah of the consequences if he did anything Horace had forbidden.

When he stormed into the office, the ninny behind the front desk didn't even try to stop him. He must have learned his lesson from the last time Horace was there.

He threw open the door to Isaiah's office. The weakling sat with his hands clasped, but he glanced up at the noise. Probably praying, just like Mercer did.

Horace had no patience with weak men. They were too easy to control. Until that last day with Mercer. He shook his head. He didn't want to think about what had happened then. Water under the bridge.

"What was Sneed doing here?"

"How—?"

"I saw him get off the elevator." He didn't care how far his voice carried. If other people feared him, that made his work easier. "I told you I would be watching you," he sneered. "And I have enough spies planted around you that I'll know every move you make before the day is over."

The lawyer stood and gripped the back of his chair. "What do you want?"

"I already asked you," Horace roared, enjoying the hint of fear the man tried to hide. "What about Sneed?"

"He..." Sanderson cleared his throat. "He wanted to know about the reading of the will."

Hoping he had mud on his shoes so there'd be a mess on the carpet, Horace stomped across the Persian rug and planted his fists against the desktop. "What did you tell him?"

"Nothing." Sanderson stiffened his spine. "I told him absolutely nothing. Just that I thought you and Miss Mercer were getting married."

"And?"

"He said Mr. Mercer hadn't said anything about the marriage before he died."

Horace stood straight and crossed his arms. "Is that all?"

"Y–yes," Sanderson stammered.

"Just remember what will happen if this marriage doesn't take place. The danger to your family."

Back on the sidewalk, Horace's aggressive steps matched his mood. He could better collect his thoughts while in motion. What could be going on? Why would Sneed contact Sanderson? Insignificant fool. But maybe too smart for his own good.

He'd have to watch out for that one. He didn't like it a bit. And he wasn't going to let a mere servant ruin all he'd worked for. The taunting words and names from his childhood echoed in his mind, trying to drag him back into the mire. He'd never be able to silence them until he'd accomplished all he'd set out to do. Then he'd be in a position of power and prestige. Nothing —and no one—would be able to stop him.

~

*F*rank stumbled down the brick street toward the mansion. A bright moon lit the way. An exploding headache burned behind his eyes, and he had trouble focusing.

The few drinks he'd had hit him hard on the way home. Never a man for liquor, he hadn't realized the sips he'd taken could combine to bring on so much pain. His only consolation was that the women would all be abed, and no one would see his inebriated condition. Never again would a drop of the devil's brew pass his lips. But he wasn't sorry they had tonight. He'd learned a lot while he nursed a few drinks and plied others with many more.

Some of the men took longer than others, but eventually all their tongues loosened. What he found out scared him. Madeline didn't have any idea what she was up against. Johnstone thought himself above the law. And he didn't hesitate to eliminate anyone who got in his way. Wonder if that's what happened with Mr. Mercer? Maybe his death wasn't an accident after all. The idea stiffened Frank's spine and sobered him a little.

Hopefully, his mind would work better in the morning. *Lord, please let me remember everything that was said to me tonight. We need to use the information to protect Madeline.* He stuck his hand in his pocket to make sure the ad from the newspaper hadn't gotten lost.

He fumbled with the gate several times before the latch opened, and the clang it made pounded against his head, intensifying the pain. The sooner he got to bed, the better. He only hoped Sarah was sound asleep when he slid between the covers. He didn't want his sweet wife to see him in this shape.

As he tried to grasp the knob, the door flew open. The astonishment on Sarah's face would have been comical if it hadn't quickly turned into a harsh frown.

"Where have you been?" she hissed and pulled him through the doorway, almost jerking his arm out of its socket. That's all he needed, more pain.

The thud when she closed the door did almost as much damage to his head as the gate had. Her fisted hands flew to her hips, and he read deep disappointment in her eyes. Pain shot through his heart. He hadn't wanted to upset Sarah. He knew she would understand when he told her what he'd done. He just didn't want to face her without clear thoughts.

He slid into a chair by the kitchen table and dropped his face into his hands. *Help me, Lord.*

Sarah followed and towered over him—a new feeling since her head only reached to his chest, and he'd always sheltered her there.

"Are you going to give me an answer?"

The sound of her disappointment hurt as much as seeing it in her face. Frank raised his head and took a deep breath.

"You reek of the terrible odors of a tavern. You haven't had a drink of alcohol since before we were wed. Why now, Frank, of all times?" She dropped into the chair on the other side of the table, her arms crossed in defiance.

"I tol' ya I'd be checking on Johnstone." After the first few slurred words, he was better able to manage his tongue. "I learned a lot."

"You were gone long enough."

"First I went to Sanderson. He wouldn't give me a straight answer about anything. Treated me like I wasn't worth dirt." Stating it so baldly sent a sword through his gut. "But the man was hiding something. He couldn't even look at me. I've never trusted a man who can't meet my eyes."

Sarah reached across the table and took his hand. "You're a fine man, Frank Sneed. He should have recognized your worth."

Just like Sarah to comfort him, even when she was mad at him. He'd give her a reason for those words to be true.

"I spent the rest of the day checking out things, at the company, on the docks, then in the tavern. It's hard to get men to open up if you're not drinking with them. The liquor really loosens their tongues." He squeezed her hand. "I only sipped mine occasionally, but I'm not used to spirits anymore. They really did me in. I hoped you wouldn't be awake, so you wouldn't see me this way."

A lone tear made its way down her cheek. "I should've known you hadn't gone back to your old ways from before you became a Christian. Too many years have passed for that. And you've become such a stalwart man of God."

Sarah's support meant the world to him. She could lift the heaviness from his heart with just a smile. Her words of praise poured like the balm of Gilead over his soul.

"I may have found a way to get Madeline out of the city until this estate and marriage thing can be worked through." He pulled out the crumpled paper and smoothed it before handing it to Sarah.

After she read it, she looked up, puzzled. "How can this help her? She doesn't want to marry anyone right now, especially not a man she doesn't know."

He nodded. "I know that. But from what I've found out about Johnstone, if she doesn't agree to marry him, her life would be in danger. I think she should answer this ad. She wouldn't have to marry the man, even if she goes to—" He glanced down at the address. "Golden in New Mexico territory. One or both of us could accompany her and protect her. And we'd only use this as an escape if absolutely necessary."

"Are you out of your mind, Frank Sneed?"

CHAPTER 6

*a*fter a seemingly endless night at Loraine's bedside, Maddy slipped into her own room for a short nap. When she awoke, sunlight spilled through the lacy panels between the heavy brocade draperies, painting a new design on the Persian carpet.

It must be close to noon. She sat up and stretched her hands high above her head, trying to get the kinks out of her back before climbing out of bed. Her body ached from all the things she'd been doing that were different from her normal routine.

She crossed the hallway to check on Loraine. Her friend slept snuggled under the covers, and her even breathing sounded more normal. So Maddy returned to her own room.

Using the tepid water in her pitcher, she finished her ablutions and donned a black house dress before hurrying down the stairs. Finding Sarah in the kitchen, Maddy perched on a stool, her feet on the bottom rung. "Where is Frank? I'm sure you both had breakfast hours ago."

"Yes. He ate after he fed the horses this morning." Sarah spooned a large helping of steaming eggs and sausage onto a plate. "When I heard you moving around, I cooked your eggs."

She buttered two biscuits and arranged the pieces beside the other food. "Frank has gone to pick up Bonnie Maguire." After setting the plate in front of Maddy, she hurried to the ice box and poured a glass of milk from the fresh bottle delivered that morning.

"I'm glad Mrs. Maguire is free to come." Maddy took a bite and chewed slowly. As hungry as she was, she was tempted to gulp down the delicious food. But she decided to take her time and enjoy all the flavors instead. "I'm really worried about Loraine."

"For sure, and we all are." Sarah nodded. "That poor thing's needed help for a long time. I hadn't realized how much. At least you and Frank have been taking food to her."

Maddy stared at the abundance on her plate. Her throat tightened, and hot tears threatened. "I just pray it was enough to bring her through this. I should have thought to move her into this house sooner. But she's really not wanted to accept much charity. I tried to respect her wishes and still be sure she had enough. Hard to balance those two things."

The back door burst open, and the freshening, cold spring wind blew through the kitchen.

"Just come on in here, Miz Maguire." Frank ushered the midwife ahead of him. "I'll be carrying your bags up to your room for you." He went back outside, closing the door behind him.

Sarah rushed to her. "Bonnie, dear, Miss Madeline had me fix up a room right next to Loraine's. Would you be wanting something to eat?"

Maddy stood. "I'm just now having breakfast. I'm sure there's plenty."

The tiny woman didn't look strong enough for the hard work of helping babies into the world. Or turning her patients, or anything else strenuous. But a crinkly smile spread across her face. "I'd rather go meet the little mother right away. I'll wait until lunchtime to eat with her. What has she been able to eat?"

"We've been trying to get her to take some good strong beef broth with noodles, but she only swallows a few bites at a time." Sarah shook her head. "I'm afraid it might not be enough for the wee one." She led the midwife from the kitchen. "And she'll need strength for the del…"

Sarah's voice faded as she ascended the stairway. Maddy sat back down and nibbled on a piece of biscuit. What more could she do for Loraine? She had to think of something.

Frank blustered through the door, carrying two carpetbags. He stopped beside the table. "And how was your night, Miss Madeline? Did you sleep at all?"

She tried for a bright smile but wasn't sure she succeeded. "The night was rough, but I've had a good nap. You go on up and help Sarah and Bonnie."

By the time Maddy finished eating, Mrs. Maguire had settled into her room and taken up her post beside Loraine's bed. Worry puckered the wrinkled brow of the midwife, validating Maddy's worst fears.

"Should I go down and get more broth for Loraine?"

Maddy's words snagged Mrs. Maguire's attention. "Yes, I'd like to try to get her to eat again. While you're gone, I'll finish cleaning her up and fixing her hair. Maybe that will perk her up a bit."

When Maddy stepped into the hallway and closed the door, a loud pounding on the front door caused her to hesitate. Why didn't the person use the doorbell? The ornate brass handle was right there in plain sight beside the doorpost.

Before she got to the top of the stairs, Frank opened the door.

"Now see here, Sneed!" No mistaking that harsh voice.

Maddy shuddered. She shrank back and stood out of sight, waiting for her nemesis to leave.

"Johnstone, how can I help you?"

Maddy smiled at Frank's cool reply. She appreciated the strength and restraint he displayed.

"*Mr.* Johnstone to you, Sneed. Let me in."

Maddy wished she could see the two men without being seen. Hopefully Frank would keep Horace Johnstone away from her.

~

rank opened the door wider and hinges squeaked as if in protest against the sleazy man standing there. "No need to get so snippy, *Mr.* Johnstone. Now what can I do for you?" He closed the door to shut out the cold wind.

Johnstone's eyes darted around as if he were looking for something...or someone. Probably Madeline. Frank didn't intend to let the man near her today.

"I don't like you shoving your nose into my business." The belligerent tone echoed throughout the foyer while the angry man's forefinger pounded a harsh tattoo on Frank's chest.

Frank stifled his urge to shout at the man. He knew it wouldn't help anything. Maybe another tack would work.

"Not sure what yer talkin' about." Frank deliberately chose his words. He wanted Johnstone to think him uneducated. Maybe it would give him an advantage down the road.

"Why'd you go to see Sanderson?" Johnstone's fists landed on his own waist as he stood glaring at Frank.

Frank stiffened. "I wanted to check on Mr. Mercer's will. Since Miss Madeline had to get rid of the other servants, I worry about her." He gripped his hands behind his back, wishing he could punch the pompous man in the snout.

"Worried about your own position, I'm sure." Johnstone barked out a harsh laugh. "Let this be a warning to you. You'll do what I tell you, or you and that wife of yours will find yourselves out on the street with nary a penny to your name. And I'll see to it you won't be able to find another position here in Boston. Stay away from Sanderson. I'm taking care of every-thing for Madeline. Now where is she?"

Once more his beady eyes studied every corner. Frank hoped Madeline would stay upstairs until he got rid of the man.

"She's still grieving her dear father's death. Had a bad night. Hope you haven't disturbed her rest." Frank worked hard to keep his gaze from going to the top of the stairs. Mustn't let Johnstone know how worried he was.

"Tell her I'll be coming back for dinner on Sunday." The man gave an evil grin. "That should give her enough time to...*rest*."

Frank shut the door behind Johnstone and sagged against it. *Lord, help me know what to do to protect our Madeline.*

"Frank."

Madeline's soft voice caused him to look up at her as she descended the stairs. "What was he talking about? Why was he mad at you?" She clasped her hands in front of her waist and stood waiting for his reply.

"Sarah and I want to discuss that with you, Miss Madeline. Can we do it now?"

"I need to take some more broth up to Loraine. Then we can talk in the kitchen." She walked past him but turned back. "This sounds serious."

"That it is." Frank agreed. *More than you can imagine.*

~

*M*addy trudged up the stairs. The knot in her stomach tightened. She tapped the door with her foot, and Mrs. Maguire opened it.

"Let me help you with that tray." The midwife took the food and set it on the bedside table. Turning, she crossed her arms over her chest. "What was all that hullabaloo? Even though she

54

was sleeping, all the noise agitated Loraine. She became restless. I think it was the tone the man used. We couldn't understand the words."

"I don't want her disturbed like that." Maddy went to her friend's bedside and watched her slowly open her eyes.

"Miss...Mercer."

The whispered words warmed Maddy's heart. Loraine looked better than she had since she arrived. Her hair was clean and combed and her skin not as pale as it had been. Maddy sensed that they *would* be able to help Loraine and her baby.

"Let's sit you up." Mrs. Maguire lifted Loraine's upper body while Maddy pushed two fat goose-down pillows behind her back. "Here's some good beef broth. You really need to eat and build up your strength. Your time isn't far off."

Maddy leaned over and pressed a kiss to Loraine's forehead. "I'm going downstairs, but when you're finished eating, I'll be back and visit with you."

Loraine's answering smile added fuel to the hope in Maddy's heart.

Apprehensive, Maddy thrust open the door to the kitchen. Frank and Sarah sat with their heads bowed, holding each other's hands. From across the cavernous room, their murmured prayers engulfed Maddy. She quietly slipped into the chair across the table from them and bowed her head. Frank continued to pray softly. She didn't understand every word he said, but the peace of sharing their worship settled over her.

"Amen." Frank's voice ending the prayer was louder.

She raised her head and opened her eyes. "Why did you want to talk to me, Frank?"

He gazed directly into her eyes. "I've been doing some checking, Miss Madeline. Several matters don't add up to me."

The hairs on her neck stood up. "What?" She had been concerned, too, and wondered if they were thinking about the same things.

Frank leaned his beefy forearms on the table. "I've never known it to take so long for the reading of a will. That should have happened long ago."

She nodded. One of her concerns too.

"I hope you don't mind, Miss Madeline, but I went to see Mr. Sanderson yesterday morning." He lifted one questioning brow.

"That was a good thing. What did you find out?" Finally, she would have some answers.

"Nothing." He gave an emphatic nod. "That man wouldn't answer a single question for me."

So no answers yet. "Do you think it's because you're my servant? I could go see him with you." She clasped her hands in her lap, gripping them tight. "Why didn't I think of that sooner? We can go tomorrow."

Frank shook his head before she could continue. "He did question me about my position here, but I don't think that's the real reason. I'm sure Johnstone has something to do with why Sanderson won't tell me anything. Sanderson was evasive and nervous."

Maddy's heavy woolen dress couldn't keep the chill from her body. A chill that didn't have anything to do with the temperature in the kitchen. The walls closed in on her as if she were in a prison cell. She shook the image from her mind.

"When Johnstone was here earlier, it confirmed my suspicions that he had something to do with the delay." The scowl on Frank's face looked out of place on the normally placid man. His Adam's apple bobbed.

Exasperated, she started tapping her foot on the stone floor. What could they do now? She *would not* let that man control her life.

Frank stood up. "That's not all."

"What do you mean?" She was ready to listen to whatever else he had to say. Then decisions could be made.

He started pacing the room. "I did a lot of snooping yesterday. Even visited a couple of taverns late last night, trying to get information."

Maddy had never seen Frank so riled up. She rose to her feet. "And what did you find out?"

He stopped and faced her. "There's no easy way to say this." Regret painted his features, darkening his eyes. "Johnstone has a bad reputation. Lots of rumors about him. He's made many enemies. Some say he wouldn't blink an eye at murdering a man. And some are questioning the way your dear father died. That maybe Johnstone had a hand in that."

Maddy widened her eyes. "Are you saying he may have killed my father?" She dropped into the chair. Unthinkable! But what if it were true? "The man's a villain. How could he get away with murder?" What could they do about it? "This is so much worse than I feared." Angry tears clogged her throat, cutting off any more words.

Sarah came around the table and caressed Maddy's shoulders. "We didn't want to upset you, but you need to know the truth." She leaned down and placed a gentle kiss on the top of Maddy's head. But no matter how much Sarah tried to soothe her, Maddy's thoughts warred inside her.

That knowledge about Johnstone changed everything. Now she knew her feelings about the man were valid. He couldn't be trusted, and she'd never marry him. Somehow she had to get out of it. But how?

Frank thrust his hand into the pocket of his trousers and pulled out a bit of torn newspaper. He laid the scrap on the table in front of where she stood, smoothing it out so she could read the words. She'd seen ads like this before. Wondered what kind of women would answer them—never dreaming anything could happen that would cause her to consider answering one.

She glanced up at him. "Why did you bring this to me?"

He rubbed the back of his neck while red crept into his already ruddy cheeks. "The newspaper had been left on a table in the tavern, opened to this very page. When I sat down, the words screamed up at me. I'd been praying for a way to protect you from Johnstone. This could be the answer to those prayers."

Aghast, Maddy turned her head to look at Sarah still standing behind her. "Do you agree with him?"

"It makes sense to me." She eased into the chair beside Maddy. "You might never need to go to this place, but it wouldn't hurt to at least write the man. Just in case."

Maddy couldn't believe they agreed on this. She leaned her hands on the table. "I don't want to marry a stranger any more than I want to marry Horace Johnstone."

Sarah patted her hand. "We're not saying you'll marry him. Going there could get you out of danger. Provide a way of escape. I'm sure a Christian man wouldn't press you into marriage unless you wanted it, and the ad does say he's a Christian."

Maddy glanced at the ceiling. "What about Loraine?"

"You might not ever go to New Mexico territory. But answer the letter so you have that option. I'm sure you'll be all right until the baby is born."

Frank stood before her like a father. "Johnstone said he'd give you a month before he'll press for the marriage. If I haven't found out enough by then, we could accompany you on the journey. We'd protect you after we get there too."

A lot of things on her mind, Maddy took the newspaper ad upstairs to her room. She'd really seek the Lord before she did anything. Then Horace Johnstone's words played over and over in her head.

Answering the ad might be a good thing. Just a note of introduction anyway. Surely she'd never need to actually go there.

CHAPTER 7

GOLDEN, NEW MEXICO

*J*eremiah enjoyed the journey from his ranch into Golden. Being out on the range beat spending time in a mine any day. Cooler breezes blew across the Ortiz Mountains, carrying the scents of warm soil and wild flowers. The lower temperature would make working on the house more comfortable than the last few days had been. A late spring rain had greened up the countryside. For today, anyway. Occasional patches of blooming sage added purple to the myriad earthen shades of the landscape. Overhead a lone hawk cried out at the few tufts of white clouds that shared the sky with it.

Riding Lightning up Main Street toward Philip's house, Jeremiah studied the progress on the addition. Several of the unemployed miners had welcomed the chance to make a little extra money. And they were working hard to quickly finish the rooms. He didn't think there was a need to be in that big of a hurry, but the sooner they finished, the sooner he'd have one responsibility lifted from his shoulders.

Reining his palomino to the right, he stopped in front of Skinner's Mercantile. The post office resided in the back corner, and Philip was sure to ask him about the mail as soon as he arrived.

Jeremiah tied the reins to a hitching post and patted Lightning's neck. "I'll be right back." He scratched his stallion on the namesake white streak down his face, a very unique blaze.

Wooden barrels and kegs displaying an assortment of items from straw brooms to nails and screws sat on the boardwalk, holding the double doors open to the welcome fresh air and customers. Jeremiah's eyes took a couple minutes to adjust from the bright sunlight to the dim interior of the building. The scents of beeswax, tobacco, and leather mingling with pickle brine assaulted him, taking him back to the general store he loved as a boy.

Several people milled around, studying a variety of merchandise. Off to his right, Cyrus Skinner, the proprietor and postmaster, talked to a miner looking at tools.

When the storekeeper turned away for a moment, Jeremiah took his chance. "Say, Cyrus, any mail for me or Philip?"

The postmaster squinted and stared out the dusty front window for a moment. Then he shoved his bushy white hair back with one hand. If he'd use the Macassar oil he sold, he'd have a better chance of keeping the strands out of his eyes. "I b'lieve there's quite a bit a mail fer Philip. Don't recollect none fer you."

Jeremiah slipped past three women deep in conversation and headed toward the wooden counter in the post office corner of the building. "I'll just wait till you're finished."

"No need fer that." Cyrus picked up a long-handled broom and gave the ceiling three hard whacks. "Helen can come down and take care a ya."

Before Jeremiah took another step, the back stairs emitted a loud squeak.

Helen popped through the curtained doorway and gave him a wide smile, revealing the gap between her two front teeth. "How can I help you, Jeremiah?"

"Wanting to pick up the mail." He waved a hand at the postal area. "Cyrus said Philip has some."

She scurried past him and took her place behind the counter. "Cyrus!" The blast of the words could have shattered a plate-glass window. Thankfully, it didn't. "Where'd you put Mr. Smith's mail?"

If the cattle out on his ranch hadn't heard her yell, Jeremiah'd be surprised.

Cyrus turned from the miner and glared at her. "Stacked on the desk." He gave a dismissive wave toward that piece of beat-up furniture.

His answer wasn't any quieter than her question. Jeremiah was glad there weren't any strangers in the store. They probably wouldn't understand all that hollering. But everyone here in Golden was used to the Skinners. None of the people in the store flinched or even turned their heads.

Helen swung around to the desk shoved against the back wall. She put her hands on her hips and studied the stacks of varied heights. "Sure a lot of letters. Maybe they're not all for Philip."

"I certainly hope not." The words were out before Jeremiah thought about stopping them. He hurried to cover his blunder. "It'd take him awhile to read all those."

Helen went over to the grocery side of the store and picked up a tow sack. "I'll just put them in this, so's they'll be easy for you to tote."

She returned to the desk and started picking up stacks of letters. She glanced at the top envelope to make sure they were for Philip before stuffing them in the bag. When she handed the tow sack to Jeremiah, it was nearly half full and the desktop had been cleared.

"Thank you, Miz Skinner." Jeremiah tipped his hat. "Be seeing you." He skedaddled before she had a chance for any of the questions he knew she was itching to ask.

While he rode the rest of the way up to the house, Jeremiah couldn't believe so many women in the Boston area would answer an ad for a bride. What kind of terrible situations must they be in to risk coming west and marrying a perfect stranger? He couldn't imagine any decent woman he knew doing such a thing.

Philip could only help one of these women. Would he get upset there were so many others who probably needed help too? Maybe some of them weren't in dire straits but saw the ad as a chance to move across the country. What if others were swindlers?

Jeremiah was determined to protect his friend. Whenever Philip chose the woman, Jeremiah would be sure he met the train and checked her out before taking her up to the house. If need be, he'd put her right back on the train, using his own money.

~

Boston, Massachusetts

After Maddy returned from a trip to the emporium to replenish her supply of handkerchiefs, she hurried up the stairs.

Mrs. Maguire was coming from Loraine's room. "Is there another place we could move Loraine, so she won't be bothered by any disturbance downstairs? You know, like the one when Mr. Johnstone was here."

Maddy automatically glanced toward the ceiling, then back at the woman. "There are servants' quarters on the third floor. My father turned two of the rooms into an apartment for Frank and Sarah. But the rest of them are smaller than the one Loraine's using."

"Can I see them?" She sounded as if her mind was made up about moving her patient.

Maddy led the way toward the back stairs. Since the house was solidly built, the steps were sturdy, but not as wide as the staircase that connected the first and second floors. At the top, she opened the door and led the midwife on a tour of the six unoccupied rooms.

After inspecting the last one, Mrs. Maguire turned toward Maddy. "These are right nice. I'm sure Loraine will think so too. Maybe we could move into these rooms." She chose the two farthest from the Sneeds' apartment so she wouldn't disturb them during the night.

"It's fine with me, if that's what you really want."

The smile that lit the midwife's face was as bright as one of the electric lights Maddy's father had proudly installed on the first two floors of the mansion. "I'll get Frank to help me move Loraine and our things after she has breakfast. I'm going to try her on scrambled eggs and toast this morning. She's been eating better lately. Some of her strength is returning. A very good thing, for sure."

∼

GOLDEN, NEW MEXICO

*B*efore Jeremiah reached the house, Philip stepped onto the stoop of the adobe dwelling. The workmen had already extended the porch in front of the two new rooms, so it went all along the south wall. Philip liked to sit in the plain, wooden rocking chair that stayed out there, especially to watch the spectacular sunsets.

Philip's eyes twinkled. "Jerry, glad ya finally got here. These men are doin' really good, doncha think?" He slipped his thumbs under his suspenders and stretched them a few inches from his chest.

Jeremiah swung his leg over the back of the horse and dropped to the ground. "I noticed the change when I rode into town." He nodded toward a couple of the men who came around the house carrying lumber. "Good job."

They returned his nod and continued carrying their burden out of sight.

After tying Lightning to the hitching post, he reached for the tow sack tied behind his saddle. The paper crinkled when he moved it.

"What ya got in the sack?"

"Something that'll make you happy."

Jeremiah slung the bag over his shoulder and led the way into the main room. As he strode across the floor, his spurs jangled to the accompanying drumbeat of his boots across the wooden floor. Some of the adobe houses on the edge of town only had a dirt floor. Nothing but the best for his friend.

Arriving at the table, he opened the top of the sack and unceremoniously dumped the envelopes across its polished surface. A few skittered over the edge.

Philip's eyes widened. "That what I think it is?"

"Yup." Jeremiah scooped up a handful. "Answers to your ad."

He glanced at the postmarks on the letters he held. Only a couple were from Boston. One was even from Chicago. He never thought about women from other places answering Philip's ad.

The smile that split Philip's face revealed straight teeth. His happiness shone like the noonday sun over the desert. "Well, I'll be."

When he reached for the envelopes Jeremiah held out, his hands shook as if he had the palsy. He didn't even glance at the messy stack on the table. He just went to his favorite rocker and carefully settled against the cushions. Instead of starting to open the envelopes he held, he laid them in his lap and placed one hand on top before squeezing his eyes shut and bowing his head.

Jeremiah knew he was praying. Philip did that a lot, but why would he want to pray over these letters?

Jeremiah headed out to check on the building progress. Before long, he jumped into working on the dividing wall between the two new rooms. Might as well help all he could. He certainly didn't want to stay in the other part of the house and watch Philip pray.

By the time they finished the wall and slapped plaster on it, Jeremiah was tired and thirsty. He went into the kitchen and gulped down two large glasses of water before he lugged a fresh bucket of water out to the other workers. While they slaked their thirst, he gave a quick glance toward the sun. Almost straight above their heads. Time to eat.

He headed toward the hotel. Caroline should have lunch ready about now. He'd save her the effort of bringing it up to the house. Instead of riding Lightning, he decided that stretching his legs on the fairly long walk would do him good. Help him clear his mind.

Three men from the stock exchange went into the bank. Several horses were tied in front of the saloons on the other end of Main Street. Too bad not all the miners and cowhands wanted to work. A wagonload of ore lumbered toward the stamping plant, reminding him why the whole town pulsed with the confounded loud pounding. Everyone tolerated the noise, because it meant money in most of their pockets. The same three women he'd seen in the mercantile headed toward one of the houses on the southern side of the street.

When he reached the hotel, he ducked inside. Light streamed through the front windows, which were much cleaner than the ones on the mercantile. No one was behind the registration desk.

"Caroline?" He took off his hat and walked into the dining room. "Got lunch ready for the workers up at Philip's house?"

The pretty woman came through the swinging doors, wiping her hands on the voluminous apron that almost swallowed her. "Sure do. I was about to go down to the livery and get the wagon."

"I can do that." He settled his hat back on his curls. "Just get everything ready. I'll bring the wagon to the back door."

"Thanks, Jeremiah. I really appreciate it."

He didn't want to consider what Philip would find in that pile of mail. So he passed the half a mile hike to the livery by forcing himself to think about his ranch. So far, the last group of hands he'd hired had stayed on. Two of the men were clever with tools. They'd almost caught up on all the repairs that had been neglected by their predecessors. Maybe he'd put them to work on making his ranch house more like a home. He hadn't made any changes from what the previous owners left. Looking at Philip's house made him realize just how inadequate the older house had become. He could even add on to what was there, expanding the size of the main area and adding a couple more bedrooms. Now why would a bachelor need all that room?

Maybe he'd want to have a community supper out there sometime. Not until changes had been made, though. The place looked more like a shack. Since he could afford a better house, he'd get the workers started on changing that as soon as they finished repairing the fences and outbuildings. Maybe even hire a few of the men working on Philip's house.

Jeremiah strode through the large open doorway of the livery stable. "Hey, Swede."

"Back here, *ja*." The older man's white-blond hair was easy to spot in the darkened building. He stepped from one of the stalls and leaned a pitchfork against the nearby wall. "So what can I do for you?"

Jeremiah met him halfway down the corridor between the two long rows of stalls. "I came to get the wagon for Caroline. I'm helping her take lunch up to Philip and the workers."

Swede led the way out the back door. "I haf the horses already hitched to the *vagn*."

Jeremiah went to the oddly matched pair—one a paint and one a sorrel. He patted each horse on the neck and whispered into its ear. Then he hopped up on the wagon and lifted the reins. "I'll bring it back when we're finished. I'll pay you then."

"Naw." The livery owner waved him away. "No one else usin' the vagn right now. No charge. Tell Philip hello for me."

Jeremiah nodded. "Sure thing."

He flicked the reins and clicked his tongue at the horses. They took off at a leisurely pace. He wasn't in a hurry. He'd just enjoy the pleasant spring day.

Caroline met him at the door. "Cyrus had some ham shipped in, and I bought one. The men should like the sandwiches I made."

She led the way toward the large worktable in the kitchen. Three platters held mounds of thick-sliced brown bread piled high with slices of meat. The men would welcome them. Her bread was some of the best Jeremiah had ever tasted.

Caroline covered each platter with a large tea towel, tucking the fabric tight under them. "I'll start carrying these out to the wagon. Could you get the lemonade?" She pointed toward the five-gallon earthenware crock with the handle of a tin dipper crooked over the top.

He hefted it to his shoulder, headed outdoors, and wedged the crock into a corner of the wagon. "Do you want to cover this so no dust will get into it?"

She brought another large piece of cloth and spread it over the crock. "You can cover the sawhorse table with this and the tea towels. That way the men won't get any splinters in their food or fingers."

Jeremiah drove the wagon carefully up the uneven street so he wouldn't dump any of the vittles. The men already had the table set up, and they made quick work of putting the cloths down and setting the food out. Each man had his own tin cup for the lemonade.

After enjoying one of the hearty sandwiches, Jeremiah grabbed another and headed inside to see Philip. "I brought you a ham sandwich. This tastes like it's been cured with honey, instead of sugar. Really tasty."

His friend looked up from the letters on the table, and his eyes took a moment to focus on Jeremiah. "Jerry, that sounds good." Philip eased back down into his rocker and took the proffered food.

Jeremiah carried one of Philip's glasses back outside to get him some lemonade. When he returned, pensiveness clouded Philip's usually sunny smile.

"What's the problem?" Jeremiah set the glass on the table beside the older man.

"None a-these are from the right woman." Philip took a bite from the sandwich.

"What do you mean? Have you read them all?"

Philip slowly finished chewing the bite before he answered. "Didn't havta."

"That's why we wrote the ad. Remember? You won't know about these women until you read every one of the letters."

Philip took a long drink from his glass of lemonade. "Didn't havta, I said. God done told me her letter ain't here yet." He took another bite from the sandwich.

Jeremiah blew out a long breath. Back to that God thing again. Surely the old man wasn't losing his marbles...or was he?

~

BOSTON, MASSACHUSETTS

*T*hings were going better than Maddy had hoped. Since moving Loraine to the third floor of the mansion, she'd perked up a lot. Maddy had gone through her own clothing and given Mrs. Maguire several night dresses for Loraine. Every day the midwife bathed Loraine and dressed her in a soft, warm gown. Today, Maddy told Mrs. Maguire to take a few hours off.

Hurrying up the back stairs, Maddy planned out their day. She and Loraine could visit and maybe sew a few things for the baby. She had sent Frank and Sarah to the Jordan Marsh Store yesterday for fabric to make diapers, gowns, and blankets. And plenty of embroidery floss.

She knocked on the door and waited for Loraine's answer.

"Come in." The words sounded stronger than yesterday.

Maddy set the bundle she carried on the table, approached the bed, and hugged Loraine. "What can I do to help you?"

"I want to sit by the fireplace and visit, please." The frail woman swung her legs over the side of the tall bed and slid her feet to the floor.

Maddy offered her arm, and Loraine took it before they walked the few steps to the two chairs set close together on the braided rug beside the fire.

After pulling the bundle into her lap, Maddy unwrapped the fabric and notions.

"What do you have there?" Loraine leaned forward, an eager sparkle in her eyes.

"I thought we could work on things for the baby." Maddy held up some white birdseye-woven fabric. "This is for making the diapers. We also have some cambric and dimity for infant gowns." She held up two more large cuts of fabric. "And this flannel will make nice receiving blankets. We could even embroider the borders."

Tears tracked down Loraine's cheeks. "I was so worried about getting well, I hadn't even thought about what the baby needs."

Maddy patted her arm. "I know you've had enough on your mind." She leaned back and smiled. "And you're so much better than you were when you arrived. You look absolutely lovely with color in your cheeks and more meat on your bones."

When she laughed, Loraine joined in. "Madeline, you've been so good to me."

With a finger to her own lips, Maddy shushed her. "Don't start that again. I'm blessed to have you in my home. Now which do you want to work on—the diapers, a blanket, or a gown?"

Loraine sat silent so long, Maddy was afraid she'd hurt her feelings somehow. "I'm sorry. You don't have to work on any of this. We can just sit and visit until Mrs. Maguire gets back."

Loraine took a deep breath and slowly sighed. "I really must talk to you about something."

Maddy laid the fabric back on the table and concentrated on her friend. "What's on your mind?"

"I have an important request to make."

Maddy laughed. "You can ask me anything, and if it's within my power, I'll be glad to do it for you."

After another moment's hesitation, Loraine closed her eyes. "Please Madeline, promise me you'll take care of my baby—if something happens to me." She opened her eyes and stared straight into Maddy's.

"Don't you think your parents will want to know about their grandchild? They'll want to help you when they find out."

"No!" Loraine's vehemence sliced through Maddy's heart. "I don't want them to have my baby if I'm not here."

Maddy jumped up. "Don't talk like that. You're going to be all right."

Loraine clutched the arms of the chair until her knuckles

blanched. "My parents rejected my husband, and they rejected me. I wouldn't want my child raised in their home. Their poisonous hate would damage a tender soul." She struggled to stand, succeeding before Maddy got there to help her. "Please, promise me. I can't rest easy until you do."

Throwing her arms around Loraine, Maddy drew her into an embrace. "Don't worry. I promise. If anything happens to you, I'll raise your child."

But nothing's going to happen to you. I won't let it.

CHAPTER 8

*D*arkness fluttered around Maddy's heart and spirit. Agitated, she stalked across the floor, carrying Loraine's baby. Wails from the infant rent the air, stiffening Madeline's spine and arms with every heart-wrenching cry. She rested the swaddled bundle against her shoulder while her own tears dripped onto the flannel blanket she'd finished hemming just yesterday. *How much more can I take, Lord?*

Mrs. McGuire had warned her that Loraine's body was so weak she probably wouldn't be able to survive labor and delivery of her child. Maddy wouldn't let herself believe those discouraging words. She'd held out hope until the very end.

The last twenty-four hours had been agony, watching Loraine's labor drain so much from her already too-frail body. The widowed mother heroically carried on, no matter the toll on her. After the baby girl was laid in her arms, she gazed upon her adoringly while tears streamed down her face. Finally, she turned her gaze toward Maddy, her eyes already losing their luster.

"Take her." The words were like a soft wind soughing in the trees.

At the slight nod toward the newborn, Maddy leaned over and lifted the tiny child, who felt as light as a goose feather.

"Please name her Pearl." Loraine's last words rasped out, then she closed her eyes and slipped away from them, peace descending on her features as she lay in repose, a half-smile on her lips.

The memory of that moment still seared Maddy's heart. "Oh, Pearl, I wish I knew what to do." Never had she felt so inadequate. Confusion and fear clawed at her restless mind. Like a deluge, all the ramifications flooded over her. She barely had enough money to provide for herself and the Sneeds. How would she be able to pay for all the things a baby needed?

And what would other people think about a woman who had never been married with a baby? What if every man thought of her as damaged goods?

Maddy shook her head vehemently. She wished she'd never let that thought enter her mind. Pearl was a gift from God. No matter what other people thought of her, Maddy would be proud to claim the baby as her daughter.

Mrs. Maguire had hurried to the Shale's Mercantile to get Nestle's Infant Food and nursing bottles so they could take care of Pearl. Maddy hoped she would soon return. Maybe feeding the baby would calm her. Or maybe the child also sensed the loss of her mother, in some indefinable way.

Why had Loraine wanted *her* to take Pearl? Even though Maddy had been kind to the mother, she was the least qualified person to care for a newborn. Having no brothers or sisters, the only place she'd been around infants was at church, and their mothers took care of them. She'd held some, but only for a few minutes before placing them back into their mothers' loving arms. They were happy and cooing when she did, not upset and fighting. But the soft warm bundle struggling against her chest reached all the way to her heart, touching a depth she'd never felt before.

Oh, Lord, please help me. I need You now more than I ever have before.

Even though Pearl continued to whimper, the peace that passeth understanding descended on Maddy's spirit, slowly at first, then like a down comforter enveloping her. If God was in control, and she believed He was, then He would help her learn. A tiny bud awakened inside her and slowly unfurled, like the petals of one of her mother's tea roses, into an unfamiliar, maternal instinct. This tiny scrap of wriggling humanity needed her. The tension in her spine drained away, leaving the warmth of summer sunshine in its place. She cuddled the baby closer as her inadequacies miraculously receded like waves from the shoreline.

Her hand on Pearl's back made lazy circles as she whispered words of comfort and love. The whimpers became an occasional snubbing, then finally the baby slept. The weight of the child's trust added fuel to her maternal feelings. No one had ever depended on her before. With God's help, she could do this. She pressed a kiss to the top of Pearl's head, the downy white hair tickling her lips in a most pleasurable way.

~

GOLDEN, NEW MEXICO

*J*eremiah walked through the two newly constructed rooms with Philip. Solid and well-built, they would be more than adequate for most anyone. Caroline and some of the women in the church had completed hanging the wallpaper yesterday. Wallpaper. Here in Golden. Jeremiah didn't know of another house that had anything fancier than painted walls.

"It's finished, Jerry." Philip had more of a spring in his step than Jeremiah had seen for a long time. "I done ordered the basic furniture, but Miz Oldman give me ideas 'bout other things fer the rooms. Doodads and such. See if Cyrus'll let ya bring the Sears and Roebuck up here. Or maybe that Montgomery Wards' un."

Doodads and such? Would it never end? "I'll head on down there. See what I can do." Another walk might help him work out some of his frustrations, what with all this folderol. "I'll be back as soon as I can."

Striding down the hill didn't do as much good as usual. The pounding of the stamping machine added a dimension to the headache that had hovered near the whole day. All he could think about was the complete waste of time and money this whole project had been. Even though letters arrived almost daily, Philip hadn't read a single one. He just prayed over them, then put them away, saying the right one hadn't come yet. Jeremiah was beginning to wonder if Philip was edging toward senile. If so, hiring a caretaker made a lot more sense than a mail-order bride. Why was the old man so stubborn about this?

If the right letter ever came and Philip invited the woman here, she'd better be worth all this effort. Jeremiah would know the first time he laid eyes on her if she was going to cause trouble for Philip. And he'd take care of her before she could. Even if he had to hogtie her to get her on the train out of here.

~

BOSTON, MASSACHUSETTS

Maddy sat in the rocker they'd brought into the kitchen. Pearl hadn't taken to the bottle right away, but Mrs. Maguire's expertise had helped both the baby and Maddy. She rocked the infant while Pearl sucked on the burgundy-colored rubber nipple. The teardrop-shaped nursing bottle lay flat on the baby's stomach with tubing connecting it to the nipple. Maddy moved the chair with a gentle motion and stared down at the blessing in her arms. One week old today. Her love for the tiny girl had grown so large that she could hardly remember not loving her.

Up until this time in her life, everyone had taken care of Maddy. She'd floated through the days almost oblivious to the real world around her. Oh, she did benevolent work, but it never really touched her heart. She gave out of her own bounty, bestowing it on the more needy, like some kind of fairy godmother.

Now her life had taken on new meaning. A deeper meaning. She would do everything she could to see that this child was loved and cared for. If it took all her time, if it took all her money—what little she evidently had left—she didn't care. Nothing was too much for this tiny gift from heaven. She'd give up everything she had, even her own life, for this child.

"Oh, she's a sweet one, that Pearl is." Sarah left off stirring the gravy long enough to lean over Maddy's shoulder and coo. "It's so nice to have a baby in the house again."

Maddy chuckled. "Since I don't remember when one was here, I'll take your word for it. But Pearl has taken my heart and awakened it. And turned my whole outlook on life topsy-turvy." She smiled as Pearl's mouth went slack and the nipple slipped out from between her lips, leaving a dribble of milk behind.

After moving the bottle onto the table, she tenderly patted Pearl's lips before lifting the infant to her shoulder to get her to burp the way Mrs. Maguire had shown her. Maddy started humming a lullaby and patting the baby's back in rhythm to the tune.

Sarah went to the stove to stir her pot of stew. "Not wanting to bring a cloud on your happiness, but did you remember that Mr. Johnstone is supposed to come to dinner tonight?"

Even though she tried to remain still, a shudder rippled through Maddy. At least it didn't disturb Pearl. "Why won't the man listen to what I've been telling him?" She gritted her teeth and forced the words through them. "I will never...and I mean *never*...ever consider marrying him. Nothing about him is appealing to me. I don't even like the man." She whooshed out a breath. "I know I should have Christian love for all mankind, and I can do my best to muster Christian love, yes, but I cannot... I cannot imagine myself being his wife. Not ever."

Sarah stopped stirring. "And who knows what the man will say about the wee one."

Maddy pulled Pearl closer to her heart. "What he says will not matter." She pressed a gentle kiss to one tiny, fisted hand.

~

*M*addy hurried to put the finishing touches on her hair. Although she didn't want to look especially nice for Mr. Johnstone, she did want to look presentable. If she didn't, Sarah would rebuke her. Her heart hadn't been concerned with her toilette, because she could hear Pearl crying, no matter what Sarah or Frank did for her. Something had the baby upset, and Maddy wanted to quickly return to her. Maybe that would calm her down.

She had planned to keep Pearl's presence a secret from Johnstone, but maybe it would be better for him to see that she now had a child. Perhaps it would help change his mind about the wedding. That thought brought a smile to her face. If so, it would be the solution to her most pressing problem.

Mr. Johnstone thought the loss of her father's money would make her need him, but she had resources he didn't know about. Her mother had left her a legacy that was in the bank in her own name. If she were frugal, the inheritance could take care of her and Pearl, and she could be frugal. She didn't need all the trappings of wealth around her. When her daughter was a little older, maybe Maddy could find some kind of position—as a teacher or governess or something like that.

She was sure Sarah and Frank would teach her about making money stretch. They'd been doing that since the household account had been drastically altered after her father's death.

Thinking about Father didn't bring as strong a twinge of grief as it used to. Perhaps Pearl was also helping her heal from that hurt.

She hurried into the nursery across the hall from her own bedchamber. Frank allowed her to take the baby before he headed downstairs to make sure everything was ready for their unwanted guest.

As she walked the floor and whispered soothing words to Pearl, her cries became quieter, but they didn't completely cease. However, Maddy was able to hear the loud knock by Mr. Johnstone. With the nursery door open, she heard the murmurs as Frank invited him in.

Another loud wail from Pearl startled Maddy. She pulled the baby closer against her and whispered loving words before humming a quiet lullaby. The baby settled her head into the crook of Maddy's arm and gave a soul-deep sigh.

"Miss Madeline." Frank stood in the doorway. "Would you like for me to take Pearl to Sarah?"

She turned toward him. "No, I'm going to keep her with me. She seems more settled in my arms." At his frown, she continued, "It will be all right. Maybe the baby will change Mr. Johnstone's mind about wanting to marry me."

Maddy swept past him and carefully made her way down the staircase. Before she reached the bottom, Mr. Johnstone swaggered from the parlor into the entrance hall.

"What have we here?" His harsh tone caused Pearl to jump.

Maddy patted the baby's bottom to soothe her. "A dear

friend asked me to take her child before she died." She continued to the bottom of the stairs.

His thunderous scowl would have frightened her before today. "What're you going to do with it?"

Standing serenely, Maddy almost smiled at him. "I'm going to take care of *her*."

If he had been a dragon, fire would have shot from his nostrils. "You will *not* be taking care of her after we marry." He pulled a deep breath into his lungs, then bellowed, "You listen to me, missy. Our marriage will take place one week from today, and that brat will not be here. If you don't take care of it, I will. Remember, I took care of your father, and I can deal with this too. You have until noon next Saturday to get it done. Otherwise, I will come and take it away."

He stared at Maddy through squinted eyes, as if evaluating her reaction. "And don't even think about trying to hide from me. No matter where you go, I will find you, and you'll be sorry you ever crossed Horace Johnstone!"

He slammed out of the house without looking back. Evidently, he forgot about having dinner, which pleased Maddy even though his threat shook her.

With Pearl once again crying in her arms, she whirled toward Frank's footsteps coming from the kitchen. "Did you hear that?" she asked when he came into sight.

"How could I miss it even in this big house?" His gentle eyes were troubled. "What do you plan to do, Miss Madeline?"

While putting Pearl on her shoulder and patting the baby's back, Maddy blew out a deep breath. "I'm not exactly sure right this minute. But I will not marry that man, and I will not give up my daughter. I may not have carried her in my body, but she is the child of my heart."

She buried her face against Pearl's neck while tears streamed from her own eyes.

Some of the things Mr. Johnstone said played over in her

mind. *Took care of your father*. Whatever that meant...*brat...take it away...I will find you...you'll be sorry*. They sounded like the pounding of coffin nails, burying her dreams.

~

*A*ll the hullabaloo upset both Pearl and Maddy. It took quite awhile for Maddy to settle the baby down to sleep. When she finished, she undressed and got ready for bed, then remembered she hadn't had dinner. Surely Sarah had something she could eat in the kitchen. She put on her robe and trudged down the stairs.

When she opened the door to the kitchen, both Sarah and Frank were sitting at the table. Sarah jumped up and went to the stove.

"I kept the stew hot. I knew you'd be hungry." She dished up a bowl of the mixture, lacing the air with the delicious fragrance of beef and vegetables, and set it on a plate, then placed biscuits beside the bowl.

Maddy pulled up a tall stool and climbed onto the seat, resting her feet on the lower rung. "Thank you. I didn't realize how hungry I was until I finally got Pearl to sleep." She dipped the warm bread into the dish and took a bite before picking up her spoon. "This is so good."

Frank leaned his elbows on the table and bowed his head a moment. When he looked up at her, his brown eyes glistened with unshed tears. "Miss Madeline, we have to make some hard decisions right away."

She nodded. "I know. My mind was on the problem. That's probably why it was so hard to settle Pearl down. She sensed my tension."

Sarah went to stand behind Frank, her hand on his shoulder. "We think we should all go to New Mexico Territory right away. Before Mr. Johnstone finds out about our leaving."

Frank reached up to pat her hand. "We've been talking about what we can do. Sarah and I have saved most of our salary for years. We have a nest egg, and we can pay for train tickets to get us there."

Now tears ran down Maddy's cheeks. She swiped at them with both palms. "You do know that I have some money from my mother, don't you? And all of her jewelry?"

Frank jumped up like a jack-in-the-box and strode across the room and back. "We know about some of that. Just not how much you have. But we really want to do this for you. Sarah and me never had any children, so you're all we've got. And you'll need your money for supplies and things." He scratched his head. "We'll have to figure out all we'll need to take with us— and how we'll get it without Johnstone finding out. That's what we've been discussing."

Maddy slipped down from the stool and went to her trusted servants and friends. She threw her arms around both of them. "What would I have done without the two of you in my life?"

Frank jerked a handkerchief from his back pocket and dried his eyes. "I can go to the other side of town and rent a wagon. And I'll make sure neither Johnstone or any of his henchmen are around when I buy the tickets."

"But how will we take care of Pearl on the long trip?" Maddy could think of a lot of complications.

"We could get Mrs. Maguire to help us buy what we'll need for little Pearl during the journey." Sarah's confident tone bolstered Maddy's confidence. "She'll know how much infant food to buy. We'll take enough for on the trip and for a while after we arrive, in case the stores there don't stock the Nestle brand. We can always order it."

Frank nodded. "I have a cousin who works for the railroad. I've been talking to him. Most of the way, we'll be on trains with dining cars. We won't have any trouble getting the warm water we need. And when we transfer to the Santa Fe line, they stop at Harvey Houses along the route."

Maddy put a hand to her chest. Everything was moving so fast. "One thing—I haven't heard back from Mr. Smith. What if he doesn't want me to come? Or what if he's accepted some other woman for his bride?"

"Won't matter. We can make a home there with you." Frank's eyes glinted with stubbornness. "Sarah can help you take care of Pearl, and I'll get a job. Johnstone won't be able to find you."

Sarah tsked. "You weren't planning on marrying him anyway."

"But if the man does want me there, how do I tell him I don't want to marry him?" *So many stumbling blocks in my path.* Maddy shuddered thinking about all of them.

Sarah pulled her into a warm embrace and cradled her against her cozy breast. "We've been talking to the good Lord about this, child. I do believe we have God's blessing. And Pearl will be removed from danger."

She couldn't have said anything that would have convinced Maddy more of the need to make haste. Pearl was more important than anything else. That man would never get his hands on her.

~

*M*addy hadn't realized just how hard and long the trip would be, and caring for little Pearl wasn't easy. She thanked God every day that Sarah and Frank were there to help her. Sarah knew a lot about caring for infants, even though they had never had a child of their own...except for her when she was a baby. That's why they felt so much like family.

Pearl awakened, and she picked her up and patted her back. Since they went through Texas, the train had a lot more passengers than before. Maddy didn't want the baby's crying to disturb them.

Frank had taken to walking up and down the aisle between the seats. He said his lumbago gave him fits if he sat on one place too long. That's where he was right now while Sarah dozed beside Maddy.

Realizing that she needed to change Pearl, she returned to their private sleeping compartment. After cleaning up the baby and changing her clothes, she mixed formula powder with the hot water the porter had supplied her earlier. By now, it was only lukewarm, so Pearl would drink it right down.

While Maddy fed the baby her bottle, she enjoyed the feel of the sweetheart in her arms. For the first time, her heart yearned for someone to love her and want to share a family with her.

When Pearl was finished, Maddy talked to her, laughing and loving to watch those sweet lips and sparkling eyes as the baby looked every direction in the small compartment. Finally, she packed up everything she had been using and headed back toward where she'd been sitting before.

As she walked toward Sarah, she grasped the backs of seats she walked beside with one hand. This train was going so much faster than she'd ever imagined it would. She had a hard time balancing with the car lurching over the tracks.

The door at the other end of the car opened, and Frank stepped through, followed by a tall stranger in a cowboy hat and boots. She dropped into the seat before they arrived. Perhaps the man was going somewhere else.

However, when Frank stopped beside her, he turned to the man. "This here's the young woman I told you about."

The stranger tipped his hat and nodded. "I'm pleased to meet you."

What should she say to him? She wasn't used to meeting strangers. What had Frank told him about her?

"The name's Dave Jefferson."

"It's nice to meet you, too, I'm sure." Heat climbed her cheeks. She had to be blushing, but she didn't know why. "I'm Maddy Mercer."

Frank stepped between the seats that faced each other and dropped down across from Sarah. "Dave, why don't you join us for a while?"

Mr. Jefferson glanced at Maddy as if he were asking her permission. She gave him a nod. He removed his hat, sat down, and hung the hat on his knee. She'd never seen a man do that before, but there was plenty of room between the seats for him to do it.

Frank reached across and pulled Pearl into his arms. He gave her a kiss on her forehead and cuddled her on his chest.

Mr. Jefferson watched Frank's every move. "And who is this tiny girl?"

Maddy hadn't told many people what happened. She wasn't sure she wanted to tell a stranger. Frank evidently trusted him, so she told him a shortened version of how she became Pearl's mother.

"I admire you for what you've done, Ma'am."

What could she say to that? All she could think of was "Thank you."

Frank rested Pearl on his shoulder and patted her back. "I invited Dave to join us, because he has quite a story to tell. We've been visiting a bit every time I walked into the next rail car."

Maddy turned her attention toward the handsome cowboy. "Please tell us. We still have several hours of riding this train."

"Well, I'm going to get off at Los Cerillos, just as you folks are, but I'm going north to Santa Fe, instead of south like you'll do."

O.K. That didn't sound all that interesting.

"Tell the women why." Frank prodded him.

"All right. Here's the short version." He smiled at each of

them. "When I was a young man, almost a boy, I was a scoundrel. It lasted many more years than it should have."

Maddy hadn't expected that. He didn't look like a scoundrel now, but what does a scoundrel look like. She really didn't know. The only one she knew was Mr. Johnstone. Surely he wasn't that bad.

"I lied and cheated my way through life, leaving hurting people scattered behind me. I'm not proud of it. But a few years ago, an old rancher introduced me to Jesus, and my life changed. Now I'm trying to make restitution for all the damage I caused. I found out that one of the men I swindled is in Santa Fe. I aim to find him and pay him back as I have done with each person I've been able to track down."

Maddy was amazed by what he shared. She could do nothing but respect him. How many people ever did anything like that? She hadn't known any. You never knew what was in anyone else's heart.

CHAPTER 9

GOLDEN, NEW MEXICO

*T*his late in the spring, the heat was starting to take hold of everything in the Ortiz Mountain region. Jeremiah let Lightning have his head and the steed's hooves flew over the rocky ground, eating up the miles to Golden. The speed created enough wind to cool off Jeremiah. Even though he enjoyed the short season of desert spring flowers, he didn't pay attention to how many different ones were blooming today.

He needed to check on Philip. And his mail. Couldn't forget his mail. Jeremiah wanted to get back to his ranch and work with the new hands. At least a few of the ones who'd left earlier to seek their fortune at the mines had returned, asking for their old jobs back. They were breaking in the new hands while he went to town.

Soon the faint rhythm of the stamping machines matched Lightning's strides, growing stronger and louder the closer he rode to Golden. Jeremiah didn't think he'd ever get used to living in town with all that racket. The few hours he spent with Philip were more than enough. At the ranch, he enjoyed the subtle sounds of nature—the wind in the trees around the ranch house, the lowing of his cattle, birdcalls, and the evening song of insects—instead of this steady pounding.

He gradually slowed the big horse before they rode up Main Street, then reined Lightning to a stop in front of Skinner's Mercantile. Jeremiah dismounted and tied the reins to the hitching rail.

When he stepped into the shadowed interior of the store, he spied Cyrus sorting the mail and headed that way. "Got anything for Philip?"

"Yep." The storekeeper/postmaster pointed to a small stack on the back table. "Even got somethin' fer you." He held out a single letter.

"Thanks." Jeremiah looked at the return address, then tore into the envelope. "Good. I've been waiting for this notification. My shipment of building materials will arrive on tomorrow's train."

Cyrus raised his bushy eyebrows. "What you plannin' to build now? Isn't Philip's house done?"

The trouble with knowing everyone in town was that they all wanted to know his business too. "Doing some building out at my ranch." That was an answer without too much information. He grabbed Philip's letters. "Tell Helen I said hello."

"Will do." The old man's words followed Jeremiah out of the store.

At the top of the hill, Philip sat in one of the rocking chairs on his front porch. Jeremiah noticed his friend watching as he and Lightning approached. But the retired miner continued gently moving the chair until Jeremiah dismounted.

"Jerry, glad yer here." He used one toe to stop the swaying motion of the chair. "Saw ya at the store. Got any mail fer me?"

Mounting the steps with the letters held in his hands, Jeremiah answered, "Got some today. Seems there are fewer and fewer now."

"Maybe the one I'm waitin' fer's here." He stood up and reached for the envelopes.

Jeremiah followed him indoors.

Philip sat in his favorite padded rocker with the letters on his bony lap. After bowing his shaggy head a short time, he looked up with a huge smile. "'Tis. Right here."

He picked up each envelope and stared at it as if he could read the words through the thick paper. With the fifth one, he held the letter tight in his grip and let the rest drop to the floor. "This'n."

The envelope didn't look like the rest. Not just plain paper. Some kind of fancy expensive stationery, like the Skinners had in the glass-front counter in the store.

"Are you sure? Doesn't look like that woman needs your help." Jeremiah caught himself before he snorted.

"I didn't say she'd be poor. Just that she'd need my help. There's all kinds a-needs, Jerry. Don't forgit that." Philip tore the letter open and started to read, forming the words soundlessly. After only a few, he held out the sheet. "Read it fer me, Jerry."

Jeremiah took the paper, and the faint scent of roses teased his nostrils. Wanting to pull it close and really take a whiff, he restrained himself. He'd been doing that a lot lately around his old friend. No use letting Philip know he noticed the perfume. He'd never hear the end of it.

"You can read."

The older man nodded. "'Course I can. You jist do it faster, and I'm in a hurry to hear it."

Jeremiah stared at the words written in a feminine script with whirls and curlicues as he read the letter aloud.

Dear Mr. Smith,

A good friend of mine gave me a copy of your advertisement. Because of a present circumstance in my life, I may need to leave Boston quickly. Although Golden in New Mexico Territory has been previously unknown to me, I might want to travel there to meet you. Since you're a Christian gentleman, I'm sure you'll not force me into a quick marriage, and if it doesn't work out, you'll forgive me.

Sincerely,

Miss Madeline Mercer

He stopped and glanced at Philip, who sat with his head resting on the back of the rocker, his eyes shut tight. Jeremiah wondered if he'd fallen asleep. He often did these days. One more reason not to let on how aggravated Jeremiah was with this letter business.

"Them's real purty words, ain't they, Jerry?" Philip opened his eyes and stared straight at him. "And her writin' looked real purty, too."

Jeremiah huffed out an exasperated breath. The man was bordering on loony. "How do you know this is the one you should answer?" He flung a hand toward the envelopes scattered on the floor near the rocker. "You haven't read any of those, or any of the others you've stuck away in drawers."

"She's the one, all righty. The good Lord done told me." He pushed to his feet, rocking a little with the movement of the chair before he steadied. "We havta write her today. Hiram'll be headin' out later in the afternoon to take the mail ta Los Se-re-yos. I want the letter in the outgoin' mail sack."

Another delay before getting back to the ranch. Jeremiah had a lot to do today, and he could trust his hands to complete what he told them to. But he hankered to be out there on the range too. A flash of memory stopped those thoughts in their tracks—Philip helping him drag the body of his partner, Charles Warner, from the rubble after the tunnel collapsed on him. The old man hadn't worried about where else he wanted to be when

89

Jeremiah fell apart and needed him. And even though he thought his old friend was just about to make one of the biggest mistakes of his life, he wouldn't stand in his way. He read determination in every line on the old man's face and in the stiff way he held his skinny arms and shoulders.

Without another thought, Jeremiah pulled out the tablet and pencil and sat at the table. "All right, what do you want to say?"

"Wish we could make it sound purty, like hers did." Philip scratched his head, mussing his white hair. "Write one of them sal-you-tashuns like she done."

"Dear Miss Mercer. That all right?"

"Shore is." He stared out the window for a moment. "You put it in them good words. Wanna tell her she can come on out here. She can jist visit. If'n she needs the protec-shun of my name, I'll marry her, but onlies if'n that's what she wants."

Jeremiah copied down all Philip said but crafted the old man's words into better sentences, then he recopied it on the stationery with ink. He added the address from the envelope, then Philip's General Delivery as the return address. When he finished, he handed it to Philip to read.

"That's jist what I wanted." A smile split his white beard that was beginning to grow back. "I wanna git another shave afore she comes too. Might as well start shavin' real often."

Jeremiah took the letter, put it in the envelope, and sealed it. "How about if I take this to the post office and mail it? Then I go on back to the ranch. I've got to come to town tomorrow. My building supplies should come in on the southbound train. I'll stop here on the way back to help you shave."

"Sounds good to me. Jerry, I take up too much of yer time as it is." Philip shooed him away.

"No, you don't." He waved, then ducked out the door. His gut told him something momentous was going to happen tomorrow, and that it might not be good.

~

*T*he early morning train from Albuquerque had gone through Los Cerrillos and already headed for Santa Fe before Jeremiah reached the livery in Golden.

"Swede?" He strode through the open doors, then waited for his eyes to adjust to the low light inside. At least some sunlight streamed through occasional cracks between the boards. "You in here?"

The tall blond stood up inside one of the stalls. "Ja, I'm checkin' out Old Gert here. She's needin' a new shoe." The big man opened the door of the stall, keeping himself between the horse and the opening, and slipped through before latching it securely. "What can I do for you?"

"I need to hire the wagon." Jeremiah took off his hat and ran his fingers through his sweaty hair. Maybe the darkness in here would cool his head some. "I need to go to Los Cerrillos to pick up some building supplies I ordered."

The livery owner headed toward another stall. "Then you'll need to keep it most of the day, for sure. Drivin' a wagon that far will take some time. Do you want to leave Lightning here? I could cool him down and feed and water him for you."

"That would be great. The southbound train comes by around two o'clock. I need to be on my way." He slapped his hat back on his head.

The two men worked together hitching two fresh horses to the wagon. Swede went over to his tack room. "I've got a jug of water you can take with you. It could turn into a real scorcher before you get back."

"Thanks." Jeremiah headed northeast out of town, thinking about all the changes he wanted done to the ranch house.

He had plenty of time to think about it. At least his planning would take away from the boredom of the long drive. By the time he could no longer hear the *thump, thump* of the stamping machines, his headache had cleared up, and he could finally admire the scenery. Areas of white or yellow flowers were decorated with occasional clumps of color—red, blue, purple. He knew the names of some of the flowers and cacti, but not all of them.

Lupins reminded him of his mother's eyes. That's about all he could remember about her. The distinct color that sometimes looked blue, sometimes purple. He knew Indian paintbrush by its flaming red blossoms on the green plant with thin leaves. His mother would have loved them. She always liked bright things.

Why was he thinking about his mother? Doing that only made him realize all he'd missed in life. A wife and a family.

The thoughts he'd been keeping at bay finally slipped in. What could he do about Philip and that Mercer woman? Just why would an educated woman who could afford really nice stationery want to come from a metropolitan area like Boston to a small desert town like Golden? It didn't make a lick of sense. Something was wrong with the whole picture. But he didn't know exactly what it was. Knowing how long it took for her letter to get here after they mailed the ad, he should have plenty of time to figure it out before they heard back from her again. Maybe she'd change her mind before the letter even reached Boston.

In the near distance, he could hear the train's whistle. Since Los Cerrillos was a watering stop for the train and a meal stop for the passengers, he should be there only a few minutes after the train arrived. And it wouldn't leave before he got there. He'd have plenty of time to load his wagon, refill the water jug, and maybe even stop for a visit at the café. Get a piece of pie. Something to fortify him for his trip home.

~

LOS CERRILLOS, NEW MEXICO

*a*t the knock on their private compartment in the Pullman car, Maddy watched Frank open the door.

The conductor stood outside. "We're approaching Los Cerrillos, the train stop closest to Golden. Will someone be meeting you there?"

"I don't think so." Frank glanced back at the women before continuing. "Won't we be able to hire a carriage to take us to Golden?"

"Things out here are different from back East. The south-bound stagecoach goes through there once a week, and yesterday was the day." The man shook his head. "I'm not sure who you'll find to take you. It's still quite a ways off."

That didn't sound good. Maddy swallowed a gasp and tried to compose herself. This trip had been hard enough already. Maybe they shouldn't have been so hasty to choose Golden, since they really knew little about the town. Pearl slept on her shoulder, and she pulled the baby even closer to her heart. The memory of what probably would have happened to her daughter at the hands of Horace Johnstone helped stiffen her spine. They could face anything they had to as long as they were together.

"Don't worry, Frank. We'll find a way after we get there." Her words held more assurance than she felt.

The conductor moved on down the car as the now-familiar train whistle split the air, awakening Pearl. Maddy patted her back to calm her. "We need to change her again before we alight from the train."

She changed the diaper while Sarah worked on the infant food. By the time the train slowed for the station, the baby was content taking her bottle, her blue eyes fixed all the while on Maddy's face. She could sense the love coming from the babe.

Pearl felt the connection between them just as strongly as Maddy did.

When the train finally came to a full stop, Frank stepped down from the car and reached back to help Maddy. After she stood on the platform, Frank went up to get Pearl so Sarah could also climb down the steps.

Holding her daughter in her arms, Maddy glanced around at the town with the Spanish name. Wondering what it meant, she looked beyond the station platform to the buildings so different from what she was used to in Boston. Built of adobe or earthen bricks, each sported a sign proclaiming more than one newspaper, a couple of hotels, and farther down a rowdier bunch of people milled around a group of saloons. Glancing at side streets, she caught a glimpse of homes and other businesses. Los Cerrillos seemed to be a thriving town, bustling with activity. Surely they would be able to hire someone to take them to Golden. If not, she wasn't sure what they would do.

CHAPTER 10

*T*he wagon joggled across the rise of one of the hills that gave Los Cerrillos its name, and Jeremiah had a clear view of the train that had recently pulled into the station. A man in a loose-hanging suit stepped down from one of the Pullman cars, then turned back, offering his hand to someone inside.

Close to the station now, Jeremiah stared at the vision that descended the last step to the platform, revealing a tiny bit of ankle above her dainty slippers. She looked like the china doll that had sat in the glass counter at the mercantile a long time. Fine features, creamy skin, a little bit of a thing, but he could tell she was a woman, not a girl. Her rich brown hair was pulled up away from her neck, and a hat perched on the pile of curls. She had to be from back East. No women he knew in Golden took the time to style hair so elaborately.

For a moment, he felt as if a whole herd of cattle stampeded through his stomach. If he hadn't been thinking so much about Philip's mail-order bride, he probably wouldn't have even noticed this woman.

Tell yourself that if you want to. But he knew it wasn't true.

This woman looked like the one in his dreams—a wife to be proud of. A mother for his yet-to-be-born children.

When the man let go of her hand, he climbed back into the car and reemerged with a baby in his arms. He handed the infant to the woman. She pulled it close and kissed the child on the head. Well, she was someone's wife. Surely not the man who helped her from the train. He was old enough to be her father or even her grandfather.

When the man went back to the train, Jeremiah kept studying the woman. Looking at another man's wife like that was wrong, but for a little while, he enjoyed her beauty, every graceful movement.

Shaking his head, he stopped the wagon beside the train platform and tied the reins to the hitching rail before heading into the station. Now the pretty woman was already inside along with the older man and an older woman. So where was her husband? Didn't matter. She wasn't his concern. He leaned against the wall and rested one booted foot against it. Jeremiah watched them from under the brim of his Stetson while they talked to the station master.

"We're going to the closest hotel to get something to eat." The woman holding the baby was the one who spoke to Charlie, instead of the man traveling with her.

Odd. Where was the man who should be protecting her? She'd need a lot of that in this rough town. Sure, some families lived here, but all the decent women were attached. Miners were always on the prowl for something besides the fare at the saloons.

"After that"—her voice, so like a song bird, drew his attention back to her—"we'll want to hire a carriage to take us to Golden. Can you tell us where to find the livery stable?"

The station master stared at her before answering. "A carriage? Don't think there's a single one in all of Los Cerillos."

The frown that puckered her brows didn't diminish her beauty in the least. "Then how are we going to get there?"

Charlie glanced toward Jeremiah.

Oh, no. He wasn't about to get roped into this mess. These people should've made arrangements before they got to Los Cerrillos.

"Jeremiah, you here with a wagon?"

The old coot knew he was coming for supplies. Why was the man pushing him into a corner about this? Probably because of how pretty the tiny woman was. She had Charlie eating out of her hand, the one that wasn't clasped around another man's child.

"Yeah, I've got the wagon." He pushed away from his resting place. "Why?"

He knew what Charlie wanted, but he wasn't going to make it any easier for the old man. He couldn't get all his supplies and these people and their luggage into the wagon at the same time.

"These here fine folks need a ride to Golden." He'd never seen Charlie smile so wide.

Three pairs of eyes turned toward him. The man sized him up. The older woman had a look of interest, and the young mother all but begged him with her gaze.

"I can pay you for your trouble."

Her soft words caressed his ears. Heated them up. They had to be burning red.

He was a goner. "Keep your money." He glanced toward the station master. "I'll come back tomorrow for the supplies. You can store them for me, can't you?" He hardened his expression, daring Charlie to disagree.

The older man stepped forward, thrusting his hand toward Jeremiah. "The name's Frank Sneed, and this is my wife, Sarah. We're traveling with Miss Madeline. I'll help you put our luggage in your wagon."

You bet you will. Jeremiah gave his hand a quick, hard shake.

He didn't plan on doing all the work by himself. He followed Sneed out onto the platform.

"We don't have a lot of time to be lollygagging before we leave. It's quite a ways to Golden." He stared at the luggage piled together and gave one longing glance toward his supplies before grabbing two of the canvas bags and heading toward the wagon.

Only then did the name register. Miss Madeline? So there wasn't a husband. Interesting. And very dangerous for her, the town of Golden—and for him.

~

*M*addy was sure that Jeremiah What's-His-Name didn't want to help them. His tangible disdain tainted the air in the station, and she didn't like it one bit. No one had ever treated her with such a lack of respect. She had heard about a *Code of the West*. People helped each other, especially a damsel in distress. And she was a damsel in distress if there ever was one. A seemingly endless train ride had worn her down, and this man's lack of kindness grated on her nerves. She really wanted to give him a piece of her mind. Uncomfortable at where her thoughts were leading her, she didn't like feeling this way. She'd never met a more exasperating man—except Horace Johnstone. A shudder accompanied that thought.

Reality settled over her. She needed to treat this Jeremiah person kindly because she must get as far away from Mr. Johnstone as possible. She hoped no one had discovered they had left Boston, but her insides quaked when she thought of all the things that could have gone wrong. At least when they arrived in Golden, she could ask Mr. Smith for his protection, even if they didn't marry. Hopefully he was a strong man who could give them a refuge from danger.

For some strange reason, the thought brought that Jeremiah

man to mind. No one would argue that he wasn't strong. And he could keep them safe. But evidently he didn't want to.

As if her thoughts called his name out loud, Jeremiah stood in the open doorway of the station, blocking out the sunlight. "Follow me." After the terse order, he disappeared from her sight.

Maddy snapped her gaze to Sarah.

"Let's go." With an encouraging smile, Sarah led the way outside.

Their trunks and luggage filled over half the wagon. She stared at the pile, wondering where they would ride.

Frank trotted toward her. "Let me have Pearl. I'll ride in the back, and I can keep her in the shadows of the baggage or the seat. She might even go to sleep in the wagon."

He took the baby from her arms and cooed at the infant.

"Miss Madeline." The words sounded derogatory coming from Jeremiah. "You and Miz Sneed can sit up front with me."

Maddy stared at the board seat. It didn't look long enough to hold three people, especially if one was this cowboy. She glanced at Sarah.

"I'll get our parasols from the luggage, so we can keep the sun off." Her servant spoke to their reluctant driver. "Just how long will it take to get to Golden?"

"At least three hours, so we better get on the road." He turned from Sarah toward Maddy and offered his hand. "I'll help you up."

How Maddy wished she didn't need his help, but this skirt would hinder her climbing onto the wagon. She looked for a step or something to put her foot on.

He leaned close to her and whispered, "The step's by the wagon wheel. The brake is on, so the wagon won't move."

She leaned away from him. His proximity made her nervous. She glanced into his eyes, and they held a serious expression. He held out his hand.

After grabbing hold of it, she held her skirt with her other hand and placed her kid slipper on the narrow step. She was sure that anyone coming by could see her unmentionables. Her foot slipped, and she almost fell, but his hand gripped harder. When she tried again and her leather sole slid once more, he released his hold on her. Then the insufferable man grasped her waist with both his hands and hoisted her up. She felt like a sack of flour.

But she felt something else as well. The heat of his hands branded her waist. Warmth spread from them like the spokes of the wheel she'd stood beside, making her uncomfortably hot, even in this dimity dress she'd bought in Santa Fe when they had a longer stop. Most of the clothing she'd brought with her was much too warm for this climate.

"Miss Madeline."

At the soft words, she glanced down. Sarah held a parasol toward her. Maddy took the lacy confection and unfurled it, positioning it so the sun no longer poured down on her face.

Jeremiah held his hand out for Sarah, and she took it. When she put her more sturdy shoe on the step, it didn't slip or slide. She quickly used his help to reach the wagon bed, but there wasn't room for her to pass Maddy and sit beside the driver.

When Sarah stared pointedly at Maddy, she shifted toward the middle. By then Jeremiah's long strides had brought him to the other side of the wagon. He nimbly leapt up and took his seat. No way the three of them would ride without touching each other. This was going to be a long three hours.

The man quickly had the wagon on its way over one of the hills, driving on a rocky path that didn't look like a road to her. With each rut the wagon listed from side to side. Maddy felt as if she were on a ship, instead of a wagon driving across a desolate wasteland. At least patches of colorful flowers broke the monotony of the landscape.

"Miss…"

She stared up into his eyes, too dark to really be brown but not quite black. Uncomfortable at his perusal, she lowered her lashes. "Yes?"

"I'm sure these are trusted servants, and they call you Miss Madeline, but I'd like a last name to tag on." His words were hard like the landscape.

"Mr...?" She cocked her head and gave him a saucy smile. Two could play this game.

"Dennison. Jeremiah Dennison." He didn't take his attention from the road, but his lips tipped up slightly at the ends.

She stared straight ahead. "I'm Madeline Mercer—of the Boston Mercers."

Total silence followed her announcement. She waited for his response. Nothing. She could wait him out. Finally, she glanced up at him.

"What brings you to our fine town, Miss Mercer of the Boston Mercers?" An insincere smile spread across Mr. Dennison's face, never reaching his inscrutable dark eyes.

"The good Lord did." Maddy showed him what a real smile should look like.

His expression turned to a scowl, as if he'd just taken a bite of a sour pickle. "I'm quite sure the 'good Lord' had nothing to do with it."

This chilly response disturbed her. The way he said the words told her he wasn't one bit familiar with her Lord, and probably didn't want to be. Maddy knew she couldn't trust a man who wasn't a strong man of God.

~

*I*diot! How could he be such an idiot? Jeremiah gulped a deep breath to keep from cursing. This was the woman he and Philip had sent a letter to *yesterday*. And here she was. On the way to Golden. Right now.

He stared at the faint road ahead. If it hadn't been for the other people in the wagon, he wouldn't try to miss the worst of the rocks and ruts. He'd just as soon shake the stiffness right out of Miss Madeline Mercer.

Why hadn't he pegged her right off? With her rose-scented letter and her fancy clothes, she'd slipped under his defenses. But he had her number now. She had to be a gold digger. Probably living off some other man's wealth she'd stolen and looking for a way to finance her high standard of living, as evidenced by her clothing and luggage, when that ran out. Well, it wouldn't be Philip's gold. He'd see to it.

Talking about God the way Philip did, she had to be a hypocrite. Evidently, this was just her way of playing on emotions to get what she wanted. It wouldn't take long to have the retired miner eating out of her hand. He had to think of something fast to keep her from meeting him. A single woman with a baby shouted immorality. She was more suited to work in one of the saloons than to marry a decent man.

He'd been so intrigued by her outward appearance that he hadn't looked deeper. Shame on him. Too late now to put her back on the train and get her out of here. He'd have to think of something else. But what?

CHAPTER 11

GOLDEN, NEW MEXICO

*T*he sun was sinking low on the horizon when the wagon topped a small rise. The outline of buildings smudged the distance, almost indistinguishable from the shadows of the low mountains. Maddy squinted to make sure she wasn't imagining them. Could they be a mirage? She'd read about them in a desert, and this was definitely a desert.

"That's Golden up ahead." Mr. Dennison's voice, gravelly from not being used, startled her.

He hadn't spoken a word since asking her name, except to offer them drinks from a large water jug. And he didn't have a cup. They all drank from the unwieldy container. At first she wiped the top with her handkerchief before she took a sip. Later, because of the heat, she turned it up and gulped the refreshing liquid, glad to have something to rinse the dust out of her throat.

She knew many men didn't talk much, but riding silently for hours while sitting so close to others was the height of rudeness. Try as she might to prevent it, during the long journey, their hips and arms often brushed. Every muscle in her body ached from all the jostling and from trying to hold herself erect.

Somewhere along the line, while they were working out transportation, the idea of going to a hotel to eat had fallen by the wayside. Her stomach screamed for attention, but the clip-clops from the horses' hooves and the creaking timbers of the wagon drowned out the unladylike noise. Nothing could help the hunger pangs that accompanied the rumbles. She hoped Golden would have a nice restaurant. Was that too much to ask?

"I spotted the town up ahead." She clipped her words as he had his. She didn't think he would even realize her lapse of good manners.

He stared down at her. She didn't glance up, but she felt the weight of his gaze burning into her, adding to her other aches and pains. Her body had never been so mistreated. She wondered how long it would take her to recover once they arrived in town.

"It'll still take almost an hour to get there. You can see a fur piece out here."

Once more his shoulder bumped hers, leaving an indelible impression. A fur piece? Surely he wasn't talking about an outer garment. Fur? Far? He meant they can see a far distance. What quaint wording. She hoped everyone in Golden didn't talk in some kind of code that was hard to understand. If that were true, a civilized conversation would take an eternity.

Before they'd gone far, a muffled thumping off in the distance caught her attention. She gazed all around, trying to find the source of the noise, which grew louder the farther they traveled. "What's that sound?"

Without taking his gaze from the road ahead, Mr. Dennison answered, "The stamping machines. They break up the ore before the gold is refined."

Maddy hoped the sound wouldn't get much louder but feared it would. She leaned forward, stretching her back. With nothing to lean against, her muscles agonized. "Mr...uh, Dennison, does Golden have a hotel where we can spend the night?"

Like twine that had been cut from a package, his muscles uncoiled at her question, pulling him farther away from her. "Yes. Actually, the preacher and his wife run the hotel."

What a relief. Not only was Mr. Smith a Christian, but a minister and his wife also lived in Golden. She felt a lot safer at that thought.

"And will we be able to get something to eat at the hotel, or is there a restaurant close by?" She moved her parasol to the other shoulder, imagining a large plate of delicious food.

Her stomach let out the loudest growl so far. Surely everyone in the wagon could hear it. She cut her eyes up toward their driver. His full lips tilted at the ends for just a moment before they flattened back into a thin line.

"Miss Mercer." His Adam's apple bobbed as if the words caught in his throat. "I'm very sorry we got distracted, and you and your friends didn't eat. How long has it been?" He stared straight ahead at the town that now was taking shape.

She didn't want the man to feel bad, because they had caused him a lot of trouble. Maddy knew he hadn't wanted to offer them a ride. The station master had practically forced him into it. At the time, she'd considered him a boor, but she hadn't realized what an imposition it would be. The ride had been long and hard, and he would have to make it again tomorrow to pick up his supplies.

"We did eat a little in Santa Fe, but I spent most of our time there purchasing clothing more suitable to this climate. I suppose I'm to blame that we're so hungry." She peeked at him out of the corner of her eye.

He had an actual smile on his face. "I shouldn't have been in such a bad mood that I didn't pay attention to your needs." The words didn't sound as grudging as his earlier ones had been.

"About a restaurant—the best place to eat in Golden is the hotel. Miz Oldman's a really good cook."

"And is that the only place to eat?" She was genuinely interested in finding out all she could about her new home, no matter how short or long their stay.

"There are other places, but I don't think a lady'd want to eat there." The tan in his cheeks deepened with a reddish tinge.

Was he blushing? Interesting. So why wouldn't a lady…?

She didn't need to finish her question. Undoubtedly, he was talking about saloons. She'd heard that some of them served food along with their other…enticements. She stared straight ahead, feeling more heat in her own cheeks.

Sarah leaned forward, around Maddy, and looked at Mr. Dennison. "Can you tell us about the town?"

"Well, gold was discovered near Golden back in 1825, years before it was found in Colorado or California. It was actually the first gold rush west of the Mississippi River." He continued to stare off into the distance.

Finally, the man was opening up to them. Maddy had a few questions of her own. "That's interesting. So how many mines are there?"

His face hardened as if made from one of the huge rocks scattered across the hills. "I haven't counted them." He paused. "Our town has a post office, several businesses—including a stock exchange—and a school."

The last words sounded like bullets they were so hard, each delivered with a slam. What was his problem? Didn't the man know how to be kind for more than a few minutes?

～

*J*ust as Jeremiah thought. This woman was a gold digger sure as shootin'. She'd really perked up when he mentioned the mines. A lump as big and hard as a boulder lodged in his stomach. He didn't like the direction his thoughts wandered. Why hadn't he kept his wits about him in Los Cerrillos? If he had, Miss Mercer *of the Boston Mercers* wouldn't be sitting beside him on the wagon seat. Several times, the worrisome woman had almost hit him with that lacy sunshade contraption she used. The softness of her arm and leg branded his own, and some flowery fragrance floated on the slight breeze, even though they'd been riding through the desert for hours. So like a long-forgotten scent, it raised memories of his mother's garden. An ache settled near his heart for what he lost when his mother died with him just a little sprout. What was he going to do with Miss Mercer now? How could he keep her from meeting Philip?

∽

*B*efore they reached the outskirts of Golden, Pearl's wail split the air. No wonder. The pounding had intensified. Maddy could feel it pulsing through her body. Pearl probably could too.

Maddy had changed her and mixed up a bottle each time they stopped, and the baby had slept most of the way, rocked by the wagon's swaying. Maddy knew she'd be sorry later. No matter how tired she felt, she wouldn't get much sleep. With Pearl staying awake longer each day, all these naps would disrupt her slumber tonight. Maddy would have to try to keep her quiet, so the other guests at the hotel wouldn't be bothered.

Suddenly the loud noise stopped. Relief washed through her like a refreshing stream. At least they wouldn't have to contend with that through the night.

She furled her parasol and handed it to Frank before he lifted Pearl toward her. It hadn't been too long since they stopped the last time, and the baby didn't need changing. Maddy cuddled her close and cooed to her. Pearl's eyes opened wide and stared straight at her—soft, blue, beautiful. Her little fists circled in the warm air and her mouth puckered, but not to cry again. For the first time, a tiny mew gurgled out. Her first coo.

The sound arrowed straight to Maddy's heart, almost bursting it. This child was so precious—and so loved.

The wagon turned down the main street of Golden, but Maddy wouldn't have called it a street. More like a country road until they reached a section of uneven cobblestones that jarred the wagon just as much as the rutted, rocky road they had traveled from the train station.

They drove in front of several saloons and other disreputable-looking businesses. Maddy didn't want to think about what they might be. Loud music played on an out-of-tune piano accompanied an off-key voice. She couldn't tell which establishment the noise came from. Just as they reached one of the saloons, the swinging doors burst open, and two men fell through, tumbled onto the cobblestones, and continued to punch each other over and over.

The doors fanned a couple of times before a crowd surged through them. Drunken men in ragged clothing, cowboys with gun belts slung low on their hips, and scantily clad women with painted faces shouted obscenities as they urged the men to continue their battle. Maddy had never seen or heard anything like it. She wished for her parasol to hide the spectacle from her eyes and to protect Pearl.

Their driver merely kept driving as if nothing were amiss. Maybe things like this went on all the time in Golden. What had she gotten them into?

Finally, Mr. Dennison stopped the wagon in front of the hotel quite a ways farther up the street. They sat in front of a two-story structure built of lumber. Maddy wondered where they got all the wood. One thing missing from the landscape here was trees tall enough to make boards. They must have shipped it in. For a moment, she wondered if the supplies their driver was picking up included lumber. That would be some coincidence, wouldn't it?

Frank jumped down from the back of the wagon and came to the side where Sarah sat. He lifted his arms and helped his wife step down. Then he held out his hands for Pearl.

Maddy hated to give her up so soon. She had missed holding her daughter on the long trip from Los Cerrillos, but the baby had been safer in the back with Frank keeping her out of the blazing sun.

When all the passengers alighted from the wagon, Mr. Dennison jumped to the street. "I'll start carrying your luggage into the lobby while you go check in."

Frank shook his head. "I'll help you. Miss Madeline and Sarah can take care of the business."

Maddy stepped up on the boardwalk and strode through the open doorway into the small lobby of the hotel. A pleasant room. Two upholstered chairs—separated by a small round table that held a decorated oil lamp—sat by one wall. Sconces held lighted candles, giving the room a warm glow in the descending twilight. A gentle breeze ruffled the café-style curtains framing the windows.

"Welcome to the Golden Hotel." A thin woman with dark hair piled haphazardly on the top of her head and a wide smile stood behind a polished wooden counter near the staircase that twisted out of sight.

Maddy glided toward her, relieved at such a welcome. What a contrast to the way Mr. Dennison had treated them.

"We'd like two adjoining rooms, if you have them." She hoisted Pearl higher on her shoulder and patted her back absently.

The woman pulled out a large ledger, laying it on top of the counter. Using her forefinger to follow the columns, she studied the entries before looking up. "We have two nice rooms away from the street. That way your baby won't be disturbed if there's any racket tonight. I'm afraid when the machines start up in the morning, they'll wake her."

"I'm sure they will." Maddy pressed a kiss against Pearl's hair. "Will there be people in the rooms beside ours?"

"Not unless someone else comes to town later tonight." The woman extended her hand across the counter. "I'm Caroline Oldman."

Maddy took her hand for a moment. "And I'm Madeline Mercer." She turned toward her housekeeper. "And this is Sarah Sneed. She and her husband Frank are traveling with us."

"We're glad to have you visit our town." Caroline held out her hand, and Sarah shook it.

Maddy glanced at Sarah, hoping it would be just a visit...or maybe not. From Sarah's raised eyebrow, she knew her old friend wondered the same thing.

"So how long will you be staying?"

The question shouldn't have surprised her, but what answer could she give? "We're not sure."

Mr. Dennison came through the door with one of Maddy's trunks on his shoulder as if it weighed almost nothing, but she knew better. "Caroline, you got a room I can rent tonight?"

Caroline's eyes widened and her lips parted slightly. "Won't you be staying with Philip? Since he built on those two rooms..."

Maddy knew why the woman stopped talking. The man's face resembled a thundercloud about to drop a storm. At this point, she would welcome rain to cool this hot, dry air.

"I'd rather not bother him tonight."

Caroline eyed the man as if he had two heads. Why was it strange for him not to stay with this Philip?

Philip? Of course the name sounded familiar. That was Mr. Smith's name, wasn't it?

"Would that be Mr. Philip Smith?" Maddy's heart pulsed in her throat. Would she be able to meet him so soon?

All eyes trained on her, even Frank's, as he carried another trunk through the door.

Caroline beamed at her. "Do you know Philip Smith?"

"I haven't met him, but he invited us to come meet him." She didn't know how much information would be too much. She didn't want to start any gossip that would be detrimental to Mr. Smith or to them.

"That's nice." Caroline's cheerful tone encouraged Maddy. "We didn't know he had friends coming. That's probably why he built on the extra rooms. Do you want to go on up there tonight instead?"

Mr. Dennison dropped the trunk with a loud thump and glared at Maddy.

She ignored his rudeness. "Actually, we want to take those two hotel rooms. I'd rather have a chance to clean up and be rested before we meet him."

Mr. Dennison clomped out the door and climbed up in the wagon seat. He drove off a different direction from the way they'd entered town, and he didn't look back. His stiff posture reinforced his displeasure.

"What's put a burr under his saddle?" Caroline stared after the man. "I don't think I've ever seen him this mad."

What did he have to be angry about? He'd been unsociable during the whole trip. Just the mention of Mr. Smith set him off like fireworks on the Fourth of July. Well, he didn't actually explode, but his anger had pulsated through the room before he huffed out. Maddy had planned to express thanks and offer him payment for his trouble, but she would be glad if she'd seen the last of Mr. Dennison. Him *and* his bad moods.

CHAPTER 12

*A*t dawn, loud thumping and pulsing awoke Maddy. She glanced down beside the high bed at the drawer from a wooden chest-of-drawers where Pearl lay nestled on a pillow. Rolled-up blankets cradled her. The beautiful, tiny face wrinkled, and a wail erupted.

Maddy picked her up and cuddled Pearl against her shoulder, amazed the baby had slept through the night without waking. That had never happened before. The train ride and the drive to Golden must have taken their toll.

"Sweet Pearl." Maddy grabbed one of the blankets and laid it on the bed, using one hand to fold it into fourths. She placed the infant in the middle of the pad and searched the luggage for clean clothes and a fresh diaper, talking as she went. "You must have been very tired, and I'm sure you're hungry. Just let Mother get you cleaned up, then I'll have a bottle for you."

For a moment, Maddy paused. She'd never called herself *Mother* when she talked to Pearl, but it felt so natural. And since Loraine extracted that promise from her, she was the only mother Pearl had. She really should start calling herself that, so Pearl would associate the name with her.

Maddy wished she had some warm water, but she'd just have to clean Pearl with the tepid water in the pitcher and bowl. Although the baby gave a little flinch when Maddy put the moistened washcloth on her tummy, she didn't cry out. Pearl must enjoy being clean because she always settled down and smiled after her bath. Maddy had heard other women say that a baby doesn't smile this young, but she knew her own child. Those turned-up lips and wide-awake eyes definitely created a smile on Pearl's face when she gazed up at her.

Almost stealing her breath, Pearl's smile made Maddy's heart flutter in her chest, like the butterfly she'd seen a lepidopterist catch in a net when she was in school. Could anything be as wonderful as a baby's smile? She don't think so. She'd barely finished mixing up the infant food and pouring it into the bottle when a rap at the door caught her attention.

"Who is it?"

"It's me, Sarah."

Maddy opened the door and welcomed her friend with a hug. Then she sat in a rocking chair Mr. Oldman had brought up for her last night and gave Pearl the bottle. For a fleeting moment, she wondered what it would be like to nurse a baby she'd borne herself. To provide all the sustenance the child needed from near her heart. Maybe someday she'd find out, but it couldn't be any more special than feeding Pearl right now.

Sarah started washing out Pearl's clothes in the basin on the washstand. "Either I was so tired I didn't hear her, or our wee babe didn't wake up during the night."

"She didn't." Maddy cuddled the infant closer. "I'm sure she was as tired as we were. That was a long trip."

"Indeed it was. I wasn't surprised the noise from the machines woke her up." Sarah wrung out the clothes and spread them across the edge of the open lid of the trunk. "Should I go down and get you some tea?"

"I'm not sure they'll have any." A cup of hot tea would really taste good right now. She hadn't had any in quite awhile. The dining cars on the train and restaurants in the Harvey House hotels served coffee instead.

"I'll go check." Sarah slipped out, closing the door quietly behind her.

Maddy brushed Pearl's wispy hair away from her forehead. In the few short weeks of her life, the baby fuzz had already started to grow, and the ends curled around her finger, soft and silky.

"You are such a blessing," she whispered, and Pearl's eyes never left Maddy's face as she sucked on the rubber nipple. "When Loraine gave you to me, I thought she had made a mistake. But now I know she didn't. I believe God wanted me to be your mother since she couldn't." Tears tracked down Maddy's cheeks. She swiped at them with the back of her hand.

Thank You, Lord, for this wonderful gift. How could I ever question whether You know what's best for me?

And if that was true, then God had sent her to Golden, New Mexico, for a specific purpose. She just wished she knew what it was.

~

*A*fter tossing and turning on his lumpy mattress most of the night, Jeremiah arose at dawn. Instead of taking that room at the hotel and opening himself up to more questioning, he'd come straight home, hoping to rest before making the long trip to Los Cerillos again. With a start at daybreak, he should be back earlier than he was yesterday.

He stopped by the cook shack and grabbed some sausage and biscuits to eat on his way. T-Bone wrapped them in a napkin for him. Before he left, he gulped down a cup of coffee that scalded his throat, bringing tears to his eyes. At least it was strong enough to keep him awake for most of the morning. He knew the long ride in the wagon could lull him to sleep, and he didn't need that.

Although most of the area was free from outlaws, an occasional man on the wrong side of the law would waylay solitary travelers. He had to stay alert. He didn't want to lose any more time than he had to. As it was, he'd lost all of yesterday.

Jeremiah wanted to get back to Golden before those people were up and around. As tired as they were when he'd dropped them off at the hotel, surely they'd want to rest up today. And they had to take care of that baby. The infant might've kept Miss Mercer up most of the night. He certainly hoped so, because he wanted to have a serious talk with Philip before he took those people to meet him.

One reason he had a hard time sleeping was that he wished he'd stopped to see Philip, instead of going off half-cocked and heading back to the ranch in such a rush. He needed to learn to control his anger. At least he hadn't taken it out on anyone else.

That woman riled him, and he hoped he could convince her to leave Golden. But now that they were at the hotel, Philip would learn they were in town. Jeremiah had to hold his cards close to his chest and play them just right to get rid of the woman and all she stood for. And he had only a few hours to do it.

～

*A*fter Pearl finished her bottle, Maddy, holding her precious bundle in her arms, followed the delicious scents that enticed her downstairs. Although they'd eaten in the dining room last night, the whole evening had blurred together. Fatigue had blinded her to her surroundings. This morning she felt alive and eager to meet the day. A little sore maybe, but that soon would work itself out.

"Good morning, Madeline. Did you and your baby sleep

115

well?" Caroline's smiling face welcomed her to the lobby. "You're just in time for breakfast."

The proprietress led the way into the dining room. Frank and Sarah sat at one of the tables with empty plates in front of them. Maddy and Caroline headed that direction.

"I've already fed your friends." Caroline stopped beside the waiting pair. "I have pancakes or biscuits, sausage, and eggs. How do you like your eggs?"

"Can you poach them?" Maddy hoped she could get them prepared the way she liked them.

"I have, but not very often." Caroline laughed. "I can just see some of the miners if I tried to feed them poached eggs. They want lots of eggs, but they've got to be scrambled. Heaping mounds of them."

"How about toast?" Maddy held her breath, willing the answer to be *yes*.

"I make a good hearty country bread that toasts up really well in a skillet. I'll have it ready in a jiffy." She picked up the dirty plates, stacking them on one arm. "Would you like hot tea, or is milk or coffee more to your taste in the morning?"

Maddy smiled gratefully. "Tea would be wonderful, thank you."

"Oh, dear." Sarah stared up at Maddy. "I completely forgot what I came down here for when Frank got to talking to me. Then we came in here and ate breakfast."

"That's all right. I'd have had a hard time managing the hot tea while I was giving Pearl a bottle."

After Caroline left, Maddy eased into an empty chair at the table. She shifted Pearl into her lap. "So was the food as good as the stew and cornbread were last night?"

Frank leaned back and gave his stomach a satisfied pat. "That woman's almost as good a cook as my wife."

"Frank, you do go on, don't you?" Sarah's smile revealed her pleasure at the compliment. "Miss Madeline, I feel rather useless with us staying at the hotel. I should be cleaning or cooking or something."

"You should not." Maddy was firm. "You helped me so much on the trip. I couldn't have done it without you, but now you're guests at the hotel as much as I am. Enjoy it."

Sarah stretched her arms toward Pearl. "At least let me hold the wee one while you eat."

While Maddy watched Sarah and Frank play with Pearl, her thoughts wandered. She had enough money for a few more days at the hotel, but it wouldn't last very long. When she wrote the letter to Mr. Smith, she really hadn't even considered marrying him. She had simply wanted a way to escape Horace Johnstone's clutches.

If what Mr. Johnstone said was true, she was destitute. The thought was too horrible to consider. Somehow she had a problem believing it, but the supply of money from her father's business had dried up, and she hadn't heard anything from the lawyer. She needed to take care of Pearl, Sarah, and Frank, in addition to herself.

Mr. Smith said in his ad that he was a Christian. She might have to consider accepting his marriage proposal—if he was the kind of Christian her father had been. Other women married for convenience, and love usually followed. If she could respect the man when she met him, maybe... Grabbing onto the thought was hard to do.

The food quickly arrived, and Caroline sat down with them after she served Maddy. "Since no one else is here right now, I want to get better acquainted with our newest guests. You were all so tired last night. I didn't want to bother you then."

Maddy smiled at their hostess. "You were very helpful. Sending up a hot bath so I could wash my hair was so thoughtful of you. And having your husband bring up the rocking chair. We have been traveling quite awhile."

"Where you from?"

Maddy considered not answering, but she wanted to make friends with this woman, since she was the preacher's wife. "We came from Boston."

"All the way from Boston?" Caroline's eyes widened. "That is a long journey."

Frank harrumphed. "'Twas indeed."

Sarah nodded, placing the baby on her shoulder, and Pearl snuggled against her.

"The train trip was long, but interesting." Maddy spoke between bites. The toast had butter melted into it, and the eggs nestled on the slices. She savored the taste, salty and smooth.

"When are you going to see Philip?" Caroline gave Maddy a pointed look.

She placed her fork on the edge of the plate, trying to decide how to answer. "I'm not sure. Does he live close by?"

Caroline waved a hand toward the door. "His house is the farthest one up the hill. He bought the old adobe after selling his mine."

Maddy took in the fact that Philip had owned a mine. Maybe he *would* be financially able and willing to help them for a while. If not, she'd have to find another means of support for all of them. She remembered noticing the adobe sitting up there a little ways from the nearest structure, but it certainly didn't look old. "How long ago was that?"

"A couple of years." Caroline got up and took Maddy's empty plate. "Jeremiah helps take care of Philip, but since he's gone to Los Cerrillos today, I'm going to take breakfast up there. Philip usually sleeps late, but he'll be hungry soon."

Maddy wondered about that. Why couldn't Mr. Smith take care of himself? Maybe he'd had a wife who took care of him and never learned how to do things for himself. Jeremiah? Wasn't that what the station master called Mr. Dennison? If he was a good friend of Philip, why didn't he tell them? But then they didn't actually tell the man who they were coming to see in Golden.

Frank rose from his chair and pushed it in toward the table. "I'm going to go outside and look around." He ambled out of the room.

Caroline started toward the kitchen, then stopped. "I'd be glad to take you with me to Philip's when I go."

Maddy wondered if that would be a good idea. She didn't even know if he'd received her letter. *Lord, what am I supposed to do?* As she pondered that question, peace descended on her heart. "I'd like that."

Sarah glanced at her. "Frank and I should go too."

That felt right. Just as well she let Mr. Smith know that people had come with her. And the baby would be with her. She didn't want to keep any secrets from him. From this moment on, she would be totally honest with him, but would only tell him what he asked about. And if he didn't want them here, they could stay in the hotel for a short time while they decided what to do next.

∼

On the walk up the hill toward Mr. Smith's house, Maddy got a better look at this town called Golden. In the morning light, the town looked friendly. Although several buildings they passed the previous evening were saloons, this end of town looked more civilized. Homes clung to the rocky terrain, most of them built of stone or adobe, instead of timber like the hotel. Caroline Oldman, carrying the basket of food, greeted the many people they saw with either a word or a wave with her free hand. And the residents included her and the Sneeds in that greeting. At least they made her feel welcome.

After their long ride from Los Cerillos, Maddy was glad to find more grass and bushes in and around the town. It wasn't as desolate as most of the area they had ridden through. Even more wildflowers clustered among the other plants. It was a far cry from the tall trees, lush grass, and abundant gardens in Boston. Still, the landscape held a quiet beauty she enjoyed.

The sun hung high above them this late in the morning, and a breeze danced through the town, playing with Maddy's skirt. She held the edge of a light blanket over Pearl's head to shade her face. The baby seemed more aware of her surroundings than she had before. She must have liked the open air, instead of air containing exhaust from industrial plants. Unfortunately, many times the wind had carried the terrible smells into their usually pleasant neighborhood in Boston.

Stretching her legs on the walk released some of the tension Maddy had felt for several weeks. She relished the freedom of not being hemmed in by her house or by that Johnstone man.

"That you, Caroline?" The voice of an obviously elderly man preceded him through the open doorway of the house perched a little ways in front of the group.

When he stepped onto the porch, Maddy wondered who the man leaning on a cane could be. Did Mr. Smith have someone else living with him? His father? A friend?

"Sure is, Philip." Caroline continued to swing the basket in rhythm with her strides. "And I've brought some people to meet you."

"Good." The old man's eyes twinkled as they studied the group approaching the house.

Maddy finally understood. *His house.* Caroline had called him Philip. This had to be Mr. Philip Smith. Maddy tried to hide her consternation. *Philip?* Not the Philip of the ad. He couldn't be. Certainly not. Why in the world would a man old enough to be her grandfather advertise for a bride? If he was, it changed everything. She would never consider being married to him, no matter how good a Christian he might be. Thoughts whirled like a typhoon in her mind. What was she going to do now?

Caroline walked up the steps onto the porch. "These people have come from Boston to meet you."

He stared straight into Maddy's eyes, his gaze never wavering. "From Boston, ya say? Well, come in. Come on in."

Maddy broke the connection of their gaze and looked at the steps as she navigated them. She didn't want to stumble with Pearl in her arms. She was thankful Frank and Sarah followed close behind.

"That my breakfast ya have there?" He peered into the basket, but Caroline had covered the food with a tea towel.

Caroline opened the door and went inside as if she was used to doing that very thing. "Sure is. Just what you like. Sausage, scrambled eggs, and biscuits."

He licked his lips, giving them a little smack.

Maddy gave an inward shudder as she followed Caroline into the pleasant room. "We can come back after you've eaten, if you'd like."

Mr. Smith hobbled over to the table and dropped into a chair. "No." The man gave a sharp shake of his head. "No reason fer that. Ya eaten yet?"

Caroline went to a cupboard and got a plate and cup. "Of course. I fed them before bringing them up here."

He nodded. "Jist have a seat. I can finish this in no time."

Maddy glanced at Caroline, who nodded, so she, Frank, and Sarah sat on the sofa against one wall. She tried to calm her thoughts by concentrating on the room. It didn't show any wear. Mr. Smith must have remodeled this house after he bought it. Didn't Caroline say something yesterday about him adding on to the house recently?

All the furniture looked new, as did the pictures, knick-knacks, and polished hardwood floor. Maddy liked the large room with its homey feeling, but it couldn't keep her attention from rushing back to her dilemma. Why were they here? What would she do now that marriage was out of the question?

Caroline picked up the basket, went to the door, and glanced back. "I'm going down to the hotel. I have to start working on lunch. Lots of hungry workers will be coming by." She looked straight at Maddy. "You want to stay here, or go back with me?"

Glad for the option, Maddy started to rise.

Mr. Smith dropped his fork onto his plate with a clatter that jangled her already stretched nerves. "Please stay and visit awhile. Wanna hear 'bout Boston."

Maddy didn't want to disappoint him before they even got acquainted, so she nodded. Might as well find out what this was all about. But watching the old man's lack of manners grieved her. Would staying in Boston have been so much worse? Of course it would. She had to remember to keep the alternative in the forefront of her mind.

He quickly finished eating and moved to a rocking chair near where they were, setting it in motion with one foot. "So tell me who y'are."

Frank stood and leaned against the wall near Maddy. She knew he wanted to let the man know that he was there to protect her, and she welcomed that assurance.

"I'm Madeline Mercer." The whispered words resounded in the silent room.

Mr. Smith stopped the rocker and took a gulp of air. "Madeline Mercer from Boston?"

Maddy sat up a little straighter. "Yes, sir."

"But we just writ ya a letter day b'fore yesterday. How'd ya git here so fast?"

She couldn't tell if he was angry or glad they came. She took a deep breath and let it out slowly. "We, uh, I needed to leave Boston...quickly. I didn't wait for a reply to my letter."

He reached a weathered hand to his face and scratched the

slight beard on his cheek. Then he nodded. "I see. Somethin' bad happenin' back there?"

Once again the horror of being in Mr. Johnstone's presence washed over her, and she shivered. For some reason, she didn't feel the same revulsion for Mr. Smith.

"You could say that." Maddy still couldn't tell if Mr. Smith was upset or just curious.

Pearl started whimpering, and Sarah took the baby to quiet her.

Tears glistened on the old man's cheeks. "I knowed it. Yer s'posed to be here." The light in his eyes transformed him from a stranger into someone Maddy wanted to get to know.

What did he mean by what he said? At least he wasn't demanding they leave his house, his town. She let out the breath she hadn't realized she'd been holding and relaxed. Perhaps they should talk about why he had sent for a bride. He didn't look like he needed or even wanted one. Especially one with a baby. Her child needed a father, not a great-grandfather. But there was more to this situation than what was evident on the surface.

Maybe a discussion would help her understand why he had advertised for a bride. For certain, something had to happen to ease her financial situation. She couldn't even try to find a position as a teacher or anything else because of Pearl. Caroline had mentioned that Mr. Smith sold his mine before he bought this house. Maybe he had the resources to help them. Perhaps he could take them in and let them work for him...care for his needs.

She knew God had sent her here. But not to be a bride for Philip Smith. She couldn't rest easy until she understood all of what had happened. Her future still hung in the balance. *Lord, I need Your help now more than ever before.*

CHAPTER 13

"What did you mean, Mr. Smith, when you said we're supposed to be here?" So many thoughts jumbled in her mind, and Maddy wanted to straighten them out.

The old man flicked his glance from her to Sarah, then Frank. "You. I said yer s'posed to be here. I don't know them."

Frank shifted closer to Maddy. She tilted her head and gave him a tremulous smile. Frank replied with a slight nod, then trained his attention back on Mr. Smith. How like Frank to stress his protective stance, but Maddy was beginning to think she didn't need protection from this man.

She turned back toward him. "This is my housekeeper, Sarah, and her husband, Frank Sneed, my caretaker and driver." She looked down at Pearl, who had fallen asleep in her arms. "And this is my daughter, Pearl."

Surprise flitted across his face, then disappeared. However, the warm welcome stayed in his eyes.

Tilting up her chin, Maddy continued, "And why am I supposed to be here? What exactly does that mean?"

Once again, Mr. Smith set the rocker in motion. His bony

elbows rested on the padded arms of the rocker, and his hands lay against his flat stomach, fingers interlaced. "Said in my ad, I'm a Christian man."

"That's the only reason I answered it." Maddy hated to bare her soul this way with a perfect stranger, but honesty was essential. "I never would have written to any other man."

Mr. Smith nodded. "I know. I can tell yer not useta this kinda thing."

Maddy wondered how he could tell. Nothing she had said or done since they'd been in his house revealed anything about her nature. Or had it? She cast a glance out the window, noticing the wind playing in the leaves of the few scrubby trees. Without that wind, the temperatures here would be completely intolerable. As it was, her skirt wilted around her legs, smothering them.

"I wouldn't a-done it, but the good Lord done told me to." He glanced across the room toward a table holding a lamp and a well-worn Bible. "I didn't understand Him at first."

That statement intrigued her. How did he know God spoke to him? She'd never heard an audible voice. God spoke to her through His Word and in her spirit. Was that the way Mr. Smith heard him? Perhaps the worn book was evidence that he did, but where in the Bible did it say to order a bride with an advertisement in a newspaper?

"But He wouldn't let me alone." He wagged his head. "The more I said no, the more He stressed the need. Finally, I had to write the letter."

"Why did you choose Boston?" Maddy knew he could have sent it many different places, and she never would have seen it.

"That's what He said." The finality of the statement caught her by surprise, as if there were no other answer that would work.

"How did you know I was supposed to be the one?" She

needed more firm details. Pearl stirred in her arms but didn't whimper.

"Well, I got lotsa letters. I jist prayed over 'em. God'd say no, and I'd put 'em away."

So matter of fact. He didn't sound as if this was the least bit peculiar—even though it was to her.

"You kept the other letters?" Maddy wondered how many there were—ten...a hundred?

"Shore did." Philip turned slightly and waved toward a desk on the back wall. "All them drawers are full. I didn't open nary a one."

Maddy glanced over at Sarah to see what she thought. Sarah gave a slight shake of her head. She probably thought Mr. Smith was more than a little crazy. Maybe he was, but somehow Maddy's peace wasn't disturbed by what she was hearing.

"But you opened mine?"

"God told me to." This time his words came out firmer. "Yer the one He done told me to send fer."

How could he send for her if he didn't even know her? And what about Pearl? God had to have known that she would have Pearl before she left to come to Golden.

"You didn't know you'd be getting a child in the bargain, did you?"

He couldn't have known that.

"Well, later on, I got the feelin' there'd be a child." His gaze traveled over the infant in her lap with a special tenderness.

Maddy liked this side of him. Her first impressions of him were wrong. She could see beyond the obvious to the tender man who loved children—and who was a strong man of God. She didn't know why God had brought her here, but she understood He didn't make a mistake. Somehow Mr. Smith would be His instrument to help her.

"That's why I built on the two rooms. So there'd be room for any children." He directed his gaze at her face. "The only suprize is them two servants. Didn't reckon on them."

Sarah shifted closer to Maddy, as did Frank.

"They are also my friends. They have been with my family since before I was born, and after my mother died, they helped my father rear me."

Maddy wondered if Mr. Smith thought they hadn't done a good job, since she was unmarried with a baby. She hoped his thoughts hadn't taken that direction.

The retired miner once again reached toward his cheek, then dropped his hand. "You ready to tell me what happened in Boston?"

Am I ready? Might as well get it over with. If she was going to ask Mr. Smith for help, he deserved an answer.

Pearl stirred and gave a fussy cry. Sarah took her from Maddy and rested the baby on her shoulder, patting her back. All the while, Mr. Smith's eyes never left the child.

Restless, Maddy stood. She stared out the window at the purple haze in the distance. "My father died. Evidently, he made some poor financial decisions before his death, so I am almost penniless." She turned back toward Mr. Smith. His eyes were now fixed on her. "My father's business partner tried to force me to marry him."

She wondered how much more to tell him.

Frank stepped away from the wall. "I checked that Johnstone man out, and there were many rumors about him and his unsavory dealings. We couldn't let him destroy Miss Madeline. I was the one who found the ad and brought it to her."

Maddy touched his arm. "It's all right, Frank. I answered the ad on my own." She settled back beside Sarah. "I don't want to mislead you, but I really didn't come here to marry you. I just needed a place to escape where Horace Johnstone couldn't find me or Pearl. He wanted to get rid of her. His demeanor made me believe that serious harm would be involved with that."

A snap of fire lit the old miner's eyes, and he sat forward in the chair. "I don't take kindly to men like that. When I answered yer letter, I said ya don't hafta to marry me. I wanna help ya." His gaze latched onto hers and clung fast. "I said if'n ya need the protec-shun of my name, I'll marry you. If not, yer welcome in my home as a guest or whatever ya wanna work out."

Just what she needed. Protection. A place to stay. "I'd like to take you up on your offer. We"—her sweeping gesture included all four of them—"would be glad to take care of you."

Sarah smiled at the retired miner. "I'm a good cook, and I can keep your place clean."

Frank moved to stand beside his wife. "And I can take care of repairs and things around the place. Run errands for you. We won't be a burden."

"And I'll try to keep Pearl from disturbing you." Maddy took her from Sarah and cuddled her close.

Another twinkle lit the old man's eyes. "Maybe I need disturbin'. Been too long since I had a babe 'round."

Maddy gave a contented sigh. *Thank You, Lord.* This really could work out for all of them.

⁓

*J*eremiah's stomach was growling and really kicking up a fuss by the time he was halfway back to Golden from Los Cerrillos. Those biscuits with sausage hadn't carried him very far after he'd wolfed them down before dawn. With all his worries, they soured on his stomach, and the ache added to his other distress.

That Mercer woman had filled his thoughts even when he tried to push her out. She wasn't worth the bother. Why were so many of the bad women beautiful? He'd never seen anyone as lovely as she was. Even after traveling so far, her brown hair shone in the sun, and that silly hat she had perched on top yesterday added to her charm instead of detracting from it.

During the night, his thoughts had jumped from disdain for the way she tried to charm money from old men to near desire as he thought about running the backs of his fingers down her creamy cheek. Would her skin feel as soft as it looked? He'd never been one to chase skirts, but the heat building inside him was about ready to explode.

The woman had plenty of allure, but she had two *big* strikes against her. First, she was a money-grubbing gold digger, which should have been enough to turn off his thoughts. Second, if she hadn't been, she would belong to his mentor, a man who really didn't need a wife. That fact, as much as anything, ate at him. Why could an old coot like Philip get a woman to come all the way from Boston when Jeremiah hadn't seen a decent woman who wasn't married in years?

Why couldn't an available woman come to Golden? One he would consider courting? One he could marry and have a family with? The ache moved to the region of his heart. Just knowing Madeline Mercer *of the Boston Mercers* was in Golden made him realize what he'd been missing. And he didn't like it one bit.

He'd driven all the way to Los Cerrillos and most of the way back, and he was no closer to a solution than he'd been when he left town yesterday. How was he going to get rid of this no-account woman and her watchdog companions? The impossibility choked him more than the dust cloud raised by the two horses pulling the wagon. Even the wildflowers that bloomed in a dazzling array against the sandy soil yesterday looked pale and wilted today.

Yesterday Caroline Oldman had welcomed the trio with open arms. No way Philip wouldn't know they were in Golden. Even if he got to his old friend before he met the Easterners, he couldn't get them out of town without Philip knowing. One of the problems with living in a small town.

Finally, Jeremiah realized the only solution at this point was to go to Philip and explain what happened. Warn him about that woman's intentions. He'd go straight to Philip's before delivering his supplies out to the ranch. With the outline of Golden drawing closer, he'd be there before long.

~

"Mr. Smith, I have another question for you." Maddy still sat with the old miner while Frank and Sarah took Pearl back to the hotel to change her and give her a bottle.

"Please call me Philip." His bushy brows scrunched, and his eyes sparkled merrily. "And I'd like to call ya Madeline."

"I'd like that, Philip." She felt comfortable in this homey place with the old man. She no longer had to be wary of him. "Something you said earlier has been eating at me. Why didn't you read all the other letters?"

"Now that we're friends, I can tell ya. I don't read real good." A smile split his scruffy beard. "Jeremiah helps me. I knowed he wouldn't wanna read all of 'em."

Jeremiah helped him read? "Did he read my letter?" Maddy almost choked on those words.

The hoary head gave an emphatic nod. "'Course he did."

That lowdown, sneaky man already knew who she was when he gave them a ride. Why didn't he tell her? She tried to keep her anger in check. "And what about writing? Did you write the letter to me?"

"I told him what to write. So's it was from me. He writ the ad too."

Maddy got up and paced across the room, trying to hide her agitation. "He knows I answered the ad?"

"Yup."

"And he wrote the answer to me?" She whirled around. Embarrassment painted her cheeks with heat. She had never been as angry at anyone in her life.

Again he nodded, his eyes following her movements back and forth.

She stopped right in front of the rocking chair and stared down at him. "And he knows my name?"

"'Course. He writ the letter." Now confusion clouded the old man's expression.

"Interesting." She dropped onto the sofa where she and Sarah had been sitting. And very disturbing.

While she pondered the ramifications of this discovery, Philip rose to his feet and headed toward the door. Only then did she realize that a wagon was fast approaching. It stopped, and Philip continued onto the porch.

"Come in, Jerry. Been expectin' ya."

Maddy didn't know who Jerry was, but a premonition of something of great importance happening settled around her heart. What was going on?

She got up and trailed after Philip. Cowboy boots scuffed against the wooden planks before her gaze traveled up the length of him. Hardened muscles encased in worn dungarees, broad shoulders wrapped in a muted plaid, the Stetson pulled low over the eyes. Dark eyes trained on Philip.

She'd recognize those eyes anywhere, and she'd seen that expression before. She stepped back into the shadows before he noticed her.

What had Jeremiah Dennison so riled up? She was the one with a reason to be angry at him. The nerve of that man. Treating them as if they had leprosy, when all the time he knew who she was and why she was here. She'd like to hear what he had to say about that. Maybe if she was quiet, he'd say something before he and Philip came into the house.

"You shore made a quick trip. Miz Oldman done told me you was goin' to pick up the supplies ya didn't git yesterdy."

Maddy could see Philip, but not Jeremiah.

"So she told you about the people I picked up?" Mr. Dennison's tone conveyed he wasn't happy about Philip knowing.

"Why didn't ya bring 'em to the house when ya got here?" Philip was staring hard at the man.

"I don't think you should have anything to do with those people." The words shot out, piercing Maddy like bullets. "I question their motives."

Philip shook his head so hard his white hair ruffled in the light wind. "Yer wrong, Jerry."

"No, I'm not." His bitterness poured poison over her heart. "You haven't told them you're wealthy, have you?"

Finally, she understood. The man had the gall to judge her and her friends before he even met them. He thought they were trying to cheat Philip. How could he be so judgmental without getting to know them first? And most of his anger had to be focused on her. After all, she was the one who answered the ad. The one they wrote the letter to.

Philip shuffled closer to Jeremiah. "Ya misjudged 'em, Jerry. They ain't like that. Madeline didn't even know 'bout the mine when she writ her letter. She didn't come here fer my money."

Jeremiah took two steps away from Philip and into Maddy's line of sight. He swiped his bandanna across his forehead and replaced his hat. "You don't know that."

"Yeah, I do. Ya judged her without knowin' anything 'bout her. 'Tain't right, Jerry."

Maddy's heart warmed at the way Philip stood up for her.

"The—"

"I know." Jeremiah rudely interrupted the older man. "I know. The good Lord told you." The way he sneered the last four words grieved Maddy's heart.

She stepped through the doorway. "Hello, Mr. Dennison."

He whirled around. The surprise in his eyes was quickly veiled with contempt as he stared a hole through her. "You heard what I said?"

"You weren't quiet, Mr. Dennison." Maddy didn't raise her voice. She wondered who was more uncomfortable—her, Jeremiah Dennison, or Philip. She turned toward her host. "Thank you for the enjoyable visit, Philip. I'm going to the hotel to check on Pearl."

He nodded as she started down the steps. Silence followed her as she stepped into the street. A hot wind blew up the hill, sweeping a dusty cloud toward her. She grabbed her skirt, to keep it from flying too high.

Where had all the crowds come from? More people than she'd realized the town contained were coming and going from stores and other businesses. The thumping of the ore press sank deep into her body. A crusty miner led his swaybacked, heavily laden donkey down the middle of the street. The animal's loud braying only added to the cacophony.

Tears sprang to her eyes, and when she swiped at them, her hand came away muddy. Golden didn't seem like the promised land anymore.

She had no idea why Jeremiah Dennison made such derogatory snap decisions about her and her friends, but she was going to find out. And she was going to prove him wrong. One day, that man would apologize to her.

CHAPTER 14

*J*eremiah stared at Miss Mercer's retreating figure. That woman had caused all the upheaval in his usually settled life. Added to the fire she'd kindled inside him, his skin flamed with embarrassment at the words she'd heard him say to Philip.

"Ya gonna just stand there and gawk, or ya gonna go after her?" Philip drew Jeremiah's attention away from the saucy woman. The older man didn't look happy.

"Why didn't you tell me she was here?" He spat the words as if they tasted terrible.

"Ya didn't gimme a chance." Philip's eyes burned as he stared at him. "Besides, yer wrong 'bout her, Jerry. Ya gotta go after her. She don't need to be walkin' alone. Look at all the miners out today. She won't be safe."

Jeremiah knew Philip would give him a push if he didn't go. He took the few steps two at a time and lengthened his stride so he could overtake her before she got very far.

"Hey there, pretty lady." A miner staggered up the hill toward the woman. "I ain't seed you 'round here before." The man stumbled but righted himself before hitting the ground, then pressed on.

The old coot had been in a saloon. Someone must have hit pay dirt at his mine today. They always had to celebrate by getting drunk. Probably bought drinks for everyone and came away with empty pockets. Why didn't they ever learn?

The thought of the man placing his dirty hands on Miss Mercer brought a lump to Jeremiah's throat. He didn't like the woman. He didn't trust her, but she didn't deserve to be accosted on her first day in Golden. Didn't want to give the town a bad name. That's all it was.

He picked up his pace, hoping to head off the drunken miner.

Miss Mercer didn't even glance at the man approaching her. Jeremiah hoped he would take the hint her snub implied.

"Now see here." The slurred words, louder than before, carried above the thumping of the stamping machines. "Ya think yer better'n me?"

The man grabbed her arm, none too gently, and her head snapped around toward him.

"Unhand me this instant!"

With her turned that direction, Jeremiah could see the icy stare she trained on the man.

The rowdy miner had to be too drunk to think clearly, because he jerked her closer. "All I want is a lil' kiss."

Instant horror then fright veiled her face. "Not. On. Your. Life." She tried to pull away, but the man didn't let loose.

Jeremiah grabbed the drunk by his collar. "You'll do as the lady says," he growled.

The man glanced back over his shoulder, then quickly looked again, but didn't let go.

"Right now." Jeremiah put all the power of his size and strength into the statement, and the drunk released her.

She stood quietly, brushing at her sleeve where the drunk's

hand had been, as if trying to get the imprint of him from her person. Something hitched in his heart as he read the confusion and pain on her face. Jeremiah didn't want to feel sympathy for the woman.

He didn't let the man go. "You owe the lady an apology." He gave the dazed miner a shake for good measure.

While the drunk mumbled out a passable apology, the thought hit Jeremiah that he was no better than this man. Philip's words finally sank in. He *had* judged her without knowing anything about her, and he shouldn't have.

When the drunk staggered away, Jeremiah turned toward her. "Miss Mercer, uh…" He gazed off into the distance as if fascinated by something on the horizon before continuing. "I apologize too."

She glanced up at him with large gray eyes that had turned as stormy as the rain clouds they needed right now. "For what, Mr. Dennison?"

No warmth in those words. Crossing her arms, she stood stiff and stared at his face.

"For saying those things at Philip's. I know I hurt you just as much as he did." He gave a dismissive wave at the man heading back toward the row of saloons.

She gave a quick nod. "That you did, Mr. Dennison."

"I'm going to escort you to the hotel." He held a crooked arm toward her. "We can't have any other man accosting you on the way."

She hesitated before slipping her hand around his elbow. "I'd appreciate that."

Her fingers rested with the weight of a feather against his forearm, almost as if she didn't want to even touch him. He didn't blame her. He'd given her enough reason not to trust him. But she hadn't given him any reason not to trust her.

He'd let it go for now, but after he finished taking the supplies out to the ranch, he'd return the wagon to the livery stable. Then he'd go see the sheriff. If there was proof of her duplicity, he'd find it. Then he wouldn't be judging her unfairly. He had to find something to get this woman out of his system.

~

*M*addy tried to stay mad at Jeremiah Dennison, but how could she when he'd been so chivalrous in rescuing her from the miner's clutches? She hadn't thought a thing about walking back to the hotel by herself, but she should have remembered the rowdiness they'd seen when they passed the saloons on their way into town. Anything could have happened to her. Next time, she'd make sure she didn't venture out alone.

"Thank you for escorting me to the hotel, Mr. Dennison." She smiled up at the tall man and quickly withdrew her hand from his arm.

He quirked one eyebrow. "Don't you want to dress me down for the way I talked about you earlier?" He glanced around the empty hotel lobby. "No one else is here, so you won't have an audience."

"Are you giving me your permission?" She couldn't hold back a laugh. "I never would have expected that."

He shrugged. "I deserve it."

"I'm sure you do. But I don't hold grudges, Mr. Dennison." She swept her suddenly sweaty palms down her skirt, hoping to hide their state from him. Why would he affect her this way? A stranger who didn't really like her, as evidenced by his behavior yesterday and today?

He reached to the brim of his big hat and tipped it toward her. "Then I'll take my leave. I need to get back to my ranch."

She watched as he walked out the door and headed toward Philip's adobe. The man was an enigma, and she didn't want to think about him. She started up the stairs.

"So you're back, Miss Mercer?" Caroline came from the kitchen into the lobby, wiping her hands on her apron.

Maddy stopped with a squeak on the fourth wooden stair. Even the carpeted runner hadn't covered the noise. "Yes."

"I thought I heard Jeremiah's voice out here." Caroline glanced all around the room, then out the open doorway.

Maddy made her way back down the stairs. "You did. He saved me from a drunken miner, then escorted me to the hotel."

A broad smile spread across Caroline's face. "That sounds like Jeremiah."

"Really?" Maddy stood, her hand resting on the ball on top of the newel post.

"I could tell you a lot about that man." Caroline laughed. "But I won't. I'll let you get acquainted on your own."

What did she mean by that? Why would Maddy and Jeremiah Dennison need to get acquainted?

"Did you have a good visit with Philip?"

"Yes, we got to know each other a little." When Madeline thought about Philip, her heart warmed toward him. But she still didn't know exactly how everything would work out with him.

"I noticed the Sneeds brought your daughter back earlier. Is everything all right?" Concern colored Caroline's tone.

Remembering that she was a pastor's wife, Maddy realized she would care about the people who came through her hotel. "They brought Pearl back to clean her up and feed her. I was just going to check on them now."

"I haven't heard her crying lately. Maybe your daughter is asleep. If she is, why don't you come down and visit with me? I'd love for us to get better acquainted." Her sunny smile lit with welcome.

"I'll do that."

Maddy climbed the stairs as Caroline headed back to the kitchen. She quietly opened the door to her room. Because it was a corner room at the back of the hotel, both the windows were open, and the breeze fluttered the curtains. Sarah laid down the Bible she'd been reading and stood from the rocking chair.

"How is Pearl?" Maddy whispered.

The drawer Pearl had slept in last night sat on the bed. Sarah leaned over it. "She's asleep. We played after she finished her bottle, so I think she'll nap awhile."

Maddy gazed down and her heart constricted at the sight of her sweet child. So innocent. So dependent. What course of action should she take to secure Pearl's future? Or did she have a choice? She leaned over and kissed the sleeping baby's face. "Is it all right with you if I go down to visit with Caroline?"

"Miss Madeline, you—"

"Maybe you should just call me Madeline. Out here in the Wild West, things are more informal than back in Boston."

Sarah nodded. "Madeline then. You go right ahead and enjoy some time with our hostess. I really like the woman, and I'll just keep reading God's Word."

~

When Maddy walked through the swinging doors to the kitchen, extra warmth and delicious smells met her. "How do you work in all this heat?" She used her hand to fan her face.

Caroline glanced over at her, then picked up a roaster pan and slid it into the oven of the black cast-iron stove. "This roast has quite awhile longer to cook. We can sit in the dining room where it's cooler."

She poured two glasses of lemonade and led the way to a table situated with open windows on two adjoining sides. "If you're hungry, I can get us some cookies."

"No, but this cool drink will refresh me." Madeline sat where she could feel the wind that blew across the table.

Caroline dropped into the chair across from her. "It'll be good to take a break."

"I noticed several saloons as we came into town yesterday, and other businesses, but I didn't see the church. You are the pastor's wife, aren't you?"

Caroline nodded. "My husband works as a carpenter, just like Jesus did, and we own the hotel, but he's been a preacher as long as I've known him. We hold services in this dining room for all the people who can come. Many of the miners are Catholic, and they attend the church on the other side of town. Some places we've lived, Catholics and Protestants don't get along, but out here, we help each other. We've even held a few weddings in their church building."

Maddy took another sip of the sweet, tangy drink. "This tastes good." She paused and studied the woman before her. Caroline was quite a bit older than Maddy, but not as old as Sarah. "Do you have any children?"

"God didn't bless us with our own, but a few of the families who worship here have little ones I dote on."

If Maddy couldn't have children, she didn't think she would be as accepting of it as Caroline. The woman really must completely depend on God. She was the kind of friend Maddy needed right now.

"Do you mind telling me why you really came to Golden?" Caroline's face expressed openness, with nothing hidden.

No shadows in her eyes. No tautness to her jaw. A woman at peace. A woman Maddy felt she could trust, and she needed someone to talk to besides Sarah.

"The situation is complicated."

"Life often is." Caroline took a drink from her glass, allowing Maddy the time to mull a little longer over the question.

When Maddy started talking, she couldn't stop. She

poured out the whole story. Her father's death. His supposed mishandling of the money. Horace Johnstone. How Pearl came to her. And their secretive escape from Boston and Mr. Johnstone's clutches. She even shared about the ad and Philip but didn't tell her about Jeremiah's unfriendly reception. By the time she finished, both glasses had been drained of the soothing liquid.

Caroline arose. "Let me pour us more lemonade, and we'll discuss your options."

Options? Of course she had the option of staying with Philip, but that wouldn't look right. And she had the option of marrying him for his protection, but did she really want to completely take advantage of an old man's generosity without giving him anything in return?

～

*B*y the time Jeremiah pulled the wagon into the livery, the sun was on its descent toward the western horizon, slanting rays across the town and into the doorway of the usually darkened stable.

Swede glanced up from where he rested on a wooden bench, the sunlight glinting off his light yellow hair.

"Sorry I kept the wagon so long." Jeremiah started unhitching the horses. "Hope no one else needed it."

"*Nej*, it would've set here waitin', for sure." The tall man moved to the other side of the wagon and started working on the harnesses. "I can do this. I'm not busy right now."

"Do I need to pay you extra?" Jeremiah reached toward the back pocket on his dungarees.

"No need." Swede waved him away.

"Thanks." Jeremiah headed out and cut across the cobblestone street in the direction of the sheriff's office and jail.

He hoped no one would be in either of the cells. He wasn't

interested in having an audience when he discussed his problem with Bill Brown.

The door stood wide open, and Bill sat with his chair tipped back and his crossed ankles propped on the scarred desktop. He dropped his feet to the wooden floor with a hollow *thunk* when Jeremiah's shadow darkened the doorway. The scrambling of something in the rocks under the building made Jeremiah wonder what kind of varmints lived in the shallow space. Probably lizards—or rats. He sure wouldn't want to spend the night in one of the cells whose doors stood open right now.

"Need you to check on something for me, Sheriff." Jeremiah dropped into one of the wooden armchairs that faced the desk.

"Had some rustlers in your cattle out to the ranch?" Bill leaned forward with his elbows on the desk.

"Naw, it's another matter."

Bill opened a drawer and plucked out a pencil and pad, then poised them where he could take notes. "Tell me about it."

"Those people I picked up in Los Cerrillos yesterday."

The sheriff relaxed. "I heard about 'em. Pretty woman. Her two companions and her baby. Lots of speculation. People are wondering why they went to Philip's house this morning."

Jeremiah frowned. He wished he could have kept that part quiet.

"Now don't go getting upset." Bill stood and propped both hands on the desk. "You know how people are around here. I ain't seen 'em yet, but I've heard enough. Heard Oscar Hamilton tried to get too friendly with the little lady and you stopped him. That's all over town too." He straightened to his full six-foot height.

Jeremiah didn't like his friend's close scrutiny. "I should be used to it, but I don't like all this talk about me. I try to keep my reputation clean."

"That didn't hurt your reputation. It might have helped it

some." When his friend laughed, Jeremiah couldn't keep from joining him.

Then Bill sobered. "So tell me what you want me to check out about 'em."

"Make sure this stays just between you and me." Jeremiah stared hard at him until he nodded and sat back down, picking up the pencil again.

Even though he didn't like recounting it, he gave Bill the details. About the ad. All the letters. The one they answered. The people arriving in Los Cerrillos the very next day. Their names. Everything, even his suspicions. "So I want you to find out if they're on the lam from the law or something like that. Maybe they've done this to other rich old men. And I'm suspicious of a woman who says she's never been married, but she has a baby. Something isn't right."

Bill continued to write on the pad. "I've gotta go to Albuquerque tomorrow. I'll send a telegram to a friend of mine who's a policeman in Boston. Maybe he can shed some light on all this."

Jeremiah hoped he could—and soon. He didn't want these people to get too cozy with Philip before he knew who they really were and exactly why they were here.

~

BOSTON, MASSACHUSETTS

*W*aiting impatiently for one of his henchmen, Horace Johnstone paced the dark, tree-lined street. Finally, a thin man disconnected from the deep shadows and approached him. "What you want with me?"

The surly man had better change his attitude or Horace would replace him. "What did you find out about the Mercer woman?"

Hunched shoulders shrugged, and the man shoved his hands into his front pockets and pulled into himself like a turtle. "Nothin'. I told you that. No sign of anyone at the house all week long."

"How could three, uh, four people just disappear off the face of the earth?" He had to work to keep his voice down. He wanted to explode but didn't need to draw attention to their meeting.

"I don't know nothin'." This time his hireling's tone was sharp. "I watched the place for the whole week."

"And you never went to sleep?" Horace sneered the words, his lip curled.

"My brother took a turn each day so I could get some rest."

He barely got the words out before Horace grabbed him by the lapels and gave him a shake. "I told you I didn't want anyone else to know what you're doing."

The man pulled away and straightened his overcoat. "My twin brother won't tell anyone. I paid him. He's as much a part of this as we are."

Horace paced to the end of the block and back, trying to think of another way to find that snobbish girl. He still couldn't believe she had refused his offer of marriage. He'd been so sure he had her eating out of his hand. She was only playing hard to get. Women liked to do that sometimes. He was looking forward to taming her.

He stopped squarely in front of his henchman. "If they've gone somewhere, they had to leave a trail. You check the train station and the overland coach line. Someone had to see a young woman with a baby and two old people accompanying her—unless they split up. You sure her servants don't have a family somewhere? They might have gone to visit them."

His watchdog stood taller. "Look, Boss, I told you I already checked on 'em. There ain't anybody else."

"Well, check again." This time his voice rose in volume, and a light went on in the upper story of the house next door. He stepped back deeper into the shadows and lowered his voice. "We gotta get out of here before someone sees us together. Do your job, and do it quick."

Horace turned and stalked away from his underling, not even looking to see if the man followed or stayed. He had to find that Mercer chit. Had to get married to her. No other way would he get his hands on the wealth.

The old feeling of being poor and scorned seeped through him like a bitter potion, darkening his outlook even more. He shook his head to dislodge the haunting image. He wasn't ever going to be that *horse-faced boy* again. The only way to get rid of his ghosts was to gain control of the money. The solicitor was getting antsy. Wanted to go ahead and release the will and fortune to the girl. And that was something Horace had to stop. Immediately.

CHAPTER 15

GOLDEN, NEW MEXICO

*E*ven though she had thought about their situation long into the night, Maddy awoke early. The sunlight seeping through the rather thin curtains made it hard to sleep any later. Today was the Lord's Day, and they would attend the services held in the hotel dining room. They'd finally get to meet Caroline's husband and other citizens of Golden who worshiped there.

She had just finished pinning her curls into a cluster on top of her head when Pearl began to squirm. Then she stretched and raised her tiny chin from the pillow to look around. Her cheek held the imprint of wrinkles. She looked so bright-eyed, and her plump lips formed an O, as if she were amazed at what she saw.

Maddy folded some blankets to protect the bed and laid Pearl on the pad. "Good morning. You're such a special blessing." She couldn't take her eyes off her daughter.

Pearl's gaze, filled with innocence and love, stayed on Maddy's face. Maddy leaned over and kissed the baby's forehead, then started changing her. Pearl hadn't taken long to learn to love her bath, and now Maddy felt more at ease handling her in the wash bowl. At first she'd been afraid she'd drop her, so slick from the soap and water. Now she made quick work of cleaning Pearl, then lifted the pink, squirmy baby onto a Turkish towel furnished by the hotel. She pulled the child close to her heart and rubbed her dry on the way back to the bed.

Before dressing Pearl, Maddy poured the last of her own Italian talc into her hand and gently rubbed it all over the baby's body. Tomorrow she'd have to start using the infant powder they had purchased, which wasn't as silky. Maybe she could get more of the imported powder soon. *If my finances straighten out.*

Looking on the bright side, she and the Sneeds had options —those from Philip and those proposed by Caroline—and they'd agreed to pray about what the Lord would have them do. Maddy planned on initiating another discussion after church today. They had to do something…really soon.

She gathered her purse and a small bag with things for Pearl before picking her up and heading downstairs. Happy, Pearl peered over Maddy's shoulder and babbled all the way down, one little fist tapping her mother in the chest and the other waving in the air.

Sarah and Frank sat at their favorite table in the dining room. Frank got up and held out his arms, so Maddy handed him the baby before she went into the kitchen to get the water to mix with the infant food.

Caroline turned from looking out the kitchen window. "How is your daughter today? I didn't hear her crying during the night."

"It's amazing." Maddy poured some of the powdered mixture through a funnel into the bottle, then added water, using the enamel dipper. While she stood shaking the bottle so it would all dissolve, she continued, "For some reason, she's sleeping longer here. Maybe it's because of the cleaner air or the lack of outside noise. Even with the windows open, we don't hear anything in our room except the wind through the trees and the other sounds of nature. What a blessing the stamping machines didn't come on this morning."

"Everything but the saloons and the hotel shut down on Sunday. Now go sit with the Sneeds, and I'll bring your breakfast." Caroline grabbed a plate and started filling it with food while enticing aromas wafted toward Maddy. "Frank said he'd help Sam move the tables and chairs when you're finished."

Pearl wasn't the only one sleeping better in Golden. So was Maddy. She didn't feel the tension she had in Boston and on the train trip. Coming to New Mexico had been a good decision. Here the only cloud in her sunny sky was...Jeremiah Dennison. And she didn't really know what to think about him.

～

"*Ya* gonna go with me today, Jerry?"

"Nope." Jeremiah hated to put a damper on Philip's optimistic outlook.

Not a Sunday went by that the older man didn't invite him to go to church with him. He did agree to drive Philip down to the hotel, but that was as far as he would go. He didn't need all that off-key singing and loud preaching by a man pacing and ranting in front of the crowd. He'd had enough of that when he was a boy, and it hadn't meant a thing when his mother was killed. Her God didn't protect her. He just let her slip away, leaving Jeremiah as a confused little boy with two men who didn't give a fig about him. And he had the scars on his back as proof.

Well, he wasn't that little boy anymore. He'd made a way for himself in this world, and he'd done a good job of it. First, the gold mine that provided the means to buy his ranch. And with all the hungry people in and around Golden, his cattle brought in plenty of money.

He'd even been selling some of his beef in Albuquerque and Los Cerrillos. Most people 'round here considered him a wealthy man, and it wasn't some far-off God who helped him achieve it. His own sweat and aching muscles had given him everything he owned—except his friends, and most of them *were* Christians. But he wasn't going to waste his time in a boring meeting when he could get so much done out at the ranch.

Philip hobbled across the porch using the cane Jeremiah had carved out of a tree limb. When he reached the few steps, Jeremiah held his other arm as Philip carefully placed each foot on the next step down but quickly pulled his arm free when they were on the ground headed toward the wagon. Philip did allow Jeremiah to help him up onto the seat.

"Sure a purty day, ain't it?" Philip took a huge breath that expanded his chest, filling out the usually loose shirt.

Seemed like just a regular day to Jeremiah. Nothing special. Sunshine. Not a cloud in the skies. The afternoon would be downright hot. He picked up the reins and clicked his tongue at the horses. They set off down the deeply rutted road.

Philip held onto the seat with both hands and shifted his weight with every movement of the wagon. He didn't look the least bit uncomfortable. Sundays were always special to him, since he left his house so seldom.

Guilt knifed its way through Jeremiah, leaving a trail of honest remorse. He needed to make sure Philip got out more. It wasn't that much trouble.

Then Jeremiah argued with himself. But he did spend a goodly chunk of his time fetching things for the old man. Hadn't he just worked more than two weeks overseeing the construction of those blasted rooms? Rooms that could soon house that woman and her baby? Maybe even those servants of hers? That would make for a crowded house.

But it wasn't his problem. He wasn't going to build another

room onto that adobe. His own house needed work, and he planned to concentrate on that when he wasn't running the ranch.

Jeremiah gritted his teeth to keep from saying what he thought about the whole Mercer situation. He'd missed his chance to rescue Philip from that woman's clutches. Why did he even try to protect the stubborn miner? With the dressing down Philip gave him yesterday, the old man sure didn't seem to appreciate all Jeremiah had done for him.

Yet, as he usually did, Jeremiah helped Philip up the steps to the boardwalk in front of the hotel. The old miner headed toward the dining room, and Jeremiah went far enough inside the lobby to make sure Philip got safely to a chair.

After Philip dropped onto the seat closest to the door, Jeremiah glanced around the crowded room. He narrowed his eyes when he encountered Madeline Mercer holding her baby and talking to Caroline Oldman.

The hotel proprietress stood with her back toward him, so he took his time studying the other woman. She didn't seem the least bit uncomfortable in the midst of all those church people. Of course, getting to know the *good* people in a town would help them accept her so she could pull off her confidence game.

His breathing accelerated, but he wasn't sure if it was with anger or something else altogether. In a white dress with yellow flowers scattered over it much like the way the wildflowers bloomed in patches over the sand of the desert, she appeared innocent and sweet. Her hair was piled on top of her head, but curls framed her face, accenting the freckles on her cheeks. The way she held the baby so close affected the rhythm of his heart, making it faster and somewhat erratic. Heat boiled in his belly as he longed for what he couldn't have. He would have liked to keep staring at the woman's beauty but knew he needed to stop. His treacherous senses battled with his mind. He knew he couldn't trust her until he'd found out what she really wanted from Philip.

Shoving his hands into the front pockets of his trousers, he started to turn away when she looked up, straight into his eyes. Their gaze held for a suspended moment while everything else around him clouded. He could get lost in the soft gray of her eyes that resembled the morning mist rising from a welcome spring in the desert. And he felt like a very thirsty man.

Suddenly he broke the spell, and his boot heels beat a rapid tattoo on the floorboards and out the front door. He left the wagon tied to the railing in front of the hotel and made his way down the cobblestones to the livery. Someone else could drive Philip home.

Swede was at the church service, so Jeremiah went to the stall where Lightning munched on hay. Letting the horse out, he saddled the stallion and rode toward his ranch as fast as he could. He'd get busy on some of the work needing his attention. That would help him push that woman out of his system.

At least, he hoped so.

~

*M*addy stared at the rancher's receding back. Didn't Jeremiah attend church with Philip? The answer to that question entered into Maddy's mind, unsettling her. The way he'd looked at her before he whirled around had been intense, giving her a sense of a connection of some kind. But a sour expression marred his face when he left, not the smile that was tilting up one side of his expressive mouth when she first saw him.

If her life in Golden was to be successful, he'd have to get over his animosity toward her, which was completely uncalled for anyway. She had nothing but respect for Philip Smith, and she'd never do anything to hurt him. That's why the decision about what had to be done was so hard. Thankfulness for Caroline Oldman's suggestion warmed her heart and lifted her spirits.

The strum of a stringed instrument brought her out of her musings. A young Mexican man sat on a wooden stool beside a lectern in front of the rows of chairs. He held a musical instrument that Maddy had never seen before. It had strings like a guitar, but the body was deeper and shaped differently too. She turned her attention back to Caroline.

Caroline's eyes met Maddy's, then she cocked her head toward the man. "That's Carlos. Most of the Mexicans in town work in the mines and are Catholics, but Carlos helps Sam with his carpentry jobs. Since they've been working together so much and discussing God while they do it, he started coming to our services. It's been nice to have him leading our singing and accompanying it with his *vihuela*." She led the way toward two empty chairs on the back row. "Before he started attending here, our singing was rather off-key, but he keeps us together."

Maddy had never seen a Mexican before coming to New Mexico Territory, but two couples with small children sat on the row in front of them.

Caroline leaned toward her. "Those are Carlos's brothers and their families. They've only recently arrived from their homeland, and they come to the service with him."

All the differences in this town fascinated Maddy. And to think that God had brought her across such a vast country to this place...

When Carlos started singing "Tell Me the Story of Jesus," everyone chimed in. Although the hymn was one she'd sung in her church back in Boston, the music didn't resemble the solemnity of those occasions. Instead, the enthusiasm expressed by this congregation lifted her heart, and she felt as if Jesus was standing beside her instead of way up there in heaven.

Carlos didn't stop playing after they finished. He merely

used a few chords to move right into "Blessed Assurance," one of Maddy's favorites. The singing in this simple service lifted her soul higher than it had ever been in her church back home.

Maybe coming to this church was a large part of God's plan for her. She could hardly wait to hear Caroline's husband preach.

When Carlos came to sit beside one of his brothers, Sam Oldman laid his Bible on the lectern and stood to the side of the podium. He quoted verses without even looking at the open book.

"'For I know the thoughts that I think toward you, saith the Lord, thoughts of peace, and not of evil, to give you an expected end. Then shall ye call upon me, and ye shall go and pray unto me, and I will hearken unto you. And ye shall seek me, and find me, when ye shall search for me with all your heart.' I believe the Lord told me to share these three verses from Jeremiah 29 with you today."

Maddy was glad he paused because she was still thinking about how those words applied to her. Without being able to seek God's counsel in her life, she'd be in the clutches of evil right now. She knew she was here in Golden for a specific purpose. And even though God knew what the expected end would be, she didn't. Hearing these words brought a peace that completely surrounded her.

When Sam continued, his sermon didn't sound like any she'd heard before. He brought Father God and Jesus into the room with them. The words weren't some standoffish memorized recitation. He spoke from his heart straight to hers.

Pearl squirmed in her arms, but Maddy was so entranced she hardly noticed. She simply lifted her baby against her shoulder and automatically patted her back until she settled into slumber. But Maddy didn't take her eyes or her mind off the words being spoken to her as if they were almost a new language. Words more understandable than all the religious rhetoric she'd heard before.

When Sam finished his sermon, he asked if anyone wanted to make Jesus their Savior. Maddy felt as if her relationship with the Lord had shifted during the brief time he spoke.

Then Carlos went to the front and strummed a few chords before starting the first line of "I Am Thine, O Lord." While everyone sang the words prayerfully, Maddy expressed them anew to God as though it were the first time she'd ever asked Him into her life. She wouldn't have missed this service for anything in the world. A fitting beginning for her new life in this place.

After the service ended, the men moved the tables back into the dining room. The women headed to the kitchen to start bringing the food they'd prepared for all to share, placing it on a long table that ran along one wall. She'd heard the Sneeds talk about an "all-day singing and dinner-on-the-grounds," though she'd never experienced one. Maybe this was something like that. She looked forward to getting to know more of the people in the town.

The men outnumbered the women here, even in church. Some appeared to be cowboys, but others weren't. Maybe they worked in the mines or one of the other businesses.

The Sneeds filled their plates, and Sarah sat at a nearby table, but Frank shifted Pearl from Maddy's shoulder to his. "Go ahead and get your food. We'll save you a seat by us."

She hurried to comply. When she returned, a stranger sat across from her. He stood when she set her plate down and waited until she was seated to return to his chair. He hadn't taken his eyes off her since she arrived back at the table, and his perusal felt intense.

Frank cleared his throat. "This here's the sheriff, Bill Brown. I met him while we were moving the tables before the service."

Maddy nodded. "Pleased to meet you, Sheriff." She picked up

her fork. She never would have guessed he was a lawman. Without a badge and gun, he looked like any other man in the room. Knowing the sheriff was a Christian was comforting. Her thoughts jumped to the one man in town she was acquainted with who wasn't. Such a shame for an upstanding citizen like Jeremiah to run from attending the service. Had he decided that before he brought Philip, or had her presence made him leave so precipitously?

"Just Bill." The sheriff's lips curved into a smile. "Especially at church."

That helped her relax.

Frank shifted Pearl higher on his shoulder. "And this is Madeline Mercer." He trained his attention on the lawman. "We've come from Boston."

The sheriff, Bill, took a bite of food and chewed a moment. "I already knew that. News travels fast in a small town."

She laughed. "I'm finding that out."

He trained his piercing gaze on her. Was he trying to discover something about her? If so, what?

Maddy lifted a fork full of roast beef and closed her lips around it, the flavors teasing her tongue. For some reason, the beef out here tasted different from what they had in Boston—stronger, more full-bodied.

"But I didn't hear anything about Mr. Mercer. Will he be joining you?"

The food stopped halfway down her throat, and she had to cough to get it dislodged. She took a quick sip of lemonade. What exactly should she tell the sheriff? Not the complete truth, that's for sure, but how could she do it without lying? After her experience in the service, Maddy knew she faced a true moral dilemma.

CHAPTER 16

*J*eremiah tried to get some much-needed bookwork done. He really tried, but his mind wouldn't settle on the numbers marching across the pages. He'd rather break a wild horse than spend time indoors looking at paper, and his brain wasn't in a cooperative mood today. Finally he slammed the book closed and shoved it into the top drawer of his desk. He didn't need this right now. He grabbed up a pad and rushed out the door, leaving it swinging on its squeaky hinges.

After going around to the back, he paced off the dimensions of the space he wanted to add to the ranch house. There'd be plenty of room. He headed to the toolshed attached to the back of the barn. He slammed the tablet and pencil down on his workbench and slashed lines across the paper approximating what he'd envisioned for the addition. He marked doors and windows, then dropped the pencil and picked up a few pieces of scrap lumber. Using his ax, he began to chop away, forming the wood into pointed stakes.

Visions floated behind his eyes. The kind of woman he

longed to marry. Someone to share his life with, instead of having to return to an empty, lonely house every night. A good mother for his children. And he really wanted to have children —a boy to bounce on his knee, a girl to cuddle in his arms.

Why did this vision now have a face instead of some vague outline? More important, why was that face crowned with lustrous brown curls? Why did laughing gray eyes twinkle at him? And the woman cradled a baby girl against her chest. A very womanly, gently curved chest.

The ax slipped and barely missed his leg. He hurled the offending instrument clear across the shed, the blade sticking in the opposite wall. It'd be safe there, so he left it hanging. He huffed out a quick breath, unable to get that woman out of his thoughts. Once again his traitorous body heat centered below his belt. Blast it all! He wasn't a Christian like Philip, but he was a good, moral man. A conniving woman like Madeline Mercer shouldn't be having this effect on him.

He almost wished he believed in going to the saloons. But after the beatings he'd endured whenever his father and uncle returned from a night spent in debauchery, he'd vowed never to let whiskey and wild women come near his mind or body. He wondered now if keeping that promise might not be as important as he'd thought. But then a sickening sensation in his gut let him know he'd regret going back on his vow—in every way that counted.

He stuck the head of a hammer in his back pocket. When the handle rubbed against his back, he ignored it. Loading his arms with stakes, he started pounding them into the hard earth, marking the corners of each room. He'd use twine to connect them later.

Smashing down the top of the stakes with the hammer felt good, releasing some of his frustration...until he missed. An expletive he'd never before uttered blew between his lips. The hammer slammed into his thumb, forcing it down the side of the wood, picking up splinters along the way. Flinging the hammer as hard as he could was a stupid thing to do. Now he'd have to go hunt for it among the rocks. It was the only hammer he had. He heard the head bounce, then the splintering of wood.

He hoped it wasn't beyond repair. More words like the ones he'd already used erupted from his gut, tainting the air around him. At least there wasn't a lady nearby to hear his outburst.

Heading to the house, Jeremiah started picking at the splinters with his thumbnail. Fool things kept breaking off. Now he'd have to dig them out or get T-Bone to help him. Naw, he'd do it himself. No need letting someone else know what a mess he'd made of things. And he sure didn't want anyone to know why. T-Bone would be full of questions.

Nothing had ever caused Jeremiah to lose control like that. What was he going to do about the Mercer woman? He hoped the sheriff would soon hear back from his friend on the Boston police force. Jeremiah wanted her out of Golden. The sooner, the better. Maybe then he would regain his sanity.

After trying to dig the splinters out with the tip of the smaller blade on his Barlow knife, Jeremiah finally admitted he needed help. He tucked his hand into his pocket and headed to the cook shack.

"Hey, Boss. Wondered when you'd come eat." The short, bowlegged man sat on the bench at one of the tables, nursing a cup of coffee. "The hands've all eaten and rode out."

"I guess I wasn't thinking about food." But just then his stomach growled loudly, betraying him.

"Maybe you ain't, but your stomach sure is." The man belly-laughed as he stood and went into the partitioned-off kitchen area. "Got some beef stew and cornbread. Have it out in a jiffy."

Might as well eat first. Jeremiah stepped over the bench and dropped down beside where T-Bone had been sitting. He'd been real lucky to get such a good cook. Kept the hands happy too. When the parson and his wife bought the hotel, they hadn't needed T-Bone, so Jeremiah hired him. He wasn't sure which one of them had the best of the bargain. Even though he paid T-Bone a decent wage, Jeremiah suspected he came out ahead.

After T-Bone set Jeremiah's food in front of him, he went back to pour a cup of coffee. He thunked the tin cup down on the table and plunked down where he'd been sitting. "What took you so long?"

"I was working on the books." He scooped up a big spoonful of the stew and shoved it in his mouth but almost spit it back out. It was so hot, the inside of his mouth felt on fire. Maybe he should let it cool a bit. "Then I went to figure out for sure where I would put the addition to the house."

T-Bone stared at him from under beetle brows fringed with unruly white hair. "Seems like a waste to me." He was honest—and opinionated about everything.

"I haven't done anything with the house since I bought the ranch. After fixing up Philip's house, I decided I didn't have to live in squalor." Jeremiah once again tried the stew—this time with better results.

Jeremiah could put up with T-Bone's opinions and inquisitiveness for food that tasted this good. He took a bite of the cornbread with butter melted in.

They continued jawing while Jeremiah ate. When he finished, he finally approached the subject he dreaded. "I need your help."

"Ain't no carpenter." Sparks shot from the man's gaze. "Just leave me in the kitchen."

"Isn't about the house." Jeremiah carefully pulled his hand from his pocket, being careful not to scrape the damaged area on the denim. The thing throbbed enough already.

"Wondered why you were eatin' with one paw shoved into

your pocket." The cook didn't have to sound so gleeful about it. "Wal, what we got here?"

"Had a little accident." Jeremiah turned it over so T-Bone could see all the broken splinters.

"Looks like someone's been hackin' at it." He cut his eyes up at Jeremiah's face. "I s'pose you done that."

Jeremiah nodded.

"Boss, you need a good wife to fix ya up."

T-Bone didn't have to rub it in. The cook got up and headed toward the kitchen. When he came back, he had a metal bowl, a bottle of whiskey, and a thin knife. He set the bowl beside where Jeremiah's hand lay on the table.

"Hold your hand over this."

Jeremiah rolled up his sleeves and obeyed the order. T-Bone uncorked the whiskey and poured a generous amount over Jeremiah's hand. The stuff burned like the dickens, but he gritted his teeth so he wouldn't make a sound.

T-Bone glanced up at him. "Knowed it'd hurt, but I needed to clean it. Gettin' an infection would hurt worst."

Jeremiah nodded. "Do what you need to."

He tried to keep his mind off what his cook was doing by looking everywhere else but at the hand. That didn't keep him from feeling every jab of the knife. He winced, jerking his hand a little.

"Some of these are buried real deep. Sorry to be hurtin' you, Boss."

"Just get it over with."

Quicker than Jeremiah thought possible, considering the number of splinters, T-Bone raised his head. He grabbed the whiskey bottle again and slowly poured it over his hand, making sure it went into every cut. The fire on his hand raged as high as the fire in his gut. Jeremiah didn't have to wait until he died to experience hell. If there was such a place, he had it right here in his own cook shack.

"You keep holdin' this over the bowl." T-Bone let go of Jeremiah's wrist. "Be right back with some ointment."

He quickly returned with a tin of ointment, some gauze, and adhesive tape. When T-Bone finished bandaging his hand, Jeremiah wondered how in the world he'd be able to use it.

"Keep this bandage on until tomorrow. I'll do a new one then." T-Bone started picking up all the things he'd brought in, taking them back to the kitchen.

Approaching hoofbeats captured Jeremiah's attention. He headed toward the door.

"Come back for dessert. I made that vinegar pie you like so much."

When Jeremiah reached the front corner of the house, the sheriff was tying his reins to the hitching post. "Bill, you must have smelled T-Bone's vinegar pie. You're just in time to share some with me."

Bill rubbed his belly. "Don't have room for even a crumb. Ate at church."

"I suppose they had a real shindig to welcome the newcomers to town." Jeremiah didn't even try to hide his disdain from his good friend.

"They're why I came out here to talk to you." The sheriff headed toward him. "But I'd like a cold drink of water while you eat your pie."

"Sounds good to me."

The two men headed toward the cook shack.

Bill glanced toward Jeremiah's hand. "What happened to you? You looked all right when you brought Philip to church."

"I was." He gave a wry grin. "Just letting off some steam by working on the house. Missed the top of a stake." He glanced down at his thumb and noticed that the part peeking out of the bandage had turned an angry shade of purple. "Afraid I let my temper get the best of me." Jeremiah didn't mind telling his good friend about what happened. He wouldn't be gossiping about it.

"Threw my hammer out into the rocks and broke the handle. Have to whittle a new one if the head isn't damaged."

Bill's laughter preceded them into the cook shack.

"What's so funny, Sheriff?" T-Bone came out of the kitchen, wiping his hands on the large apron that covered most of his body.

"Jeremiah's smashed thumb. Never knew him to make a boneheaded mistake like that before."

"Not really funny." T-Bone came to his defense. "I had to work to get all the splinters out and the cuts clean. Don't want Boss-man to lose his hand."

By now Jeremiah's whole face flamed. His ears even felt hot. "All right, enough about my hand. T-Bone, please get me some pie and coffee, and bring Bill here a glass of cold water."

"I'll go to the spring and get some real fresh."

They watched the old man leave before they settled onto opposite benches.

"So what do you have to tell me about our newcomers?" Jeremiah didn't see any point in beating around the bush.

"They were in church." Bill laid his hat on the bench beside him.

"I noticed."

"That what got you in such a tizzy that you banged your thumb and broke your only hammer?"

Sometimes good friends could be a real pain.

"Yeah. That woman's like a burr under my saddle. Have you found out anything about her?"

"Not yet. I only sent the telegram yesterday."

T-Bone came in with a tin pitcher of water. He poured some in a glass and set it in front of the sheriff. "I'll get your pie now." He headed toward the kitchen, carrying the pitcher with him.

"I'm not really sure your conclusion is right about those people. I watched 'em during the service. They were really worshiping with us. I know." He held up his hands. "You're not a believer, but I don't think they were faking. They're nice, and I'm sure they're Christians."

Jeremiah scowled at that. "I've known people who claimed to be Christians but were really criminals."

"I have too, but I usually sense it right away." Bill took a long swig of the water. "This really hits the spot after the hot ride out here."

T-Bone came in with a piece of pie. He set it and a cup of coffee in front of Jeremiah. "Here you go, Boss."

"Thanks." Jeremiah took a bite, savoring the tart, sweet flavors.

"I've changed my mind, T-Bone." Bill raised his hand. "Please bring me a small piece. I can't just sit here watching him enjoy it."

"Sure thing." The older man hurried away.

"Funny thing happened at dinner." Bill leaned his crossed arms on the table.

Jeremiah put down the cup of coffee. "What?"

"I sat at the same table with Miss Mercer and the Sneeds. I didn't let on that I knew anything about 'em. When I asked if Mr. Mercer was joining them, I thought her eyes would pop out of her head, she opened them so wide."

Bill had Jeremiah's full attention now. "So what did she say?"

"She looked like she was trying to decide what to say, but then her baby woke up. She started crying, then threw up all over Frank. You should have seen the look on that man's face. Surprise, but he wasn't mad. Madeline took the baby, and she threw up again all over her mother's dress. Needless to say, that was the end of our conversation."

Jeremiah would bet his bottom dollar Madeline Mercer welcomed the interruption, even if the baby did make a mess she had to clean up.

"I'm just saying, I'm going to keep an open mind until we

163

know something for sure about her." Bill picked up his glass again.

Jeremiah stuffed another forkful of pie into his mouth. He knew something for sure. He couldn't get the woman out of his mind. And that's wasn't a good thing...not good at all.

~

*M*addy sat rocking Pearl after everyone was all cleaned up. Her daughter didn't seem to have a fever. She had no idea why Pearl threw up so much. She'd had occasional times when she spit up a little, but not like today.

She hadn't figured out what to say to the sheriff, but she'd never dreamed of getting out of it this way. With a chuckle, she looked up at Sarah, who was washing Pearl's clothing in the washbowl.

"What's so funny?"

"Did you see the sheriff's face when this happened? I was wondering what he thought about everything. It really put a stop to our conversation, and not a minute too soon." She gazed down at Pearl, who had fallen asleep.

Maddy got up and laid the baby in the drawer, making sure the pillowcase wouldn't obstruct her breathing. Because of the afternoon heat, she didn't cover her daughter.

"At least you didn't have to answer him." Sarah wrung out the tiny gown. "I was wondering what you were going to say."

"So was I." Maddy gathered up her own clothes and piled them in the corner.

Caroline had said they could do laundry with her tomorrow morning.

"Where is Frank? I'd like to discuss some things with both of you."

"I'll go get him and bring him in here." Sarah hurried out the door and soon returned with her husband.

Frank stood with his back to the door. "What did you want to talk about, Miss Madeline?"

Maddy sighed. "Frank, I wish I could get you to just call me Madeline as Sarah does now. We don't need to be so formal out here."

"I'll try to remember, but you've been Miss Madeline to me since you were born." He laughed. "Was that all?"

"No." Maddy clasped her hands in her lap. "It isn't. We've been through a lot together, especially the last few weeks. Now our finances are almost depleted. Mr. Smith said he'd marry me with no strings attached, but I'm not sure that's the best decision at this point. Caroline Oldman offered to let us stay rent free. They'll give you jobs here at the hotel. She needs help with the cleaning and cooking, and Rev. Oldman might use you, Frank, to work with him and Carlos. He's kept quite busy. What would you two think of that?"

Frank and Sarah stared at each other as if reading each other's thoughts. Then they both smiled.

He turned back toward Maddy. "That might be the best thing for right now. We could get better acquainted with Mr. Smith and see exactly what he had in mind when he sent the advertisement, but you wouldn't feel rushed to decide right away. This situation needs a lot of prayer."

"I couldn't agree more." Maddy went to hug her old friends.

"And I'd like to keep busy." Sarah leaned away from Maddy and gazed into her eyes. "You've become such a good mother for Pearl. You don't need our help as much as you did at first."

"Then it's agreed. We'll stay here for the time being." Maddy knew this was the best decision all around.

And she liked the idea of having more time to seek God. In addition to helping around the hotel, she planned to spend more time with Philip. He had enjoyed having Pearl in his home. Maybe she could divide her time between the hotel and Philip's house. If she could just figure out when Jeremiah

Dennison wouldn't be there. She didn't need him working against her in her relationship with Philip.

Too bad the cowboy was the most handsome man she'd ever met. Just thinking about him made her heart beat faster. But he evidently wasn't a Christian, and he really didn't like her being here. Well, that was just too bad. Nothing he could say or do would make her leave Golden.

CHAPTER 17

hree weeks. It didn't seem possible to Maddy that they'd been in Golden almost a month. The town was a nice place, and the people were friendly. Come to think of it, she hadn't really missed Boston that much, and she definitely felt safely out of Mr. Johnstone's clutches.

Philip hadn't been what she'd expected, but she liked him—a lot. She'd taken Pearl up to Philip's house almost every day. Funny how the elderly man and the baby really took to each other.

While Philip held and played with Pearl, Maddy made sure his house was clean and he had plenty to eat. Just listening to Pearl coo when Philip talked to her made Maddy's heart soften even more toward the man.

On Tuesday Philip had asked Frank to go to Skinner's Mercantile and buy the baby bed the proprietors had recently acquired and had him order another one for the hotel room. After Philip gave Pearl her bottle, Maddy helped him put the baby in the crib in the extra bedroom. Philip told her that room was hers when she wanted to move in, but she wouldn't give anyone else in town a reason to question her virtue or integrity.

She enjoyed spending time helping Philip. Maddy knew he would reciprocate if she would just let him. And the time might come when she'd have to accept his help. But not right now. For her and the Sneeds to work and pay their own way gave her a feeling of satisfaction—and she wasn't beholden to Philip or anyone. Instead of others taking care of her, she contributed to their lives. She'd been able to time her visits with Philip so she wasn't at his house when Jeremiah Dennison came, so everything was going well for her.

Maddy stepped onto the boardwalk in front of the hotel. This morning, a breeze blew from the east, and she covered Pearl's face with a light cotton wrap. She glanced up and down the cobbled street. Although a number of people were out and about, she didn't see any of the drunks by the saloons, so she felt safe to venture up the street alone. Frank wouldn't need to accompany her. She lifted her skirt with her free hand to keep from tripping on the hem as she descended the steps.

The walk to the adobe was easier each time she made the trip. Her legs and back felt stronger from all the exercise. And her breathing was no longer labored when she reached Philip's house high on the slope. The door stood open as usual, inviting her presence.

"Philip, we're here." She glanced around the homey room to see what she needed to do today.

The retired miner came from the kitchen. "Glad yer here, Madeline. Lemme sit down, so's I can hold lil' Pearl." He shuffled to his favorite rocking chair.

She followed him and laid Pearl in his waiting arms before removing the covering from the infant's face. The baby smiled up at Maddy, then noticed Philip. Both his face and that of her daughter brightened as he leaned close and cooed to her, clicking his tongue and laughing.

When Maddy started toward the kitchen, Philip and Pearl

commenced their nonsensical conversation. Maddy hummed under her breath as she cleaned. She had been working about half an hour when she went out the back door to empty the dishpan.

The pleasant morning captured her attention as she gazed across the flat desert toward the hazy purple mountains in the distance. The landscape in between had seemed too barren when she first saw it, much like her own life had lacked purpose before God gave her a daughter. But now she enjoyed discovering the hidden beauty of the New Mexico territory.

Every time she gazed around the area, she found something new and amazing, like the semi-arid area that held an abundance of flora and fauna. Her eyes traveled to the scrubbier trees and bushes in widely scattered clumps, surrounded by sand, rocks, and sparse grass. She smiled at the occasional wildflowers scattered here and there that managed to show off their magnificent colors. A few tall fir trees were a lovely addition to the landscape.

A little ways down the hill, she spied a rabbit of some kind hopping from a cluster of grass to one quite a distance away. So much like her. She'd managed to exchange one place for another, and she prayed this move would prove to be a good one for all of them.

Skittering in the sand brought her eyes back to the ground around the house. A lizard climbed up the back wall, then stood completely still, as if waiting for something. She shifted her weight from one foot to the other, and the creature darted up and over the top of the wall onto the flat roof. This was a barely tamed land, but she felt at home here—almost as much as she had in Boston.

Off in the distance, a lone rider was headed toward town. She wondered how many other people lived within riding distance. She felt sure not all the people who attended church last Sunday lived in the houses scattered through Golden. And, probably, some of the homeowners went to the Catholic church.

She headed into the house to make Pearl a bottle. Playing with Philip always tired the baby enough that she took a good nap. Maddy looked forward to her time with Philip when they could sit and visit without interruption.

~

*A*s Jeremiah approached Golden, he noticed Madeline standing outside the back of Philip's house. She hadn't been there any of the times he'd visited Philip, but he'd seen signs of her work. Philip had never kept his house so clean. And, according to the old miner's claims, she and her friends kept him well fed. That relieved Jeremiah from much of his worry about Philip's physical needs, but he worried what other damage they were doing to him emotionally and financially.

He stopped Lightning outside the sheriff's office in a cloud of dust and tied him to the hitching rail. The battered wooden door stood open, so he strode into the cool interior.

Bill dropped his boots from resting on the edge of the scarred desk and straightened up in his chair. "Jeremiah, what're you doing in town this early in the day?" He slowly rose to his feet and held out his hand.

Jeremiah shook it. "Just wanted to see if you'd heard anything from your friend in Boston. I'm really anxious to know about those people...especially the Mercer woman."

The sheriff came around the desk and leaned back against it, crossing his ankles. "I've been keeping an eye on 'em, and I have to tell you, I haven't seen anything out of line. Your assumptions are most likely wrong."

Jeremiah rubbed the back of his neck where the muscles

bunched and ached. "I hope, for Philip's sake, I'm wrong. He's really taken with that baby. He talks about her all the time when I'm there." Now the ache in his forehead rivaled the one in his neck, so he rubbed the weathered ridges there. "I'm really uncomfortable around that woman."

A smile spread across his friend's face. Almost a smirk. "Probably doesn't have anything to do with her past." The laugh that burst from him almost blistered Jeremiah.

"This is no laughing matter." He turned to exit, but Hiram filled the doorway.

"Hey, Sheriff. Just got back from Los Cerillos with the mail. Got a telegram for you." He plopped it down on the desk. "Gotta go on over to the Skinners'."

Thank goodness the man didn't stay. Jeremiah stared at the envelope as if it might be a rattlesnake waiting to strike. Hopefully the message was from the police in Boston. He crossed his arms and leaned against the door facing, waiting for Bill to open the thing.

The sheriff took his time, turning the envelope every which way before tearing into it. "Well, what d' you know? Sheldon says he's just received a wanted poster naming Madeline Mercer. Something about her stealing jewelry, including an heirloom cameo. Said he'd mail me a copy of the handbill."

Jeremiah knew what a cameo was. His mother had one. The only piece of genuine jewelry she owned. For a moment he wondered whatever happened to his mother's. Probably sold to buy whiskey for his father and uncle. Everything of value vanished that way.

He whooshed out his breath. "I told you something wasn't right about that woman. You gonna go arrest her?"

"Now wait just a minute. Might not be the same woman. Let's wait for the wanted poster and see the picture and description. I'm not gonna do anything until it arrives. They're not going anywhere. Besides, I haven't seen her wear any jewelry except those earbobs on Sunday."

Jeremiah swallowed all the words he wanted to say and almost choked on them. Given the stubborn tilt to Bill's chin, saying them wouldn't do any good. He'd just have to wait for that mail to come, but he'd keep a closer eye on her himself. Wouldn't do to let her get away if she were a criminal. 'Course if she were, it'd break Philip's heart.

But some things couldn't be helped.

~

*A*nother Sunday morning dawned bright and clear. Maddy could hear some kind of bird greeting the sun, and a cool breeze blew across the room. She pulled back the curtain and looked out. A small black bird, with a yellow head and breast and a white slash on its wing, sat on a tree branch not far away. With its head thrown back and its throat vibrating, it had to be the one doing the singing. The sound was different from any bird she'd heard back in Boston. For a moment, she was surprised she hadn't thought of Boston as home instead of naming the town. Did that have some deeper meaning?

Maddy had even gotten so used to the thumping of the stamping machines in Golden that she hardly ever noticed the noise. Of course, today those machines were shut down.

She knew that, later in the day, the temperature would rise to almost unbearable heights, so she studied the clothes she had hanging in the wardrobe. She'd left her heavier clothing packed in a trunk and only took out the lighter dresses she'd purchased in Santa Fe. After she helped serve breakfast to the guests in the hotel, she'd come back upstairs to get ready for the service. She wanted to get as much done as she could before Pearl awakened.

She laid out a silk dress in a lovely shade of peach. Tiny

brown horn buttons trailed from the slightly scooped front neckline to the hem, and a brown grosgrain ribbon defined the slim waist. Her mother's cameo would look good with this dress. She lifted the satin drawstring bag that held all her mother's jewels she'd hidden deep within one trunk, tucked under other clothing. She spread them on the top of the bureau, each item filling her with memories of times when Mother wore a particular piece. Mother had loved pretty jewelry. Father had given her many of the pieces, but some, including the cameo, had belonged to Maddy's grandmother. Carved from a rusty brown soapstone, the delicate face of a woman looked much like the portrait of Maddy's grandmother hanging in the parlor in Boston.

She chose a grosgrain ribbon the same shade as the buttons and laid it beside the brooch. Then she added her grandmother's pearl drop earrings. If she wore both of these, she'd feel a connection to her past as well as her present.

~

*A*fter deciding to attend church with Philip the next morning, Jeremiah had a terrible day. When he arrived home from Golden, his foreman told him they'd found ten butchered cows in the south pasture. He rode out to see if there were any clues to who committed the crime, but when they reached the hill where they'd been grazing, they found nothing except the hides, hooves, and some of the bones with bits of fresh meat attached. Vultures circled overhead. Plenty of footprints and hoofprints on top of each other beat down a large area of the scrubby grass, but they led off in several different directions, most of the pathways strewn with stones.

He sent Ramirez to get the sheriff but didn't figure they'd be able to catch the culprits. Since the cattle were slaughtered instead of herded off the land, could be some people that were just hungry. If they'd have come up to the ranch house, he'd have given them food. But it really galled him that they stole the meat and left all this mess.

He told Martin to bury the remains after the sheriff saw them. Didn't want those vultures hanging around.

While riding back to the ranch house, he was stopped by his wrangler, Manny. Two of Jeremiah's prize mares were foaling, and both of them were having a hard time. First-time mothers often did. So he and Manny stayed with the horses until well past three in the morning, when both foals were finally delivered alive and well. He left Manny to take care of the mothers and babies and went to the house to clean up before falling across the bed for some much-needed shut-eye.

The sunlight streaming in through a hole in the tattered curtains of his bedroom woke him too soon. If the sun was high enough for the light to hit him in the face, T-Bone hadn't awakened him when he should have.

Jeremiah jumped up and threw on some of his best clothes, thankful he'd bathed last night. He raked his fingertips down the side of his jaw, feeling the prickly whiskers. He'd just have to go without shaving anyway. No time.

Didn't have time to tell T-Bone what he thought about the old man ignoring his orders, but he did grab a cup of coffee and gulp it down, searing his mouth and throat on the way. One of the things he liked about T-Bone was that he kept the coffee hot, but today he'd have liked it a little cooler.

Manny had Lightning saddled when Jeremiah arrived at the barn. He glanced around the cavernous building, one of the best in the area. In a lot better condition than his house. While he was at church today, Jeremiah'd talk to Pastor Oldman to see if the man had time to do some carpentry work for him.

He jumped into the saddle and gave Lightning his head as they flew across the miles toward Golden. Philip would be antsy, waiting for him so long.

After leaving Lightning in the livery stable, he jumped onto the seat of the wagon Swede had waiting for him and drove up the main street toward Philip's house. As he expected, the old man sat in the rocker on the front porch. He stood as Jeremiah pulled the wagon to a stop.

"Hey, Jerry. Yer mighty dressed up today." Philip hobbled toward the steps. "Ya goin' somewheres special?"

He'd known he'd face this kind of question when he arrived, but he hadn't had time to think about a quick answer. *Maybe the truth.* "Thought I'd stay for the service with you."

He didn't even glance up. He didn't want to see the surprise or smug smile, whichever Philip used. Besides, he wasn't going to participate, just keep his eyes on the Mercer woman. He climbed out of the wagon and went to help Philip down the steps.

"Glad ya came to yer senses."

"Don't go making a big deal out of it. Just want to check it out."

They carefully took the steps, one at a time, then he helped Philip over the wagon wheel.

Philip settled on the bench seat. "Sure a pretty mornin', ain't it?"

The change of subject suited Jeremiah fine. They filled the short trip down to the hotel with inconsequential spurts of conversation.

Jeremiah heaved a sigh of relief when they pulled up in front. He'd noticed the music halfway down the mountain. And it wasn't the draggy, off-key singing he'd heard in church when he attended before his mother died. When he and Philip slipped into the last row of seats, no one noticed, except the sheriff in the next chair. Philip dropped into his chair and added his thready voice to the song. Even Bill belted out the words...in tune.

Jeremiah glanced toward the front. A young Mexican man

sat on a tall stool playing a strange-looking guitar. Really different from the one Martin played out in the bunkhouse some nights. Besides that, Jeremiah thought all the Mexicans were Catholics. Big surprise to see one in this church. He was pretty sure it wasn't a Catholic service, since they had a church building on the other side of town.

Madeline Mercer sat straight in front of him on the first row. Her shiny hair was piled on top of her head in a mass of curls, revealing her slender neck. Some sort of ribbon drew his attention to the smooth skin. A few stray curls fell across the band, swaying as she moved in time with the music. She reached a delicate hand back and lifted the ringlets, tucking them into the others. The baby peeked over her other shoulder.

He'd never seen her in a dress with a lowered neckline. The beginning slopes of her shoulders intrigued him, and his gut tightened. He was in church, for pity's sake. He wasn't interested in her, just keeping an eye out. Wish he knew the words to this song. It'd take his mind off that woman.

When they finished singing, everyone sat down, and Sam Oldman took the Mexican's place on the stool. He started talking to the people in a strong but gentle voice. After opening his Bible, he read something about not judging other people. Then he began to explain what it meant—in calm and reasonable tones.

After a few minutes, Jeremiah wondered if the sheriff had told him what they'd been discussing because he talked about not judging people without knowing all the details of any situation. 'Course the sheriff hadn't even known Jeremiah was coming to church. He'd never come before, and he'd only decided after he'd left the sheriff's office yesterday. Must be another reason for the man to preach on the subject.

Off and on throughout the sermon, Jeremiah's eyes kept straying to the woman in the pinkish dress. He memorized everything he could see. He knew that later he might regret his scrutiny of Miss Mercer. She'd invaded his thoughts enough already. For some reason, he felt drawn to her, even though he couldn't trust her any farther than he could throw Lightning.

Reverend Oldman didn't belabor anything he talked about. He merely explained enough so the listeners could understand and moved on. No long, drawn-out sermon filled with hellfire and damnation like his mother's pastor had pounded into the pulpit. As soon as he was finished, Sam invited everyone to join them for a fellowship meal. Evidently the women fixed dinner every Sunday for those attending church. Wouldn't hurt to enjoy some of the food if the smells coming from the kitchen were any indication of the taste.

After the final prayer, Bill turned to shake his hand. "Sorry I couldn't find out anything about who slaughtered your cattle. But we'll continue to investigate."

"Thanks. Do you stay and eat with them?" Jeremiah tilted his head toward the crowd.

The sheriff nodded. "We all do. Some really good cooks in this congregation."

"I'm sure Philip will want to anyway, so I might as well stay too."

"All the men help move the chairs and tables back in place." Bill went over to Philip and helped the older man up, then moved his chair so Philip could sit down out of the way of those men who were working.

When Jeremiah turned around, Madeline Mercer headed toward Philip. She deposited the baby in his arms. Philip beamed and cradled her against his chest, making nonsensical sounds to her. Something strange thumped in Jeremiah's chest, making him uncomfortable in an entirely different way than before.

The Mercer woman turned back toward the kitchen. Without the baby in her arms, his gaze was drawn to the piece of jewelry fastened to the ribbon around her neck. Looked a lot like the cameo his mother always wore to church.

He'd have to get Bill alone and call his attention to the cameo. Pretty good proof that she was the criminal he'd thought she was all along. For some reason, that thought brought a sour taste to his mouth, ruining his appetite.

CHAPTER 18

*E*ven though they were already singing, Maddy sensed when Jeremiah brought Philip to church. The air became more alive. Instead of waiting by the door, he followed the older man into the dining room...and he didn't leave. She was tempted to turn around and see what was going on, but she didn't. All through the service, the skin on her back tingled. Was he looking at her? Had he noticed her sitting in front of him?

With him there, the room that had been plenty large for the group gathered now had a crowded feeling to it. The front door and back door, as well as the windows, were open, letting in the gentle breeze, but all the air felt steamy. Hard to breathe.

She made herself concentrate, or she would have missed most of Pastor Oldman's sermon. And she needed to hear it. At the same time, she hoped the man behind her was listening as closely as she was. Hadn't he been judging her without knowing all the true details about what brought her to Golden?

Maddy didn't want to tell him what had happened in Boston. He'd probably turn the situation around and make it her fault. She shouldn't care what he thought about her. She really shouldn't. But every word he'd said to Philip that day still rankled. Chafed her like corset stays cinched too tight.

Pearl must have sensed her discomfort, because she didn't settle down and sleep during the sermon as she had last Sunday. Instead, she wiggled and squirmed. Maddy held her against her shoulder, and Pearl kept her head up, bobbing it occasionally as she peeked toward the back of the room. She was probably looking at Philip. At the end of the final prayer, her baby started babbling. The same coos she used with Philip, so Maddy took her to the dear old man. He held out his arms to welcome her.

When Maddy straightened, she came face to face with Jeremiah. Close enough that she could see each whisker dusting his cheeks. Catch the unique masculine fragrance that surrounded the man.

A slow smile spread across his full lips, curling something buried inside her. She took a deep breath. He stared at her, a thundercloud descending on his expression as his eyes fastened just below her chin.

She lifted her hand to her neckline. Surely it wasn't too low. Her fingers encountered the brooch. Maybe he was looking at her grandmother's cameo, but why would that make him angry?

"Miss Mercer." His voice sounded sharp as a razor. He quickly turned away and headed toward the sheriff.

What was that all about? She hadn't spent much time with men, but she'd never met one who was more exasperating—and on a totally different level from the problems with Horace Johnstone. Those didn't feel quite as personal.

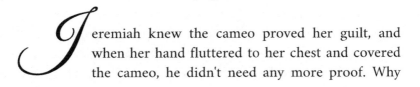

eremiah knew the cameo proved her guilt, and when her hand fluttered to her chest and covered the cameo, he didn't need any more proof. Why else would she be so nervous? He couldn't get to the sheriff fast enough.

Bill looked up from placing a table where it usually rested in the dining room. "Give us a hand, Jeremiah."

He grabbed two chairs and slid them under a table the sheriff had just put in place. "I need to talk to you."

Bill stared into Jeremiah's eyes as if assessing his intent. "Can't it wait until after our fellowship meal?"

Jeremiah hesitated. A few minutes longer wouldn't make any difference, would it? He gave a grudging nod.

When Jeremiah turned to glance at Philip, Mrs. Sneed was taking the baby from his arms. Miss Mercer watched while Philip carefully got up from his chair, then she accompanied him on a trip down one side of the tables. She carried his plate, and he told her what he wanted to eat. She kept up friendly banter with the old man, and both of them laughed often. This didn't fit with his picture of her as a conniving woman, but maybe she was just using her charm to keep Philip interested until they could fleece him of every dollar he owned.

After Jeremiah sat with three other ranchers and talked about cattle, the weather, and prices of supplies, all while consuming several plates of delicious food, he noticed Bill heading out the front door. He excused himself from his companions and hurried after the sheriff.

"Come on, walk with me." Bill pulled his badge out of his pocket and pinned it on his shirt. "I don't wear this in church, but I've gotta go down and check on things near the Golden Spur. I don't know why they have to raise a ruckus on Sunday. But drunks don't observe the Sabbath. We can talk on the way."

Jeremiah matched his stride to that of the lawman. "I wanted to ask if you saw that cameo she wore today?"

"Who?"

Jeremiah stopped in his tracks, then hurried to catch up.

"Who do you think I mean? That Mercer woman. That should prove she's the outlaw, so you can arrest her now."

Bill stopped and turned toward him. "I wish you'd just let me do my job. I noticed how nice that cameo looked on her. And I have more pressing needs than bothering a nice woman on Sunday."

Jeremiah had been biting back a lot of words around this man lately.

"Maybe it's the same cameo. Maybe it isn't," Bill said calmly. "I'm going to wait for the handbill to arrive before I do anything. Don't need to upset everyone if she isn't the person they're looking for." He started walking again.

Jeremiah didn't join him. He stood on the boardwalk, stewing in the hot sun. To him, it was as plain as the nose on his face that the Mercer woman was the one the law was looking for. And he had to find a way to prove it.

When he got back to the hotel, Philip stood in the lobby talking to the Oldmans. He glanced toward the door. "I'd a-thought ya forgot me if'n I hadn't seen the wagon."

Jeremiah stepped into the shaded room. "I wouldn't forget you. And, anyway, I want to ask Sam something."

~

*M*onday morning, Jeremiah went to the barn to talk to Manny. Both of the foals were doing fine. At least something was going like it should. And he hadn't lost a horse during the process.

Ramirez rode in hell-bent for leather. Jeremiah had never seen him ride his horse so hard. He stopped beside the barn in a cloud of dust. "Boss, sandstorm's a-comin'. A gigantic one. Looks like a massive wall movin' across the desert."

"Where'd you see it?" Jeremiah signaled for Manny to saddle Lightning.

"I was up on the high ridge on the far west end of the ranch. You can see a long ways from there. The storm is way out in the desert, but it's headin' straight towards Golden." He jumped from his horse and led it into the shady barn.

Manny brought Lightning to Jeremiah.

"Make sure everything is battened down. I'm going to check on Philip. He has a lot of trouble breathing when sand and dust are blowing." He vaulted into his saddle and headed out much the same way Ramirez came in.

When he topped the final ridge before the last leg of the journey into Golden, the enormous brown cloud had moved across the surface of the earth at an alarming speed. He'd barely make it to Philip's in time.

Jeremiah rode Lightning into the barn of the empty house that had belonged to Philip's closest neighbor. He jumped from the saddle and led the horse into a stall, then closed the gate behind him. At a dead run, he made it the rest of the way up to the adobe and leapt up onto the front porch. He burst through the door and slammed it behind him. When he turned, he read terror in Madeline Mercer's eyes.

~

*M*adeline had been leaning over Philip trying to get him to drink some water. He'd been coughing and wheezing ever since the wind had risen to a roar. Something was wrong with him, and she didn't know how to help him. At least Pearl slept in the back bedroom, so she wasn't disturbed by the ruckus Philip was making.

When the door slammed open, she looked up. Her nemesis stood silhouetted in the doorway for only an instant before he shut the door with enough force to wake the dead. Maybe not the dead, but Pearl heard it. A loud wail joined the eerie squeal of the wind.

She fought the tears clogging her throat and filling her eyes. "Just what do you think you're doing?" Even though she tried to put up a brave front, her voice trembled.

"Monstrous sandstorm's about to hit the house." Jeremiah grabbed a bandanna from his pocket and quickly tied it around Philip's mouth and nose. "Go see about your baby."

While she grabbed Pearl and changed her, she could hear the man moving around and doing something in the other parts of the house. Soon he came into the room where she had just finished changing the baby. He carried an armload of towels and sheets. He stuffed them close around the edges of the windows.

"I'm trying to keep as much of the dirt out as I can. These will help." He glanced at her.

Pearl snubbed against Maddy's shoulder.

"This your first sandstorm?"

She nodded, trying to soothe Pearl.

"You got a lightweight cover for the baby?"

She'd never seen him this frantic. "Yes." She pulled a white dimity blanket with pink roses embroidered on it from a drawer.

"Give her to me." He held out his arms toward Pearl.

Even though she wasn't sure she wanted him to touch her daughter, she relinquished the child to him. Ever so gently, he began to talk to Pearl as he wrapped the thin fabric around her, even covering her face.

"This will act like a filter to keep her from breathing in whatever dust seeps through the cracks." He carried Pearl into the room where Philip had settled against the back of his rocking chair, breathing a little easier through the bandanna mask.

Still holding Pearl, Jeremiah sat on the sofa. He rocked his upper body back and forth and patted her back while she huddled against his chest.

A broad, muscular chest. Why did she even notice such a thing? This was neither the time nor the place. And certainly not the man she should be noticing that way.

She coughed, and her stomach felt a little queasy. Not exactly as though she would lose her lunch, but very unsettled in a sick sort of way. She sat on the sofa and leaned her head back, trying to control her stomach.

With one fluid motion, still holding the baby on his shoulder, Jeremiah stood and went into Philip's bedroom. He returned with another bandanna. "Here. Tie it around your face and breathe through it."

While she complied, he went to the kitchen, and she could hear him moving the handle of the water pump. It made a funny squeak on the downstroke. When he returned, he carried a glass of water.

He handed it to her. "Here. Drink this slowly. It'll wash some of the dust you've already swallowed out of your system."

She took a sip. The cool liquid soothed her throat and calmed her stomach a little. She leaned back again, listening to the wind howl. She'd never heard anything like it. The storm sounded like a living creature crying and moaning as it pushed against the house. And as the sand hit the glass in the windows, the grains made pinging sounds, almost sounding musical, in an odd sort of way.

With the doors and windows shut tight and the window facings stuffed with towels, the house was dark as twilight. Everything about this made her nerves stand on end. Here she was in a dark house with two men, surrounded by an impenetrable storm. She crossed her arms and shivered, feeling helpless.

"How..." She cleared her throat and took another sip. "How long does a storm like this last?"

"Not usually very long." He kept patting Pearl's back rhythmically as she rested against him. "But this one is larger than any I've ever been in. I don't have any idea how long it'll take to blow through."

"At least Philip stopped coughing." Maddy didn't know what else to do for her dear friend, so she was glad Jeremiah had come along and taken over. "And it's not the hottest part of the day yet...even though it's getting stuffy in here."

The air in the house now had enough dust in it that everything looked hazy. She had never seen anything like this. Storms back in Boston had thunder, lightning, and rain. Possibly a lot of wind—even hail or sleet. No telling what would have happened if Jeremiah Dennison hadn't arrived when he did.

The man sitting beside her began humming a tuneless song while he leaned his face close to Pearl. Maddy never would have thought of the man as being paternal, but right now, that's how he looked. Like a good father would, calming his daughter during a storm. Maddy's ideas about the man had just taken a drastic turn. And that disturbed her more than the storm did.

~

*J*eremiah would never have chosen to hold that baby during the storm, but when Madeline thrust Pearl into his arms on his command, something in his heart broke loose. He'd cuddled her and done his best to keep her calm.

While he cleaned up the mess the sandstorm left at the ranch, he couldn't sweep the feelings out of his heart. That baby had touched places no one had ever reached. Swooping in and saving her and Madeline had left damage that he had no idea how to deal with.

Tuesday afternoon, Jeremiah was showing Sam Oldman what he wanted added onto the ranch house when the sheriff rode up and dismounted. "Be with you in a minute, Bill."

"So do you think you and Carlos can tackle the job right

away?" Jeremiah studied the man who looked very different than he had on Sunday in the church service.

"Don't see why not." Sam nodded toward his helper. "I've been getting a lot more done since he's been helping me. If we can hire a few of the unemployed miners, we'll get finished even quicker."

"I'll agree to that, if you can find some that are good with building materials. I think most of the ones who helped with Philip's house either went back to the mines or left town. So when can you start?" The sooner the better as far as Jeremiah was concerned.

"Since you have most of the supplies needed, we can start right away. How about tomorrow morning, bright and early?"

When Jeremiah agreed, the preacher carpenter offered his hand to seal the deal.

As the two workers rode out of sight, Jeremiah turned back to his good friend. "So what brings you out here today, Bill? Some of T-Bone's coffee and gingerbread? I think he made some after lunch. The men will get it with supper."

"I must have smelled it all the way into Golden. No one makes gingerbread as good as T-Bone's."

The two men headed toward the cook shack. After they were seated with a plate of the dessert in front of them and cups of hot black coffee in their hands, Bill took one bite followed by a swig of coffee. Then he set everything down and pulled an envelope out of his shirt pocket.

"Hiram brought this today." He handed the missive to Jeremiah.

After sliding the papers from the already-opened envelope, Jeremiah studied the handbill. The drawing was rather crude, but the woman did bear some resemblance to Madeline Mercer. However, she could also be someone completely different.

He unfolded the other piece of paper. The words told about the Mercer woman traveling with two other members of her

187

gang named Frank and Sarah Sneed and an orphan baby girl. The words hit his gut like a load of lead. There couldn't be two Madeline Mercers with the exact same traveling companions. The handbill went on to describe a number of pieces of jewelry stolen from a prominent family in Boston, and one of them was a cameo carved of reddish brown stone. Just the color that Madeline wore yesterday.

Jeremiah raised his gaze toward his friend's. "So does this mean you're going to arrest them?" Try as he might, Jeremiah couldn't keep his voice from sounding disappointed.

When had he stopped wanting Madeline to go to jail? And what was that about an orphan baby girl? Jeremiah hadn't ever seen a mother love her baby more than Madeline loved Pearl. For some reason, everything they'd heard from Boston about Miss Mercer sounded too convenient, almost like a setup. At least some part of him wanted to believe so now.

CHAPTER 19

"*D*o you mind if I ride into town with you?" Jeremiah took a bite of the spicy cake and washed it down with coffee.

"That would probably be a good idea, especially if Miss Mercer is up at Philip's house." Bill didn't seem to be in any hurry to leave as long he had any gingerbread left on his plate, and T-Bone had cut him a generous helping.

"According to what he's been telling me, she goes up there almost every day." He stuffed the last bite in his mouth, hoping the sheriff would take a hint.

Evidently he didn't, because when T-Bone offered Bill another piece, he accepted. After spending another half hour trying to fill the time with conversation, no matter how meaningless, Bill finally pushed back from the table.

He patted his stomach. "That's really good. Don't get the gingerbread anymore since T-Bone came out here instead of working at the hotel." He picked up his hat and headed out the door.

As they walked to the barn, another stiff breeze blew, but not

189

with the force of the sandstorm. While Jeremiah saddled Lightning, Bill sat on a bale of hay.

"Were you out in the sandstorm yesterday, or were you close enough to one of the buildings to take shelter?" The sheriff leaned his forearms on his thighs and clasped his hands between his knees.

Jeremiah really didn't want to go into all that had happened, so he gave a brief answer. "Had enough warning that I rode into town to make sure Philip was taken care of. Remember how much trouble he has with his breathing? Those storms really bother him."

He headed outside to where the other horse was tethered. Bill followed him, and they mounted up.

"Wasn't Miss Mercer up there yesterday morning?"

Not wanting to explain anything else, Jeremiah rode out ahead of the other man. What could he tell him? That Madeline had been there helping Philip? That he showed her how to deal with a sandstorm? That holding that baby felt better than anything he'd done in a long time?

No way was he going to ride down that path. Bill didn't need to know how confused he was right now about Madeline and her child. This was the first time he'd really thought out all that happened. Didn't want to give Bill any wild ideas. He came up with enough on his own.

When they reached Philip's house and reined in the horses, Bill hadn't forgotten. "You didn't answer my question."

Jeremiah took a deep breath, then whooshed it out. "I know." With that, he climbed the few steps and rapped on Philip's door before opening it. "Philip, I've brought the sheriff with me."

The old miner was dozing in his rocking chair. He raised his chin from his chest and gave Jeremiah a wide smile. "What does he think I done? Is he comin' to arrest me?"

"You old rascal." The sheriff played along. "Are you hiding something from me? Should I arrest you?"

Philip's cackle greeted those questions. "If ya don't know, I ain't gonna tell ya."

"Actually, we were wondering if Miss Mercer is still here. We want to discuss something with her." The sheriff stood with his back to the open doorway. The sun outlined his silhouette and threw his tall shadow across the floor.

Philip turned his attention toward Jeremiah. "Now, Jerry, don't ya go botherin' Madeline. We had us a long talk yesterdy. She's been a real help to me, and I cain't get her to take any money fer her trouble. Says she enjoys comin' up here with Pearl. And I've taken a real shine to that baby. She likes me too."

Jeremiah swallowed at the lump in his throat. He hated for anyone to hurt Philip the way it would if Madeline really was a criminal. "We just wanted to discuss something with her."

Philip's piercing gaze raked over him. "Ya cain't hide nothin' from me, Jerry. Yer up to somethin'. Ya might as well know I've almost convinced her to marry me."

The harder Jeremiah held in his emotions, the more he felt as if he might explode. Right here, all over Philip. Even though he had softened a little toward Madeline, he didn't want her marrying Philip. For a whole lot of reasons. Heat flooded his cheeks, reaching the tips of his ears. Now why did he have to blush like that? Both Philip and Bill would make all kind of assumptions.

"Now don't go gettin' yer dander up, Jerry. That's why we writ that letter. To bring her and her babe out here. The good Lord done told—"

Jeremiah pushed past the sheriff and out the door. He didn't want to hear another word about *the good Lord*. Not today. He hurried across the porch and down the steps. He could hear Bill talking to Philip, and he didn't care what the sheriff told the old man. He just had to get himself some air. Cool down his cheeks.

After only a couple of clipped statements, the sheriff

followed him. "Let's head down to the hotel and see what she has to say about the handbill."

He was sure she'd have plenty to say, but would they be able to believe her? Jeremiah didn't share his thoughts with the lawman who rode beside him. Soon enough for him to hear them after they'd talked to the woman.

~

*M*addy laid a sleeping Pearl on the pallet Caroline made for her near the back door of the kitchen, where the breeze would keep her cooler during her nap. She straightened, rubbing her lower back. All those years when other people took care of her, she'd had no idea how hard they worked.

Caroline used a wooden spoon to stir liquid in a metal pitcher. "Is Sarah coming down to have some lemonade with us? Skinner Mercantile received a new shipment of lemons from California, and Cyrus gave me first pick of the ones that made it."

"Yes, she's on her way. I'm ready for a break." Maddy moved a chair where she could see Pearl and dropped into it. What a relief.

Caroline poured three glasses of the pale yellow liquid. "You really don't have to work as hard as you do around here. The Sneeds do enough to pay for your rooms and board. That's why we've started paying them a little too. Take the time to enjoy Pearl."

Maddy took a sip of the refreshing drink. "Helping has made me understand Loraine better."

"Pearl's mother?" Interest sparkled in Caroline's eyes.

"Yes, she came from a wealthy family, too, but her parents forbade her to marry the man she loved. They disowned her. She enjoyed working beside her husband, trying to build a good life together. After he died and she had to move to shanty town, I got to know her and help her, because she was going to have a child. We talked a lot. I never did understand until we came here what she was talking about. Working for yourself and your future gives you a lot of satisfaction, even if you get tired."

Sarah slipped into one of the other chairs and picked up her glass. "I've never minded working."

Maddy leaned across the table and touched Sarah's arm. "I hadn't realized how much you and Frank did for me. And I never thanked you properly."

The praise seemed to fluster Sarah. She blushed, and her hands fluttered to her chest. "We believed God gave us a gift when He allowed us to work for your father and help raise you."

Maddy knew they were a gift from God to her too, but she didn't want to add to Sarah's discomfort right now. "Caroline, our church services in Boston were different from these here. I've loved the Lord a long time, but I think I'm getting to know Him better now—on a different level."

"Sam will be glad to hear that."

Their conversation turned to other things, but Maddy didn't share what was uppermost in her mind since yesterday. Had she misjudged Jeremiah? He had the right to wonder about them, since he loved Philip so much. And his distrust could be under-stood. She wished she felt comfortable enough with him to tell him the truth about why they had come to Golden. Maybe someday she would.

And, of course, she still needed to decide what to do about Philip's proposal. She probably should call it a proposition. He wanted to marry her and give her all the money she needed. Some proposition! She'd get all the benefits, but Philip insisted that she and Pearl had brought nothing but joy into his life. Their conversations about God helped Maddy as much or more than the service on Sunday.

But was that reason enough to marry a man? Where was the

love like her father and mother shared? Without her inviting it, a picture of Jeremiah Dennison helping her yesterday invaded her mind.

$\sim$

*J*eremiah and the sheriff rode their horses at an easy walk toward the hotel. Plenty of people were coming and going about the town. Business and industry had transformed Golden from a lazy mining village to a thriving community, almost as busy as Albuquerque though not nearly as large.

"Do you know that man on the large palomino?" Bill nodded toward a stranger stopping outside his office.

"I haven't seen him before, but I think that's one of the horses from the livery in Los Cerrillos. I've stabled Lightning there when I've taken the train to Santa Fe. You know how I like Palominos."

Wearing a suit with an Eastern cut to it, the man looked out of place. And that bowler hat added to the perception. Why didn't the man shed his jacket? The temperature had really climbed today, making it a scorcher. Only a fool would keep a coat on in this weather. A wonder he didn't pass out in the desert on the way here.

"Let's head on over there and see what he wants with me." Bill turned his horse's head and rode on.

Jeremiah followed behind.

By the time they reached the building adjoining the sheriff's office, the stranger had already gone inside. Bill didn't ever lock the door when he left. Nothing in there was worth stealing, and most outlaws stayed away from the sheriff's office and jail.

Bill stopped his horse a ways from his office. "I don't know why, but I have a hunch that man is up to no good. And I can usually trust my hunches."

Jeremiah had to agree. "Funny thing about hunches. You want to leave the horses here?"

"Yeah." Bill dismounted and tied his reins to the limb of a piñon tree.

Jeremiah did the same. They walked down to the building, then sneaked along the wall to the window. Bill peeked in.

"What's he doing?" Jeremiah whispered.

"Going through my desk."

"Reckon you know what he's looking for?"

"Only one way to find out."

Bill quickly opened the door, startling the man. The stranger straightened behind the desk, then his eyes darted to the badge on the sheriff's chest and his eyes widened. He quickly hooded them with his heavy lids, leaving only slits.

"Were you looking for something?" Bill stood with one hand resting gently on his holstered revolver.

The stranger raised both hands. "Sorry. I didn't find anyone here, and I wanted to leave a note for the sheriff."

Bill's stare zeroed in on the pad and pencil on top of the desk. "You want to try that again? This time with the truth." His fingers wrapped tighter around the handle of his pistol.

Jeremiah moved off to the side, and the stranger's eyes followed him.

"You aren't both going to shoot me, are you?" The stranger's voice didn't carry the strength it did when he first spoke.

Jeremiah crossed his arms over his chest. "My gun is only for snakes and coyotes. You're not one of those, are you?"

Fear flickered then disappeared from the man's eyes. "I'm just a law-abiding citizen needing to talk to the sheriff."

Bill took one step closer to the desk. "So start talking before I shoot you for rifling through my desk."

The stranger wilted right before their eyes, like a vegetable garden that had been too long between rains. "May I sit down?" He inched around the desk toward one of the chairs, then dropped into it. "I'm not used to being interrogated by the law."

Bill leaned against the front of the desk but kept one hand near his gun. "What are you used to?"

The man bowed his head for a moment, then straightened, stiffening his spine. "Can we start over?"

Something about the man didn't sit right with Jeremiah. Could be his shifty gaze that darted all over the room instead of looking Bill straight in the eyes. Could be the fact that he was caught red-handed in the sheriff's desk. Could be something else. He just wasn't what he seemed to be. Jeremiah would bet his bottom dollar on that.

"You come from Los Cerrillos?" Bill's voice sounded casual, but Jeremiah heard the hidden steel beneath it. "I recognize the horse."

"Yes...yes. I hired the horse from the livery when I got off the train. The station master told me it was the only way to get to Golden today." He rubbed his hand together, then placed them on his thighs.

"And why did you come to Golden?" Bill didn't take his eyes off the man, pinning him to the chair with his intense gaze.

"I'm looking for someone. A criminal." Sweat beaded on the man's forehead, but he didn't wipe it off. "A woman."

"Are you a bounty hunter?" Jeremiah couldn't hold his tongue any longer.

"A bounty hunter?" The man looked confused. "Oh, yeah, I'm a bounty hunter, and I have a wanted poster and handbill here." He held up his hands. "Can I reach into my pocket, Sheriff?"

Bill nodded.

The man pulled out papers identical to the ones Bill had in his pocket. The ones Jeremiah had read out at the ranch. The stranger handed them to Bill.

He took them and hardly glanced at them before laying them on his desk. "Where you from?"

"Boston." The man looked relieved.

"I don't see any reward on this poster. Why would a bounty hunter come all the way out here when there isn't any reward?" Bill stood up straight, towering over the man still sitting in the chair.

"Actually, I'm the woman's guardian." The man relaxed, crossing one leg over the opposite knee. "When I find her, I'll take her home."

Bill harrumphed. "If you're her guardian, you didn't do a very good job of taking care of her since you let her run with a gang."

"I...I didn't...let her." The stranger sputtered. "She just got away."

Somehow his words set off all kinds of alarms in Jeremiah's mind. The man didn't sound like a loving guardian. More like a jailer. Had he locked Madeline up? Was that why she escaped? Or was it something else altogether? He glanced at Bill, hoping his friend also saw through this man.

"Besides, how do you know she's with a gang? You didn't even read the papers I gave you." The man's belligerent voice cut through the tension in the room.

Bill pulled his paper from his pocket. "I have a set right here. I've read them completely."

"Do you know where Madeline is?"

The sound of her name coming from the other man's mouth lit a fuse in Jeremiah. The man looked like a two-bit hustler himself, with his greasy, slicked-back hair and shifty eyes. Jeremiah had to fist his hands to keep from grabbing the man and shaking him. What had he done to Madeline? And what did he want to do with her now?

"What if I do?" Bill cut into Jeremiah's thoughts. "Do you want me to arrest her?"

"No." The stranger jumped up. "I want to take her home."

We'll see about that.

Where had that thought come from? Jeremiah didn't care. All he knew was that he wasn't going to let this stranger railroad Madeline into doing something she didn't want to do. If she wanted to stay here in Golden, she would, even if she married Philip. The heat that betrayed him before churned in his gut. Somehow he couldn't imagine her married to his friend. What could he do to help Philip realize that was wrong in a lot of ways?

"So, since there isn't a reward posted, and since you want to take Miss Mercer with you"—Bill stared straight at the stranger —"are you the person who had the poster and handbill printed?"

If Jeremiah hadn't been watching, he would've missed the flicker that passed through the stranger's eyes. Now, more than ever, Jeremiah didn't want this man to get what he came for. But what could he do to prevent it?

CHAPTER 20

After Pearl awakened, Maddy took her upstairs. When she removed the baby's white gown, her daughter kicked her legs and laughed out loud for the very first time.

Maddy grabbed her up and hugged her tight, covering her head with kisses. "You are such a gift from God." Her heart expanded until she felt it wouldn't fit in her chest. How could such a tiny human bring so much love into her life? If only Pearl had a father to love her the way Maddy's father had loved her. She wished her father had seen Pearl. He would have accepted her as his granddaughter, just as she had become Maddy's daughter. Emotions clogged her throat, and tears blurred her eyes.

When she laid Pearl back on the bed, the baby kicked and waved her little fists while Maddy worked to change her diaper and slip her dimpled arms into another dimity gown. A blue one to match her eyes. Tiny tucks across the front flared into the long, full skirt that hung below the baby's feet. With the new powder that had arrived at the mercantile, Pearl smelled sweet enough to match her disposition. But dressing the wiggling baby was a new adventure every day.

"Mommy is so blessed to have you." Maddy picked her up and held the baby against her left shoulder while she gathered the soiled garments and placed them in a basket in the corner. Time enough to wash them early in the morning.

Maddy locked the door to her room and thrust the key into her pocket before heading down the stairs. When she reached the bottom step, the sheriff stood in the front doorway. Tall. Silhouetted by the strong summer sun. Maddy gave him a smile until she noticed who followed the man. She stopped dead in her tracks and clutched Pearl tighter.

Horace Johnstone! What was that man doing here? More importantly, how did he find her? She felt the blood drain from her face, and she hoped she wouldn't faint. She had to protect her daughter from that monster.

Over the man's shoulder, she noticed that Jeremiah Dennison followed him and the sheriff. This couldn't be happening. Now what was she going to do?

Hearing a slight noise at the top of the stairs, she glanced up in time to glimpse Sarah before she ducked out of sight. Maddy looked to see if any of the men had heard her friend. No one seemed to notice. They were making plenty of noise. The two men from Golden wore cowboy boots and spurs. With all the drumming and clanging, everything else was drowned out.

"Are you about ready to fix Pear—?" Caroline stopped short in the doorway that led to the kitchen. "Sheriff, what can we do for you...and your friends?" Her gesture encompassed the other two men.

After glancing toward the proprietress of the hotel, Maddy's gaze slid back toward the men who'd caused the most turmoil in her life. Why were they together?

Bill Brown pulled his cowboy hat from his head and held it down by his side, rhythmically patting it against his leg. "We actually want to talk to Miss Mercer." He turned and smiled at her. "If that's all right with you, ma'am."

His good manners calmed some of Maddy's agitation. If she were in trouble, wouldn't he frown?

Caroline came and stood beside Maddy. "Would you like to sit in the parlor?" Caroline ushered the entourage into the room that often sat empty.

With her legs feeling like jelly, Maddy dropped onto the red velvet horsehair sofa. Right in the middle. She spread her skirts wide so none of the men could sit beside her.

"Would you like me to take Pearl and give her a bottle?" Caroline hovered at the end of the sofa.

Maddy shook her head. "She's not fussy. I'll keep her with me."

Caroline stared into Maddy's eyes as if reading her thoughts. "How about I join you? Just in case I need to take her out."

Maddy gave her a shaky smile and a nod. Having a friend with her might help her keep from losing control of her emotions. Emotions that boiled and churned inside her, making her wish she hadn't eaten. Each of those men caused turmoil in very different ways. She shifted toward one end of the sofa, and Caroline sat on the other.

"Now what is this all about, Sheriff?" Maddy hoped her voice didn't sound as shaky to them as it did to her.

The sheriff took a seat on a chair facing the sofa. So did Horace Johnstone, but Jeremiah stood behind both men, almost like an avenging angel. Or a guardian angel. She hoped it was the latter, not the former.

Mr. Johnstone glared at her, making her want to squirm, but with determination, she remained still. She would not let that man get to her. He had no control over her out here in New Mexico Territory. Hadn't God assured her that this was the place of her golden opportunity? Horace would not steal it from her as he'd tried to steal her freedom in Boston. He. Would. Not.

The sheriff cleared his throat and turned his hat around and around. "Miss Mercer, this man is looking for you. He wants to take you back to Boston."

"I am not going anywhere with Mr. Johnstone." Every word she spoke sounded stronger than her last sentence had.

"He had a wanted poster and handbill printed about you."

Maddy couldn't believe the gall of the man. Had he no honor whatsoever? Of course not. She'd realized that before she left Boston. He was the very reason she came to Golden. She'd realized that God had used what the man intended for evil to work something good in her life.

"A *wanted* poster? What reason does he give for *wanting* me?"

"The poster claims you're a criminal who has a gang. The handbill names the Sneeds as part of your gang. Supposedly, you stole jewelry from a wealthy family in Boston."

Bill Brown never took his eyes from her face. He seemed genuinely interested in what she would say.

"I cannot believe he would go to such lengths." She stared at Mr. Johnstone with contempt. "The only jewelry I have with me belonged to my mother, who died when I was very young, and I can prove it. I inherited it when she died. It all belongs to me."

"Interesting." The sheriff slowly nodded. "How can you prove it?"

"When I packed to leave Boston, I brought along the few photographs I have of my mother. She's wearing many of the pieces of jewelry in those pictures."

As if sensing the tension in the room, Pearl started moving around but didn't utter a single whimper. Maddy began patting her back. She didn't want to relinquish her daughter to anyone, especially not until this matter was straightened out.

The sheriff smiled for the first time. "I believe you, Miss Mercer. So why is this man trying to find you?"

"I tol—" Horace Johnstone tried to interrupt the conversation between Maddy and the sheriff.

"I was talking to the lady." Bill stared at the interloper. "I heard you out. Now I'll listen to what she has to say."

Maddy heaved a sigh, turning her gaze from one man to each of the others before answering. "The Oldmans and Philip already know the whole story, so I guess it won't hurt to tell you, Sheriff. I just didn't want it bandied about town."

"You have my solemn promise not to divulge a word, Miss Mercer." The sheriff turned and glanced up at Jeremiah. "And I'm sure Mr. Dennison will give his promise as well."

Jeremiah stared straight into her eyes and gave a stiff nod, a hint of a smile raising one corner of his mouth.

"I understood Mr. Johnstone was just an employee of my father's until my father died. Then Mr. Johnstone came to the house to tell me that he was Father's partner." She looked everywhere but at Horace Johnstone. Even at Jeremiah, who listened attentively. "I couldn't understand why Father would make him a partner. I've never felt comfortable around the man. He told me Father made some bad business investments, and most of our money is gone. We barely received enough money each month to cover essentials. I had to let most of the staff go. Only Frank and Sarah stayed on. They've been with me all my life. They're like members of my family."

The sheriff scowled at Mr. Johnstone, then turned a smile toward Maddy. She felt better all the time. Stronger somehow.

"Then Mr. Johnstone announced that Father promised I would marry him. I knew Father wouldn't do that without consulting me. But Mr. Johnstone was persistent, inviting himself to our house for meals and treating Frank and Sarah with contempt. He gave me a deadline for our marriage, without giving me a choice…and without giving me the proper time to grieve my father's death."

Jeremiah shifted position. "What about your father's will, Madeline?"

That was the first time she'd heard him say her name

without rancor. The word slid from his tongue straight into her heart. No one had ever given it the same inflection. She wished she had more time to analyze it.

"That's just the thing. Mr. Sanderson, Father's solicitor, took months and still hadn't read the will for me. And then Loraine died after making me promise to take Pearl as my own daughter."

~

For the first time, things started falling into place in Jeremiah's mind. But who was Loraine? He'd have to ask Madeline later.

Evidently, Pearl really was an orphan, but she was also Madeline's child. So much began to make sense. He smiled at Madeline, but she didn't notice.

"When Mr. Johnstone came to the house and realized that Pearl was living there, he gave me an ultimatum about giving her away. He told me that if I didn't, he'd take care of getting rid of her. Neither Frank and Sarah nor myself would consider letting him follow through on his threat. We were sure he meant to do her harm." Tears welled in Madeline's eyes, then one trickled down her cheek. Jeremiah wished he were close enough to wipe it off for her. "I couldn't take a chance on that happening."

Just then Frank and Sarah Sneed walked through the doorway to the lobby. Jeremiah studied the pair with new eyes. Knowing everything Madeline had told them made him admire the couple.

"Everything Miss Madeline said is true." Frank took up a protective position beside Madeline. "I'd done some checking around the taverns in Boston to see what I could find out about this man, and all of it was bad. Lots of talk about people coming up missing after crossing him. Even a hint that maybe he'd had something to do with the death of Mr. Mercer. We couldn't let him hurt Miss Madeline or Pearl, so we helped her slip out of Boston."

Madeline sat up straighter. "That's right." She stared boldly at the interloper. "So, Mr. Johnstone, how did you find me here?"

The man crossed his arms and sneered. "I don't have to tell you a thing, Miss High-and-mighty. I said you couldn't get away from me. You should've listened. Then we wouldn't be out here in this godforsaken place."

Jeremiah wanted to use the man as a punching bag. He'd seen a few bare-knuckle boxing matches when he'd traveled farther east a time or two. Seemed like a just punishment for part of what the man did to Madeline. But he had to be a criminal too. Maybe there would be an arrest today, but at least it wouldn't be the beautiful woman sitting there holding a baby she'd probably rescued from being put in an orphanage.

Jeremiah hated that he'd misjudged her so much. But that opened up all sorts of other problems in his mind. How could he restrain himself and keep from coming between Philip and Madeline? They weren't right for each other, and they shouldn't marry. Surely there was another option for her. *Like me.* That thought slipped into his mind before he could close the door on it. And it sounded just right to him.

~

*M*addy winced at the harsh words Horace said but continued to stare him down.

"I believe the lady asked you a question." The sheriff's voice held the weight of strong authority. "I suggest you answer her." One hand lifted to rest on the butt of his gun.

Evidently Mr. Johnstone noticed too, because he became very talkative. "I convinced the stupid lawyer that you hadn't been seen for a while and something might have happened at the house. Maybe all of you had caught some dread disease and were dead or something. Only then would he unlock the door of the mansion and let me in. I hadn't ever been on the upper floors. Quite a fancy layout. I'll really enjoy living there."

Maddy made a face. "Just getting inside the house wouldn't tell you where we were."

"No, but this did." He reached into his pocket and extracted an opened letter.

Jeremiah stared at it. Maddy wondered what about the missive fascinated the man so much.

"Let me see that." Determination firmed Jeremiah's jaw until it looked like carved marble.

Why would Jeremiah want to see the letter?

Mr. Johnstone started to stuff it back into his pocket, but Jeremiah grabbed the man's wrist. He squeezed it so tight that Mr. Johnstone released the envelope.

Jeremiah turned it over and over, then speared her with his gaze. "This is the last letter Philip and I wrote to you—the one you never got. That's how he knew to come to Golden."

Maddy covered her mouth with one hand. Now what?

The sheriff stood. He grabbed Johnstone's arm, lifted him from the chair, and snapped handcuffs around the man's wrists. "Johnstone, you're under arrest. I'm not sure what all the charges will be, but I do know that it's against the law to open other people's mail. And you were rifling through my desk, which is also against the law. I might have quite a few other things to charge you with as well."

Horace Johnstone's face turned beet red, and he looked about to explode. "You can't do this to me. I came out here of my own free will, and I'll get what I came for. Didn't you listen to a thing I said? You don't believe me, but you didn't even ask her to show you the pictures she claims to have. What's fair about that?"

"Should I add resisting arrest to the list?" The sheriff quirked one eyebrow, then turned toward Maddy. "This man won't bother you again, Miss Mercer. I'll see to that. He'll be in jail until the territorial judge comes around. Could be at least a couple of months."

He marched the man out the door, but Jeremiah didn't follow.

Pearl picked this time to let out a wail. Maddy arose from the sofa, patting the baby's back.

Sarah reached for the infant. "Madeline, I'll take her and start feeding her."

Caroline jumped up. "I'll help you fix the bottle."

The two women quickly exited together, and Frank followed them.

Maddy stood there, trying to decide what to do. Jeremiah hadn't moved. The silence between them expanded like the rising bread dough she was learning to bake, filling the room. Nothing but the rhythmic thump of the stamping machines broke the silence. Funny how Maddy hardly ever noticed the sound anymore, but today it matched the beating of her pulse. She placed a hand on her throat to hide the throb.

"Madeline." Her name from his lips once again affected her equilibrium. She dropped onto the sofa and sat on the edge, her knees and feet together and her back straight.

"I must apologize to you." He rubbed the back of his neck as if it hurt him. "I misjudged you." He paused, and she didn't feel any inclination to fill the space with words. "I said things that hurt you, and I'm sorry. Do you think you could ever forgive me?"

The way he stood there with his hat in his hands touched her heart. It must be hard for a strong man like him to speak those words. What else could she say?

"Yes, Mr. Dennison, I can forgive you. Forgiving is what Christians do."

A slow smile crept across his face, bringing a light to his eyes she had never seen before. "Thank you, Madeline. Could you call me Jeremiah?"

She hesitated. Should she take that step? Did she want to be more than an acquaintance with this man?

"Yes, Jeremiah." She liked the way his name felt on her tongue, almost as if it belonged there.

He stared at her before pivoting and leaving the room.

This softer, kinder Jeremiah Dennison would be a different man to deal with. After the way he'd treated her, Pearl, and Philip during the sandstorm, and now with his apology, she was in danger of losing her heart to the man. And she couldn't afford to do that.

Philip had asked her to marry him. If she accepted his proposition, she'd be seeing even more of Jeremiah. And she couldn't do that either. She didn't dare let her heart become entangled with a man who didn't know and love her Savior. Somehow she'd have to figure out a way to treat him as a man she respected and nothing more. She'd have to rethink her future in Golden. Make all the pieces fit in a way that didn't hurt Philip, Pearl, or herself.

Did Jeremiah Dennison fit in that picture anywhere? She didn't think so.

*a*s Jeremiah's boots hit the boardwalk in front of the hotel, he glanced toward the sheriff's office. Bill struggled with Johnstone, but he finally shoved the man through the open doorway of his office, and Jeremiah figured he got the man into a cell.

Maybe he should go see if his friend needed any help. Striding down the cobblestone street, he flexed his hands. He'd been gripping them so hard to keep from reaching out and touching Madeline that they ached. What he'd wanted more than anything would've been to take her in his arms and comfort her. Even finger her dark brown curls to see if they felt like silk as he imagined. The next best thing would be to make sure her tormentor stayed behind bars until the judge arrived. Judge Barker could be held up a long time. At least Jeremiah hoped so. The territory was large, and sometime lawlessness reigned in various places, although this area from Albuquerque to Santa Fe had settled down. Usually Bill was able to keep the peace in Golden, but not always.

Jeremiah wanted Johnstone to rot in jail and worry about what was going to happen. The man didn't deserve anything better. When the judge did come, Jeremiah planned to be present for the trial to make sure the weasel suffered for the crimes he'd committed against Madeline.

A vision he'd tucked away stole into his mind—Madeline stepping from the train, like a mirage in the New Mexico sun. Her beauty had overwhelmed him before he knew who she was. All brightness and light in an otherwise dismal day. Although beauty was often skin-deep, as his mother had told him when he was a little boy, Madeline had a good heart and sweet spirit. Why had he allowed himself to be blinded to that fact?

He should have recognized it from the start instead of judging her as he did. He hated to admit that even to himself. But if people had made that kind of mistake about him, he'd have been angry. Would've had a hard time forgiving them. After that sermon Sam preached, Jeremiah's judgmental attitude hadn't let him rest. He was truly sorry for the way he'd treated her.

Why had he let Philip's ad for the mail-order bride get in his way of accepting her when she first came? Of course, that had to be it, didn't it?

Admit it, Jeremiah. You're jealous of Philip. Of his old friend's claim to the beautiful woman. And jealousy did ugly things in his mind. It took a man and twisted his gut until he was tied in knots so tight, they hardly ever came apart. At least, that's what had happened to Jeremiah. Why had he allowed it? He wished he knew. And more than anything, he wanted to be rid of those knots.

His muscles clenched so tight, the ache returned to his stomach. His anger at himself matched what he felt for the stranger who'd forced Madeline to run from the only home she'd ever known. Although Jeremiah hadn't treated her quite as badly— except for those words she overheard at Philip's house that day —he wasn't much better than that skunk Johnstone.

When Jeremiah finally reached the doorway to the sheriff's

office, Bill was sitting behind his desk. Johnstone, behind bars and slumped on the hard, narrow bed, was sulking—his eyes like fire.

"I see you got him into a cell." Jeremiah moved into the coolness and pulled off his hat, then rubbed the sweat from his forehead with his shirt sleeve. "How soon do you think Judge Barker'll get here?"

Bill crossed his arms and leaned on the top of his desk. "Well, it hasn't been long since he left. Might take several weeks. Depends on whether he has a trial somewhere else. Could have more than one trial. Hard to tell."

With each phrase the sheriff uttered, the prisoner sounded more agitated. Jeremiah couldn't understand how Bill could ignore the muttering coming from the man.

"Guess that means the town'll have to feed Johnstone for a while." Jeremiah was all for feeding him bread and water.

Bill nodded. "Like always, the Oldmans'll bring meals to him. I figure it'll be Sam most of the time."

"Probably. Wouldn't want Caroline to have to."

"Hey, I'm hungry now."

The growl from the direction of the cells sailed right past Jeremiah. He wasn't about to give Johnstone the satisfaction of knowing he heard. "You going to have to hire a deputy to stay here during the night?"

"Sure will." Bill leaned back with his hands behind his head. "Thought I'd get Swede to come by and let me go home to the missus most nights."

"Sounds good to me." Jeremiah dropped into the chair across the desk from his friend. "If you need any of my ranch hands, I can send one to town. Let me know."

"All right. Might just do that. Not sure Swede'll want to do it every night."

The bed creaked, and Jeremiah heard Johnstone's shoes scuff across the rock floor. "When am I going to get something to eat?" The harsh words were loud enough that anyone nearby on the street could hear them.

Bill stood and stared at the man. "Might as well settle down. You'll get to eat when the food comes and not a minute before. All your bellerin' won't change a thing."

"Got a question for you." Jeremiah rested his arms on his thighs, clasping his hands between his knees. "You know who Loraine is? The one Madeline mentioned awhile ago?"

Something slapped against the bars, and Jeremiah turned to look at the prisoner, who now clasped his hands around the steel rods enclosing him.

"I know who she was." Contempt dripped from every word. "Some no-account piece of trash, living out in shanty town. Miss Do Gooder just had to help her and ended up saddled with her kid. If she hadn't run away, I'd have taken care of the brat."

Remembering the sweet weight of little Pearl when she rested on his chest during the dust storm, Jeremiah jumped up and headed toward the cell. He'd reach between the bars with his fists and teach the man a lesson.

"Don't do anything stupid. He's not worth it."

The sheriff's icy tone sliced through Jeremiah's anger, and he stopped in his tracks. He wanted Johnstone to suffer for what he'd done to Madeline and her daughter, but maybe the judge should get here soon, before Jeremiah completely lost his temper with the scoundrel.

As he turned back toward Bill, he forced his hands out of the fists they'd formed. "I'll mosey on up to see Philip before I return to the ranch. Got a question or two to ask him."

Mosey wasn't exactly what he did. In his anger, his pace increased until his breaths came harder than usual. Arriving on Philip's front porch, Jeremiah took a minute to control his breathing and flex his aching hands.

"That you, Jerry?"

With his thoughts in turmoil, Jeremiah hadn't even noticed Philip stepping into the open doorway.

"Come on in here." Philip turned back toward his rocking chair. "Somethin' sure is eatin' at ya. What's on yer mind?"

Jeremiah swept his hat from his head and followed his old friend inside. "Lots of things."

"Well, spit 'em out. Got plenty a-time to listen." He dropped into the cushioned seat and set the chair in motion, the familiar squeak bringing a degree of comfort to Jeremiah.

He hung his hat on a hook beside the door but didn't sit down. He could think better on his feet. His strides measured the distance to the window opening toward the west. On the other side of the vast expanse of scattered trees, desert, and sagebrush, mountains rose toward the sky. He studied the jagged line drawn by the peaks. A different world existed out there on the horizon. Maybe even more of the gold that had made their town thrive, but its siren call didn't affect Jeremiah. He'd had all of the mining he wanted. Ranching fit him better. He did thank the gold for paying for the ranch, though.

He could hear Philip's chair creaking against the floor, but his friend gave him plenty of time to gather his thoughts. When he turned back toward Philip, the old miner's eyes held a warm expression that showed acceptance of whatever Jeremiah had to tell him. A man didn't have many friends like that in his lifetime. Jeremiah was glad he'd found his.

"I'm not sure how to start." He scratched his head. "You know I haven't been too keen on Miss Mercer since she came."

"I did notice a time er two." Philip shook his shaggy head. "But not always."

"That's been a problem." Jeremiah stuffed his hands in his front pockets. "I was afraid she was just a gold digger, coming out here to fleece you out of your money."

Philip snorted. "I knew she weren't the minute I seen her."

"The first time I saw her, before I knew who she was, I

thought differently too." The admission brought a flush to Jeremiah's face. "Actually, I was drawn to her beauty." He hadn't mentioned that to anyone else and wasn't sure he should have mentioned it to Philip.

"Who wouldn't be?" Philip's cackle filled the room. "She's right purty, that one. But her beauty goes clean through."

The words echoed Jeremiah's previous thoughts. The fact that Philip had sunk his pick in the heart of the ore didn't make him feel any better. And all those words Sam Oldman had preached still tumbled in his head.

"Remember I went to the service last Sunday?"

Philip let out another cackle. "I wondered when you'd come to yer senses and talk about it."

"What's to talk about? I went with you. That's all."

"Then why'd ya bring it up?" The old man's piercing eyes drilled straight through Jeremiah like they were heading for the mother lode.

He wondered if Philip could read his thoughts. "Been thinking about what the preacher said. You know, about judging other people."

Philip nodded but didn't say a word, even though his eyes held Jeremiah captive.

"I didn't even realize how wrong I was about Madeline"—her name tasted like a sweet dessert on his tongue—"until just a little while ago."

Philip stopped the chair from rocking and inched forward. "What happened?"

"A scoundrel came to town and accused Madeline of terrible things."

Gripping the armrests, Philip scowled at Jeremiah. "Horace Johnstone's here in Golden?" The question roared through the room.

"How'd you know his name?" Jeremiah didn't know what to think about his friend's reaction. "Did someone come up here and tell you before I came?"

"No, Madeline told me 'bout the man. I think he's a swindler who's done stole Madeline's father's wealth. She don't realize it yet, but I hope she sees him fer what he is real soon."

Jeremiah knew Johnstone had done bad things to Madeline, but could he be a crook too? A new thought, for sure. But Philip knowing all about this man and his coming was a surprise to Jeremiah.

He dropped onto the sofa. "Madeline told you about him?"

Philip nodded. "No secrets between us. I done asked her to marry me, so she and Pearl can be my heirs. 'Course, I could jist make a will to say that, I guess."

Those knots in Jeremiah's gut were tightening again. He hadn't realized marriage between Madeline and Philip was really on the horizon. He loved Philip like a father, more than he ever loved the man who took such pleasure in beating a helpless boy. But nothing inside him wanted Philip to marry Madeline. What could he do now?

"So what happened when Johnstone made his appearance?"

Jeremiah was so lost in his own thoughts, he almost didn't catch the question. "She…disproved the man's accusations, and the sheriff threw him in jail."

A smile crept across Philip's wrinkles. "Wonder how long Bill can keep him?"

Jeremiah shook his head, trying to get his mind back into the conversation, which had taken a real detour from what he had in mind when he came to Philip's. "He opened Madeline's mail back in Boston, plus we caught him rifling through the sheriff's desk. Sheriff's planning on holding him until the territorial judge comes back around. Could be quite awhile."

Philip slid to the back of the chair and set it to rocking again. "Now why did ya want to talk 'bout Sam's sermon?"

The man was lightning fast in changing the subject. Jeremiah had a hard time keeping up. "Ma took me to church before she died. I'd never heard a sermon like the one Sam preached. The old ones were all about the fires of hell, and they scared me to death. Sam seemed to be talking to the life I've been living. Like he was walking in my boots."

Philip chuckled. "He's really good, ain't he? A sermon's no good if'n it don't set ya to thinkin'."

"I've been doing plenty of that, 'specially since I found out how I'd misjudged Miss Mercer." He decided maybe he should call her that since Philip planned to marry her. Maybe it would help him put a barrier between himself and her. A barrier he wouldn't dare cross now that he knew about the upcoming wedding. Or could he?

Philip held up one hand. "I know ya don't like me to talk 'bout the good Lord, but He's tryin' to get yer attention, Jerry. A spiritual thing." Philip shook his head with certainty.

Philip's words stabbed at Jeremiah, making him even more uncomfortable than before. And why? He wasn't a rank sinner like some. He lived right—at least he tried to. Treated his fellow man with kindness—usually. He just wanted to know how bad it was that he'd misjudged Madeli...Miss Mercer. Maybe he'd go to church with Philip again. Couldn't hurt. Last time it didn't. Except for this terrible knot in his stomach.

He stood and snatched his hat from the hook. "Sorry to rush off, but I need to get back to the ranch."

It wasn't exactly a lie, but he was leaving because he didn't want to discuss anything *spiritual* with Philip. Besides, he sure didn't want to blurt out his feelings for Madeline in a weak moment and hurt Philip. Probably the older man knew he was running away. Jeremiah hastened his pace even as he tried to figure out what it was that had him on the run. He wished he knew. Something was eating on him. Could he face whatever it was when it really came down to it? He sure hoped so.

CHAPTER 22

*Y*esterday had been such a busy day, Maddy hadn't spent any time with Philip. Today she'd remedy that situation. As soon as she finished feeding, cleaning, and dressing Pearl, she headed up the hill toward the lovely adobe house. This walk was becoming a familiar part of her routine, greeting those who were out and about in Golden, noticing the differences in the landscape from Boston. Even though the dwelling was small in comparison to her mansion in Boston, she loved visiting there. In many ways, it felt more homey. Her visits with Philip were enjoyable too. He'd lived an interesting life that he freely shared with her.

Truly, her life had changed since she came to Golden. She had more purpose, and here there were no mansions that shut out the poorer people in town. There wasn't a sense of difference between classes. She'd gotten to know all the women who worshiped at the hotel. They welcomed her with open arms, making her feel accepted, as if she'd always been one of them. On several occasions, she'd been invited to lunch or to help with a quilting bee or sewing circle.

She could almost forget how coddled she'd been, but she

didn't want to completely forget how wonderful her father and mother had been. Those memories were precious. However, she never wanted to be so dependent again. Although she thanked God for her family and the way she'd been reared, Golden was becoming more home to her, since it was here she'd really blossomed into a responsible woman. Even if she didn't actually have her own place.

Of course, Philip had offered to marry her so she could move into his house and make it her own. Was that what she should do? She wasn't so sure. She didn't feel a peace about doing that. Philip was a good man, and she had come to love him, but not as she should a husband. In the back of her mind, Maddy still clung to the chance that she would one day give Pearl brothers and sisters. But her financial situation since coming here was precarious, and if she married Philip, all Pearl needed would be provided. He'd already helped Maddy financially by buying things for her and Pearl, but she didn't feel right continuing to accept his help if he wanted more from her.

"Good morning, Madeline."

She had been so lost in thought she hadn't noticed Martha Henderson coming toward her. "Good morning. Isn't it lovely out here today?"

Martha peered at Pearl. "And your daughter is enjoying being out in the sunshine, isn't she?"

Pearl jumped in her arms, and Maddy had to grab her before she fell. "She's a handful when we're out here."

"Just wait until she starts walking. I remember chasing my Rosie down this road many a time."

Maddy glanced down at the dirt, since they'd left the cobblestones behind. "I'm glad Pearl isn't walking yet. Actually, when do babies usually start?"

Her friend studied the few clouds for a minute. "Well, Hank walked when he was only nine months old, but Rosie and Lynette didn't start until they were almost a year old. Of course, they crawled all over the place before that." She shaded her eyes with one hand and stared down toward town. "I've got to go. Nice talking to you, Madeline."

Crawling, then walking. Maddy hadn't considered the ramifications of these. Pearl didn't have much room for either in the hotel room. Something had to happen—and soon.

If she married Philip, she wasn't sure how other people would react. Would they think less of Philip or her? A sham marriage would be an easy answer, but Philip deserved better than that.

She didn't want to lose their easy relationship, but somehow her situation had to change. Maybe she could sell some of her mother's jewelry. But she didn't want to let any of the pieces go, because they were all she had left of her mother.

Pearl squirmed, and Maddy shifted her to one hip and started up the hill again.

She enjoyed taking care of Philip and making his home more comfortable for him. After all his stories about what it was like when he was one of the first settlers in this area, she wanted to make his later years better. Her final decision wouldn't be an easy one either way.

Pearl loved going to the house on the hill. Even though her weight offset that of the food basket in her other arm, Maddy'd be glad when they reached the front porch.

A laugh burst from Pearl's lips as she waved her hands in the air. Hanging onto her was becoming harder.

"You love being outside, don't you, my Pearl of great price?" Maddy held her closer and dropped a quick kiss on her cheek. "We're almost there. Soon you'll get to see Philip."

Pearl patted a slobbery hand against Maddy's cheek. Maddy quickly turned so she could kiss the sweet fingers, not caring about the wet mess on her own face.

"Saw ya comin'." Philip stood on the edge of the porch. Leaning on his cane, his balance looked precarious.

He'd become more unsteady on his feet lately. Maddy hoped he wouldn't topple over before she climbed the steps. She worried about what would happen to him if no one came to check on him. He might not live very long. That thought squeezed her heart. She didn't want him to die.

"How's my girl this mornin'?" His eyes gleamed as he studied the baby.

Maddy reached the porch. "You can hold onto my arm while we go inside. When you're seated, I'll give Pearl to you."

"Yer a good woman, Madeline." He grabbed onto the arm carrying the food basket and tottered into the house beside her.

"I know you love being outside on such a beautiful morning, but I wish you'd wait for me inside. Then I could accompany you when you go out." Maddy set the basket on the table while Philip went to his favorite chair.

She nestled Pearl into his arms, but the baby sat up and stared into his face. Her expression radiated glee. And his matched hers.

"That baby looks forward to being with you just as much as you love having her." Maddy took the basket into the kitchen and started unloading the food.

"She's a special lil' darlin'." When Philip started talking gibberish to Pearl, she cooed and jabbered right back until both were laughing out loud.

"Are you hungry?" Maddy called to Philip, hoping he would hear her over all the noise the two were making.

"Sure am."

She quickly pulled a plate from the shelf and filled it with scrambled eggs, bacon, and buckwheat cakes. Then she took the food into the front room. "I can put Pearl on a pallet while you eat. She can play with those spools and the ball I put in the armoire."

After she'd spread a quilt in the middle of the floor, she lifted

Pearl from his arms. Philip seemed reluctant to let go of the baby.

"You can hold her again when you're finished eating."

Maddy went back into the kitchen to get the butter, syrup, and a fork for him. When she came back, he was seated at the table chewing on a piece of crisp bacon. She set down the items and headed back for the coffee she'd carried up in a fruit jar. She poured two mugs full and carried them to the table.

She glanced at Pearl, who had a spool in each hand and was waving them in the air, occasionally clacking them together. "I'm going to sit down with you, because we need to talk." She sat on the edge of the chair, leaning toward him.

"What's on yer mind, Madeline girl?"

She took a sip of the now tepid drink and wished she hadn't. Hot coffee tasted much better. Now how should she approach the subject? "I've been thinking about your proposal."

While she was trying to decide what to say next, he put down his fork. "I don't wanna force ya into anythin'."

"I know that." She reached across the table and clasped his hand. Age spots and wrinkles gave it character, and his grip was surprisingly strong. "I don't want to bring shame on either of us. If I were to marry you, people would think I was taking advantage of you, and I'd never do that."

When he raised his hand to interrupt, she rushed her words, so she could finish before he said anything. "I've come to love you as if you were my grandfather. And I want to honor you that way. If we married in name only, as you suggested, it would be a mockery of what I feel for you and a mockery of the real marriages around us. I like what we have right now. A friendship that is strong as a family bond. And I want that to continue."

She paused, and he took his chance. "Ya finished?"

After she nodded, he continued, "I like what we have too.

You, me, and Pearl. Ya feel like family to me already. So let's jist keep it that way."

Relieved, she sat back in the chair. "That's what I was trying to say."

"Madeline, ya know I might not last much longer." He continued to clasp her hand tightly in his.

She ducked her head and took a breath. "I know. But I want to make your last days comfortable and happy. Taking care of you and your home gives me great pleasure."

"Make a deal with ya, girl. Let me pay ya fer takin' care of me."

Maddy stretched to her full height. "Family members don't pay other family members for taking care of them."

A twinkle lit his eyes. "If I'm yer grandpappy, I'd give ya presents then. Sometimes money." He shook his head as if for emphasis.

She heaved a deep sigh. "Philip, what am I going to do with you?"

"Jist love me, girl. Jist love me and let me be yer grandpappy."

"I do that already." She realized she meant every word. "I didn't know what I would find when I got here, but I didn't expect to love you like you were family."

A lone tear slipped down his wrinkled cheek. "Yer too good to me, Maddy."

"No, I'm not." She arose and went around the table, clasping her arms around him from behind. "God truly brought us together for His purpose."

I just wish I knew what that purpose was. Surely it wasn't simply to watch this man slowly slip away.

~

*W*hen Sunday arrived, Jeremiah arose with the dawn. Birdsong greeted the sun as it made its way over the mountains. He loved listening to the different birdcalls—especially the doves. They brought a feeling of peace. As though everything was right in the world. But everything wasn't right. Turmoil waged war inside him.

After he dressed he made his way to the cook shack. A woodpecker tapped in rhythm on one of the oaks that surrounded the ranch house, and a jay flew up out of the tree. Maybe there was a nest up there. He'd thought so in the spring. Probably by now all the eggs had hatched and the nest would be empty. Just like his life was empty without a wife and family. A jackrabbit headed out of the brush toward a cluster of cactus, flushing a roadrunner that took off like a flash, leaving a trail of dust in its wake.

Jeremiah loved this ranch. He felt in tune with the land and the animals, the tame ones and the wildlife. If only he had that same kind of peace in his heart. The smell of ham sizzling on the fire tickled his nostrils as he entered the cook shack.

T-Bone had flapjacks and a slab of ham waiting for him. "Yer up early for a Sunday, Boss. Dressed kinda nice. What ya plannin' to do today?"

Jeremiah lifted the mug of coffee and took a swig. The heat traveled down his gullet and hit his stomach like a wildfire. He took a deep breath through his mouth to cool it off. "Going into town."

"Yeah, but ya don't usually dress up like that." The burly man crossed his beefy arms.

"Takin' Philip to church. Thought I might stay awhile." Jeremiah stuffed a huge bite in his mouth, hoping T-Bone would back off.

"Good, I made gingerbread. Ya can take some to the old man."

Jeremiah watched T-Bone saunter back to the kitchen area. Good. Now he could finish his breakfast in peace. Most of the hands would be sleeping late after a night in town. He didn't mind them letting off steam on Saturday night as long as they didn't drink on the ranch. He'd had more than his fill of drunks losing control. Didn't need it here.

T-Bone returned to the dining area with a wrapped package just as Jeremiah finished eating. He thanked T-Bone for his thoughtfulness and headed toward the barn.

As he rode out on Lightning, a pair of red-tailed hawks soared over him almost as if they wanted to go too, but the horse soon outpaced them as they climbed higher and rode the wind current back toward the ranch. Even birds had a mate. The deep, empty ache inside him throbbed. Wasn't he as good as a stupid bird? Philip did pretty good for himself ordering a mail-order bride. Maybe he should write for one too. Naw, she wouldn't be Madeline.

Swede had the wagon ready for him when he arrived in Golden. After handing off Lightning to Swede's good care, Jeremiah drove the wagon up the hill. He arrived a bit early, so Philip was still inside, snoozing in his rocking chair with his chin resting on his chest. Jeremiah hated to wake him, but he knew Philip really looked forward to the church service. After studying the older man for a few minutes, noting how frail he had become, Jeremiah gently touched his shoulder.

Philip's head popped up, and he blinked a couple of times. "Jerry? Time to go to church?"

"Sure is. Here, I brought you something from T-Bone. I'll leave it on the table." Jeremiah wanted to lift the old man and carry him out to the wagon, but he knew that would embarrass Philip.

He offered his arm, and Philip took hold of it to rise from the chair. The older man didn't let go while they walked slowly out on the porch, down the steps, and the few feet to the wagon.

Philip struggled to get his foot up on the step, but he finally managed. And Jeremiah lifted him the rest of the way, setting him gently on the seat.

"Nice mornin', ain't it?" The old miner took a deep breath that turned into a cough, which he covered with his hand-kerchief.

Jeremiah tried not to let Philip know how worried he was about him. His friend looked as though a good stiff breeze could blow him right off his perch. Jeremiah tried to miss the ruts and bumps on the way down to the hotel. The ride was smoother when they reached the cobblestones.

After Jeremiah helped Philip into a chair, he dropped into the seat beside him. The service hadn't quite started, so everyone milled around, visiting. He studied the various clusters of people until he spied Miss Mercer. He couldn't keep his attention from honing in on her.

Wearing a fluffy pink dress, she looked like some kind of penny candy, which made his mouth water, but he wasn't sure whether it was the reminder of candy or her. And on a ribbon that matched the color of her dress, the cameo rested against the hollow of her throat, rocking gently as she talked. Her hair was swept up from her neck as it had been last Sunday. Her eyes sparkled, making him wish she was talking to him instead of a couple ladies. One was holding Pearl, letting the baby play with the ruffles on her dress, but he only glanced toward her, his attention drawn back to the mother. Just gazing at her brought back Jeremiah's longing for a wife and children of his own.

Miss Mercer seemed to belong in Golden. When had that happened? Maybe she looked that way all along, but he had been blinded by judging her motives. Those words he'd spoken on the porch of Philip's house, the ones she'd overheard, tasted bitter in his mouth even today. Why hadn't he watched what he said? He'd never been that critical of anyone before. If she was going to marry Philip, he'd have to train his thoughts to stay far from her. He couldn't have his old friend realize how he felt about his wife.

He glanced up when Sam Oldman headed toward him. "Mornin', Sam."

"I see I didn't scare you off last Sunday." The preacher held out his hand.

Jeremiah stood and clasped it. "Not at all. The service was different from what I'd expected."

"In a good way, I hope." Sam gave a throaty chuckle. "Can't be running off important ranchers."

"Don't know how important I am, but nothing you did or said would run me off." Jeremiah wondered where this was heading. He hoped not into some deeply spiritual discussion.

"Carlos and I just wanted to let you know we'd be out at your ranch early tomorrow morning." He nodded toward the man who had led the singing. "We'll be working there until the remodeling and construction job is done."

"That sounds good to me." Something to keep his mind off Philip and Madeli—Miss Mercer.

The two men headed toward the front of the room to start the service. During the singing, Jeremiah heard phrases he remembered from when he was a boy. But these people sang with pep and enthusiasm, as if they meant every word and weren't bored with the song. On a couple of songs he even got caught up in the melody and rhythm. When some sections were repeated, he found himself joining in. It felt good. Must be something about the music.

Sam laid his unopened Bible on the podium. Then he stood in front of it and talked to the people. "Caroline and I have been providing the meal for Bill's prisoner. I've been taking the food down to Mr. Johnstone."

When Sam said that, Jeremiah grimaced. He didn't even like to hear the man's name. And he sure hoped the man was miserable in that jail cell. He didn't deserve anything better.

"Horace has had a difficult life. Some of it has been his own fault, but he didn't have the kind of raising your kids do."

Doesn't excuse what the man did to Madeline. People were always making excuses for their bad behavior. Now the preacher was doing it for the scoundrel.

"I believe God brought him here so he could hear about our Savior. I've been listening to him and talking to him. Answering lots of his questions. Because I don't want to reveal what he has shared with me, I'm just going to ask you one thing. Please put Horace Johnstone on your prayer lists. Pray for the man every day. I believe he's about ready to make a drastic change in his life, and I want us to be a part of holding out the hope of the Lord to him."

Jeremiah's hands squeezed into fists, so he unfurled them and shoved his fingers into his pockets. Fine words coming from a good preacher, but not very realistic in the world where they lived. Johnstone deserved whatever punishment the law would bring against him. Probably even more than the law allowed. No way would he hope the man changed his life.

Besides, he could merely be stringing the preacher along, hoping things would go easy for him. Jeremiah was glad he wasn't a part of this church. He could never agree with what the preacher asked.

Now Sam was coming out to Jeremiah's ranch to work. He sure hoped the preacher wouldn't try to get him to change his ways. Jeremiah wasn't exactly a reprobate. Didn't Sam just call him an important rancher? Well, his life was just fine the way it was, and he'd tell the preacher so if he started talking religion out at the ranch.

CHAPTER 23

*E*ven though he'd had a hard time falling asleep last night, Jeremiah once again awakened at dawn. All the turmoil going on in his mind kept his belly in an uproar. Maybe T-Bone could give him something for it. But he didn't want to face the man's questions.

He went out to the side of the house where he'd pounded in those stakes. In his mind's eye, he pictured the walls standing and the roof...even the windows that lined the sides letting in the morning sun. When the rooms were finished, they'd expand his house to more than twice its size. A place where he'd be glad to bring a bride, if he could find one.

Madeline.

Jeremiah squelched the name that whispered in his mind.

Even if he had a wife, he wouldn't know how to treat her. He knew most of the people who went to the church services at the hotel probably had good marriages. He could only imagine what went on in the privacy of their homes. All he'd learned growing up was how not to treat a woman. The memories that flashed through his mind were horrible, making him shudder. Women brought to the house were used and abused in ways he wished he'd never witnessed. Even as a boy, then a young man, he'd vowed he'd never do things like that to a woman. And he'd kept that promise. He wouldn't have wanted anyone to treat his mother that way if she'd lived longer. And with the way his father and uncle drank, her dying probably had saved her from later abuse.

The churning in his gut increased. Maybe he should go see T-Bone. He hustled toward the cook shack, leaving a trail of dust in his wake.

Bursting through the open doorway, he nearly ran into his cook. "You got something for a stomachache?"

"Sure thing, Boss." T-Bone hurried to the back and poured water into a glass, vigorously stirring the white powder he added.

Jeremiah hoped the hard whacks the spoon made as it whirled around wouldn't shatter the glass, sending shards flying his way.

"What's got ya in an uproar?" The cook handed the glass to him.

"Just been trying to figure out some things. Nothing major." Except in his own mind.

Jeremiah finished downing the horrible-tasting baking soda and water and let out a loud belch. It brought some relief, but not enough.

T-Bone wiped his hand down the big apron that covered him from knees to chin, leaving greasy streaks. "Ya ain't been this stirred up since I've worked for ya. Only in the last few weeks."

The man had the time period down, but Jeremiah hoped he didn't cipher out the real cause. He didn't want anyone to know how much he longed for a woman like Miss Mercer.

"Hey, T-Bone, you got any good coffee for some hard workers?" The familiar booming voice invaded the tension in Jeremiah.

The cook glanced toward the doorway, and his eyes lit up like Chinese fireworks. He headed toward the coffeepot and mugs. "Sure do. Sit down, Preacher. Can fix ya some eggs too. Got biscuits...ham steak. Jeremiah here ain't et his breakfast either. Maybe I'll join ya too."

The arrival of Sam and his sidekick, Carlos, kept Jeremiah from having to answer T-Bone's other question. At least that was a relief to his mind and heart. Nothing seemed to help his gut.

"You men jist sit down and enjoy the coffee." The cook plopped three mugs on the end of the long table. "Won't take me but a minute to get the rest."

Jeremiah stepped over the bench and sat down. "You're out here bright and early."

Sam and Carlos took their places across from him.

After taking a swig of the coffee, Sam set his cup down. "We wanted to get an early start. See how much we could accomplish today."

Jeremiah understood that rationale. He always liked to jump right into a job and get it done. No need fooling around and dragging things out. "How long you think it'll take?"

"I've looked over the plans you gave me. If I can hire a few extra workers, we might be finished in a week...two at the most."

T-Bone interrupted the conversation by setting heaping plates in front of the two visitors. Steam wafted through the air between the men, carrying a fragrance that could bring a growl to a dead man's stomach. Jeremiah wasn't anywhere near dying. His stomach rumbled loud enough for the hands out on the range to hear.

"Umm, smells good, *señor*." Carlos picked up his biscuit and sank his teeth into it. "Good butter too. You churn it yourself, *amigo?*"

"Sure do." The cook hooked his thumbs under his suspenders. "Cain't have biscuits without butter, you know." He headed back toward the kitchen area for the other two plates.

There was enough churning going on inside Jeremiah to make a couple pounds of that butter if he were trying. He chuckled. "I've gotta thank you, Sam, for telling me first that your wife would be doing the cooking at the hotel. Someone else would have hired him before I could've, and I'd have been in a bad way having to feed all my hands."

"I guess the good Lord wanted you to have him, since you were at Philip's house when I went up to meet him that first day."

Jeremiah winced when the preacher said "the good Lord" just the way Philip always did. There he was already with the God talk. The next week or two might seem like a thousand years if every time Jeremiah was around the preacher and his workers, he was bombarded with that kind of thing. Maybe he should stay out on the range as much as possible.

~

*M*addy knew Sam and Carlos were working on Jeremiah's house this last week, but she had missed seeing the rancher. Somehow, since the moment Mr. Johnstone arrived in town, she hadn't felt the usual animosity emanating from Jeremiah. She wondered if he would continue treating her differently. And she wondered what kind of work they were doing on his house.

She'd never been out to his ranch, so she didn't even know what kind of house was there. Probably an adobe one, since there weren't many trees for lumber. All Philip had told her was that Jeremiah had helped build onto his house, and it made him want to add to his own.

Maddy had spent a lot of time with Philip this week. Her heart ached as she watched him grow weaker. He tried to hide it but wasn't successful. His slow steps often faltered, and when he thought she wasn't looking, he relaxed. Tremors took over his arms and hands—sometimes even his head and neck.

She wished she knew more about what she could do to help him. The wonderful man had made such a difference in her life that she wanted to return the favor. And Pearl loved being around Philip. Maddy marveled once again at how well the two connected. She'd never thought about babies really taking to the aged. But nothing was sweeter than watching them interact with each other. They had a language all their own.

Enough dawdling. She needed to get dressed before Pearl awoke. Then after she took care of her daughter's needs, they'd go to church.

Maddy remembered that Jeremiah had come to the services a couple of times. She wondered if he would be there today. Since he insisted on coming into town to bring Philip to church, there was no reason for him not to stay. Just thinking about him caused elation to surge through her, leaving a strange fluttering in her midsection. She tamped down the feelings. If only...

Because dressing and feeding Pearl took longer than usual, Philip was already in the dining room when Maddy arrived. Disappointed that Jeremiah wasn't sitting beside him, she glanced around to see who all was there. Like a piece of iron drawn to a magnet, her gaze arrowed straight toward the tall rancher talking to the sheriff.

With his Stetson removed, Jeremiah's curls fell haphazardly across his brow. He raked his fingers through his hair and patted the waves down, probably trying to tame them. Evidently he hadn't had time for a haircut lately because his hair fell past his collar in the back. For just a moment, Maddy wondered what it would feel like to tame those curls herself. Sarah often cut Frank's hair. If Maddy were working on Jeremiah's hair, she'd probably leave it a little long in the back anyway. She liked... What was she thinking?

Shaking these thoughts from her mind, she headed toward Philip. Pearl had spied her friend and almost leaned too far toward him. Maddy caught her before she fell and set the baby in the old miner's lap. The two started their nonsensical conversation—with lots of jabbers and giggles by the baby, accompanied by Philip's gibberish.

Maddy laughed out loud at their antics. How her manners had changed since she left Boston. She felt a freedom to express herself openly without having to question if it was appropriate. Besides, the Bible said that laughter was good medicine. She'd never felt better in her whole life.

~

Jeremiah had been in an intense conversation with Bill, so he hadn't noticed Miss Mercer arriving with Pearl until her laugh rang out. He shot a glance at her, and the way she looked captured his attention—relaxed, at ease with her world. He'd never seen her so beautiful. A special glow surrounded her.

His breath hitched, and he turned back toward Bill, hoping his friend hadn't noticed. "So what did you do about it?" Maybe that was the appropriate question. He hoped.

Obviously not, since Bill shook his head and laughed. "You weren't paying any attention to what I was saying." It wasn't a question. Just a statement of fact.

Jeremiah couldn't deny it. "Not really."

Sam called everyone to prayer, so Jeremiah bowed his head, glad for the preacher's interruption of that conversation. He hoped Bill would let him off the hook, but he was afraid they'd revisit this topic later.

Jeremiah didn't close his eyes. He turned them once again toward Philip and his soon-to-be family. The old man, young woman, and baby would make a good family, but Philip looked more like a grandfather for Miss Mercer than a husband. She needed a younger, stronger man to protect her and provide for her family. A deep hunger gnawed on him, but it had nothing to do with food.

With all his heart, he wished he felt a freedom to pursue a relationship with Madeline since she was the kind of woman he dreamed about. But Philip was the first man who'd treated Jeremiah with any respect. He'd taken Jeremiah under his wing and helped him make wise business decisions. Over the years, he'd come to love the old miner as a father. A decent man would never try to take a woman away from his best friend. And, like it or not, Jeremiah considered himself a decent man.

After Sam finished praying, Carlos strummed his strange guitar, and the people started singing. Jeremiah wondered if he should've gone on home instead of staying for the service. He didn't belong with this group. He was an outsider, no matter how well they treated him. The wall that separated them was religious, and he hadn't been willing to tear it down.

When the singing ended, Sam said he had an announcement to make. "I've been talking to the prisoner every evening when I take him his supper. Thank you for praying for him. Mr. Johnstone has asked a lot of questions, and we've been reading the Bible together. Last night he gave his life to the Lord. His whole attitude is different today. When I took him breakfast, he sounded like a completely different man."

Several praise-the-Lords erupted from all over the room—some quiet, a few resounding. The phrase kept repeating in Jeremiah's head and reached down toward his heart. This feeling upset him—emotionally and even physically. He didn't know what to do about it. At least this type of stirring didn't bring the churning to his gut that had been burning there for weeks.

Jeremiah had a hard time staying focused on what Sam was saying. His thoughts bounced from Philip and his influence on Jeremiah's life to a scoundrel like Johnstone becoming a Christian. How come a man like that could change in an instant and become accepted by the congregation? Shouldn't he face the consequences of his actions? Where was the justice in that?

What if it wasn't real? Maybe Johnstone only said what he thought the preacher wanted to hear. When he got out of jail, if he did, he could turn back into the unprincipled man he was before. Jeremiah had heard of jailhouse conversions. He'd never believed any of them were real. But Johnstone wasn't really facing death, was he? Jeremiah wasn't sure what charges Bill had against the man. Maybe he should find out.

"Forgiveness." Sam's word penetrated his swirling thoughts. "Forgiveness is the key to a satisfied life. If you harbor unfor-giveness against anyone, it'll eat on you and do you more harm than it does the person you're not forgiving."

Jeremiah was still chewing on the point when Sam opened his Bible.

"It's important to God that we forgive others. In the portion of the Sermon on the Mount found in Matthew 6, the Lord stresses that we must forgive others if we want His forgiveness. He even included it as part of the model prayer He taught His disciples."

Some of the things Sam said didn't mean a lot to Jeremiah. He hadn't heard these ideas before. But something felt right about what the man was saying. Having to forgive before you could receive forgiveness. And right now, Jeremiah wanted a clean slate. He wanted to be forgiven for all the things he'd done wrong.

"You must forgive people even when they've committed grievous wrongs against you."

Whoa. Grievous wrongs? Jeremiah knew what those were. He carried the scars of many on his back. He didn't even know if his old man and his uncle were still alive, and he hadn't cared to find out...until now. Could he forgive them? He didn't think so. Where did that leave him?

CHAPTER 24

*P*astor Oldman's message settled into Maddy's heart and started putting down roots.

Pearl had fallen asleep toward the last of the sermon. Even the song at the end didn't awaken her. All her playing with Philip, and then Martha Henderson and Harriet Stone, had tired the baby out. Maddy shifted her daughter from her lap up to her shoulder and arose from the chair.

Sarah glided toward her. "Would you like me to take the sweet babe up to her bed? I'll stay with her, and you can visit some more. I know how much you enjoy that."

When they transferred Pearl from one person's shoulder to the other, she raised her head, then plopped it down again but never really woke up.

"Thank you. I wanted to talk to Pastor Oldman."

While visiting with Martha and Harriet, Maddy waited her turn to talk to the minister. That made her the last person in line.

Pastor Oldman took her hand, engulfing it in his large one and covering it with the other. "I always enjoy seeing you in the services, Madeline. And Philip has a good time with your daughter." He glanced around. "Where is Pearl? She really made the rounds this morning."

"Sarah took her up to bed. I'm afraid your sermon put her to sleep." Maddy smiled so he would know she was joking.

He threw back his head, and his rich laugh echoed in the large room. "That's a good one." Everyone turned to look at them.

Maddy withdrew her hand. She made her tone serious. "But I listened to every word. Your message went straight to...where I have...hidden unforgiveness."

The same seriousness entered the pastor's eyes. He glanced around long enough to ascertain their relative privacy before continuing in a voice just above a whisper, "I wanted to talk to you about that, Madeline. I wasn't sure how to approach the matter, but you've given me an open door."

Maddy wasn't sure where he was heading with this conversation. Did he have perception to read her heart? "So what are you talking about?"

"Horace Johnstone." After pronouncing the name, Pastor Oldman stood there as if waiting for her to assimilate what he'd said.

As if she could at that moment. Mr. Johnstone was the one man who had treated her the worst. The memory of how authoritarian he'd been back in Boston made her clamp her teeth on her lower lip. She had tried to tell him what she wanted, but he cast her desires away as just so much garbage and forced his plans on her. The only way to escape from him and keep her daughter safe was to make the long trip across the vast United States to this western territory.

And he called her a thief. She caressed her mother's cameo, fingering the intricate carving. How could he desecrate something so precious to her with his lies? Did she want to forgive him? No!

After she, Pearl, and the Sneeds settled into the community

here, she had been able to push the man out of her mind, thinking she was out of his reach. She could forget that he ever lived. But she hadn't considered forgiving him.

Then his arrival in Golden had put her off balance. Brought back all those memories of the horrible things he'd said and done to her. After the sheriff arrested him, Maddy finally realized she had changed since she left Boston. Horace Johnstone no longer had any hold on her.

But could she forgive him? That was a hard question.

The words from the sermon tumbled over and over in her mind. To receive God's forgiveness, she would have to forgive even Horace Johnstone. She didn't really feel like it, but she could choose to forgive him because God had forgiven her. The Bible hadn't said anything about having to *feel* like forgiving the other person. It would have to be a conscious decision. Was this a decision she could make?

~

Jeremiah stood a short distance from Madeline and Sam Oldman and managed to hear their conversation despite their lowered voices. How could the man expect her to forgive Horace Johnstone after all he'd done to her? Yes, he had preached about forgiveness, but wasn't this instance beyond what any human could be expected to do?

"Madeline." The preacher's gaze never left hers. "Mr. Johnstone asked me to bring you to see him. He wants to beg your forgiveness in person. Do you think you could face him?"

No! Why in tarnation would the preacher ask her to go and put herself through such an ordeal? Jeremiah wanted to step in and tell the man off. Oldman had no right to take her there. She should be protected from men like Johnstone. A jailhouse was no place for a lady like her.

Madeline smiled up at Sam, her gaze never wavering. "After

carefully considering all this, I really believe that's what the good Lord would have me do."

This time when Jeremiah heard the words *the good Lord*, they didn't bother him as they had before. If God wanted her to face the man and forgive him, maybe there was still hope for Jeremiah.

He stepped forward. "I'd like to go with the two of you when you talk to him, Miss Mercer, if I may."

She looked confused for a moment. Then she nodded, lighting a tiny flame of hope in his heart. "Thank you, Jeremiah. I'd like that...if it's all right with Pastor Oldman."

When Madeline glanced toward the parson, he agreed.

"I know they're working on putting the meal out for all of us, but could we go right now?" Sam stared straight at Jeremiah.

"It's fine with me."

"Then that's settled." Madeline's firm tone brought Jeremiah's attention back to her.

So many things about her that he liked, besides her obvious physical beauty. She was a good mother, she took loving care of Philip, and she had compassion for others. She even showed a surprising strength in this situation.

The two men walked on either side of her. When they stepped off the boardwalk to cross the road, Madeline unfurled her parasol. The New Mexican sun beat down on them, and the lacy fabric shaded her very little from the unrelenting rays. Jeremiah didn't think that thing really made much difference, but holding it above her head enhanced her beauty. Because her hands were trembling, the ruffles around the edge of the sunshade shook, and she started twirling the handle with nervous fingers. Jeremiah wondered if he should try to talk her out of continuing toward the jail. Would it do any good?

She glanced up at Sam. "How is Mr. Johnstone...really?" Her voice sounded more tentative than it had while they were back at the hotel.

"As I said before, he is a different man from the one that rode into Golden."

Jeremiah couldn't let the idea alone. "Do you think he meant it? Or was he just saying what he knew you wanted to hear?"

Madeline cut her eyes up at him, and this time she didn't look too friendly. "How can you ask that, Jeremiah, without even giving the man a chance? Wouldn't you want a chance for a new life?"

He was speechless. How could she know so much about what was in his heart? Yet her question stated exactly what he did want. To be sure he had a chance for forgiveness. But he wasn't anywhere near ready to offer forgiveness to the two men who'd hurt him the most. His chances weren't looking too good right now.

"Bill got here ahead of us." Sam nodded toward the sheriff's office.

Standing in the doorway, Bill was every inch a lawman. His badge caught the sunlight and shot a glimmer toward them. He even wore his six-guns.

Madeline stepped up on the boardwalk outside the open doorway and snapped her parasol closed. "Hello, Sheriff. I thought I saw you at the service this morning."

Bill tipped his hat toward her. "You did, Miss Mercer, but when I heard you talking about coming down here, I decided I should look official. Since you want to talk to the prisoner and all."

The sheriff led them through the doorway. Madeline followed, flanked by Sam and Jeremiah. He didn't plan on leaving her side during whatever was about to happen in the jail.

Madeline stopped beside the desk and turned to the sheriff. "Are we going to meet in here or in there?" She glanced toward the walls of bars but quickly averted her gaze.

"I don't want to take the prisoner out of the cell right now." Bill shifted from one booted foot to the other.

She nodded. "Then Pastor Oldman and I will just go in there." Since her hands trembled, this firm declaration sounded weak in Jeremiah's ears.

He moved closer to her. "I'll go with you too."

Madeline's gaze tangled with his, then she stared into his eyes as if she wanted to read his mind. He couldn't turn away from her assessment if he'd wanted to.

"Thank you, Jeremiah, that will be nice." Her lilting tones sang in his heart. This woman would be the death of him yet.

Bill unlocked the cell door, and Sam picked up the chair that sat in front of the desk. He dragged it across the wooden floor into the enclosure. "Here, Miss Mercer. You can sit on this. We don't mind standing."

While she sat and arranged her skirt, the sweet aroma of flowers filled the cell...and Jeremiah's head. Finally, she laid the parasol in her lap, holding it with both hands. She appeared so out of place in a jail cell.

Bill pushed the door closed behind them, turning the key with a loud squawk. Then he leaned both arms on one of the crossbars, his eyes scrutinizing every inch of the area.

By the time Madeline was settled, Johnstone stood beside his hard bunk. "You brought quite a group with you, Pastor."

Sam chuckled. "I did, didn't I? Hope you don't mind."

Johnstone stared at Jeremiah a moment, then looked away. "It's all right with me, if it's all right with Miss Mercer."

The man looked at Madeline, but Jeremiah didn't see any of the animosity and possessiveness in his expression that he'd exhibited that first day. Maybe this would turn out all right. He sure hoped so.

Sam cleared his throat. "Why don't I pray before we get started?"

"Sounds good to me, Preacher." Johnstone bowed his head.

Jeremiah glanced toward Madeline. Her head was bowed, her chin trembling. Everyone had their heads down, except him. So he lowered his but didn't close his eyes. Didn't want to give Johnstone a chance to jump them when they weren't alert. He especially didn't want the man to touch Madeline in any way. Just because the prisoner had cleaned up for this meeting didn't mean he wouldn't try something.

"Amen." Sam shot a glance toward Johnstone. "It's all up to you now, Horace."

The prisoner sank onto the thin mattress of his bunk, making him more on the level with Madeline. He leaned forward with his hands clasped between his knees. If the man got one inch closer to her, Jeremiah was poised to intervene.

"I owe you a number of apologies, Miss Mercer." His voice took on a husky tone, a surprise to Jeremiah. "I'm not proud of what I tried to do. I knew it was wrong, and I'm sorry I almost messed up your life."

When he stopped talking, every eye turned toward him, waiting for him to continue. Surely that wasn't all the man was going to say. Jeremiah knew Johnstone hadn't said nearly enough to Madeline.

"There's no excuse for what I did. But I will explain the best I can. When I was young, I was orphaned. Lived in a stable. Took care of the horses." Johnstone cleared his throat, and Jeremiah caught a glimpse of moisture gathering in the corners of his eyes. "I was teased and bullied...a lot. You can just imagine what they did with my first name. Horsey, Horse Boy, and other more unsavory names. I hated it, and all I wanted to do was become powerful enough that no one could ever intimidate or torment me again."

Johnstone rose to his feet and strode across the small distance to the barred window. He stared out as he continued, "I worked hard until I finally was nearing the prize." He turned to look at Madeline, who hadn't taken her eyes off the man. "Your father hired me and gave me a responsible job. I planned to work myself into a partnership. He was getting older, and he didn't have a son. I wanted to make myself indispensable to him."

Madeline's posture stiffened, her hands clasping the folded parasol so tight her knuckles whitened. Jeremiah wished there was something he could do to keep her from being disturbed by this man. He wanted to smash Johnstone's face against the adobe wall. Instead he took a deep breath and released it gradually.

"Before I could do that, your father dropped dead." The poison of the stark words hung in the air.

Madeline gasped. Tears slipped down her cheeks. She dropped her head and pulled a hanky from her sleeve to pat them away.

"I'm sorry to bring up your grief again, but you have to know why I was trying to force you to marry me. That was the only way I'd ever get my hands on his business…and enough money to make me powerful." He stopped and slumped against the wall, all the starch gone out of him.

Madeline raised her head to a regal height. "I knew you didn't love me, Mr. Johnstone. I just couldn't imagine why you would want to marry me."

"What I want to know, Miss Mercer, is…could you ever forgive me for what I did? I didn't mean to scare you. Or make you leave everything you know and run so far away. For that I'm truly sorry." He stood, dejection in every line of his face and body.

Madeline stood. "I came here, Mr. Johnstone, because I believe God would have me forgive you. I don't feel like it, but I choose to do so."

The surprise in Johnstone's expression would have been almost comical, if Jeremiah hadn't been mad at the man for hurting Madeline.

"Now, Pastor Oldman, Jeremiah"—she glanced from one man to the other—"I'd like to go eat dinner, wouldn't you?"

"But I'm not finished, Miss Mercer." Johnstone tried to approach her, but Jeremiah stepped between them. "I need to tell you what else I did."

"Don't push your luck, Mr. Johnstone." The firmness in her tone was like a rock. "I have forgiven you, but don't try my patience. I will tell you this, though. What you planned for evil in my life, God intended for good, and coming to Golden has been a wonderful thing for me."

Bill unlocked the door, and Madeline led the way from the cell. She continued out into the street and unfurled that parasol. Without saying another word, she headed up the middle of the road toward the hotel.

"I certainly hope there's still some food left for us." Her words floated back toward Jeremiah and Bill.

Even though she was a tiny woman, her pace made Jeremiah lengthen his stride to keep up with her. He admired her and the strength of her belief in God. But more than that, he allowed the small flame of hope in his heart to grow. If a man like Johnstone could be forgiven, maybe Jeremiah should learn even more about God, who could make a person strong enough to offer that kind of forgiveness.

Right after dinner he needed to talk to Philip.

CHAPTER 25

*E*very step Maddy took toward the hotel brought her a sense of relief. Strength gradually returned to her trembling limbs. While Pastor Oldman and Jeremiah chatted, she mulled over all that had happened.

Maddy had dreaded the meeting with Mr. Johnstone more than she'd ever dreaded anything, but the event was far different from what she imagined. Parts were really hard to take, but she could understand, a little bit, why he'd done what he did. That didn't make it right. And that's not why she forgave him. Only the love of the Lord had helped her do that. But in another way, she had a hard time not pitying the man. Evidently, he never knew what it was like to have true friends. How sad. Where would she be without her friends? *Perish the thought.*

Dinner at the hotel was wonderful. She could relax and enjoy herself with friends who had been nothing but good to her. They accepted her for who she was. And they liked her. What a relief.

She heaped delicious food on her plate before she sat down. Later, while she helped the women clean up, she couldn't remember what she ate. But she remembered the shared conversations. The fellowship had been much more important than the meal. It satisfied a hunger no food could touch. Having faced the difficult decision to offer forgiveness to Mr. Johnstone and coming through unscathed made her feel stronger. She was truly blessed.

Jeremiah jumped right in and helped the men set the room back the way it needed to be for the rest of the week. Now he was heading out the door with Philip.

Maddy hurried over and gave the old miner a big hug. She loved him more than any man alive. Almost as much as she'd loved her dear father.

Jeremiah hovered over them with a smile. "I need to get Philip up to his house. He looks really tired."

"Don't go talkin' 'bout me like I'm not here." The humor in Philip's eyes belied his gruff statement. "'Sides, I'm never too tired fer a hug from a pretty lady."

He gave Maddy a saucy wink, so she kissed him on his cool, leathery cheek.

Philip grinned up at Jeremiah. "See what happens when yer nice to her. Take a lesson."

When she glanced at Jeremiah, a red tinge darkened his cheeks. Was he blushing? She'd never noticed a man do that before. And she wasn't sure how she felt about it. Why would Philip's joking cause this reaction in Jeremiah? He should be used to it after all the years they'd spent together.

Something else to ponder.

~

Jeremiah couldn't get out of there quickly enough. He didn't want anyone to guess what he was thinking. That he'd like a hug and a kiss from her too. The heat in his cheeks told him they were probably red. He hadn't blushed like that since he was a young whelp.

Watching how the stress of the meeting affected Madeline, and enjoying how she relaxed in the company of friends, opened his heart to her more than ever. The very idea of a future with her caused a longing inside he couldn't quell, no matter how hard he tried. Philip was one lucky man, no doubt about it.

After he had Philip on the seat of the wagon, Jeremiah drove up the bumpy road.

"Good service today, wadn't it?" Philip grinned wider than the mouth of the mine he'd owned.

"Uh-huh." Jeremiah didn't want to talk about anything out here in the open. His questions were better asked in privacy.

"So what was so all-fired important that you, Sam, and Madeline lit out after church?"

"Sam wanted us to talk to the prisoner." Jeremiah clamped his lips together. He sure hadn't wanted to take her down there, but he wasn't about to let her go without him.

"That so?" Philip's brows drew together. "Cain't imagine why."

"I'll tell you all about it after we get inside." He tried to keep his words from sounding harsh.

Philip nodded as they arrived in front of his house.

Jeremiah helped him inside and got him settled in his favorite chair. "I really want to have a serious talk with you."

"Good." Philip nodded. "I knowed ya would someday."

"Oh, you did, did you?" How could Philip have known when he didn't know it himself until today?

He pulled a chair close in front of Philip and dropped into it, leaning forward. "I'm not sure where to start."

"The beginnin'd be good." Philip set his chair in motion but didn't take his eyes off Jeremiah.

The old man's gaze probed into the depths of Jeremiah's mind. He hoped Philip couldn't read the thoughts residing there.

"I've told you a lot about my raising...or the lack thereof." He paused, trying to decide what words to use. "Some things I've never told anybody."

"Don't tell me anything ya don't wanna." Philip looked relaxed.

Jeremiah felt wound as tight as a watch spring. "It's kinda hard to talk about personal things. I'm not used to doing that, but I need to. Since Ma died, I haven't had much use for...God. I thought He wasn't there for me when I needed Him." He shifted in his chair, trying to find a more comfortable position. There wasn't one. "You've talked a lot about *the good Lord*, and I passed all of it off as the ramblings of an old man."

A smile teased the corners of Philip's lips, but he didn't say anything.

"I've come to know Sam Oldman and Carlos more while they've worked on my house. I trust them and think they might have something I don't. The sermons I've heard Sam preach have picked at my thoughts a lot. I can't seem to keep them from intruding." He scratched an itch on one cheek but couldn't touch the itch inside his mind. "That one today was really something."

"Sure was a mighty fine sermon." Philip stopped the chair's rhythmic movements. "What's that got to do with you, Sam, and Madeline talkin' to the prisoner?"

"You know how the man treated her before she came here, and how he was when he first arrived. Well, last night he asked Sam to pray with him to become a Christian, and Johnstone told him he wanted to beg Madeline's forgiveness in person. I really didn't want her to go, but it wasn't my place to stop her. So I went along with them...just in case."

That must've pleased Philip because he grinned and set the chair back in motion.

"I wanted to be sure the man didn't do anything to hurt Madeline." At least that's what he told himself.

"Ya didn't think Sam and the sheriff could protect her?" Philip had a way of cutting through a subject to get right to the meat of it.

Jeremiah cleared his throat. "Yeah, they could. I guess I just wanted to be there."

"So what happened?" Philip's color had improved, and he was more animated than Jeremiah had seen him in quite awhile.

Maybe he hadn't been coming to see Philip often enough. The old man needed to be involved in what was happening with the people who were important to him. Jeremiah would make sure he came by more often simply to shoot the breeze.

"Johnstone explained what he'd been doing when he tried to force Madeline to marry him." He told Philip all the details he could remember.

He left out how much he'd been watching Madeline and her responses to what the man said. This discussion wasn't about how he felt, but about what Madeline went through while they were there.

"She told Johnstone she didn't feel like forgiving him, but she chose to because that's what the good Lord wanted." He laughed. "She sounded just like you. I'm not sure how either of you know what God wants you to do, unless it's something you heard in a sermon."

"Lots more to it than that." Philip stopped the chair and gazed squarely into Jeremiah's eyes, compelling him to listen. "Sermons and things like that er good and all, but there's a lot more to knowin' the Lord. He's a real person. Ya havta ask Him into yer life. When He comes in, ya git to know Him real good."

To break the strong visual connection between them, Jeremiah stood and paced around the room. "I went to church with my ma, but all those preachers did was shout about hellfire. Sam doesn't do that."

"'Course not. God wants to love ya into heaven, not scare ya outa hell."

That's what those preachers had been doing—scaring everyone with all their shouting and harsh preaching. *How does God love a man into heaven?* Jeremiah didn't realize he'd voiced the question until Philip answered.

"He loved ya so much, He sent Jesus to die on the cross fer all yer sins." Philip settled back. "The book a-John in the Bible tells about it. Chapter 3, verse 16. 'Fer God so loved the world, that He give His only b'gotten Son, that whosoever b'lieveth in Him should not perish, but have everlastin' life.' God said whosoever. He meant everyone who'd b'lieve in Jesus. I have. Madeline has. Whosoever means you too, Jeremiah."

Jeremiah turned that thought over and over in his mind. He'd celebrated Christmas and knew it was about Jesus being born on earth. He'd heard about Jesus dying, and he'd been around people who celebrated Easter, when Jesus rose from the dead. But he'd never put it all together.

"Let me get this straight. God did all that to love people into heaven?"

Philip gave a vigorous nod. "Not just people. You, Jeremiah. God did that to love *you* into heaven."

He dropped back into the chair facing the old miner. "I'm beginning to understand. And I've seen how different your life, and Sam's, and Madeline's are from mine. You all have a quietness and peace about you. That come from knowing God?"

"Sure does."

He was glad Philip wasn't pushing him faster than he wanted to go with this. The man just waited for Jeremiah to think over every point. "I got a hankering for that peace. How do I get it?"

Philip's eyes closed, and his chin dropped to his chest. Jeremiah was afraid he'd died or something. He didn't want that to happen before he found out what he needed to know about all this. Then he noticed Philip's lips moving. The man was praying. *Like to scared me to death.*

After raising his head and opening his eyes, Philip's gaze cut toward Jeremiah. "That's the question I've been waitin' a long time to hear. All ya havta do is ask Jesus into yer heart. Give Him control of yer life. I'll introduce ya to Him right now."

They bowed their heads, and Philip prayed a prayer that included an introduction of Jeremiah to Jesus. Then he told Jeremiah to just talk to the Lord.

"Well, Lord, uh…" Jeremiah began to talk haltingly to Jesus, but soon the words almost stumbled over each other in their haste, like a clear mountain stream tumbling over rocks, rushing down to the valley. He poured out all his sins and asked Jesus to take them from him. "And that's about all I've got to say, Lord." He sat in silence…waiting.

A miracle happened.

He felt as if everything had been cleansed from his past. He was a new man in a way he didn't really understand, but he liked the feeling.

He raised his head with tears in his eyes. "I couldn't imagine how this would work, but it's real. I'm different."

"'Course ya are." Philip swallowed and blinked his eyes. Then he pulled out his handkerchief and swiped at his cheeks. "Thank Ya, Jesus, fer answerin' my prayers."

Jeremiah started laughing, and he couldn't stop for a few minutes. Soon Philip joined him. Their merriment filled the room. And for some reason, it felt as if someone else was there with them. *That You, Lord?*

Yes, My child.

How he'd heard that soft voice through all the noise, Jeremiah didn't understand, but he'd heard it clearly. As if the Lord stood beside him, whispering in his ear.

Finally, the laughter died down, and Jeremiah could talk. "I've still got a question. What about that forgiveness thing? I haven't ever forgiven my father and my uncle for what they did to me. Don't know if I can."

"Ya can do just like Madeline did." Philip's wise words were a balm to his spirit. "Choose to forgive 'em here and now. Ya don't havta see 'em to do it."

"I'm not even sure if they're still alive."

"Don't matter. Forgive 'em. More fer yourself than fer them."

Jeremiah stood and stretched as tall as he could. He raised his eyes and arms toward the ceiling. "I choose to forgive my... father and my uncle for...all their cruelty."

Flashes of the harsh faces, loud voices, and leather strap filled his head, and pain shot through his heart as if he were in a fierce gun battle. Then, like an eraser on a chalkboard, the visions began to disappear, and peace settled like a mourning dove on his heart. A final weight lifted from his shoulders. He felt ten pounds lighter.

"I've waited years fer this to happen, Jerry." An occasional tear made its slow way down Philip's cheek. "I've been hangin' onto my life. Couldn't let go until it did."

What did Philip mean by that?

"Now I've gotta tell ya some other things." Philip wheezed out a breath, followed by a cough. "When I sent fer Madeline, God wanted me to rescue her. But more than that, He wanted me to bring her here so you could have a wife."

"What are you talking about?" This time Jeremiah couldn't keep the question inside. "I thought you asked her to marry you."

"I did, but not fer me." Philip sucked in a deep breath. "Showed me how ya feel 'bout her. Was hopin' ya wouldn't like it. Boy howdy, it made ya mad. Ya didn't think I noticed, did ya?"

Jeremiah shook his head and rubbed the back of his neck. Philip hadn't caused this pain in his neck in a long time, but right now the muscles knotted like an old rope.

"And I noticed how you been lookin' at her lately, when ya didn't think anybidy was watchin'. Don't have much longer in this life."

Jeremiah scooted closer and took the old man's hands in his.

They felt like thin parchment stretched over a skeleton. "Don't talk like that. We're going to take care of you."

"Nothin' ya can do, Jerry. Don't know how much time I've got, but I plan to spend it with the people I love." Philip squeezed his fingers. "That's you, Madeline, and Pearl. Ya need to start courtin' Madeline. Maybe I'll dance at yer weddin' if'n the good Lord's willin'."

Jeremiah hoped so. Maybe the old coot would live long enough to see their children. What was he thinking? He didn't know if Madeline would even consider letting him court her, much less marry her. And here he was thinking about children.

"Ya don't havta worry none about what Madeline feels. She watches ya a lot too." Philip punctuated that sentence with a cackle that turned into a cough.

After he and Philip visited a little longer, the older man looked like he could nod off to sleep. Jeremiah helped him into his room to take a nap.

When Jeremiah stepped into the afternoon sunlight, everything looked different to him. Brighter...cleaner somehow. Did knowing the Lord change the world around him, or was he just seeing it with new eyes? And what relationship did Philip's revelation about Madeline have to do with the way he saw everything?

He leapt up on the wagon seat and drove down toward the livery. A horse was tied out in front of the hotel. He recognized it as one from Los Cerrillos. Evidently another stranger had come to town. After he turned the wagon in to Swede, he mounted Lightning and rode over to the sheriff's office.

"Bill, I'm glad you're still here. One of the livery horses from Los Cerrillos is tied up at the hotel. I'm going to check on who rode it in. Want to come with me?" He wasn't sure whether his friend would go or not, but Bill stood and stretched.

"I'll just walk up there. Won't take me much longer than it

will you." Bill snagged his hat from the corner of his desk and settled it on his head.

Jeremiah rode up the cobblestones. When he tied Lightning's reins to the hitching rail, he could hear, through the swinging doors, a woman crying softly. Without hesitating, he hurried inside and spied two people in the parlor. The man, dressed in a fancy Eastern suit, had his back to Jeremiah, but the crying woman was Madeline. Whoever he was, the man wasn't going to get away with hurting her.

No matter that Jeremiah had just accepted the Lord into his life. No man should make a woman cry...ever. And he wasn't going to stand by and let anyone else hurt the woman he loved. He stomped through the doorway and raised his voice. "What do you think you're doing?"

CHAPTER 26

While dabbing tears from her cheeks, Maddy stared at Jeremiah, who had burst through the doorway like a raging bull. What was wrong with him? She arose and stood beside her visitor.

The fierce frown on Jeremiah's face didn't alter one bit. He looked as if he might take a swing at poor Mr. Sanderson. She had to stop him.

"Jeremiah?"

Finally he looked at her instead of her visitor.

"You haven't met my father's solicitor, Mr. Isaiah Sanderson. He's come all the way from Boston to see me." She didn't take her eyes from Jeremiah's face, willing him to relax.

Mr. Sanderson thrust out his hand, but Jeremiah ignored it, continuing to study her.

"Jeremiah Dennison owns a ranch near here, and he's a good friend of the man who sent the letter to me." Maddy expected Jeremiah to shake the proffered hand, but he just stood there and stared at it as if it were holding a gun aimed at his heart.

What had happened to Jeremiah after he'd left with Philip? She couldn't imagine any reason for him to act this way. She frowned at him, then noticed over his shoulder that the sheriff had entered the lobby behind him. Maddy couldn't believe a meeting between herself and her father's lawyer would cause such a ruckus.

"Sheriff Brown, this is my father's solicitor, Isaiah Sanderson, from Boston." She smiled at the lawyer. "And this is Bill Brown, our sheriff."

At least Bill reached toward the man and shook his hand. Then he stepped back. "What seems to be the problem?"

Maddy glared at Jeremiah. "I don't know of any problem, but Jeremiah seems to have one."

He had the good sense to turn his attention toward the floor and keep his mouth shut.

"Mr. Sanderson was telling me that he came to give me a copy of my father's will. Remembering my loss made me cry, and Jeremiah burst in on us. He may have thought something else was going on." She gave the sheriff a tremulous smile.

Bill looked from her to Jeremiah and back. "Do you want me to stay? Do you think you need protection?"

"Not really, but I need a friend. Frank and Sarah have taken Pearl over to the Hendersons'. Sarah is visiting with Martha, and Frank is helping Hank deliver their mare's first foal. I would like someone here with me during the reading of the will." One more tear made its way down her cheek, and she swiped it away before stuffing her hanky into her sleeve.

Bill doffed his hat. "I'd be glad to stay, Madeline."

Jeremiah removed his too, turning his gray Stetson round and round in his hands. "I'd like to stay if you'll allow me…after the way I burst in here." Sincere regret shone from his eyes and colored his tone.

She nodded and took her place at one end of the sofa. Mr. Sanderson sat beside her. Jeremiah and Bill chose two wingback chairs across from them.

Mr. Sanderson cleared his throat. "I was just getting ready to apologize to Miss Mercer. I'm afraid I've contributed to many of her problems without realizing I had."

Maddy couldn't imagine what the man was talking about. He'd always been more than kind to her.

"When we read the will, you'll find that your father did bequeath Mr. Johnstone a one-fourth portion of the business for his faithful service. When Mr. Johnstone told me to not read the will for you until he said it was time, I thought he had that authority. He kept putting off the actual reading, even though I wanted to proceed." He took out his handkerchief and wiped the perspiration from his forehead.

Maddy felt the warm temperature too, but large drops of sweat streamed down Mr. Sanderson's face. She wondered if he couldn't take the heat so well or if he were bothered by his confession.

"At that point, Mr. Johnstone took over doling out the money to you. I didn't know until Mr. Sneed came by my office that Johnstone was actually withholding the money. I tried to get him to change what he was doing, but he threatened my family with grievous harm. And there were all those rumors of horrible deeds the man had done. I couldn't put my family at risk."

"Of course you couldn't." Maddy patted him on the arm. She didn't want the solicitor to take the blame for what Horace did. She was saddened that the man had caused such havoc in Mr. Sanderson's life too.

She noticed Jeremiah's fists flexing as if he wanted to hit someone. Surely not Mr. Sanderson. Jeremiah's brooding presence cast a greater pall on the proceedings.

"Then when Mr. Johnstone made me unlock the house for him, and we found that letter, he opened it right away, even though I told him he shouldn't. He was very angry. I thought he would come after you, but he isn't here, is he?" His probing gaze begged Madeline to agree.

"Yes, he is. The sheriff has him in jail right now." Maddy clasped her hands in her lap. "I actually talked to him today."

"Oh, dear...oh, my." Mr. Sanderson ran his finger around his collar. "You know there had been rumors that Mr. Johnstone had killed your dear father."

She gasped.

"Thankfully, that wasn't true." Once again the lawyer patted his forehead with the damp cloth. "I talked to your doctor, and he said your father had suffered from heart trouble for several years. He hadn't wanted you to worry, so they never told you. Finally, he succumbed to a heart attack. I was relieved it wasn't murder."

"*Murder?*" Maddy clutched her hands to her chest. "Such an ugly word. I had heard about the rumors, but I'd held out hope they weren't true."

Mr. Sanderson stuffed his handkerchief back into his pocket. "When I couldn't find Mr. Johnstone, I investigated for myself. I discovered the rumors were started by none other than Mr. Johnstone himself. He wanted people to fear him so they would do what he told them."

Maddy remembered how she'd felt when the man tried to force her to do what he wanted. She could understand why the lawyer feared Mr. Johnstone.

"But I decided I was no longer afraid of the man." Mr. Sanderson sat up straighter. "I had an accounting of your estate prepared. I brought a bank draft and some cash to tide you over until we finish settling all the legal and financial matters."

Maddy sat up straighter. "Are you telling me that I'm not poor?" That would be good news indeed. Most of her worries would blow away with the desert wind.

"Oh my, no. You're a very wealthy woman, Miss Mercer." He bestowed a big smile on her with that pronouncement.

She stared at him for a minute, trying to take it all in. Not only did she have money, it must be a tidy sum for Mr. Sanderson to call her *very* wealthy.

Unsure exactly what that meant, she turned toward Jeremiah and the sheriff. Jeremiah appeared stunned. "I'm glad to know I'm not penniless. Philip won't need to help me anymore. And maybe I can pay back what he's already spent."

Jeremiah leaned forward in his chair. "I know Philip isn't worried about that."

"Probably not, but I really didn't feel right about letting him spend money on me, even though he assured me I was doing as much for him as he was for me." She'd been learning to get by with as little as possible, just so Philip wouldn't buy much for her and Pearl. Maybe she wouldn't have to be so thrifty now. "What kind of money are we talking about, Mr. Sanderson?"

"Do you really want me to tell you in front of these men, Miss Mercer?" He cocked his head toward Jeremiah.

"Actually, they are very good friends of mine who know the whole story of why I came to Golden. It's all right for them to hear the details."

He didn't look convinced. "If you're sure?" He opened his satchel and withdrew several papers. "According to your father's will, you own three-fourths of his company. I've been over-seeing the import-export portion until you or Mr. Johnstone return to Boston. Your father left a generous amount to the Sneeds, but that still leaves you with well over five hundred thousand dollars in cash and the business, several commercial buildings, and the mansion. I brought you one hundred dollars and a bank draft for ten thousand dollars. You do have a bank in Golden, don't you?"

"We most certainly do." Bill sounded almost insulted that the man would think otherwise.

Maddy had never seen or even heard of anyone owning so much money. Now she would be facing a different dilemma. She hadn't really managed finances in the past. She just used the money her father gave her, and when it ran out, she asked him for more. Which he gave with an open hand. She might need help.

All of this meant she had to make some important decisions. Having a lot of money at her disposal would allow her to do good for other people. People had needs in Boston, and many in and near Golden could use a helping hand.

This led to another question. Would she stay in Golden, or would she return to Boston? Although she'd like to return to Boston from time to time, she'd fallen in love with Golden, New Mexico. She'd grown from a timid, child-like person into a strong woman eager to shape her own destiny. Realizing all this, she wanted to put down roots right here.

With the railroad connections from here to Massachusetts, more options were available to her. She could have the best of both worlds.

"So, Mr. Sanderson, when can we have the reading of the will?" Madeline hoped it would be soon. Now that she knew what had happened, she wanted everything settled quickly.

"Since all of the people mentioned in the document are here in Golden, I don't see any problem with getting them together." Mr. Sanderson shuffled the papers in his hands.

"How about this evening after Frank and Sarah return to the hotel and we've eaten supper?" Madeline glanced toward Bill Brown. "Do you suppose you could bring Mr. Johnstone to the hotel for the reading?"

"I don't see why not, if you'll let me stay with him. After all, he's still my prisoner."

At least the sheriff was amiable. A thundercloud had settled on Jeremiah Dennison's face. Obviously, he didn't agree. But he didn't have a say in the matter, did he?

~

*a*fter Sam offered to keep a close eye on Philip, Jeremiah made a trip out to the ranch. All the cowhands had been off this weekend, and he made quick work of throwing out the feed for the cattle. Then he bathed in the shower he'd rigged up near the windmill and spruced up a bit. He wanted to look nice when he went to the hotel for the evening meal. Somehow he had to be included in that meeting with the lawyer. Just to make sure no one took advantage of Madeline. She had no idea how many men thought women didn't have a brain in their heads. He knew she was plenty smart, but would the others realize it?

Philip filling his mind with the idea of marrying her had reinforced what he'd been wanting for quite a while. That's all he could think about, besides how wonderful he felt now that he finally understood about God and how much He loved him. Both of these things were a wonder to him.

Come to think of it, when he first saw Sanderson with Madeline, he finally admitted to himself that he loved her. If only he could figure out how to get her to love him. Then there was the matter of her fortune. With so many options open to her now, she might pull up stakes and head back East before he could convince her to marry him. Another reason he wanted to keep a close eye on her. Maybe he wasn't as fancy as some of the men back East, but the money he'd made from selling his mine matched hers, and he did own the most successful ranch in the territory.

He rode up to the hotel and dismounted, tying Lightning's reins to the hitching rail. His boot heels drummed a steady beat on the wooden boardwalk. As he stood in the doorway to the dining room, Madeline's gaze slid past him then back again.

She waved. "Jeremiah. Come join us."

Her words were music to his ears. The very thing he'd wished for. Madeline, with Pearl on her lap, shared the table with the Sneeds and Mr. Sanderson. They shifted around, making room for him to pull up another chair. Close enough that he caught a whiff of that flowery scent always surrounding her. He took a moment to enjoy its fragrance, and to enjoy sitting this close to her. Maybe when the meal was over, he could tag along for the meeting.

Sure enough, no one questioned him when he followed everyone into the parlor. Bill was already seated at the side of the room with Johnstone in handcuffs beside him. Jeremiah sauntered over and leaned against the wall behind the two men, crossing his arms and trying to look relaxed. Appearances could be deceiving. Jeremiah knew that for sure.

Sanderson took center stage by pulling a straight chair close beside the sofa, where Madeline, Frank, and Sarah sat. The older woman lifted the baby into her arms, relieving Madeline of her distraction.

The lawyer perched spectacles on his nose and pulled a sheaf of papers from his satchel. He glanced around the room. "It looks as if everyone is accounted for."

When his gaze reached Johnstone, Sanderson paused a long moment before returning the man's smile. Without further ado, the lawyer started reading the will.

Why did legal documents contain so many big words and confusing phrases? Jeremiah had to listen carefully to understand the details. *No surprises.* The document said pretty much what Sanderson had told them earlier in the day.

Johnstone received one-fourth of the Mercer import-export business as well as an amount of money. Although it wouldn't make him wealthy, the number would be enough to take care of him for some time if he used it wisely. Of course, he was part owner of the business, so he could be set for life. It didn't seem quite right to Jeremiah—that the man would get part of her father's fortune. He felt sure Mr. Mercer wouldn't have written his will this way if he'd have known what Johnstone was capable of doing.

The next item was a stipend for Frank and Sarah Sneed. Their fifty thousand dollars would be considered a fortune by most everyone in Golden.

Jeremiah watched them when they realized just how much Mr. Mercer had given them. Their shocked expressions turned to delight. Sarah pulled Pearl close to her heart and buried her face against the baby's curls. Jeremiah detected tears glistening in her eyes.

Frank put his arm around his wife and cradled her against his shoulder. "Are you sure that's what it says?"

Sanderson smiled at them. "I believe Mr. Mercer wanted to reward you for all the years you helped him rear his daughter without her mother. He expressed to me how valuable your service has always been to him."

Madeline turned her attention toward her friends. "You deserve every penny, and even more."

"The rest of the estate goes to Miss Madeline Mercer. Your father expressed his desire to see you taken care of. He didn't want you to ever be in need. And with this bequest, you never shall."

Well, the man had done right by Madeline. Jeremiah relaxed. Maybe Sanderson was on the up and up after all.

~

"Thank you for taking care of all this for me, Mr. Sanderson." Maddy glanced around the room until her gaze landed on Johnstone. "Now we must decide what to do about the business. Sheriff, what exactly are the charges against Mr. Johnstone?" *It might be time for me to really live out that forgiveness I professed.*

Bill mulled over her questions for a moment. "Most of them

stem from his treatment of you, Miss Mercer. He opened your mail without your consent, but we can see about dropping the charge that goes along with that misdemeanor if you're not going to press charges."

Maddy turned her attention toward Sanderson. "Since most of the information we believed about Mr. Johnstone wasn't true, and since Father made him a partner in the business, what do you think we should do? I did choose to forgive Mr. Johnstone earlier today."

"Horace knows more about the business than I do. He would be valuable in keeping everything running smoothly, if you trust him now. And I would keep a close eye on the finances. Is there any way he can come back to Boston with me?" Mr. Sanderson stared at Mr. Johnstone, who hung his head as if in shame.

"And when will that be?" Bill stood and took a step closer to the lawyer.

"I plan on staying until everything is completely settled with Miss Mercer's estate. It could take a couple of weeks or more. These things do take time. Why?"

"What should I do with Johnstone in the meantime?" Bill looked over at the prisoner, who sat up straighter even with the handcuffs on.

"If Miss Mercer will drop her charges against him, he could stay in the hotel with me while we decide exactly what to do with the company." He turned his attention toward Madeline. "Could you agree to this?"

Horace Johnstone glanced at her. All she could read in his expression was hope. None of his former attitude still clung to him. *God is the God of second chances.*

Maddy nodded. "Mr. Johnstone and I need to discuss how to proceed. Having him with you is a good idea."

The man stood with his manacled hands in front of him. "I'd really be glad to be out of that cell. And I do need to talk to

Madeline and Sanderson to work everything out. But after that, I want to head back to Boston as soon as I can."

That might work out for the best. If the man truly had changed, maybe he could take over the running of the business, and Maddy could be a silent, majority partner, since Mr. Sanderson would protect her interests. With that, and her newfound fortune, her future was looking more and more interesting.

For a moment, the thought came into her mind: *Can I really trust these two men? Please, Lord, let it be true.*

CHAPTER 27

"*S*arah, would you take Pearl up to bed for me?"
Maddy wanted Philip's undivided attention when
she went to share her good news with him.

Knowing how interested he was in her welfare, she knew
he'd be pleased with the way everything was turning out.
Besides, she wanted to make sure he was all right. He looked
weaker than before and shaky when Jeremiah took him home
after lunch.

"It'll be a pleasure, Madeline." Sarah started up the stairs with
the baby peeking over her shoulder.

Pearl laughed and grabbed a fistful of Sarah's hair. Maddy
smiled at her. *Thank You, Lord, for giving me this special gift.*

She turned toward the swinging doors and found Jeremiah
standing there with a broad smile and twinkling eyes. He was
devastatingly handsome when he smiled like that. Maddy's
pulse fluttered, and her mouth suddenly felt dry. She cleared her
throat. The man could really upset her equilibrium. She hoped
he couldn't tell. How embarrassing that would be. And she had
to keep reminding herself there could be no future for them,
because he didn't really know the Lord.

"What are you going to do now, Madeline?" His deep, rich voice settled comfortably over her.

"I wanted to go see Philip." She placed her hand against her heart, trying to still it.

"I thought you might." He crooked his arm, his gaze snagging hers, almost daring her to refuse. "I'd like to see him too. May I accompany you?"

Maddy let out a slow breath. "I'd appreciate that. It'll soon be dark, and I wasn't looking forward to walking back down the hill alone."

Jeremiah left Lightning hitched outside the hotel, and they strolled in the deepening twilight. Several stars glittered in the part of the indigo sky where the sun had already withdrawn its rays. With every step they took, more points of light appeared. Maddy liked this vast expanse of heaven with its twinkling display. She'd never noticed so many stars in Boston. Large trees grew around her house and in most of the areas where she went in town.

On the horizon, the afterglow of the sinking sun still cast faint orange and purple streaks before extinguishing its light completely. A gentle breeze stole away the oppressive heat of the day. Maddy would have felt a chill if Jeremiah hadn't been beside her. His body exuded enough heat to keep that from happening. For just a moment she wondered how it would feel if he were to cradle her against his shoulder as Frank did with Sarah earlier. She needed to control her errant thoughts.

When she took the next step, she moved a little farther from Jeremiah. To quiet her mind, she needed to find something to talk about. "What did you think about Mr. Johnstone's idea of going back to Boston?"

Jeremiah stopped walking and peered down at her, his eyes roving her face until she felt vulnerable. "Are you going back to Boston soon too?"

His question startled her. Why would he want to know? She

had expected an answer about Mr. Johnstone, not a question about her intentions.

"I'm not making any plans to go."

He nodded, then started walking again. Did he look relieved? Maddy hoped so.

"I wasn't really comfortable with Johnstone being let loose from jail, but it's not my place to object." His tone belied the casual way he said the words.

"I believe he has changed, Jeremiah. And God does give second chances." She tried to keep reproof from her tone.

After a moment, he answered, "Yes, He does." His strong assertion sounded almost as if he were a believer.

How Maddy wished that were true. If it were, she wouldn't have to guard her heart against him. "Do you really believe that, Jeremiah?"

Once again, he stopped and turned toward her. "I haven't had a chance to tell you, but I do believe in God."

"Why have you been hiding it? I would've wanted to know." She needed to make sure he wasn't just saying what he thought she wanted to hear.

"I haven't had much use for God since my mother died." He never took his eyes from hers. "You choosing to forgive Johnstone has kept my thoughts in turmoil. I've heard several sermons that Sam preached, and they wouldn't let me go, either. I had a long talk with Philip after I took him up to the house."

Jeremiah stopped talking and tilted his face heavenward. He paused, as if listening to someone. "I asked Jesus into my life, and He forgave me for the sins I've committed. I pledged to give Him control, but I have a lot to learn."

Overjoyed, Maddy couldn't hold back her thoughts. "That's wonderful, Jeremiah. Philip and I have prayed for you so many times. I rejoice with the angels in heaven. The Bible says they rejoice every time someone comes to know the Lord."

Tears welled up in Maddy's eyes, and she tried to blink them back. One escaped down her cheek.

He glanced at her face, and his gaze traveled the path the drop took. Then he reached up and wiped the moisture away with his callused thumb.

Shivers cascaded down her spine and settled deep within her where a previously unknown warmth churned. The gentle touch of this man sparked a remarkable reaction in her. How would she ever be able to protect her heart now? *Do I really need to?*

Jeremiah leaned his face toward hers and didn't stop until he was so close she could feel his warm breath. For a moment that lengthened into an eon, he stayed there, gazing tenderly into her eyes. She wondered if he could read her thoughts. What was he going to do?

Then he moved away. "Madeline, I wish we had more time to talk, but we must get up to see Philip. Sam and Caroline have been with him while we were at the hotel."

Maddy fell into step with him, her thoughts in a jumble. She'd never been that close to a man, and he drew her interest as no man ever had before. For just a moment, she'd wondered if he was going to kiss her right out here in public. She was glad he hadn't crossed that line, but a part of her wanted to feel his kiss. Somehow she had to forget her feelings about that and concentrate on talking to Philip. Once she was in her room tonight, she could pull out the memory of this walk and relive every second.

∽

*J*eremiah helped Madeline climb the steps to the porch. Caroline stood in the open doorway.

"Has something happened to Philip?" Jeremiah would never forgive himself if he'd let his old friend down.

"No. It's just that he's so weak." Caroline stepped back to let them enter. "Sam is in the bedroom with him. I came out for a breath of fresh air."

For a moment, Jeremiah wondered if she'd noticed him and Madeline standing so close together. So what if she did? Soon enough everyone in town would find out how he felt about the woman by his side.

"Do you think it would tire him too much if we both went in to see him?" Madeline's words sounded wistful.

Caroline gave a sad smile. "Even if it did, Philip wouldn't want to miss seeing you."

Her words made Jeremiah realize how much it would hurt Madeline to lose Philip. Probably as much as it would hurt him. He swallowed around the lump in his throat and blinked back the moisture in his eyes.

He ushered Madeline in front of him as they went to the bedroom. "Don't worry. Philip gets tired easily, and today was a long day for him." Although he tried to reassure her, somehow his words didn't convince himself.

Sam noticed them at the door. "Come in. I know Philip wants to talk to the two of you anyway. I'll join my wife."

Madeline sat in the chair beside the bed and picked up Philip's hand, holding it in both of hers, a tender smile on her lips. "I had to see how you were doing."

The old miner turned his face toward her. In the lamplight, Jeremiah noticed that his skin seemed to be stretched over his skull. His cheeks were even more sunken than when Jeremiah had left earlier today. His stomach lurched. *No! God, please let me have more time with him. I need his wisdom—especially now.*

Philip gave a weak smile to Madeline, and Jeremiah could read the alarm on her face.

"Better…now that…yer here." Philip took shallow breaths between the words.

Jeremiah worried about the old man's complexion. It had

turned chalky and dull. A vise squeezed his heart. *I love this man. God, please*. He didn't know what else to pray. Philip had said that he didn't have much longer in this world. Jeremiah knew the old miner would be eager to be with God, and finally, Jeremiah understood why Philip felt that way. So he couldn't hold his good friend here on earth in his suffering.

Tears streamed down Madeline's face, but she didn't let go to wipe them away.

"Jerry...tell ya?" This time his breath held out longer.

She nodded. "About him becoming a believer?"

Jeremiah barely caught the old man's slight nod.

"Yes, I'm so happy for him. It was an answer to our prayers." Madeline's words were soft, as if she didn't want to disturb anyone.

And Jeremiah felt like screaming.

"'Fraid don't have...much time. Have Jerry...tell the real reason I brung...ya out here. Only want...the best." His words deteriorated to a wispy sound.

Madeline looked confused, and Jeremiah didn't blame her. She glanced up at him as if in question.

What should he do now? Tell her the truth?

Philip stared at him. "Tell her...now."

Talking appeared to have drained more life out of the old man. Jeremiah had to do what he asked. He hoped the truth wouldn't chase Madeline away. The scene out under the stars flashed through his mind. He'd been sure she would have let him kiss her if he tried, but he respected her too much to take advantage that way.

He pulled another chair up beside Madeline and proceeded to tell her about his previous conversation with Philip. While he talked, he carefully watched her reactions, as well as the old man's.

When she heard about Philip bringing her out to marry Jeremiah, Madeline's eyes cut toward her dear friend. He gave another slight nod, his eyes begging her for forgiveness. Then her attention turned toward Jeremiah. Emotions flitted across her face, telling their own story. He hoped he read it right. Amazement turned into a question. Then acceptance, like she understood Philip's motives. But underlying all of this, Jeremiah saw a flicker of a deeper emotion. One that mirrored what he felt for her. At least, that's how it looked to him.

She leaned toward the old man and kissed his cheek. "I know you were doing what you thought was right."

Her words eased some of the turmoil on Philip's face.

"Thank you for all you've done for me." She dropped to her knees beside the bed, still holding his hand. "I've grown to love you very much. I'm not upset with you."

Removing one hand from his, she smoothed the wrinkles on his forehead. "You're the reason I don't want to return to Boston. I love you, and Pearl loves you. You've made Golden into a real home for us."

"Love ya...too." Philip's lips stretched into a weak smile. "What 'bout...Jerry?"

Madeline took her time answering that question. Finally, she glanced up at Jeremiah with a twinkle behind the tears. "I've come to appreciate him in many ways."

That wasn't enough to satisfy the old man. "He...court ya?"

The earnestness in the question hit Jeremiah hard. He stood up, afraid Madeline would agree with anything Philip wanted just to make him rest easy. That's not the way he wanted her. When—if—she agreed to marry him, he wanted it to be because she loved him completely, not because of a promise to a sick old man.

Madeline reached to move her skirt out of her way and tried to stand. Jeremiah offered his hand. She took it and arose to take her place beside him. Philip watched every movement.

She studied Jeremiah's face and stared deep into his eyes. Was his heart and soul uncovered to her? He hoped she couldn't see how desperately he wanted her to agree. She needed to see him as strong, not as a man who waited breathlessly for her answer.

Without taking her gaze from his, she smiled. "Yes, I'd be honored if Jeremiah wants to court me."

Her sincerity rang through the room, lighting her eyes and making him feel as tall as a ponderosa pine. Want to court her? Not a doubt in his mind. She was the very woman he'd been looking for his whole adult life.

"I want to court you." He placed the weight of his whole heart and life into each word.

$\sim$

*M*addy couldn't believe the turn of events. She'd come up here to Philip's to tell him about her good fortune, but he fell asleep right after Jeremiah made his assertion. Did he really mean it, or was he merely trying to please the old miner? She hoped it was the former.

Ever since she met Jeremiah Dennison, she'd felt drawn to him, even though she'd fought those feelings because he wasn't a Christian. That roadblock now had been removed. The fluttery feeling returned to her chest. Could the man possibly love her the way her father loved her mother? Even though she was a child when her mother died, she remembered the warmth and scope of that love that filled every room of their home. She wanted a chance to find out.

She glanced down at Philip. He looked so peaceful. She was glad they'd agreed with him if it gave him that peace. When she leaned over and tucked his quilt around his shoulders, he didn't stir.

"Are you ready to go back to the hotel?" Jeremiah stood very close to her.

She turned her gaze up into his eyes that glittered like black jet. One curl drooped over his forehead. She wanted to brush it back, but it was too soon for such an intimate touch. "Yes."

His hand barely touched the small of her back, but it sent tingles throughout her body. They went into the main room of the cabin. No one was there. Sam and Caroline must have gone back to the hotel.

Jeremiah stopped and turned toward her. Without thinking, she moved closer to him. "Madeline, I don't want you to feel like you have to let me court you, but it's been my desire for quite a while." His probing gaze never left her face. "Do you really mean you want me to?"

So hopeful sounding, like he might be afraid of her answer.

She wouldn't keep him in suspense. "I meant what I said. It wasn't just to please Philip."

A dazzling smile bloomed on his face. He reached for her, and she slid into his arms, laying her head on his muscular chest. All the imaginings of being in his embrace became reality. She felt protected—safe, happy. She could hear his heartbeat that answered her own strengthened pulse.

"You know that means I'm interested in marrying you, don't you?" His words rumbled in his chest as well as into the air around them.

"I know," she whispered.

He pulled back so he could see her face. "We've had a very busy day, with lots of things to think about. We can discuss this more when I come see you tomorrow."

She nodded, hoping tomorrow would bring them even closer. Anticipation shot through her.

Before they reached the door, Sam arrived. "How is he?"

Maddy stayed quiet, letting Jeremiah take the lead. "He went to sleep, but he's really weak. I want to accompany Madeline back to the hotel. Could you stay with him while I do?"

"When you were with Philip, I took Caroline to the hotel. I came back to tell you that I'd spend the night watching over him." Sam clasped one of Jeremiah's shoulders. "You go on home after you say good night to Madeline."

Maddy read the indecision in Jeremiah's face. Evidently, so did Sam.

"You need your rest, my friend." The pastor's compassionate tone enveloped Maddy. She hoped Jeremiah felt it too. "We don't know what tomorrow will bring."

Finally, Jeremiah agreed, and they headed out into the dark night. This time Maddy walked very close to him, welcoming his presence, the touch of his hand, his murmured words weaving themselves into her heart. Nothing could take away her happiness.

CHAPTER 28

*M*adeline's womanly softness in his embrace brought a longing to taste her luscious lips. He lowered his head until their lips were only a breath apart...

A loud explosion jerked him awake, piercing the warm, loving embrace. Jeremiah groaned as the dream faded and Madeline vanished like early morning fog in the warm sunshine. What had awakened him? Something in his dream?

He listened to the silence of the night, then burrowed his head deeper into his pillow, willing the mental image back, wishing it were real. Would her lips feel as soft and dewy as they looked?

Pounding on the front door started again, bringing back the familiar sound that had destroyed his vision. He jumped out of bed and grabbed the trousers he'd dropped on the floor. After buttoning the fly, he snagged the shirt hanging on the back of a chair and pushed his arms into the sleeves while he made his way through the house. His eyes didn't detect any light, not even faint moonlight through the uncovered windows. He stubbed his toe on something and bit back an exclamation that, since yesterday, wouldn't be right for him to utter, even in private.

He stopped trying to button the shirt and used his hands to feel his way through the dining room and living room, favoring his sore toe. Would be nice when he got used to all this space and knew where to dodge the furniture.

"Jeremiah, open up." Sam's voice accompanied another onslaught on his door. "I need to talk to you."

Jeremiah pulled the new door open wide before starting to button his shirt. "What's going on, Sam?" Then it hit him. "Philip. He's gone, isn't he?"

"I'm sorry to say he is." Sincere regret threaded through Sam's words.

Jeremiah dropped his chin against his chest and squeezed his eyes closed. Tears pricked at his eyelids and a few escaped. The loss hit him harder than he'd imagined it would. Then a previously unknown peace about his friend's passing dropped into his heart. He would miss the old codger like the dickens. Philip had been such an important part of his life for many years. He had to blink to hold back the flood of tears that threatened.

"Does Madeline know?" His heart told him she would be devastated too.

The waning stars provided enough light for him to detect Sam shaking his head. "Not yet. I want you with me when I tell her. According to Philip, you're courting her. He said you should be there to comfort her."

Jeremiah wanted to laugh at how quickly the word had gotten out, but the ache in his heart prevented mirth. Strange how that peace and the ache could coexist.

He stepped back. "Come in while I finish dressing. What time is it?"

Sam closed the door, and everything went totally black.

Jeremiah lit a match to find the kerosene lamp, then applied the flame to its wick, adjusting it so smoke wouldn't leave soot in the chimney. "Come on back. We can talk."

He set the lamp on the chest of drawers and grabbed a pair

of socks from the top drawer. "It's got to be the middle of the night."

"Last time I checked, it was about 3:00 a.m." Sam stood, arms crossed, in the doorway. "Should be about 3:30 or 4:00 by now. Philip told me about your conversation after church yesterday." He stepped forward and held out his hand. "Welcome to the family of God."

Jeremiah shook it. He realized it was special to acknowledge his new faith to his friend. He felt accepted in a way he'd never experienced before.

Quickly he reached for his boots. "Sounds like he was talkative last night."

Sam laughed. "He tried. Wheezed out a few words at a time, and I caught the gist of it."

"What else did he say?"

"A lot, really." Sam paused before he continued. "Said he wants to be buried today. Said you and Madeline should talk to that lawyer from Boston. Said he really loved you and Madeline and little Pearl. Other things too." His voice sounded husky before he finished.

Jeremiah got a bandanna out of the same drawer as the socks. He wiped his eyes before stuffing the handkerchief in his hip pocket. Picking up the lamp, he led the way to the front door, opened it, then turned down the wick to extinguish the flame and set the lamp on the table by the door.

"Wanna stop by the cook shack to grab some coffee?" He headed outside. A faint tinge of light outlined the horizon to the east.

Sam mounted his horse and turned toward the barn. "No thanks. But go ahead if you need to."

Jeremiah headed to the barn as well. "Let's get to the hotel as fast as we can."

For some reason, Maddy slept fitfully, waking at the smallest sounds. She heard the top step on the stairs squeak, then scuffing footsteps down the hall toward her bedroom. When they stopped, she held her breath.

She'd never been afraid in this hotel, but she didn't like the idea of someone skulking outside her door. Every night she used the key so she and Pearl would be safe. Even so, tonight she sat up in bed and pulled the covers around her chest, waiting for another sound.

"Madeline." The whispered word barely made it through the door.

What did Caroline want at this time of night? Or morning? Predawn light had brought a glow to the horizon outside her window.

Maddy slipped from under the covers and went to unlock the door. After opening it only a slit, she peeked with one eye at her landlady. Caroline wore a dressing gown and a mobcap on her head, as if she'd just gotten out of bed herself.

"Yes? Did you want something?" She kept her tone low so she wouldn't awaken Pearl.

"Can you come out into the hallway so I can talk to you?" Caroline still kept her voice breathy.

Maddy moved the door enough to slip through, then closed it. Caroline's eyes were serious, and her usually smiling lips formed a tight line.

"What's wrong?" That's all Maddy could think to say.

"I've come up to sit with Pearl. You need to get dressed and go down to the parlor. Jeremiah would like to talk to you."

When she first heard his name, her heartbeat quickened. Then questions rolled through her mind. Why would Jeremiah be here at this time of night? And why was Caroline upset?

She turned and led her friend into the room. After lighting the lamp, she stepped behind the folding screen beside the wardrobe and quickly dressed. When she came out, Caroline sat in the rocking chair.

"Is something wrong?"

"Don't keep Jeremiah waiting." Caroline shooed her toward the door. "Don't worry about Pearl. I'll stay as long as I'm needed."

Maddy hurried down the stairs into the parlor. Jeremiah stood with his hands clasped behind him, staring out the window at the early morning. He must have heard her, because he turned. His eyes glistened with tears.

She rushed to him. "Tell me what's wrong."

He gathered her into his embrace and rested his chin on top of her head. "Philip…" He tightened his hold on her.

She pulled away and stepped back a bit. "Please don't tell me he's gone." Tears clogged her throat, and she couldn't say another word.

He grabbed a large, colorful handkerchief from his back pocket and gently dabbed at her cheeks. "You did realize how weak he was, didn't you?"

The gentle way he said the words soaked into her aching heart. She stared into his eyes, reading the pain and peace. Such a change had happened to this man. Had it been only yesterday? Things were happening way too fast for her. Her whole world was changing at breakneck speed. She needed something solid to hold onto.

"I knew, but I hoped I was wrong." She crossed her arms, holding tightly to her upper arms. "Such a special man…" She couldn't continue.

Jeremiah pulled her close to him once again. This time she didn't resist. Tears streamed down her face, accompanied by sobs from deep within. The salty water pooled on the front of his shirt under her cheek. She let his soothing words wash over her and his arms give her comfort as he whispered into her hair.

God had given her a special gift to help her face this flood of grief.

~

*J*eremiah's heart broke right along with Madeline's. He'd never given in to tears, even when he was being beaten as a boy. But this shared loss opened a place in his heart where deep hurt had hidden. His quiet crying mingled with hers as they shared this burden, making it lighter.

When they both came to the end of their tears, he once again pulled out his bandanna and dried her cheeks, still holding her in his embrace. She stared straight into his eyes. He knew she saw his tears as well, but he didn't care.

"I'm glad I have you, Jeremiah. I couldn't get through this alone. Philip..." She swallowed. "Philip knew we needed each other."

"I agree." Yes, he needed her in a way he'd never needed anyone in his life. Facing a single day without her was unthinkable. *Thank you, Philip...and God.*

A throat cleared behind him. Jeremiah turned but kept his arm around Madeline's waist. Sam and that lawyer guy stood in the doorway, waiting to be acknowledged. Jeremiah led her toward the sofa.

"Come in and join us." Jeremiah sat close beside her, the desire for her to be next to him overwhelming.

When the two men took the wing-backed chairs across from them, Jeremiah noticed the morning light coming through the windows behind them. "Sam, I just now remembered you said Philip wanted us to talk to this man." He looked at the lawyer. "Why would he say that?"

Mr. Sanderson's bearing belied the early hour. His suit didn't show a crease, and not one of his white hairs was out of place.

"Mr. Smith had me draw up a will for him. He wanted the provisions followed to a T."

How could that be? Jeremiah didn't think Philip had ever met the man. "Just when did you write this will?"

"Yesterday afternoon, when you went back to the ranch. Mr. Smith sent the pastor to get me. He wanted everything in order." Sanderson's Adam's apple bobbed, and he cleared his throat. "I believe Mr. Smith knew that his death was imminent."

Jeremiah felt Madeline tremble. He glanced down at her, and she leaned even closer to him.

"When will we have the reading of the will?" Jeremiah didn't really care when it would be, but Madeline might.

"We can do it right now, if that's all right with you and Miss Mercer." The lawyer waited for them to nod their approval. "Pastor Oldman, would you ask Mr. and Mrs. Sneed to join us?"

After Sam left, the lawyer took over the proceedings. "We'll read the document as soon as they arrive. Actually it's a very simple will."

Jeremiah didn't care what was in it. He didn't need the money, and neither did Madeline. But he knew they must go through the formalities.

Evidently the Sneeds had already been contacted, because they didn't have to wait for the couple to dress. Within a few moments, Sam returned with them in tow.

Sam looked first at Madeline, then at Jeremiah. "I can leave, if you want me to."

"Please don't go. Your presence is comforting." She pulled her own hanky from her sleeve and dabbed at her nose before settling back beside Jeremiah.

The lawyer dug in his satchel for papers, then shuffled them into order. He read the usual legalese about Philip being of sound mind and then continued, "First, I want to be buried today. Don't want much fuss. If Jerry will allow it, I want to be buried under that lone tree on the hill at the ranch. He'll know which one I'm talking about. Maybe he can start a family plot in that pretty place."

Even without Philip's accent, the words sounded like what he would say in person.

"And I don't want a big ceremony. Just friends at the graveside. Sam'll say all the right things." The lawyer paused and looked at the preacher.

Sam nodded. "Be happy to."

"And I know you'll be sad, but don't make it too long. I'll be jumping and running all over glory with Jesus."

How the man could read Philip's words in such a monotone, Jeremiah didn't understand. Those words carried a huge load of emotion.

"I want to match Madeline's father's bequest for the Sneeds. They've become good friends, and I appreciate them taking care of Madeline and helping me."

Jeremiah wondered that the old man had enough air to get all this information to the lawyer. Maybe that's what robbed him of his breath, making him so weak last night. But he was glad Philip had done this for Madeline's former servants. They deserved every penny.

"I want a matching amount to be put in trust for Pearl when she is eighteen."

Madeline shook with a sob. Jeremiah cradled her up close to his side.

"My house will go to Madeline and Pearl, so they have a home here."

Just the right thing. Jeremiah was glad they wouldn't have to live at the hotel any longer.

"The rest of my money should be divided evenly between Madeline Mercer and Jeremiah Dennison. Of course, since they're courting, it'll all come back together soon." Mr. Sanderson looked up at them. "At this time, he gave a cackle, as if he had made a joke."

"He was serious." Jeremiah glanced around at all those in the room. "He was the only other person who knew I'd decided to court Madeline and she'd agreed. Just like Philip to tell everyone first. Musta gave him a real charge."

Mr. Sanderson divided the papers, handing a copy of the will to the Sneeds, one to Madeline, and one to Jeremiah. "My business is almost finished here. Miss Mercer, after the burial service, could you meet with Mr. Johnstone and me before we go back to Boston?"

"I'd be glad to, Mr. Sanderson, but"—she glanced up at Jeremiah—"I want Mr. Dennison to be present too."

Something inside Jeremiah's chest expanded almost too big to be contained. Madeline was treating him as her protector. Just what a husband was supposed to be.

Dear Lord, I don't deserve this. Please help me be the man she needs.

~

The simple service on the hillside at the ranch touched Madeline more than any funeral she'd attended in a large church in Boston. Philip was laid to rest in the place he chose under the wide-open sky. She'd found a black dress at Skinner's Mercantile that was made from a lighter weight fabric than the mourning dresses she'd brought on the trip with her. The wind blew her skirt around her while the men filled in the grave. One more man she loved would be waiting for her in heaven.

"Are you ready to go?"

She was so lost in thought that she hadn't noticed Jeremiah come up beside her. "Yes. I'm ready for things to settle down."

He led her to the wagon and when she put her foot on the step, he circled her waist with his hands and swung her up. He made her feel light as a bird. She unfurled her parasol to protect them from the sun on the trip back to town.

"Mr. Sanderson has gone on ahead. He and Mr. Johnstone will be waiting for us when we get there. Are you sure you're up to another meeting with them?" Again Jeremiah was protecting her.

"It's all right. I want all of this to be over."

She enjoyed the ride. She'd noticed the ranch house quite a ways farther into Jeremiah's property from the hill where Philip was buried. "Tell me about your house."

He told about living there for several years and not really making any changes. Then, after he'd added onto Philip's house, he'd decided to build onto his own. He wanted it to be a place where he could invite friends from town to celebrate holidays and other things.

"I ordered furniture for the rooms before I knew you. Philip had ordered his furniture from the Montgomery Ward catalog, so I did too. I hope you like it. If not, we can change it. I had no idea I'd be courting a wonderful woman so soon."

His words brought warmth to her face. Maybe he'd think she'd been in the sun too long.

Maddy had never even seen a Montgomery Ward catalog. She'd heard about them, but she just went to a store and bought what she wanted or needed. She wondered what kind of furniture Jeremiah would order. No matter what style it was, she decided to be satisfied with everything he ordered. What would be most important to her was making a home with him.

She wondered how long he planned to court her. Should they wait several months to show honor to Philip?

When they stopped in front of the hotel, Jeremiah's gaze traveled over her face, as if he were memorizing every feature. She could almost feel it as a caress.

"I need to take the wagon down to Swede."

She wasn't ready to be separated from him right now. "I'll go with you. We can walk back here together."

"If you're sure."

At her nod, he clicked his tongue to the horses and headed toward the livery stable. Outside the door, he helped her down, then hollered into the shadows, "Hey, Swede. Here's the wagon. Madeline is with me."

The blond giant came out into the sunshine, smiling broadly. "Good day, Miss Mercer. Ja, nice to see you."

"You too."

Jeremiah placed a proprietary hand on her back and escorted her up the boardwalk to the hotel. On the way, they greeted several people from church. From the speculative smiles, word of their courting had evidently spread through town. Madeline didn't mind one bit.

At the hotel, Mr. Sanderson and Mr. Johnstone waited in the parlor for them. After several minutes of discussion, Madeline gave Jeremiah a questioning look. He must have understood what she wondered, because he nodded.

"Mr. Sanderson, we'll look forward to having regular monthly reports from you on the finances, and Mr. Johnstone, you will keep us informed about the business. Right? We're putting our trust in you, even though you haven't really earned it."

Both men assured Jeremiah that they would take care of Madeline's affairs.

"I'm sure, after we're married, Miss Mercer and I will come to Boston often as well."

When they finished taking care of business, the lawyer and her business partner took their leave, planning to ride to Los Cerrillos right away so they could catch the next eastbound train.

Madeline and Jeremiah were finally alone in the parlor. She glanced up at him. The light in his eyes warmed her from the top of her head to the tips of her toes. His gaze mesmerized her. She couldn't look away, even if she'd wanted to. But oh, she didn't want to. She swayed toward him, and he pulled her into his arms.

"When I awoke this morning, I was dreaming I held you in my arms. My lips"—his head dipped until their noses were only a hair's breadth apart—"were almost touching yours. Anticipation filled me with the thought of finally kissing your beautiful mouth."

She would have swooned if he hadn't been holding her.

"May I?" He waited for her reply, giving her a chance to say no. What a gentleman!

She lifted up on tiptoes, angling her face slightly so her lips finally touched his. Tentatively. She'd never done this before.

He let his lips linger softly against hers for a moment before cradling the back of her head and pulling her even closer. His touch like a butterfly landing...lifting...landing...caressing ever so lightly. Bringing a deeper desire for more. Then his mouth moved against hers more firmly.

With the meeting of their lips, she felt her very soul fuse with his. As their mouths shared their love, her spirit danced within her. This man of God loved her in a way she had never imagined. She couldn't get enough of the nectar of his kisses. Tasting, knowing the love they shared.

When their lips parted, Madeline breathed deeply, taking in the outdoorsy, masculine scent of the man, so much a part of him. Now so much a part of her.

Finally, her life was settled. Nothing could ever disturb it again.

CHAPTER 29

A new day—and hopefully a more settled one.

Pearl's hand gripped the spindles on her crib, and she stared at her mother. Maddy started toward the baby bed. Her daughter reached higher and tried to pull herself up.

Maddy swooped her into a hug. "I didn't hear a peep out of you all night."

Actually, she wouldn't have minded if Pearl had awakened. Feeling the loss of Philip, she would've loved snuggling her baby close to her breast and singing her back to sleep.

While washing and changing Pearl, Maddy kept chattering to her, and her daughter babbled nonsense right back. Soon they were both giggling. When she was finished, she swept her baby into her arms and hugged her close, savoring the baby smell.

After dressing Pearl, she took her down to Sarah in the kitchen.

"Are you sure you don't mind watching her while Jeremiah helps me move our things into Philip's house?"

Sarah took Pearl and hugged her. "Such a pretty girl." She sat in one of the chairs beside the table where Caroline was preparing breakfast. "Pearl and I will have a good time. Would you like Frank to help the two of you?"

"Thank you, but I don't have that much to move. I'm sure Jeremiah and I can manage."

Caroline filled a plate with bacon, scrambled eggs, and biscuits. "Here. You need to eat because you have a lot of hard work ahead of you today. Just sit down and enjoy this. I'll pour you some tea."

"You're right." Maddy took the plate and sat in the chair closest to Sarah. Pearl reached toward her plate. "How soon can I start feeding Pearl scrambled eggs?"

"It wouldn't hurt to let her try some. Just be sure you mash them into tiny pieces. Even a bit of biscuit won't hurt her." Sarah turned the baby in her lap so she faced her mother.

Maddy put a tiny bit of egg on her fingertip and held it out to her daughter. Pearl sucked on the end of her finger, and Maddy felt a tiny scrape. "Ouch." She ran her finger along Pearl's swollen gums. "Could she be teething? I think I feel the tip of a tooth."

Sarah wiped her hand and felt inside the baby's mouth. "I believe you're right. I've heard of babies starting to teeth this young, but it's a little early. No wonder she was so fussy yesterday."

"You didn't tell me she was fussy while I was gone." Maddy reached for her fork. "I'm sorry I left her with you."

"Now don't be worrying about that. I love this little girl. A little fussiness didn't hurt me. But we may have more of this for a while." Sarah hugged Pearl closer to her chest, but the baby wiggled and whined until Sarah sat her back up. "She really isn't a tiny baby anymore. She has a mind of her own."

What Sarah said was true. Pearl was growing and changing faster than Maddy had anticipated. Of course, that's what children did, but she didn't want her daughter to grow up too fast. She'd wanted to experience and savor every moment. And it would be all right for her daughter to have a mind of her own. Maddy wanted her to grow up strong—able to care for herself. If Maddy hadn't been able to think for herself, her life in Boston would have been a lot different from what she had here in Golden.

Maddy buttered her biscuit and spread pink jelly on it. She took a bite, wondering at the strange but delicious taste. "What kind of jelly is this?"

"Prickly pear. Mrs. Stone makes it for us every year." Caroline continued to stir a pot on the stove.

"What's a prickly pear? I haven't seen any pear trees." Maddy took another bite. "But it's delicious."

Caroline laughed. "Actually, it's a cactus fruit. They're hard to work with because of the spines on the plants, so I've never bothered. But Sam really likes this jelly." She turned back to her cooking.

Maddy still had a lot to learn about this rugged country and the people who populated it. She finished eating and took her plate and mug to the sink. After rinsing them off, she turned toward Sarah. "Are you sure she won't be too much bother?"

"Our little Pearl of great price? A bother? Never."

"So this is where all the women are hiding."

Jeremiah stood in the doorway, almost filling it completely and her heart as well. A towering man, all strong muscles and handsome features. Learning more about this man was something she looked forward to the most.

"Madeline, are you ready to start?"

"Yes."

When they stepped out on the boardwalk, Madeline noticed a large wooden trunk in the wagon. "What do you have there?"

"It's empty. I brought it so we could pack away those things of Philip's that we want to keep."

The life-sized memories she carried of him wouldn't fit into something as small as a trunk. She put one foot up on the step of the wagon. "That's a good idea."

Jeremiah swung her up the rest of the way. She could get used to being handled by this man.

"After we clean out all his things, we can come back for your trunks and move them into the house." He climbed up beside her, his solid frame so close their hips and shoulders connected with every sway of the wagon.

Maddy decided she liked this courting. She'd never been touched by a man so much, and every time she liked it more than the time before.

After two hours, they had divided everything Philip owned into piles. Some things weren't worth keeping—like those letters answering his newspaper ad. Looking at all the envelopes stacked on the table, Maddy marveled at how God made her letter prick Philip's heart. There were so many others. No reason to save them—except the ones she wrote. She reached toward the first stack, planning to find them.

"You looking for these?" Jeremiah held two envelopes in his hand, and his gentle gaze touched her heart.

"How did you know?" she whispered.

"I thought we should keep these, even though we're throwing away all the rest." He shoved them into the shirt pocket over his heart.

Maybe they meant as much to him as they did to her.

They packed the keepsakes into the trunk and also had a stack of things to let Pastor Oldman have on hand to give to people who needed them.

Maddy swept and mopped the floor. Jeremiah took the clothing and linens that needed washing to the Chinese laundry at the other end of town. He hadn't wanted her to have to take care of them. She could have her wash done by someone else all the time if she wanted to. She'd have to think about that.

When they went to the hotel for lunch, Sarah had already

put Pearl down for her nap in the room she shared with Frank. After they were through eating, Maddy went upstairs and finished packing while Jeremiah took down the first trunk.

In the time she'd been in Golden, she'd amassed several things. With the crib she had up at Philip's house, *now her house*, and the one in the hotel room, they had more than they needed. She decided to seek Sarah's advice.

"What should I do with the extra crib?"

"You could leave one with Frank and me. We'll want the sweet little thing to spend time with us, as if we were her grandparents." She twisted the corner of her apron.

Maddy hugged her. "You are all the grandparents she will ever have. So I believe I'll do just that."

With that problem taken care of, she returned to the hotel room in time to stuff the rest of their belongings into the last trunk before Jeremiah came to take it away. She followed him out to the wagon and watched him heft the heavy luggage up on his shoulder before setting it in the bed of the wagon. His muscles rippled against his shirt. She praised the Lord for bringing such a strong man into her life. Strong. Wise. A lover of Jesus. And he'll make me a wonderful husband. What more could she ask for? Nothing at all.

The wagon creaked under its heavier load as they drove up the hill. She leaned against Jeremiah, one hand through the crook of his elbow and her other on his upper arm. With each movement, she felt his muscles bunch and release. Tingling started deep within her. She didn't know anything about being married, but being next to him made her long for the day she'd know everything it meant to have someone to love. Maddy wanted to be the best wife in the world for Jeremiah.

He pulled on the reins to stop the horses. "So, Madeline, do you want your things in the room Philip had built for you, or will you move into the other bedroom?"

"I don't think I could sleep in there. I'd keep remembering

that last time we spent with him. How he could hardly talk. How weak he was. Just put my trunks in the other room."

He helped her down from the wagon, and his hands remained on her waist longer than necessary. She enjoyed the feeling. When he finally moved away, she wanted them back. But enough of thoughts like that. She had work to do.

When the house was finally the way she wanted it, she stood staring out the window that overlooked the desert. No flowers at this time of summer, but beauty still prevailed. Scattered brush and scrubby trees filled her view along with the purple outline of that mountain range in the distance. So different from back East, but artistic in its own way.

Jeremiah came up behind her. He pulled her back against his chest and held her within his arms. He kissed the top of her head then turned her around and stared into her eyes. Unspoken communication flowed between them. She held nothing back, and neither did he. The abundance of love she read on his face and in the depths of his dark, sparkling eyes almost overwhelmed her.

"I love you, Madeline."

Maddy hadn't realized just how much weight those three words carried as they winged their way to her heart, suffusing it with indescribable sensations completely foreign to her. For a moment, she couldn't catch her breath. She stared into those fathomless eyes, trying to express with her own just how much he meant to her.

"I love you too, Jeremiah." Her words started tentatively but gained strength.

His lips skimmed across her forehead. Each touch sent flashes of heat through her veins. Then he tenderly kissed the corners of her mouth, teasing her, not really settling on her lips. He tasted of her chin, and she dropped her head back, reveling in the sensations that tingled all the way to her toes.

When his lips trailed down the length of her neck, her

breathing deepened. Then he settled on the hollow of her throat where she felt her pulse beat like the wings of a hummingbird. He tasted of her, awakening sensations she'd never imagined.

Finally, his lips settled on hers again. Firmly. Giving and receiving a depth of love beyond her wildest dreams. Desire swept through her like a raging fire, beautiful and fearful at the same time. She yearned to find new ways to express her love to him, not able to imagine another way.

When he lifted his face from hers, she felt bereft, as if something important was missing. She pulled him to her once more, but this time she initiated the kiss. Then awkwardness seeped in ever so slightly. She stepped back at the same time he did.

"Maddy, my Maddy." His husky voice played a symphony on her heartstrings.

"No one but my mother and father ever called me that."

"Then I won't, if it brings sadness."

"I want you to. I always think of myself as Maddy."

He hugged her close and drew her head against his chest. She could feel the gallop of his heartbeat in tandem with hers. "It'll be my special name for you in our private moments, Maddy."

The sound of her name on his lips sealed her love to him forever.

"How long will I need to court you, Maddy, before we can be married?"

She had no idea. She couldn't even think. His love had captured her so completely.

~

As soon as Jeremiah took Maddy back to the hotel, he left for the ranch. He needed to get away from her and the deep longings she stirred in him. He had to clear his head and plan how he could spend time with his beloved without desiring her so much it hurt.

She had responded to his love in ways he hadn't imagined. Ways that inflamed his desire, but not in a bad way. He knew God would want them to feel this kind of pure desire for each other, but he didn't want his human longings to lead them down a road they shouldn't take.

Being with Maddy made him feel alive as never before. She brought out the protector in him, and he respected her above every woman he'd ever known—even his mother. He'd loved his mother, but because she'd died when he was very young, he didn't know enough about her to respect her as much as he did Maddy.

Jeremiah kept every lamp in his house lit. He paced from room to room, reliving the moments he'd spent with her in his arms. In the middle of the night, when he couldn't fall asleep, he went out to the woodpile and started chopping. By the time he quit, he had enough to last a month. He'd hoped it would make him tired enough to finally sleep.

Every time he closed his eyes, Maddy was there. Her pure spirit. Her beautiful face. Her kisses that lit a fire in him that he couldn't quench.

He went out to the shower. Even several minutes under the cold stream didn't help. Finally, he picked up Philip's Bible, which Maddy had given him, hoping some of the writing in the margins would give him the direction he needed so he could read the right verses.

Poring over page after page, he couldn't find anything that applied. There was only one other place to go for help. Finally, he dropped to his knees beside a chair and prayed. Longer and harder than he'd ever done before. He begged God to guide him in this matter.

When the peace finally settled in his mind and heart, he closed his eyes for just a moment.

T-Bone clanging the bell for breakfast woke him. His whole body felt stiff and creaky, but his spirit contained peace.

He shaved, dressed, and went out to eat with the ranch hands. Then he gave the orders for the day before heading into Golden. Anxious to see Maddy, he rode straight to the adobe. No one answered his knock.

He opened the door and walked in calling her name. No one was in the house. He knew it was too early for Maddy to have fed Pearl, dressed her, and gone somewhere else.

Something was wrong.

He had to find her.

CHAPTER 30

$\mathcal{M}$addy had just finished dressing Pearl when a sharp rap on the hotel room door caught her attention.

"Madeline, are you in there?"

Jeremiah! He sounded almost frantic. She strode to the door with Pearl resting on her hip. When she opened it wide, her eyes feasted on him. His dark hair with that curl falling on his forehead. This time she did reach up and push it back. Their eyes connected. Her hand slid down across his smooth-shaven jaw. A hint of something spicy and sweet clung to him, enhancing his usual masculine aroma.

Had it only been a few hours since she'd seen him? It felt like a week or more, the way she'd missed him.

A perplexed expression slid from his face, replaced by a warm smile. He opened his arms and cocooned Maddy and Pearl inside his embrace. She lifted her face to him, and he brushed his lips across hers. Then he transferred his kisses to the baby's forehead. Her daughter laughed and wiggled until she could look up into his face.

"She loves you too, Jeremiah."

"I hope so, since I'm going to be her daddy."

Maddy couldn't keep from teasing him. "No one has asked me to marry him yet."

"But you agreed that the courting would lead to marriage." Confusion brought a hint of pain to his eyes.

"Yes, but I want a proposal."

He left the door wide open and led her to the chair beside the window. After she was seated, he dropped to one knee beside her.

"I was teasing, Jeremiah."

"But I'm not." He kissed the back of her hand. Then he kissed Pearl's tiny hand, and the baby jabbered happily at him, patting his face with her other one.

"Maddy, will you marry me, and let me be a father to your daughter, Pearl?" He pressed a kiss on the baby's cheek.

She took a deep breath. "Of course I will."

His smile rivaled the sunlight streaming through the window. "And we'll give Pearl lots of brothers and sisters?"

A slow burn started deep in her belly and spread throughout her limbs as she remembered the kiss they'd shared yesterday. She knew that was just a prelude to what would follow, even if she didn't understand the details.

"I hope so." Maddy leaned forward and kissed him square on the mouth.

He stood and lifted her from the chair. "Now, are you going to tell me why you're in this hotel room when you have a perfectly good house up on the hill? I went there first, and it worried me when you weren't there."

She stepped away from him. "I took Pearl up there, and she was fine for a few minutes. But she kept looking around as if she were trying to find something. She kept staring at the rocking chair. Then she looked toward his bedroom. I went in there so she could see it was empty. That's when she started crying and nothing would calm her."

Jeremiah reached for Pearl and held her close. "You think she misses him?"

"Babies are smart. He's always been there, and he played with her every day. I tried everything. Put her in the crib. Walked the floor with her. She cried and cried until I brought her back down here."

He lifted Pearl high and made a silly noise at her. She laughed and drooled on him, her blond curls bouncing around her face.

Jeremiah pulled out his bandanna and wiped his cheek and the baby's mouth before he kissed her neck, making her laugh even more.

"That's not all. She's started teething. When I got to the hotel, Caroline gave me some paregoric to rub on her gums. That helped settle her down, and she slept all night."

He glanced toward the crib by the wall. "Did you bring this from the house?"

"No. Frank brought the one I left with them into this room."

Jeremiah jiggled the baby on his hip. "Have you had breakfast?"

She shook her head.

"Well, neither have I. Let's go down and eat. Then we can take Pearl back up to the house and see if she's better up there today. We may have to make some different arrangements." He led the way out the door, talking and cooing to the baby.

What a good father he was going to be.

~

Jeremiah could get used to sitting across the table, watching Maddy feed Pearl in between taking bites of her own breakfast—her hair a halo around her China-doll face. But this woman wasn't fragile. Her strength and faith amazed him. Today the warmth in her gray eyes lit up the room. The Lord helped him tamp down his strong desire for her to a manageable level.

And Pearl was a bonus. He hoped God knew what He was doing. He didn't have any experience being a husband, let alone a father, but he'd do everything he could to be the best.

Maddy gave the baby a tiny bit of eggs, then glanced at him. "What are you thinking about? You look so serious."

He rested his hands on the table. "I understand the great responsibility that rests on my shoulders, and I want to be the best husband for you and father for Pearl and our other children."

One hand reached toward his arm and clasped it. "I believe in you, Jeremiah."

Those words dove deep into the final pool of insecurity that hid in the back of his heart, scattering it. Bringing light to even that far corner. Maddy would be very good for him. He could do no less for her.

"Are you finished?" He stood and reached for Pearl.

She came eagerly into his arms, so trusting too.

Maddy laid her napkin beside her plate and gracefully rose. He liked her in the colorful dresses she'd been wearing, but even the gray one this morning swished around her, setting off her pleasing form. "Are we going up to the house?"

"I think we should." He placed his hand on the small of her back, and they walked out into the sunlight. "Would you like me to get the wagon?"

"No, I enjoy the walk, especially since you're carrying Pearl."

"Hey! Jeremiah—" Mr. Skinner's loud shout carried up the street. The owner of the mercantile stopped sweeping the boardwalk in front of his store and leaned on the handle of the broom. "Heerd you was gettin' married. That right?"

Might as well have been a public announcement, because everyone who was out stopped to see what was going on.

Jeremiah glanced down at Maddy. She blushed but didn't look upset.

He tipped his hat toward the storekeeper. "Sure is." Then he turned back toward the adobe.

All the way up the road, Maddy commented on the various plants and trees, the early morning sunshine, even a lone hawk sailing across the cloudless sky. Pearl chewed on his collar and played with the buttons on his shirt. He felt like a family man already.

Maddy led the way into the house. Pearl's babbling and laughter stopped. No matter where he went in the room, she turned her head to look at the rocking chair. Her face slowly crumpled, and she stuck out her bottom lip. Then she whined before bursting into tears.

He patted her back and walked to the window, talking to her and pointing out everything he could see. She stopped wailing but continued to whimper. Then she looked over his shoulder and started crying again.

Maddy followed them as he walked to the kitchen and back. He went into the bedroom where all of Maddy's and Pearl's things were already unpacked.

Pearl kept looking back over his shoulder and crying like her heart would break. He didn't know what else to do. Her crying was breaking his heart too. When he turned around, he saw tears in Maddy's eyes.

He leaned his head close to her ear. "This isn't working."

"I know." She took Pearl from his arms and stood rocking her from side to side.

The baby dropped her head on Maddy's shoulder, but she didn't stop crying.

"Ready to go back to the hotel?" He lifted Pearl into his own arms and ushered Maddy out the door.

The walk to the hotel was accompanied by the baby's tears. If he couldn't comfort her, what kind of father would he be?

Sarah met them in the lobby. "Here, let me take her up to our room and give her a bottle."

When Sarah cuddled Pearl, the baby settled against her chest and stopped crying.

"Before you go—" Maddy stopped her friend. "Now that you and Frank have resources to do what you want to, are you going back to Boston?"

Sarah shook her head. "You're all the family we have. We want to stay here near you, and we'll be like grandparents to this wee one…and any other babies you have." Merriment twinkled in Sarah's eyes.

"Aren't you tired of living in the hotel?" Jeremiah had to ask.

"Well, there is that house up near the one Philip left to Maddy. We could see about buying that place." She started up the stairs but stopped on the second step and turned around. "We really haven't decided anything yet."

Jeremiah took Maddy's hand and pulled her into the empty parlor. He had an idea, but first he wanted one thing. He turned her into his arms and pulled her close. "I love you, Maddy."

The last word he whispered against her lips before settling his where they belonged. Her honeyed sweetness thrilled him. He couldn't let her go. Trailing kisses along her cheeks, he dropped one on each eyelid before returning to taste her lips once again. He'd never before understood the connection between a man and a woman in love. His commitment to her strengthened like a strong rope that was wet when tied together and pulled tighter as it dried. His heart and soul were connected to hers with knots that would never come loose.

Reluctantly he pulled back from the kiss and rested her head against his chest. "I will never, ever leave you or forsake you." That was a promise he knew he could keep.

Finally, he led her to the sofa. They sat close together, holding hands.

"I can't have you coming back to the hotel to stay."

The question in her eyes as they gazed up at him let him know she didn't know what to do about it.

"I have a couple suggestions."

"What are they, Jeremiah?"

He needed to think clearly, so he stood and crossed the room to the front window. Then he turned back to face her. "You can't live in the house Philip left you. Pearl doesn't understand what happened, and we don't want to upset her any more."

"I know." Maddy clasped her hands in her lap. "I'm at my wits' end."

"You and Pearl could move into my house. She won't expect Philip to be there."

The shock that covered Maddy's face was almost comical. "Jeremiah!"

"I don't mean with me. I could sleep in the bunkhouse. If you think people would still talk, I would sleep in Philip's house or even the hotel."

She stood. "I don't like either of those ideas." She straightened her back.

He liked her spunk. Living with Maddy would be interesting. They wouldn't agree on everything, and he liked the idea of having lively discussions.

"Then here's a better idea. We could get married right away. Tomorrow. The next day. Next week. Whatever suits you. I don't want to wait. I want you with me. The sooner the better." He hoped he didn't sound like he was begging.

She didn't say anything for a few moments.

"And then we could give Philip's house to Frank and Sarah. That way they wouldn't have to spend any of their inheritance on property."

Maddy still didn't say anything. He waited in agony for her answer.

"We could do that. Get married soon. Maybe day after tomorrow. I want a little time to get ready."

She'd agreed with him! Though he wanted to whoop and holler, he restrained himself. But he did rush to her and clasp her hands. "Are you sure? I did promise to court you."

"Courting is to get to know each other and discuss the future." She smiled up at him.

He let out a big breath he'd been holding, afraid she'd change her mind.

"We've gotten to know each other over the time I've been here. And we know what our future will be. So the wedding will be day after tomorrow at sunset."

He thrust his arms around Maddy and held her close, breathing in the light flowery scent that always surrounded her. He could hardly believe it. He would be married to the woman of his dreams in only two days.

~

When Maddy told Sarah and Caroline about their wedding plans, these two good friends went into a frenzy of activity. All the people who attended their church were invited. Many of them offered to help cook for the celebration. Martha Henderson and Harriet Stone took over that part. Caroline was baking a spicy wedding cake full of dried fruit, and Sarah took Maddy to Skinner's, looking for a dress for Maddy to wear.

Mrs. Skinner had just gotten in a shipment of ready-made dresses. The only one that fit Maddy was a deep golden-colored dimity with lace, ruffles, and flounces. And when Carlos heard about the wedding, he brought a gift from Mexico for Maddy— a lovely lace mantilla to wear on her hair. It would be the closest thing to a bridal veil they would find in Golden.

Sarah insisted that Maddy try all of it on to make sure she liked it all together. Maddy chose to wear her mother's string of pearls, because they looked wonderful with the dress.

After changing into her house dress, Maddy went down to the kitchen to see if she could get a sandwich or something light for lunch. Her stomach was too fluttery to eat much. Just before she reached the door from the lobby to the kitchen area, the stagecoach pulled up outside the hotel.

She moved to the doorway in time to see an older couple, dressed in clothing much too heavy for the weather here in New Mexico Territory, climb down from the coach. They would be right at home in Boston, but not here.

Before she could step away, the woman's gaze slid over her, then back. "Is that you, Madeline Mercer?"

How does she know my name? Maddy didn't even have time to answer.

"You look just like your mother." The woman lifted her skirts and quickly ascended the steps to the boardwalk while the man accompanying her and the driver worked together to get their luggage off the boot of the coach.

"Did you know my mother?" That caught Maddy's interest.

"Yes, we were friends at finishing school. I was sad when she died so young."

"I'm sorry. I don't know who you are." Maddy didn't want to appear rude, but something didn't feel quite right to her.

"Millicent Osgood, and that's my husband, William." She waved a gloved hand toward the man in the heavy suit. "We understand you knew our daughter, Loraine Henry."

Loraine's parents? What were they doing in Golden?

"May we speak with you for a few minutes? We've traveled a long way to see you."

I'm sure you have. Now it was all falling into place. These people were here to try and take Pearl away from her. She prayed that Sarah would keep her daughter upstairs in her room. Maddy would try to get rid of these people as quickly as she could.

"Come into the parlor." She turned and led the way, not even caring whether they both followed her or not.

After she was seated in one of the wing-backed chairs, the Osgoods entered and sat on the sofa.

"How did you know that I was a friend of Loraine's?"

Mr. Osgood tugged at his collar and didn't say a word.

His wife stared straight at Maddy. "It's rather a long story."

"I'm listening." Maddy wasn't going to make this easy for them. She held nothing but disdain for parents who would disown their daughter the way they did Loraine.

"Our neighbor's daughter came to her parents' house for her lying-in. Bonnie McGuire was her midwife. Sometime during her labor, Mrs. McGuire mentioned that she delivered Loraine's baby and that Loraine had died. She was commending our neighbor for calling her early enough to keep something bad from happening."

Maddy felt the color drain from her face. She hoped she wouldn't faint.

Mrs. Osgood pulled a hanky from her sleeve and wiped the perspiration from her forehead. "Harriet knew I would want to hear the story. She sent for me and had Mrs. McGuire repeat all she had told them. I was shocked. I never even knew Loraine was having a baby or that her husband had passed away. My heart broke. I cried for days. Finally, William and I talked about what a terrible thing we had done to our own flesh and blood."

When she said that, Maddy knew what was coming next. She jumped up. "Loraine made me promise to raise her child as my own. She never wanted you to raise her."

Tears glistened on Mrs. Osgood's cheeks. "We know. And we understand she was right. But I can't rest easy until I know that the child is well cared for and loved."

"Oh, she is loved all right. By a number of people. She has a mother, soon will have a father, and grandparents. She's very much loved and cared for." Maddy's chest heaved. She would never give Pearl up. To these people or anyone else.

"My dear—" Mrs. Osgood stood and stepped closer. "We're not trying to take her from you. But we have repented and asked God's forgiveness for how we treated our daughter and her husband. We wish we could have asked Loraine's..." She dabbed at the moisture on her cheeks. "What we want to know...is there any way we could be a part of her life too?" The woman stood with expectancy and fearfulness warring in her expression.

Maddy could understand the anguish these parents had suffered. If they truly had changed, could she deny them access to their own grandchild?

Before she could answer, Jeremiah appeared in the doorway. "Is something wrong, Maddy?" He came to stand beside her, slipping his arm around her waist.

"This is Mr. and Mrs. Osgood from Boston. They've come to check on their grandchild, my daughter."

He glanced at the man, then the woman. "You're Loraine's parents?"

Mr. Osgood moved to stand beside his wife. "Yes, we are."

Jeremiah studied them as if he were looking for something. A few moments later, he relaxed. "After the wedding this evening, I'll be Pearl's father. She'll be well taken care of."

"Pearl? You named her Pearl?" More tears streamed down the woman's face. "My middle name is Pearl. How did you know?"

Maddy stared at her. "I didn't know, but Loraine did. She named her daughter."

The four of them spent several minutes discussing Pearl.

Finally, Maddy said, "Jeremiah and I would welcome you to have contact with your granddaughter, but she will be living here in Golden. You may come visit when you want to. It'll be good for Pearl to have two sets of grandparents."

Jeremiah tightened his arm around her. "And Maddy and I will visit Boston from time to time."

Maddy marveled at the wisdom of her husband. He'd helped her work this out to be in the best interest of all the people concerned. "We're getting married at sunset. Mr. and Mrs. Osgood, you're welcome to attend the ceremony and celebration afterward."

She hoped they would actually come.

~

*A*s the waning sun cast an array of colors across the sky, Maddy and Jeremiah stood in front of Sam Oldman, their pastor and friend. When she'd first received that newspaper ad back in Boston from the man in Golden, New Mexico Territory, she'd had no idea what a treasure would come into her life. And she didn't mean the money.

The man who stood beside her had come to know the Lord. Then he had offered her the treasure of his love and a future filled with all kinds of possibilities. Her happiness was complete as she watched the golden rays of the setting sun play across his handsome features and heard his husky voice pledge his life to hers. *Thank You, God.*

Did you enjoy this book? We hope so!
Would you take a quick minute to leave a review where you purchased the book?
It doesn't have to be long. Just a sentence or two telling what you liked about the story!

Receive a FREE ebook and get updates when new Wild Heart books release: https://wildheartbooks.org/newsletter

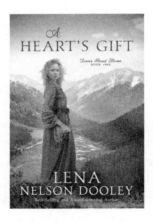

Book 1: A Heart's Gift

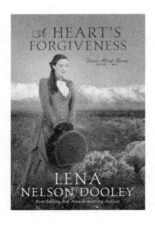

Book 2: A Heart's Forgiveness

Book 3: A Heart's Forever Home

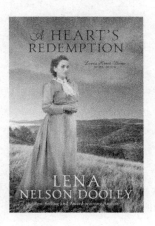

Book 4: A Heart's Redemption

ABOUT THE AUTHOR

Multi-published, award-winning author Lena Nelson Dooley has had more than 950,000 copies of her 50+ books sold. Her books have appeared on the CBA and ECPA bestseller lists, as well as Amazon bestseller lists. She is a member of American Christian Fiction Writers and the local chapter, ACFW - DFW. She's a member of Christian Authors' Network, and Gateway Church in Southlake, Texas.

Her 2010 release, *Love Finds You in Golden, New Mexico*, won the 2011 Will Rogers Medallion Award for excellence in publishing Western Fiction. Her next series, *McKenna's Daughters: Maggie's Journey* appeared on a reviewers' Top Ten Books of 2011 list. It also won the 2012 Selah award for Historical Novel. The second, *Mary's Blessing*, was a Selah Award finalist for Romance novel. *Catherine's Pursuit* released in 2013. It was the winner of the NTRWA Carolyn Reader's Choice contest, took second place in the CAN Golden Scroll Novel of the Year award, and won the Will Rogers Medallion bronze medallion. Her blog, A Christian Writer's World, received the Readers' Choice Blog of the Year Award from the Book Club Network. She also has won three Carol Award Silver pins. In 2015 and 2016, these novella collections—*A Texas Christmas, Love Is Patient,* and *Mountain Christmas Brides* have all appeared on the ECPA bestseller list, one of the top two bestseller lists for Christian books.

She has experience in screenwriting, acting, directing, and voice-overs. She is on the Board of Directors for Higher Ground Films and is one of the screenwriters for their upcoming film Abducted to Kill. She has been featured in articles in Christian Retailing, ACFW Journal, Charisma Magazine, and Christian Fiction Online Magazine. Her article in CFOM was the cover story.

In addition to her writing, Lena is a frequent speaker at women's groups, writers groups, and at both regional and national conferences. She has spoken in six states and internationally. The Lena Nelson Dooley Show is on the Along Came A Writer Blogtalk network.

Lena has an active web presence on Facebook, Twitter, Goodreads, Linkedin and with her internationally connected blog where she interviews other authors and promotes their books. Her blog has a reach of over 55,000.

- Website: https://lenanelsondooley.com
- Blog: http://lenanelsondooley.blogspot.com
- Blogtalk Radio:
  https://blogtalkradio.com/alongcameawriter/2

facebook.com/Lena-Nelson-Dooley-42960748768
instagram.com/lenanelsondooley
pinterest.com/lenandooley
goodreads.com/lenanelsondooley
twitter.com/lenandooley
amazon.com/author/lenadooley
linkedin.com/in/lenanelsondooley

ALSO BY LENA NELSON DOOLEY

The McKenna's Daughters Series:

Maggie's Journey: Near her eighteenth birthday, Margaret Lenora Caine finds a chest hidden in the attic containing proof that she's adopted. The spoiled daughter of wealthy merchants in Seattle, she feels betrayed by her real parents and by the ones who raised her. But mystery surrounds her new discovery, and when Maggie uncovers another family secret, she loses all sense of identity. Leaving her home in Seattle, Washington, Maggie strikes out to find her destiny. Will Charles Stanton, who's been in love with her for years, be able to help her discover who she really is?

Mary's Blessing: When her mother dies, Mary Lenora must grow up quickly to take care of her brothers and sisters. Can love help her to shoulder the burden? Mary Lenora Caine knows she is adopted. As she was growing up, her mother called her "God's blessing." But now that she's gone, Mary no longer feels like any kind of blessing. Her father, in his grief, has cut himself off from the family, leaving the running of the home entirely in Mary's hands. As she nears her eighteenth birthday, Mary can't see anything in her future but drudgery. Then her childhood friend Daniel begins to court her, promising her a life of riches and ease. But her fairy-tale dreams turn to dust when her family becomes too much for Daniel, and he abandons her in her time of deepest need. Will Daniel come to grips with God's plan for him? And if he does return, can Mary trust that this time he will really follow through?

Catherine's Pursuit: In book three of the McKenna's Daughters series, Catherine McKenna begins a journey to find her lost sisters that turns into a spiritual journey for the entire McKenna family.

Lena's work is also featured in the following recent collections: *8 Weddings and a Miracle Romance Collection, A Texas Christmas: Six*

Romances from the Historic Lone Star State Herald the Season of Love, Warm Mulled Kisses: A Collection of 10 Christian Christmas Novellas, and April Love: A Collection of 10 Christian April Fool's Novellas.

Want more?

If you love historical romance, check out our other Wild Heart books!

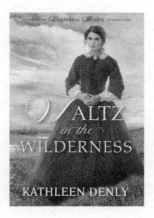

Waltz in the Wilderness by Kathleen Denly

She's desperate to find her missing father. His conscience demands he risk all to help.

Eliza Brooks is haunted by her role in her mother's death, so she'll do anything to find her missing pa—even if it means sneaking aboard a southbound ship. When those meant to protect her abandon and betray her instead, a family friend's unexpected assistance is a blessing she can't refuse.

Daniel Clarke came to California to make his fortune, and a stable job as a San Francisco carpenter has earned him more than most have scraped from the local goldfields. But it's been four years since he left Massachusetts and his fiancé is impatient for his return. Bound for home at last, Daniel Clarke finds his heart and plans challenged by a tenacious young woman with haunted eyes. Though every word he utters seems to offend her, he is determined to see her safely returned to her father. Even if that means risking his fragile engagement.

When disaster befalls them in the remote wilderness of the Southern California mountains, true feelings are revealed, and both must face heart-rending decisions. But how to decide when every choice before them leads to someone getting hurt?

Lone Star Ranger by Renae Brumbaugh Green

Elizabeth Covington will get her man.

And she has just a week to prove her brother isn't the murderer Texas Ranger Rett Smith accuses him of being. She'll show the good-looking lawman he's wrong, even if it means setting out on a risky race across Texas to catch the real killer.

Rett doesn't want to convict an innocent man. But he can't let the Boston beauty sway his senses to set a guilty man free. When Elizabeth follows him on a dangerous trek, the Ranger vows to keep her safe. But who will protect him from the woman whose conviction and courage leave him doubting everything—even his heart?

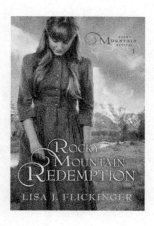

Rocky Mountain Redemption by Lisa J. Flickinger

A *Rocky Mountain* logging camp may be just the place to find herself.

To escape the devastation caused by the breaking of her wedding engagement, Isabelle Franklin joins her aunt in the Rocky Mountains to feed a camp of lumberjacks cutting on the slopes of Cougar Ridge. If only she could out run the lingering nightmares.

Charles Bailey, camp foreman and Stony Creek's itinerant pastor, develops a reputation to match his new nickname—Preach. However, an inner battle ensues when the details of his rough history threaten to overcome the beliefs of his young faith.

Amid the hazards of camp life, the unlikely friendship growing between the two surprises Isabelle. She's drawn to Preach's brute strength and gentle nature as he leads the ragtag crew toiling for Pollitt's Lumber. But when the ghosts from her past return to haunt her, the choices she will make change the course of her life forever—and that of the man she's come to love.

Printed in Great Britain
by Amazon

28785206R00185